D0350719

ALSO BY REED ARVIN
The Wind in the Wheat

THE
WILL

A Novel

Reed Arvin

SCRIBNER

NEW YORK LONDON TORONTO SYDNEY SINGAPORE

SCRIBNER
1230 Avenue of the Americas
New York, NY 10020

This book is a work of fiction. Names, characters, places, and incidents
either are products of the author's imagination or are used fictitiously.
Any resemblance to actual events or locales or persons, living or dead,
is entirely coincidental.

Copyright © 2000 by Reed Arvin

All rights reserved, including the right of reproduction in whole
or in part in any form.

SCRIBNER and design are trademarks of Macmillan Library
Reference USA, Inc., used under license by Simon & Schuster,
the publisher of this work.

Designed by Colin Joh
Text set in Janson

Manufactured in the United States of America

1 3 5 7 9 10 8 6 4 2

Library of Congress Cataloging-in-Publication Data

Arvin, Reed.
The will/Reed Arvin
p. cm.
1. Inheritance and succession—Fiction. 2. Homeless persons—Fiction.
3. Millionaires—Fiction. 4. Kansas—Fiction. I. Title.

PS3551.R85 W55 2000
813'.54—dc21
00–026012

ISBN 0-7432-0148-5

FIC
ARVIN

For my father, who taught me the meaning of integrity.
Unlike this book, he cannot be bought.

THE
WILL

Chapter One

Margaret Crandall fluttered open her eyes at five-thirty and felt the warm sheets and covers around her. She hadn't needed an alarm clock in years; every day she awoke at the same time, her life a predictable routine of meals and laundry and sleep. She licked her lips, sighed into her pillow, and turned to wake her husband. He lay with his back to her, and she pushed him, her fingers spread against his cotton pajama top. Her hand pressed into his fleshy back, and he rotated forward slightly with the pressure. She pushed harder, and his arm fell suddenly, woodenly down over the edge of the bed. She lowered her hand and felt his skin; he was as cold and still as winter fields.

She did not move. For several minutes she lay silently, her breathing unanswered, hands balled up at her chin. Then she rose, put on a pale pink robe, and walked out of the room. She closed the door behind her quietly, carefully, as though not to disturb her husband. She walked down the hallway to the stairs, descending into the living room. Her balance began to disintegrate as she walked, her equilibrium slipping further away with each step. She began listing, leaning. She entered the kitchen but came to a halt just inside the door; focusing her eyes unsteadily on the sink across the tile floor, she righted herself and began inching forward. After a few last steps she collided with the kitchen table, knocking two plates and a cup to the floor. The dishes spun lazily downward and broke into pieces as they struck the tile, scattering sharp, colored chips to every corner of the room.

Upstairs, the dead man's son awoke with the sound of smashing china. Roger, tense and listening, pulled on his pants and entered the hallway. He passed his sister Sarah's room, descended the stairs, and saw his mother collapsed into an awkward sitting position on the kitchen floor, slumped over with her back to the sink.

Roger took his mother's shoulder in his hand; she moved easily in his grip, her limbs loose. At that moment the house was filled with a high-pitched scream of agony.

Roger took the stairs three at a time. He entered the bedroom, saw Sarah, and understood instantly that his father was dead. Sarah was clinging to the body, her head buried in the chest. Roger disengaged her, her nails leaving marks in the pajama top as he peeled them back. He pulled her out into the hallway; she resisted, reaching back uselessly toward her father. But he was too strong, and forcing her away from the door, he managed to reenter the bedroom, close the door behind him, and lock it.

Now the dead man and his son were alone. For a moment, he stood close by the door, staring. He could hear his sister whimpering and sobbing through the door, and eventually he moved away from the noise, walking slowly toward his father. A leg had fallen gracelessly off the bed during the struggle, and the body lay like an enormous stuffed doll, mouth open, limbs akimbo. Roger reached a hand out tentatively, but pulled slowly back; the eyes were still open, staring up at the ceiling. The son reached the bed and stood over the body, his eyes locked on his father's. Then, with an abrupt motion, he reached out and slapped the dead man's face, a brutal strike directly across the cheek. The crack of his hand echoed in the bedroom like a gunshot.

Tractors were running by sunup all over Cheney County the morning Tyler Crandall died; there was rain in the forecast. Kit Munroe, the chief of the Council Grove volunteer fire department, was already out working his fields when his wife received the call. She had to drive a pickup truck twenty minutes across five gated fields to find her husband. Munroe listened quietly, shut the tractor down, and rode back with his wife. He called for some help; Crandall was a big man, and it would take two people to hoist him onto a stretcher. He didn't want the Crandall boy to have to do it.

It was some work getting Ty up off the bed and onto the stretcher with any dignity. Munroe and Carter Dixon wrestled him to the stretcher, lowering it briefly to the floor to rearrange the limbs. Then Munroe pulled a white sheet up over the face and tucked it in over the head. He signaled with a grunt and they heaved the body up, steadying themselves.

It was warming up outside, and Munroe and Carter sweated in the June sun as they hoisted Crandall down the front steps, down the long walkway to the driveway and the car. They loaded him in and Munroe slammed shut the big, swinging back door of the ambulance. The car pulled out into the driveway in a cloud of grit and gravel dust, and was gone.

Roger entered his father's office an hour later. He pulled the big chair back from the ornate desk and sat, feeling his weight in the chair, adjusting its height to fit his own lighter frame. After a moment he took a key from his pocket and unlocked the right bottom drawer of the desk. Inside were a black long-barreled revolver, a half-empty metal flask, and a large manila envelope. He grasped the flask and screwed open the top; sniffing the contents, he took a quick swallow. He was an experienced drinker, and his face was unchanged by the jolt of straight whiskey. He screwed the top back on the flask lightly and returned to the drawer. He removed the envelope, opened it, and pulled out several typewritten pages. He scanned the top page silently, his expression blank. Setting it aside, he picked up the phone and dialed.

Chapter Two

Earlier that morning Henry Mathews, Jr., had been fighting the usual Chicago drive-time traffic, another day of automotive peristalsis that left him switching radio stations obsessively, tapping on his steering wheel in time to the music. Calculations flickered behind his eyes as he glanced down at his watch; alternative routes passed briefly through his brain, were considered and discarded. He looked at a passing street sign and added minutes: nine for driving, three to park, five for the elevator. He didn't like to be late, but Elaine had stayed over and she had been in a playful mood. After what she had put him through, he was lucky to be at work at all. He pulled into the underground parking lot at the Equitable Building on Michigan Avenue and grabbed a lucky parking spot near an elevator.

Henry ascended several hundred feet from the shoreline of Lake Michigan to the offices of Wilson, Lougherby and Mathers, smiled at the receptionist, and turned down the long corridor toward the office of Sheldon Parker. He knocked at Parker's door and stood silently in the hallway, knowing that Sheldon would make him wait. He pictured Parker leaning back in his oversized leather chair, hands locked behind his head, a self-satisfied grin on his face. Parker managed eleven junior associates in the firm and, due to a personality clouded by a vague, broadly aimed sadism, took frequent pleasure in trivial abuses of his authority.

Henry checked himself in a mirror at the end of the hallway, scanning for Parker fodder: dark olive sport coat, conservative but fresh; thin-striped shirt and silk tie; tailored pants, gold Gevril watch. His darkening blond hair was short and cut expensively, his pale blue eyes level and inquiring. But impeccable appearance just meant Parker would find some other topic upon which to focus his sardonic abuse.

After several long seconds a muffled voice said, "Enter," and Henry stepped into the office. As expected, Parker was smirking, a highly communicative expression composed of equal parts arrogance, power, and prissy tattletale. He looked for all the world like a high school principal, except for the nine-hundred-dollar suit. A small man, he had compensated for his lack of physical presence with a kind of overworked, slicked-down finesse. His hair was jet-black, with eyebrows Henry sincerely believed were regularly plucked to perfection. He was tanned—remarkably so, given that the summer was only beginning—and he radiated a sense of wealth so comfortably that it could only have been inherited. He was also brilliant, with a win rate in the 90 percent range, and Henry had settled in for a two- or three-year stint of pain at his feet, determined to glean whatever crumbs the man might let fall from his table.

Parker gestured toward a seat opposite his desk. "You know something, Henry?" he began in his silky Ivy League voice. "These Monday morning shakedowns are my favorite time of the week. Know why that is?"

Henry took the chair opposite Parker's desk and set down his briefcase. The ritual abuse had begun. "No, Sheldon, I don't."

"It's because we both know our place. Every man has a part to play in life, and the universe decrees that he plays it. Otherwise, order breaks down."

"I thought that was how lawyers made money. Order breaking down, I mean."

"Of course. But our roles are decreed by fate. You, for example. What is your part in our little weekly drama?"

"I am to deliver work to you so perfect it defies analysis."

"That is correct. And what is my purpose in this happy scenario?"

Henry smiled. "Your role is to tell me I'm shit."

Parker's eyes gleamed. "Henry, you're shit."

Henry relaxed; the world was once again comfortably predictable. "Thank you, Sheldon. Was there anything else?"

Parker grinned, his mouth a thin, shallow curve. "You think by agreeing with me you can avoid my pain. But I didn't make partner by not picking up little misdirections. I'm afraid you have to sit here for the full hour while I deconstruct briefs you thought were works of art. Then I'll bury you with research because you're still young enough to be brilliant on caffeine and doughnuts, whereas I have better things to do with my nights. This is work, ironically, for which you will not receive one whit of credit. Long before it's seen it will bear the proud name of Sheldon Parker."

"The universe does have a sense of humor."

Parker's mouth widened into a smile. "Do you know why I like you, Henry?"

Henry shrugged. "My innocence?"

"Very droll."

"Is it possible I offer the firm something professionally?"

"Be serious. You're lucky you're even here. I mean, the *University of Kansas.*"

"Unlike you, Sheldon," Henry replied, "I had to actually pay for my education."

Parker waved his hand dismissively. "You had some decent clerking . . ."

"Excellent clerking, Sheldon. At the state supreme court."

"That would require calling Kansas a state, which, naturally, I won't.

But miraculously, you now find yourself living beyond your limited pedigree. You find yourself, in fact, buried in the legal backwaters of the firm of Destroy, Dismantle and Debase. You work sixty hours a week and have no life other than work at all. You have a girlfriend—inexplicably desirable, by the way—that you see intermittently. Perhaps you've developed the ability to write briefs and screw simultaneously. But that's not what really amuses me, Mathews. What amuses me is the fact that every day you get up, look at yourself in the mirror, and tell yourself the same pathetic thing."

A trace of irony filtered involuntarily through Henry's voice; Parker was being unusually wicked, and he was tired of playing whipping boy. "And what would that be, Sheldon?" he asked. "Please enlighten me."

Parker shrugged. "You tell yourself that if you can stand kissing my ass a couple more years, you will receive your payoff."

Henry responded with a grim smile. He had, in fact, muttered something very like those words to himself that morning. "What is the payoff, Sheldon?" he asked. "Now, with my nose shined so shiny brown, would be a golden time to remind me."

Parker smiled. "House in Lincoln Park, and a staggering capacity to borrow money."

"That's it, then? That's what I get in return for my immortal soul?"

Parker looked at his protégé indulgently. "I understand you, Henry. You're smart and ambitious, and you thought that made you special. Now, two years into your career, you're realizing that it merely made you a cliché."

Henry contained the desire to execute a perfect backhand with a tightly strung tennis racket on Parker's face by letting his mind settle instead on Elaine Mitchell's immaculate backside, which an hour earlier he had been caressing with the kind of pleasure he sincerely hoped Parker had never experienced. Parker was smiling smugly, but then, predictably, his expression clouded. Henry knew what was coming. It followed in these sessions as night followed day.

Parker's voice dropped. "Yet one thing you withhold from me," he said quietly. "This morsel you keep in the dark. It eats at me, and I don't like that." His eyes searched Henry's face. "I speak of the little black spot on your otherwise stellar résumé, Henry. The failure. The disappointment. The only thing about you someone like me could possibly find interesting."

"You don't find my excellence entertaining?"

"God, no," Parker said earnestly, leaning forward. "Look at it from my point of view. Before me flows an endless stream of superlative résumés, nothing but fawning recommendations. Losers don't apply here, for obvious reasons. It's a nightmare. You can't think I would ever have hired you if you had been merely excellent. It was your disturbing flaw that made me care about you at all."

"I've wondered about that, Sheldon. Why would you hire less than the best? What's this attraction to the fallen?"

Parker smiled, perfectly aligned teeth in an alligator row.

"Go ahead, Henry. Be my analyst. You tell me."

Henry knew the answer, judged his response, and took one of the reckless liberties that he risked from time to time, risks that none of the other junior attorneys at the firm dared. Lately he found himself going over the line more often with Parker, a kind of behavior not unlike being attracted to stepping off a cliff. It was dangerous, and it kept him sane. "Could it be that abusing armor-plated lawyers isn't any fun for a guy like you?" he asked, his voice absolutely level. "That the masochist needs weakness to feed on?"

The word "masochist" hung in the air like mustard gas, dangerous and mobile. Parker's expression was very nearly unchanged; only his eyes widened perceptibly. After a long, perilous moment, he laughed. "There it is," he stated, as though uncovering the determining fact in a difficult case. "You're a piranha, Mathews. Presented with fresh meat, you can't help yourself. You have to go in for the kill. That's what makes you different from the other well-dressed robots around here."

Henry exhaled; once again, he had survived. It actually seemed that the more he pushed his luck, the more Parker appeared to enjoy it. It suddenly and horribly dawned on him that Parker might actually be one step ahead of him, in control of the process, running him like a foreign agent. Was it possible that being turned into an impulsive asshole was part of Parker's plan for him, a step in his training? The thought gave him a momentary sense of vertigo, mostly because that was exactly what he knew he was becoming: a dangerous, efficient mercenary. For lack of a better word, a *Parker*. Looking at his managing partner across the desk, he found that he wasn't relieved, exactly, that Parker hadn't fired him for his remark. "You love to use my little past excursion to bring that out in me, don't you, Sheldon?" Henry asked. "Anyway, I never hid anything about that time, my so-called black spot. It's all in the paperwork."

Parker smiled. "The subject graduates with a business degree, cum laude. How thoroughly blasé. But does he enter law school? He does not. He goes to Kentucky, land of marrying cousins, sagging porches, and outdoor appliances. What does he do there? He enrolls in an academically inauspicious *seminary*. He goes, ladies and gentlemen, to find God."

"Study God," Henry corrected. "I spent some time in seminary after undergraduate school. What of it?"

"And dropped out in the second semester," Parker interrupted. "Three weeks from the end of an academic year."

"We've been through this, Sheldon. I changed my mind. Rather than finish the year, I dropped out. Four months later I was in law school."

"It wasn't leaving seminary that was the mistake I'm so drawn to." He leaned forward, putting his slender fingers on his mahogany desk. "Leaving seminary is something I have absolutely no trouble understanding."

"Then what's bothering you, Sheldon? What is this fatal flaw?"

"Entering it in the first place. It's so wonderfully needy. So vulnerable and . . . hell, I don't know, optimistic."

Henry stared at Parker, a man utterly at peace with his cynicism. "And for these few months of inquisition into the eternal I have a parson's collar tattooed around my neck."

"Permanently, and no amount of after-hours martini swilling with the boys is going to change that fact."

"Look, Sheldon," Henry said, "not that this isn't fun, but don't you have my week to destroy?"

Parker eyed him for a long time, and Henry began to suspect that for once he would press on and try to force an answer about leaving seminary. But Sheldon blinked, then released him as usual. It couldn't possibly be from weakness. Why he allowed Henry to maintain his secret continued to be a mystery. "All right, Mathews," he said, "but I'm going to get you good and drunk one day and make you spill. It's just a matter of time."

"I'll cherish the moment," Henry replied. "Bereft of human emotion yourself, you squeeze the feelings out of your subordinates like toothpaste." Henry nearly winced, stunned by the liberty he had just taken, ready for a withering response. But Parker exploded with laughter.

"Damn, you need a wheelbarrow for those balls?" He waved his hand. "Of course, rednecks are known for their brass ones. Having been born smart, rich, and pretty, I can appreciate that." To Parker, a Connecticut native whose family had been inextricably woven through the highly educated East Coast elite for a hundred years, a lawyer from the Kansas backwater was like a kind of rare, exotic bird: fascinating and mostly decorative. "In gratitude for your amusing banter," he went on, "I will leave time for some no doubt obscene dinner plans with that lovely girl from Hargrove and Lecherous you've been hanging around."

"Hargrove and *Leach*," Henry corrected. "And her name's Elaine."

"Whatever. Whenever I think of that woman, I lose some fine muscle control. Blood rushing from the brain and all that." Henry absorbed the tactless comment stoically.

Parker reached for a sheaf of papers that was sitting neatly on his desk;

apparently, playtime was over. He opened the top file. "You remember the Centel thing. We put together their takeover by Technology Enterprises."

"Must have been two hundred pages. That was what, six months ago?"

Parker nodded. "Already going bad."

Henry looked up, surprised. "It looked airtight."

"Seems the Centel folks didn't understand that their jobs were a part of the deal. Losing them, I mean."

"TE canned Centel's management after the buyout?"

Parker nodded. "Those who were sacrificed were not pleased."

"I can imagine."

Sheldon's expression didn't change; other people's tragedies didn't faze him. He was a professional, like a pathologist; he could turn over the internal organs of a corporation and stare at them without regard for the people involved. "Batting second, we have our favorite health-care provider, Dr. Lindsay Samuelson. Apparently he's once again been misunderstood by a former patient."

Henry grimaced; he hated those kinds of cases. The firm did little of that kind of work, but Samuelson was a friend of one of the partners. "Messy?" he asked.

"Plastic surgery gone horribly awry, apparently." Parker smiled.

"Mercy isn't one of your strong suits, is it, Sheldon?"

"Litigation pays better," Parker replied easily.

Henry sat quietly, mentally calculating the hours it would take to pull the projects together. Sheldon loved shoveling the big stuff on him, which was, he knew, a kind of compliment. In spite of the ritual abuse, Henry knew from the caseload that he was rising in the firm. The Centel case, in particular, was tricky stuff, the kind of law that the firm had made its reputation on. Parker wouldn't trust it to someone in whom he didn't have confidence. At a minimum, withstanding Parker's tortuous workload was demonstrating a capacity for pain that was getting him noticed. He pulled out a legal pad and prepared to take notes. "Let's get started," he said. "We can't have any millionaires feeling like we don't care."

Parker chuckled again, a deeply satisfied sound. He opened another folder, but before he could speak his intercom buzzed.

"No interruptions, Suzie," Parker said. "I'm in my weekly meeting with the brilliant young comedian, Mr. Mathews. We're much too busy to talk to any millionaires today."

"I'm sorry, sir," a breathy, female voice answered over the speakerphone. Parker hired his secretaries for their measurements, not their dictation. "I explained to the gentleman several times that you and Mr. Mathews were in conference. But he insisted Mr. Mathews take his call immediately." Henry raised an eyebrow, but said nothing.

"Oh really," Sheldon answered grandly. "And who might this very important caller be?"

"It's a Mr. Roger Crandall, from Council Grove."

"Council what?"

"I believe he said Kansas, sir."

A smile spread across Sheldon's face as he turned to Henry. "How odd, darling. That's Henry's hometown. The Mathews spawning ground."

"That's right, Sheldon," Henry said. "That's in the paperwork, too."

"*From Council Grove to Chicago.* Sounds like Mark Twain." Parker stood up from behind his desk. "Tell you what, Henry. I've got to go to the can anyway. You can take the call from the insistent Mr. Crandall, of the Council Grove Crandalls, from here." Parker handed Henry the phone, and pushed the intercom once again. "Here he is, darling," he said, and walked out of the room.

Henry rolled his chair up to the front of Parker's desk and spoke into the phone. "Roger?" he said. "Is that you?"

Roger's flat, midwestern voice came over the phone. "Daddy's dead," he said. "So I'm calling you."

Henry sat back in his chair, absorbing Roger's words. Tyler Crandall had been a legend in Henry's own childhood, a kind of symbol that had seemed eternal. He had been the king of Council Grove, the most powerful man in the county. The idea that he was dead seemed impossible. "I'm very sorry, Roger," he said. "I had no idea. That's terrible news."

"I got a paper says you got all the legal stuff. And it says you got the will."

Henry's own father, also a lawyer until his own death, had handled the Crandall legal affairs for decades. But with his father's death those responsibilities had been transferred to Henry. With Crandall's apparent good health and relatively young age he hadn't dug in; an oversight, but Sheldon was working him night and day as it was. "That's right," Henry answered tentatively. "I can go through the papers for you."

"The funeral's Wednesday, eleven o'clock." Henry hesitated; Sheldon had just completed his usual surgery on his week. It was short notice, but of course that was how funerals normally were. "This here says you're the executor," Roger said curtly. "You gotta be there."

Henry made a snap decision. "Of course, Roger. I'll have to juggle some things, but I'll come in late tomorrow and be there for the service." Sheldon wouldn't like it, but there really was no choice. He would have to go and work it out some way.

"Bring the papers," Roger said flatly.

"I'll take care of everything, Roger," Henry said quietly. "Send my condolences to your mother and Sarah."

"We'll meet Wednesday night and we can go over everything then."

"All right, Roger. Try to get a little rest and take care of yourself."

"Yeah."

There was a click, and Parker reentered the room. "Sheldon," Henry said, "I've got to go home."

SIMMS LIBRARY ALBUQUERQUE ACADEMY

For early June, Chicago was clinging tenaciously to a cool spring; near the lake the north wind came off the water from Canada with the shrill whine of an ancient, crabby relative. Henry rolled up his window as he drove the shoreline to the freeway, wishing for the summer that seemed to wait so long to appear. He parked at O'Hare and walked across the lot clutching a jacket, his briefcase, and a small travel bag.

Parker had given him the time without much dispute, to his relief. Personal matters were allowed to intrude, as long as they were legal personal matters. Not seeing Elaine was something else; he had called to explain, and she sounded disappointed, which pleased him. They had been a little tense together lately—except in the sack, where the chemistry was undeniable—but Henry had been chalking it up to their brutal schedules. Between the two of them, seeing each other in the daylight was becoming a faint dream. But she had sounded almost . . . *sweet*, he thought, and then rejected that idea out of hand. Elaine wasn't sweet, he had to admit. Or tender, exactly. But the important thing was that maybe their awkward period was ending. She had blown him a kiss over the phone, and he had hung up with a smile. He hadn't dated much in law school, just the usual stress reliever with the others. But Elaine had come into his life with a combination of erotic power and professional ambition that he had found intoxicating. She was money, not family money like Parker but self-made, which to Henry was more impressive. A rising broker at a securities firm near his office, they made a formidable team—not just in bed but in career terms as well. Lately he had found himself beginning to think long range about her, and surprising himself by not killing the thought the second it occurred to him.

Henry boarded the plane and took his seat in first class, a bonus from working at the firm. The office had its own travel department, and it could usually wrangle an upgrade. Henry leaned back in the chair, thinking about what Tyler Crandall had meant to Council Grove. The man hadn't bothered to hold any office, because any one of them would have been beneath him. He got what he wanted from intimidation rather than cooperation. And Roger had been his lieutenant, although an uneasy one. Father and son were known to snap at each other, sometimes quite publicly, oblivious to onlookers. Henry had seen them fight more than once, appalled at the messiness, the lack of discretion. Apparently the power the

Crandall family wielded in Council Grove was so complete that the idea of embarrassment didn't occur to them. They simply did as they pleased, and they didn't care who watched.

Henry opened the big bundle of papers detailing the Crandall family holdings. Almost immediately his eye was drawn to one of the few sights with the emotional power to dismantle him. He looked down and saw his own father's handwriting, the loose, slightly chaotic scrawl on a note attached to a large manila envelope that was sealed by a notary. *Only to be opened in the presence of the immediate family of Tyler W. Crandall,* the note said. *Sealed this day January 17, 1993. Signed, Henry L. Mathews, Sr., attorney-at-law.*

With the sight of that note Henry's father materialized, disheveled and frayed, in his mind. He was smiling, tossing his keys to his secretary as he walked out the door of his little office just off the town square. Henry watched his father's back recede as he walked down the sidewalk, his image fading, getting smaller. Henry blinked and took a drink of the wine he had ordered; the picture disappeared, cast back into a compartment he didn't willingly open. But there were times it opened on its own, over his objections, and he was forced to indulge a memory, knowing that he would burn himself on it.

He blinked again and he was back at seminary. The open sore, the blot that had required constant explaining during the interviews for jobs. One year of his life, represented by a single line on linen résumé paper: 1994, Trinity School of Divinity. *Incomplete.* He had been told to leave the whole episode off—to lie, in effect—but he refused. The line would be there and it would say incomplete, because Henry's faith had left him three weeks before the end of a semester while sitting on the second floor of the religion building.

Seventy-two hours earlier a car containing his father and mother had been hit head-on by a drunk driver drifting across the center line as he crested a hill; one second sooner or later and they would probably still be alive. But the perfect, obscene timing of the driver's alcoholic stupor had stolen both parents from him, smashing into his life and stealing from him a past, present, and future. His father's car had careered off the road into a steep embankment, turning over in a horror of twisted metal until it came to rest upside down, thirty-five feet below the highway. The driver of the other car was killed as well. The autopsy showed a blood-alcohol level three times the legal limit.

In the wake of his parents' death belief had evaporated off Henry like a sudden shower off hot asphalt. There had been a memorial service in Council Grove, little more than a collection of platitudes from William Chambers, pastor of the Evangel Baptist Church. A dinner afterward, steaming-hot plates of food, succulent and repulsive, carried into his empty house. Looks of strained compassion, more hollow words, an aunt and uncle arguing over when to leave. Then the flight back to Louisville, Henry taking his pain back to Trinity and finding himself alone in a classroom, sitting and thinking. His books were stacked up on his desk, Bible commentaries and treatises: Pliny the Elder; the Gospels in Greek; the book of Exodus in Hebrew. Metal hit metal in his mind, smashing glass, and then an awful silence on an open road.

Henry had pushed his books from the desk in a sweeping movement, the dust of them scattering upon impact with the floor like a holy cloud, little particles exploding into the sunlight that streamed through the windows. He sat in the chair, numb, the lives of his father and mother rolling across his memory. Lives that seemed, in the pain of death, absolutely meaningless.

He was losing the memory of his mother, not by attrition but by forcing it away until only a few blurry images remained, impenetrable to the blotting, covering force of her death; one, a scene of her down on her knees planting beans and summer squash in the backyard, and another, a glimpse of her standing in the front doorway of their house leaving for church, tired, indifferently dressed. She had needed to be industrious; Henry's father had spent his life doing small-time legal practice in a Kansas backwater, establishing the equivalent of a rural legal-aid office but without even the pathetic government funding. He had spent most of his time vainly fighting farm foreclosures with out-of-state creditors. Farming was dying in Kansas, family legacies turning inexorably into ten-thousand-acre agribusiness. Farm after farm was lost. Foreclosures led to divorces, theater of the absurd warfare for people with nothing left to fight over. Between that and the biggest pro bono workload in the county, his father had worked twelve-hour days, lost more than he had won, and at his death left a mortgaged house and thirty-eight hundred dollars in the bank. Henry sold the house at a loss, and there was just enough money left to bury them. After the funeral Henry gave away most of their possessions, unwilling to keep the pathetic reminders of his father's underachievement.

Henry ordered another drink and closed his eyes. He had come back to Trinity after the funeral and sat alone in a classroom. Once again the words came to him, just as they had that day. They were words of power, silent and liberating: *It's not true. I don't believe it. God is silent or He does not exist. Both come to the same thing. There's nothing for me here.* His father and mother were in the ground, and that was all. There was no "by-and-by," no preposterous streets of gold. He left his books on the floor and walked out of the building. He left Louisville the next day. Then, a string of successes: graduating in the top 5 percent of his class, law review, the state supreme court clerking job. Finally, the pinnacle: a job offer from Wilson, Lougherby and Mathers, a firm that specialized in corporate takeovers, junk-bond issues, and IPOs. Inevitably in such actions, there were enemies to be crushed. Under the tutelage of Sheldon Parker, he was thriving, becoming as lethal as a shark in an aquarium.

The plane landed with a jolt, bringing Henry back to reality. The Chicago-to-Wichita flight was short and it was just before seven in the evening when Henry picked up his rental car. The air access to Council Grove was lousy; Wichita was too far south, Kansas City too far north. Inevitably, a drive of a couple of hours followed either flight. He pulled into light traffic for the drive, heading north. The traffic quickly thinned and he watched the numbers of the cross streets grow: 63rd Street, 91st, and, improbably, 125th—by then he was merely driving through farm country—then 197th Street, which marked nothing more than a blacktop road cutting through a cornfield, and on and on, the city zoning commission stretching its authority farther and farther into the optimistic absurd, until the numbers took on the grandeur of a borough of New York. Long after the last traffic light or stop sign he passed 275th Street, and then, fantastically, 303rd Street. At last, however—a good fifteen miles after anything possible to confuse with city life had passed—the numbers died out and the comfortable Kansas rural route system appeared. With those numbers he reentered a different world, a world as far away from Chicago as his own practice was from his father's.

Henry relaxed into the drive, and in an hour and a half he entered the Flinthills, his rental car rolling out over enormous, languishing waves of earth. Some unknown crop had just been planted off to his left, and the seeds lay hidden under great black dunes of exposed soil stretching out beside him. To his right, tall range grass grew. Henry had learned to drive on these endless ribbons of straight blacktop that cut through the Flinthills of northeastern Kansas. That land hadn't changed appreciably for five hundred years, and the roads were a kind of brand, burned into the ground over Indian ranges with hot asphalt to show who now owned it. It was a curious feeling now, coming from his new life, to ride out on the path of a bullet into the horizon, mile after perfectly straight mile, no stoplights, no traffic, no people.

The light gradually failed as Henry drove. The fields were broken by occasional farms, usually consisting of a weathered barn, a gathering of smaller outbuildings, some scattered farm equipment, and a frame house, all arranged close in on each other as if sheltering from the wind. Henry crested a hill as the sun vanished behind him, and the world seemed to gently fall away into a shallow valley, the distance across it so great that the air darkened into gray fog at a wide, distant horizon. Tall bluestem grass now filled endless fields on both sides of the road, a shifting, darkening blue and green that trembled in the growing shadows. Wild sunflowers lined the right, their black eyes seven feet high staring silently back at the sun as it vanished. Henry rolled down his window; the air was cool, and he breathed it in, smelling black dirt and humus. This was the world of AM radio, of country jamborees and wailing preachers at midnight on clear-channel stations three states away.

A lone windmill stood a half mile distant, dark against the last light, and a string of black dots stretched out toward it as cattle marched in for the night. Henry recognized the windmill; it was on the Triple Z, Rory Zachariah's land. Council Grove was fifteen miles past that.

Zachariah's ranch passed, and then the south side of the Crandall ranch itself opened up before him, the road skirting around nearly two thousand acres of prime cattle land. A great cattle pen loomed on the left, harshly lit from above by tall floodlights on poles, like a prison yard. Beneath the lights was a crisscross of sagging, fenced runways that led to a raised platform where the animals could be weighed and loaded onto trucks for slaughter. A Crandall truck was the last thing the beasts would see before the inside of a packing plant and darkness.

By the time Henry approached the outskirts of Council Grove, it was well past nine. As he passed the city limits the highway transformed itself into Pawnee Street, the main drag. He slowed to twenty miles an hour, picking up little changes in the town, subtle but discernible. He had become accustomed in Chicago to a certain noisy impermanence in things, but Council Grove had changed quietly, in small ways. Here a streetlight was burned out, there a house was abandoned and boarded up. He rolled through the scattering of old houses on the edge of town and slowed at his old high school, unglamorously named USD 492. It wasn't the kind of building that generated schoolboy nostalgia, but was merely a graceless collection of stacked bricks and impenetrable windows, rusting air conditioners hanging in an obedient row. The ball field was to the left, with rickety wooden stands and a tall wire backstop for foul balls.

A few blocks later he impulsively turned down Hazelwood, his old street. He came to a gentle stop in front of his old house. It was still empty, Council Grove struggling for existence like most other small Plains towns. The people could only sell their real estate back and forth to each other for so long, and eventually things became more or less frozen. White paint was separating from the wooden planks of the sides of the house, splinter-ing off the porch. The balcony above it gently sagged, as if an accumula-tion of memories were breaking it slowly down. He scanned the street; most of the houses were in the same condition, vainly holding back the inevitable decline. But a lingering immigrant pride still faintly flickered, and a few of the places remained well kept, covered with clean white paint, with decent lawns and small gardens.

An open expanse lay behind the house. While Henry was still a boy his father had cleared a flat spot there for a play area and erected a steel basketball goal. They would play for hours, Henry beating him like a drum but his father never tiring of the game. Henry had developed a theory about those games, one which explained his father's mostly failed practice: his father didn't need to win. He didn't go for the kill, searching instead for consensus. That made him a good father but a mediocre lawyer. Parker, for example, would have had him joyfully for lunch. The basketball court wasn't discernible now, all their pounding and running long ago grown over into an unbroken green.

Henry looked across to the Martin place next door; the families had known each other well, something inevitable in small towns. Martin's two sons had married and left Council Grove soon after high school. A sign in the front yard silently proclaimed, ASK ME ABOUT AVON.

Henry stared for only a minute or two before starting the engine and heading back through town. Two miles later he had arrived at the Flinthills Motel, a single-story, twenty-room clapboard affair. Three of the neon letters were burnt out on the sign, resulting in a meaningless collection of characters. He checked in and hung up his clothes, setting a small travel alarm for early the next day. The room was musty, as though it hadn't been opened in some time. He crawled into the worn-out bed and thought of Chicago and of Elaine, willing a dream to his mind. In fifteen minutes, he was asleep.

Henry awoke unwillingly with the dawn, an oppressive sense of solitude violating his sleep. He stayed in bed, half awake and dozing until his alarm went off. Then he quietly rose, splashed some water on his face, and walked to the window in his underwear.

Henry pulled back the curtain slightly and peered out past the gravel parking lot. There wasn't a tree to the horizon. The sun was crawling out through cirrus clouds lying low in the sky, settled in a pale, thin blue. He had forgotten that blue, living in the more industrial air of Chicago. On the plains, each day yielded up its own unique colors: this was light and luminescent, as if it had come straight from a paint tube.

After his shower he laid out his clothes on the bed and dressed carefully, pulling dark trousers up over his legs, pushing arms into an expensive linen shirt, meticulously buttoning and tucking it. He had picked out a blue tie with a subdued stripe of blood red, a pair of slender black shoes, and last, a perfectly tailored dark suit coat. He had always been a careful dresser, and it was exactly as it had been six years earlier, dressing for the funeral of his parents. The crease of his pants had been just so, cutting through the oppressive air of death when he walked, his clothes a suit of armor against the chaos and indifference of the universe. His tie had been perfect on that day as well, set against the randomness of the car crash, an act of control in opposition to the mindless nothing of life. Shoes shined, hair in place, collar pressed, all futile, desperate, unconscious. And now the film rolled out again for Tyler Crandall, rolled out in a polished button, a straightened tie. Henry checked his watch again: it was nine-thirty, and the funeral was set for ten. It was only a short drive, but there would certainly be a crowd and he didn't want to risk entering late.

Henry drove down Pawnee to the town square, which was dominated by the county courthouse, a dusty corner of which served as the town museum. As a boy, Henry had often gone there, drawn by the old monochrome photos and artifacts of the last farmers with a personal link to the pioneer days. They posed leaning on plows and fences, the men in loose-fitting handmade overalls and the women in black dresses that were surely insufferable in the summer heat. Henry had been struck by the sober expressions of each face, even of the children, with their formal poses, chests out and heads up, like soldiers. In one of the pictures the people prayed, some with heads bowed but others with faces turned up to the sky. God had fashioned an earth for them so full of promise and yet so essentially inhospitable and untrustworthy that they fell on their knees like repentant gamblers, eagerly making deals with a capricious weather master. That pioneer world still faintly echoed through Council Grove, but it was merely a whisper now, drowned out when the highway and satellite dishes brought the modern world to it and lured many of the residents away. Now Council Grove clung uneasily to its rural personality as a Pizza Hut and a video store crowded it from the highway.

Henry turned down Chautauqua toward the Evangel Baptist Church. The church building rose in pure white clapboards, with a tall white box steeple in front. Concrete steps led to the wide front double doors, and a scattering of flowers lined the walk from the gravel parking lot. A line of dark suits and dresses moved through the doors of the church like a centipede, vanishing into the building.

Henry parked and walked across the parking lot. There was little talking among the people there, the somber stillness of a funeral having already settled on the crowd, but several spoke quietly to him as he approached. He was remembered, certainly. His father, for all his faults, had been loved, and Henry nodded soberly to those near him as he entered, seating himself near the back of the sanctuary. He looked around; Frances Yancey was there, matronly and soft, all breasts and hips in a flowered dress. Old man Carr, coerced into a Wal-Mart suit but still looking like hell, the night's drink not yet drained away. The whole Breedon family, huddling together as they entered the church door like ducks in a rainstorm. Gradually he was surrounded by faces from his past, people filling every seat and pressing in on him, children on laps, the adults shoulder to shoulder. At the front of the hall lay the casket, a great oak shape covered with flowers and bows. The American and Kansas flags stood to the left, the Christian flag to the right.

A side door opened, and the first Crandall face Henry saw was Margaret's. Henry grimaced when he saw her: she appeared ill, as if some of her own life had been drained from her when her husband's slipped away. He hadn't seen her in some time, but she looked considerably aged, with new lines in her face. Her hands were pushed down as fists into her black dress as she walked unsteadily into the church.

Roger followed close behind, wearing a dark, Western-cut suit and spit-shined, black leather dress boots. Henry had forgotten how imposing he was: barrel-chested, broad-framed, and full of self-aware, ill-contained masculinity. But his galling flaw was there as well; there roamed through the Crandall men a genetic fault, and Roger had been unlucky. One leg was a good two inches shorter than the other, and his gait loped, his head moving slightly from side to side when he walked. Roger had hated the defect, torn between wearing corrective boots and the stubborn practice of smoothing out the motion. In the end, he refused the boots, which anyone could detect at a glance.

Sarah, Roger's sister, followed, her shoulder-length brunette hair pulled back with an unadorned barrette. Physically, she had stolen the best of each of her parents, with Tyler's dark, almost Gypsy good looks and her mother's remarkably clear, smooth complexion. But she had obviously been crying, and her eyes were red, the mascara smudged.

The last notes of the organ sank down into echo, and a stillness settled on the church. Three large ceiling fans whirred overhead, a slow, humming pulse. Henry glanced around; the sanctuary was packed with at least five hundred people, a good seventy-five more than it was designed to hold. *A fitting tribute to Ty Crandall, King of Council Grove,* he thought. Then, from the shadowed side of the church, a door opened on to the podium. William Chambers, pastor of the Evangel Baptist Church, entered the sanctuary.

Chapter Four

"This sacred place isn't filled to overflowing to honor some man way down in the book of life, beloved. Nobody's here to honor some low private in the army of God. We're here to celebrate a man what's gonna walk into God's heaven by the front door, beloved, with his head held up high."

Thus began the memorial service for Tyler William Crandall. Pastor Chambers was a short, stocky man, with the rough dimensions of a brick and a shock of thick black hair on top. His body was crammed into a dark blue suit, his substantial bulk sticking out from his spine like a well-dressed barrel on a post. A white handkerchief stuck out of his left chest pocket like it was struggling for air. "We come to this house with the joys of life and the sorrows of death," he said. "There's room enough for our laughter and our tears. So that's why we're here. To laugh and to cry. But over whom, beloved? Over Tyler William Crandall. And in that name is everything needs be said." Chambers moved from behind the podium, perching on the edge of the platform. He softened his tone to sweet tree sap. "Every child of God has a destiny, beloved. Ain't no soul on this earth without a purpose, and there's comfort in that fact. It means God's got His plans for livin' and dyin', and ain't no use to struggle against it. But what was Tyler Crandall's purpose? Ain't that the eternal question we got to answer on this day? What did the Lord God put that one man on this earth to do, and was he able to do it? Ain't that what makes a man's life worth livin'?" Chambers' face was intense, pleading. "Yes, beloved. The Lord brought Tyler to this town to be His instrument. God needed somebody to be His hand. And brother Tyler answered that call. He was our protector and our provider."

Chambers' mouth stretched into a melancholy smile. "Beloved, I'm gonna tell tales. I'm gonna break a little confidence. But we're family here, ain't we?" He paused, listening, his eyes cast out across the congregation. "Ain't we?"

The crowd murmured its assent, and Henry could feel the energy in the room beginning to rise. This was the ritual of his boyhood church, the slow beginning, the crescendo of the call-and-response, the climax when Chambers drove heaven and hell home and white soul would rise off the preacher like steam off ham hocks. The first beads of sweat were already forming on Chambers' face.

"I don't think I'm doing anything wrong," the pastor said, "to tell you that the brother Crandall wasn't ashamed to support the work of God in this town. He gave, beloved. There was times he gave when there wasn't nobody else to give. But that ain't what made it beautiful. What made it beautiful was that he didn't want no kind of credit for it. He didn't walk around town expecting congratulations like one of God's chosen people. Tyler Crandall didn't do nothin' to impress men." He paused again, thoughtfully. "So then why did he do it, beloved? Tell me why."

Chambers dropped his voice to a whisper. "He did it because he knew that God don't forget, beloved. The Great Heavenly Accountant got to balance the books. Tyler put his trust in heavenly treasure that moths don't eat and thieves don't steal.

"Now, brothers and sisters, ain't many in this world would count me wise. Ain't many accused me of bein' a sophisticated thinker." Chambers smiled, secure in his self-deprecation. "But I learned a thing or two ain't in books. I've seen a terrible thing with my own eyes. What is that thing, beloved? What is that demon?" Chambers pointed to the casket. "*Death*. Death, beloved. I have found that thing in hospital beds, in nursing homes. I've battled him for my flock right on through the night." Chambers' speech became dark and slow, hot asphalt slowly spreading over the still crowd. "Death comes in the night, and it breaks down every door, splinters flyin' from the mace of the devil himself." He pulled his handkerchief out of its tight cage and dabbed his eyes briefly before stuffing it, rumpled and moist, back into his pocket.

"They say every man is different. But that's a lie, because we all got the grave. That's the curse we share in this evil world. That's the day them college boys stand shoulder to shoulder with us farmers and welders and cattlemen. That's when the philosophers of this world got to shut on up and the Lord God Almighty gets His say." Chambers thrust his finger out toward the congregation. "God's gonna have the last word, beloved. Count on that. And when the Almighty clears His throat you either gonna be sleepin' the innocent sleep of blissful rest in the arms of the Redeemer, or you gonna get hauled down by the Deceiver into a hell of iniquity." He paused, terrifying and passionate. "Take stock of your lives, brothers and sisters. Check your account with the Lord God Almighty!"

Henry sat in the midst of the congregation, and he had no doubt Chambers believed every word of what he said. But he was dead to the power of his performance. The part of him that had listened as a boy to descriptions of the fires of hell was gone, murdered with his parents. Years earlier it had been alive, vividly receptive in its innocence. It had been in the heat of just such a terrifying moment that Henry, then fourteen years old, had found himself hurtling down the church aisle toward the pastor in embarrass-

ment and release. He had sinned, and he would repent. He would not be
dragged down into hell. He would answer the call of the god who shouts.

Chambers pointed down at the casket with a sigh, bringing Henry back
to the present. "But that fiery holocaust will never fall upon this dear
brother." The pastor looked up, and his face was beaming. "I see a vision,
a vision of God, beloved. I see Tyler Crandall entering the gates of heaven
and God is smiling right at him. I hear the Lord God speak. *Well done, my
good and faithful servant,* He says. *You come on in to the great feast. Come in and
dine with my special friends, my faithful friends."*

Chambers was spellbound in his own epiphany. He clutched the sides of
the podium, transported, taken up into the heaven he saw. Then he looked
out into the congregation; his voice was permeated with anguish. "What
we get is a flicker of time, beloved. We got a moment until death snuffs us
out like candles in a rainstorm. God waits at the end of our road, ready to
judge the quick and the dead! Our dear departed brother Crandall chose
right. Let us all choose so right!"

With that proclamation Chambers slumped over the podium, spent.
After some time he turned and made his way back to a large red velvet
chair on the dais. He fell into it, pink-faced, sweat beading up on his
forehead.

There was silence in the sanctuary, and Henry could feel the fear creeping up from the floorboards into the congregation. Into that vapor the
music minister stood and sang, his voice a melancholy, solemn baritone.
Several in the congregation softly took up the tune, humming and murmuring. Henry watched as Margaret collapsed and began sobbing against
Sarah.

The singing ended and Chambers nodded gravely to Roger, signaling
the eulogy. Roger stood, and when he rose every eye in the sanctuary was
fixed upon him. Soon he would be the lifeblood upon which the entire
town would depend. He would be their supply of materials and equipment
and, with the bank hurting under so many failed farms, their credit. He
could dictate the laws and the policies that ruled the few businesses he
didn't control. He would be the most important man in their lives.

Roger walked up the stairs, each step a careful measurement to level his
hated gait. He took the pulpit and looked down at the casket; for a
moment, he appeared to be in some indecision. When he began, his voice
was quiet and hard, and he seemed to speak more to the gleaming wooden
box than to the congregation. "I'm supposed to say somethin' about my
daddy now," he said. "Pastor says I might recollect some good memories
of him." He breathed deeply, never taking his eyes off the casket. "But the
fact is, I don't think about things that way, and it don't do no good to look

back. My daddy is dead. Here shortly he'll be in the ground. Then it'll all be over, every bit of it."

Roger stared blankly downward for a few brittle seconds, then continued. "Like the pastor says, ain't nobody knows when their time is up. But I had twenty-nine years of him, and I figure it all boils down to those lessons I got when he was alive. Daddy was a teacher. That's what I'll always remember. He never stopped teachin' me, not one second of the day. He'd take the broom right out of your hand, just to show you the right way to sweep. He'd make you tear down a fence just to build it up what he called straight." He paused a moment, and Henry thought he could hear his voice catch, although from what emotion it wasn't clear. "I don't reckon Daddy stopped teachin' me one second of my life. So I learned. One time I checked in a load of wheat and read the water content wrong, read it clean wrong, by two percent. Daddy taught me that day, taught me good. He never stopped teachin'." Roger ground to a halt, his voice unsteady. Then he looked up into the congregation, looking surprised to be surrounded by people. His voice cleared. "Some say this town is dyin'," he said. "But I say it ain't gonna die if I have anything to do with it. It's like Daddy used to tell me: *The difference between doin' and dreamin' ain't nothin' but the will to act. You got to have the will.* I figure that's right. What matters now is movin' this town forward and that's what I aim to do. Ain't nothin' gonna change." He paused again, looking at the pastor. Finally he muttered, "Amen," and bowed his head briefly before descending from the platform.

Chambers rose solemnly, dismissing the congregation for the interment. The organ began to play, and the Crandall family rose to leave, walking across the front of the church to the side door, vanishing back into the hallway. After the door closed behind them, the pastor motioned for the congregation to exit through the back. Henry filed out of the sanctuary with the others, blinking at the bright sunlight as he left the building.

The burial was a short affair. Henry drove in the motorcade the short distance to the Everlasting Rest Cemetery, where the Crandall family had plots. The crowd stretched out around the grave site, spilling out over the grass. Henry stood some distance away, surprised by a sense of awe at seeing Crandall actually lowered into the ground. Death was still death, and it seemed improbable that such a small bundle of polished wood and brass could contain a man's life. Henry glanced over at the family; they stood together beneath a dark green tent adjacent to the open grave.

Henry walked over and took Margaret's hand; she offered it to him limply, and her glazed expression made him wonder if she were in some kind of shock. Sarah nodded through her tears, and to his surprise, hugged him briefly. He had scarcely disengaged from her when Roger stuck his hand out, commanding his attention. "Be at our house at two," he said.

Henry showed mild surprise; the meeting had been planned for that evening, after the family had a chance to regroup. Roger, as though reading his thoughts, said, "No reason to drag things out. Best to just get it behind us."

"That's fine," Henry answered, "if the rest of the family feels up to it."

"They do."

Henry glanced at Margaret; she, at least, didn't appear up to anything more than several days of rest. But Sarah nodded to him, and Henry moved on past the family, taking his place on the periphery of the crowd. When he looked back, Roger had picked up a bright silver-colored shovel and was pushing it hard into the freshly exposed earth beside the grave. The deceased's body was laid to rest under a bright blue sky at the Everlasting Rest Cemetery, Council Grove, Kansas. The gravestone read: LET HIM WHO HAS RECEIVED MUCH GIVE MUCH. The wind ran along the greening grass, and Roger threw the first shovelful of black dirt onto his father's casket. The dirt landed with a hollow sound, the clumps of topsoil exploding into tiny black granules, the particles running across the top of the last resting place of Ty Crandall. Without speaking to anyone, Henry turned back to his car and drove to his motel.

Chapter Five

In spite of Roger's change of plans for the reading of the will, Henry still had time to kill before heading out to the Crandall place. He thought briefly of sleep; he hadn't realized how hard Parker had been driving him until he got some distance from it, and now, the numbness of sixty-hour weeks only a single day removed, he began to feel deeply tired. But driving through town from the church toward the motel pulled up a set of emotions that drew him down street after street in spite of his fatigue, back into his old life.

He had left town first in a fit of misplaced optimism, eighteen years old and anxious to put as many miles between himself and Council Grove as possible. His vehicle had been college, and he had excelled there. The second time he had left Council Grove he had left the bodies of his parents behind him, and he had felt nothing—merely a numb wounding. But to feel it now; to reenter that world voluntarily for a time and then to leave it definitively, passionless, intentional; that was what he wanted now. He wanted to shake the dust of the place off his feet, and that meant getting dusty first. He would look at every street, every house, and flick them off his finger as he headed back to Chicago to his life and lover and work. So he drove down Chautauqua toward the square, his face set, scanning the streets as he drove.

Just before the square were railroad tracks, a symbolic line that severed the town cleanly, separating the prosperous from the redneck. On the west the shopkeepers and a small handful of commuters lived; on the east were the hourly workers and the failed pig and chicken farmers that had been forced off their land. Henry turned along the railroad where it curved past the high school, running behind the Crandall Feed and Farm Supply.

The farm store was the financial center of Council Grove. Farmers funneled their existence through it, buying seed, hardware, supplies, and heavy equipment. They sold there as well; a row of grain silos just behind the store stood over the town like enormous banks, ready to spit out money if any farmers were prayed up enough with God and friendly enough with Crandall.

The Crandall family towered over Council Grove as surely as the granary did, and Henry rolled past the huge silos with an involuntary, adolescent respect. Their size alone inspired awe; a row of monsters nearly a hundred and sixty feet tall and more than fifty around, they cast gargantuan shadows across three blocks when the sun moved behind them. They were caverns of dreams, a holding place for farmers who played roulette with grain prices controlled by people and governments continents away. Henry passed by them and swept back out toward the square, still passing Crandall holdings: the grocery store, the bank building, a number of rental houses. Beyond his sight was the real Crandall wealth, over eighteen hundred acres of good grazing land, large even by Flinthills standards. Those fields contained the prized possession: seven trickling oil wells, mostly played out but the historic center of the family's money. It had been oil that made Ty Crandall's luck run gold; he had bought the land on the cheap and soon afterward found the precious, underground pools. Twenty-five years of pumping had slowed them to practically nothing, but the wells were still famous for a freak accident that had killed a field worker in their drilling. One second the roustabout had been working on the well casing, and the next a sudden, lethal updraft of sulfur gas choked his brain and dropped him on the spot. That started a trend that linked good fortune for Crandalls with bad luck for everybody else.

Eventually Henry entered the square, the junction of the town's four main streets: Chautauqua, Elm, Main, and Pawnee, each an arrow-straight thoroughfare running directly from the center to the outskirts of town and endlessly beyond. Originally made for several wagons abreast instead of for cars, the streets were now unnecessarily wide, and in front of the town's only café an actual hitching post stood. Now trucks parked in front of the long wooden pole, and at Christmas it was decorated with ribbons and electric lights. Outward from the café spread a run-down smattering of craft stores selling trinkets and handmade kachina dolls, a beauty shop, and a Radio Shack.

Just off the square was his father's old office, and as Henry drove past he kept his eyes firmly on the road, refusing to be drawn into that painful memory. Even to see the run-down place would have put an arrow in his heart. Henry glanced reflexively at his watch; there was still an hour to kill, and unwilling to have the time filled with thoughts of his father, he turned toward the town park to fill his mind with another man.

Henry had spent a good deal of his adolescence wondering about this man—more than wondering, at times obsessed with thoughts of him, and the idea of seeing him again filled him with both dread and curiosity. He was called the Birdman, and he was an anomaly in a town that badly needed one. Night and day the man staked an outpost on a concrete bench in a corner of Custer's Elm Park, a small area named for a spreading tree that Custer and his men had mustered under one night on their way to their graves. The tree was still there, an enormous, stretching umbrella that gave shade twenty yards across. The Birdman endured harsh Kansas weather there like a wooden statue—only high winds and rain would occasionally beat him indoors. His only concessions to the elements were a shapeless coat he wore in the cold and an infamous floppy Stetson that had been so beaten down by sun, rain, and wind that it had become moldy and stiff. With the Stetson pulled down low over his eyes, it was hard to distinguish where the man's grizzled face finished and the hat began. But when he looked up he showed simple features, with a small nose, brown eyes, and a pale mouth with lips dry from constant exposure. Raggedy hair fell down over his ears, with wiry arms that looked like solid bone.

The Birdman stank, and it was work to get near him. He rarely washed, and his pants were always shiny with grime and sweat, especially during the hot summer months. He wore flannel cotton shirts, often penetrated by a hole or two and hanging loosely about him.

The Birdman's circumstances fueled the speculation about him. In spite of living on the streets he owned a small house: a meager place close by the park over on Owendale. His owning the house created one of the longest-running mysteries in Council Grove: how the Birdman paid his bills. Even a run-down place meant county taxes, and there was certainly no visible income to the man. But the Birdman always paid in cash, rumpled green bills stuffed into envelopes left in the night box at the post office.

The source of the Birdman's nickname was a large carrion bird—a kind of vulture that flies high and alone over the plains looking for carcasses to pick apart. The bird was covered with purplish-black feathers and had a vicious-looking yellow beak that he squawked through. With his wings extended he was nearly four feet across, and when agitated he would stand up on wirelike talons, stretching his wings out wide and shrieking in a loud voice. The bird had a mean streak, and people didn't need much encouragement to keep their distance. It was plain scary as it flapped across town, landing here and there on the courthouse or some other building. But he would always return to the Birdman's concrete bench. Worst of all was the smell; the bird stank worse than the Birdman, and had a habit of relieving himself on the park bench and sidewalk, making a white mess on the concrete.

Now Henry turned onto Owendale and drove slowly toward the big elm on the edge of the park, rolling to a stop and lowering his windows. He scanned for signs of the Birdman, hoping to spot him at his usual bench. After a few minutes of sitting quietly he thought he might have heard the harsh calling of a bird, but it was distant and he couldn't be sure. He got out of the car and walked toward the bench; there was scratching in the dirt nearby, and the telltale droppings that meant the bird, at least, was still around. But there was no trace of the man, and Henry had the sinking feeling that something might have happened to him. It had been a long time—the aborted year of seminary, three more for law school, then more than two with the firm—since he had seen him, and a lot could happen to someone living such a rugged lifestyle in that amount of time.

Henry leaned against the tree, and in his mind he could hear the man's voice crackle out into the park. The Birdman talked almost ceaselessly, sometimes shrill, sometimes mumbling, but always a bizarre combination of foulmouthed cursing and religious sermonizing. The incoherence of such religious speech and obscene language had held the town's children spellbound for years, and Henry had been no different. But unlike the others, his fascination continued, and even as a teenager he had come many times, hiding behind a tree to listen. He never tired of watching the Birdman rise to preach to some invisible congregation, his voice cracked and urgent.

"Come to me, all ye merciless bastards," the man would say. *"Ye of talon, beak, and feather. Come to me, ye who rip and kill and tear. Come, ye murdering sons of bitches, for I will give ye rest."* Such words were accompanied by grand, electrifying motions sent into the air and sky. Henry's young mind was transfixed by the sight of madness and faith entwined and alive, the two powerful forces locked together in a single, tortured mind. It was the most potent combination he had ever seen, an explosion of dangerous, brilliant color in the black and white of Council Grove. Faith, deranged but real, ran through the Birdman's veins like electricity through a circuit. By comparison, Henry's own had been a trickle. But faith had been their silent bond, although Henry had never spoken to the man. They both believed, the Birdman in his imagined forces, Henry in the god of William Chambers and the Evangel Baptist Church. Now, his faith destroyed, he found himself wanting to see the man again, wanting to feel that the electricity between them had at last been cut.

No one appeared. Minutes passed, and after some time Henry reluctantly walked back to his car, still hoping to see the man suddenly appear from behind a tree or even out of thin air. But there was nothing, and at last he got in his car and started the drive to the Crandall place with a sense of melancholy. He wanted, at a minimum, to know that the Birdman was all right, that none of the ugliness of children had fallen too hard on him, or that simple disease hadn't taken him away. But in a few minutes he was turning into the circular drive that led to the Crandall home, and the seriousness of what he was about to do filled his mind.

The Crandall house itself had changed through the years, transforming itself as the Crandall fortunes grew from a large but straightforward two-story frame home into a rambling structure with two additions, each almost as large as the original home and obviously built at different times. The effect was unsettling, creating a great hulk put together from unrelated parts. Henry stared for a moment before he got out of his car; the Crandalls were intensely private in spite of their power, and he realized that he had never actually seen the inside of the house. After a moment he grabbed his briefcase and walked to the entrance. Before he had a chance to ring the bell Sarah opened the door, looking a little better than she had at the interment. She had changed into more casual clothes, and her deep sadness seemed to have lifted somewhat.

"It's good to see you," she said quietly. "I wanted to say more at the funeral, but there wasn't a chance."

Henry gave a solemn nod as he crossed the threshold. "How are you holding up?" he asked. "Did you get any rest?"

"A little," she answered. "I laid down for a few minutes, but Mother's needed a lot of attention." She smiled sadly. "She's taken things so hard. I'm not letting myself feel anything until she gets settled. It won't help if I fall to pieces."

"She's lucky to have you."

"Of course, we're in Roger's good hands now. Everything will be fine." She turned and led him down a hallway toward the rear of the house.

Henry glanced discreetly into a few of the rooms as they walked. The unifying force in the decor appeared to be the overt display of wealth, or what passed for it in Council Grove. There were no signs of the kind of real money Henry had been introduced to in Chicago, but instead rooms littered with items that smacked of upscale mail-order catalogues. Some of the pieces were attractive, but there was no real feeling imparted by the sum of the parts. There was one lovely painting of a landscape in a sitting room, but it was contained by a frame so overwrought that the picture was spoiled.

Sarah led him into a large family room where her mother sat on an ivory-colored couch, her expression as blank as it had been at the funeral. Roger stood beside her and then moved quickly toward them. He was still in his suit.

"Mathews," he said. "You're on time. That's good."

Henry stuck out his hand. "Hello, Roger. You okay?"

"This town's ground to a halt. You couldn't cram another living soul in that church today."

"It was a beautiful service, Roger."

Roger motioned Henry to sit, and Henry smiled at Margaret as he took his seat near her, but no connection was made. She looked through him for a moment, then turned to stare at a wall. Roger sat down heavily in an expansive, well-worn leather chair facing the two of them. *His father's chair,* Henry thought.

"So," Roger said, "you're up in *Chicago.*" He said the word as if he had said "Africa," or "Mars." Henry nodded. "What's the name? Wilton and something?"

"Wilson, Lougherby and Mathers."

Roger smiled languidly. "Why ain't your name in there, Henry?" he asked. "What's the problem?"

Henry found, to his relief, that it was easy to ignore Roger's tasteless competitiveness; he had expected it, in fact prepared himself for it unconsciously. Even in high school Roger had needed to win every game, every argument, every competition no matter how trivial. Seeing him again, it hadn't taken long to discover that he was stuck, still mired in the same adolescent compulsions. "It's a pretty large firm," Henry said easily. "Getting my name on any doors could take a while."

"Yeah?" Roger leaned back in his chair. He seemed suddenly interested in the idea of a Chicago law firm. "How many lawyers you got up there, anyway?"

"About a hundred and eighty," Henry answered, assuming it was at least ten times what Roger had imagined. Roger stared, and Henry had the satisfaction of seeing that his point had been made.

"Hell," Roger said, "I hate to think how many crooks it would take to feed a hundred and eighty lawyers."

Henry reminded himself that the best thing he had learned since leaving Council Grove was that nobody anywhere else in the world gave a damn about the Crandalls or how much money they thought they had. He smiled without answering, enjoying the distance between his old and new life. It made tolerating Roger so much easier. It would all be over soon enough. In a couple of days he would be back in Chicago and Roger could keep on living the pipe dream he loved, the pipe dream in which he was the new hero of a tiny world called Council Grove.

Roger scowled and rose. "Well, looks like you're the only lawyer here. So let's get this over with."

Henry stood, feeling that Crandalls were going to be the best dust of all to lose. "Where to?" he asked.

"Daddy's office. We'll grab a couple of extra chairs." Roger motioned to Sarah to go ahead, and she obediently rose, leading her mother. When they had passed out of earshot, he turned, his expression serious. "I got somethin' to say."

"What is it, Roger?"

"Thing is, you've been gone a good while. By my reckoning you ain't really from around here no more." Henry could taste the satisfaction in that statement, but said nothing. Roger continued: "So I figure you need to be brought up to speed."

"Which means?"

"There's things you don't know. Like I've basically been running things around here for some time now. Daddy had it in mind for me to take over, and I been doin' just that for a good while. The farm, the businesses, everything."

If what Roger said was true, it was certainly a change from what Henry remembered. In those days Tyler had treated his son as little more than a water boy, dismissing him publicly. It was, in fact, the one place where Henry had ever felt any empathy for Roger; it was hard to imagine him not despising his father, the way he had been treated. But he merely nodded and said, "I appreciate the information, Roger. I don't expect any problems."

"Just so you know," Roger said, walking out toward the study. "Daddy and me didn't have no secrets."

Henry nodded and followed Roger into Ty Crandall's office. Like the rest of the house, it was ornate and overstated. The room was dominated by a large desk with a polished birch top, supported by highly filigreed legs that tapered down to elaborately carved lion's claws. Behind the desk the wall was cluttered with framed certificates, photographs, and memberships: Rotary Club, Lions Club, Evangel Baptist Church Fund Drive, Chairman of the Deacons. Clustered to one side were the invitations to the inaugural balls of four governors. Track lights were focused on the invitations, illuminating them against the dark, paneled walls.

Roger pointed to the big, well-worn chair behind the desk. "Right over here," he said. Henry, mildly surprised that Roger would relinquish center stage for even a moment, took the seat. Roger walked over toward the little bar situated at the other end of the room. He popped some ice cubes into a tumbler. "Can I get you a drink?"

A wave of embarrassment flashed across Sarah's face, which Henry scrupulously ignored. "Not at the moment, no," he answered. "I'm fine." It occurred to him that perhaps Roger had begun his drinking earlier in the afternoon; his eyes appeared bloodshot, and his motions seemed deliberate.

"Suit yourself." Roger casually poured himself a straight scotch, swirled the ice cubes noisily, and positioned himself in a wing chair directly in front of the desk. Sarah and her mother flanked him, so that the trio made a half circle in front of Henry. *And now these little possessions will be passed on, as if any of it mattered*, Henry thought. Out loud he said, "I know this is a hard time for all of you. We'll take things one step at a time, and I'm sure everything will be clear." He picked up the will, fingering the envelope. "Tyler stipulated that this be opened only in your presence. As you can see, the seal is intact." Grasping the envelope, he tore it open and carefully pulled out a short, typewritten document.

There was no point in delaying; the tension was already thick in the room. Tyler Crandall hung over them like a specter, a ghost come back from the dead for a few last words about the small fortune he had amassed on the backs of the people of Council Grove and the oil underneath it. Henry began to read.

Being of sound mind and disposing memory, I, Tyler William Crandall, do hereby give my last will and testament.

Margaret, who until that moment had been silent, now gave a low, unsteady wail that ran up Henry's spine. He ground to a halt. *One line and she's already losing it.* Sarah turned to her mother and took her hand, stroking it softly. The sobbing eased slightly, and Sarah nodded to Henry to continue.

Henry took a breath and went on: *This document represents my unencumbered and free decision. It is my express wish that all decisions written herein be honored immediately and without delay.* Henry glanced briefly up at Roger, who was staring back at him unevenly. *Yes*, he decided, *he had been drinking.*

He continued: *Article One: This will is to be held* in terrorem.

"What's that?" Roger interrupted. "That *terrorem* stuff?"

Henry read the line silently again, but didn't show his surprise. *It means the dearly departed didn't think you were going to like this*, he thought. But Margaret had only just stopped sobbing, and he felt the need to press ahead. "Tell you what," he said. "Once we're through the whole thing I'll explain any legal terms anyone's not clear on, in case there's anything else we need to talk about." Roger swirled the ice in his glass and leaned heavily back in his chair, submissive for the moment.

Article Two: Dispossession of property. First, to my beloved wife, Margaret.

Ty's widow fell completely apart at the sound of her name, sobbing and heaving in her chair like a child. Henry put down the papers, unnerved by her unashamed grief. "We could do this another time," he said quietly. "Maybe in the morning, after some rest."

"Read on," Roger said, gesturing with his glass. "Read on, she's all right."

Henry looked for Sarah to intervene, but she merely tended silently to her mother. He stared at Roger a moment, profoundly annoyed. He attempted to show as much with a look of displeasure, but Roger was too preoccupied with his own thoughts to receive the message. Henry picked up the will again; it was fairly short, and if he kept on, he could get it all out in a few minutes and then regroup. To his surprise, Crandall's words turned personal.

I know I was a difficult man. I kept you out of a lot of things, for better or worse. But if you're hearing this then all that's behind me now. I can't undo my wrongs. Not as far as you and me are concerned.

To my beloved wife, Margaret, I bequeath sole possession of the family home and lot, and all the contents therein. I also leave to her the seven hundred and forty acres east of the house, including all buildings and assets located on that land. In addition, she is to receive the sum of three hundred thousand dollars in cash.

Henry paused, subtracting assets from the total he had familiarized himself with on the flight. It appeared, strangely, as though Crandall had left his wife the absolute minimum required by law in the state—one third of the assets.

He read on. *To my daughter Sarah: You never gave me any trouble, girl, and for that I'm grateful. To Sarah Eleanor Crandall I leave the sum of thirty-five thousand dollars a year, paid annually from a trust established for this purpose at the Cottonwood Valley Bank, until the time of your marriage. On your wedding day you will receive a payment of one hundred thousand dollars. In addition, I want you to have the two fine lithographs I bought in New Orleans, and the oil painting of myself that hangs in the feed store. It's my wish that you would keep that painting in your home, wherever you live.* Henry knew the painting; it was nearly six feet wide, and dominated the front of the store. It portrayed Ty Crandall as a kind of western hero, on horseback with a wide-brimmed cowboy hat and a long leather jacket.

He left Sarah next to nothing, Henry thought. *But the* in terrorum *didn't mean anything. Roger is the big winner.* He looked at Crandall's son; Roger's slightly mottled face stared back at him, a thin, humorless expression of triumph. In that expression an unpleasant thought came to Henry: for Roger, this was the completion of a final, grim competition. If he couldn't control his father, at least he could outlive him. Left in the estate were eleven hundred acres of prime land. The enormous granary, the feed and equipment store, the rental properties, together worth hundreds of thousands of dollars. Over a million dollars in cash and securities. The wells, which, although mostly depleted, were still the symbol of Crandall family power. And what to Roger meant much more: control over Council Grove. As long as he stayed in his little world, he would never again have to take an order from a living soul.

Henry began to read. *To my son Roger: I've made my share of enemies, although I never wanted one in my own house. But it came, and I accepted it. All that's over now. You may not understand my way, but that doesn't matter to me now. I know my mind. Maybe you can make something of yourself. That would please me. I'd like one Crandall to do right before it's all said and done. To Roger Tyler Crandall I leave my canary yellow Cadillac Eldorado, and the sum of fifty thousand dollars in cash.* There was a paragraph break, and Henry glanced upward reflexively; Roger was staring back intently, his smile had evaporated. Hostile energy radiated from him across the table.

"Go on," Roger commanded tersely. "Get to the rest of it. He's leaving me the rest of it. Read."

Henry looked back at the will. *All possessions not previously named I hereby bequeath to Mr. Raymond Josiah Boyd, 313 Owendale Street, Council Grove, Kansas. The executor will transfer all necessary documents to this effect without delay.* There followed a lengthy description of assets, but Henry was unable to read them. With his previous sentence, a kind of chaos seemed to fill the room. Roger reached out in a blinding motion, ripping the papers from his hand, and Henry released them to avoid their destruction. Roger gripped the papers and stared down at the last page for several seconds, his face red. Then he jerked his head back up at Henry and shoved him hard, ramming him back into the big chair, sending it sliding on its rollers across the hardwood floor. Henry was thrown backward into a bookcase and several books spilled down onto the floor. In the midst of the chaos there was a second crash, and Henry saw Roger, already back across the room, staring unsteadily down at a floor lamp he had toppled in his rage. Sarah and Margaret were clinging to each other, retreating into as small a space as possible.

Henry, initially taken by surprise at Roger's outburst, pushed books from his lap and leaped to his feet, instinctively preparing to defend himself. But a voice in his head said, *Associates of Wilson, Lougherby and Mathers do not get in fistfights. This is a career move.* He marshaled his anger with some difficulty and said, "Give me the will, Roger. We'll go over it again and sort all this out."

Roger spun toward him like an animal and spat, "Were you listening to what you read? It says I been cheated out of what I deserve! It says I waited twenty-nine years for nothing!" He strode across the room, face-to-face with Henry once again across the desk. Spittle flew from his mouth. "You don't even know who Raymond Boyd is, do you?"

Henry looked back blankly. "I don't," he admitted.

"Raymond Boyd," Roger spat derisively, "is the *Birdman."* He stared, eyes bulging. Then he sputtered, "Daddy left his money to the lunatic in the park."

The meaning of Roger's words overwhelmed any immediate response. The best Henry could do was mutter, "I don't understand."

Roger turned savagely toward his mother. "Do you understand what's happened here? Daddy left his money to the fool that talks to the bird!"

Henry sat heavily back down in the big leather chair. *Then he's still alive,* he thought. "Give me the will, Roger," he said. "I want to look at it again."

Roger shoved the papers across the desk. Henry read the final paragraph and read it again. It was crystal clear. If Raymond Boyd was in fact the Birdman, then the county's most famous sideshow was now the richest person in Cheney County, its largest employer, and its biggest landowner. He literally held the future of the county in his weathered, sunburned hands. "I don't follow this," Henry said. "Why would your father do something like that?"

Roger looked at Henry derisively. "To keep me from getting anything, of course."

Henry forced himself to think rationally in the midst of Roger's emotional outburst. "He didn't have to give the money to Boyd to do that," he said after a moment. "He could have given it all to your mother, for one obvious choice."

Roger's agitation, if anything, increased. "How the hell do I know what he was thinking? I never saw him say a word to that lunatic," he said bitterly. "And why should he? What the hell would they have to talk about?"

"Then what is this? Think, Roger. You've got to have some clue as to what this is about."

Roger's face hardened, but the rage drained away, replaced by a deep, unresolved pain. He paused a moment, then uttered a single word. "Punishment."

Henry stared. "Punishment for what, for God's sake?"

"For being me, damn it. Punishment for being me."

In more than two grinding, busy years of practice, Henry hadn't represented many individual clients, attractive or not, and the select few that the firm represented had made a career out of not falling apart. They were, on the contrary, the highly efficient carnivores who ate the smaller, weaker animals. Henry was repulsed by Roger's open avarice and greed, but he knew that growing up at the hands of Tyler Crandall would undoubtedly leave its mark on anyone. This, Henry realized with a start, was the law his father had practiced, the law of dissolving hopes and desperation. "Then why punish the whole family?" he asked quietly, determined to stay logical. "You're not the only one affected here, Roger."

Roger ignored the question. "I've got to think," he muttered. "Just shut up and let me *think.*" He sat for a moment, clenching the armrests of his chair so tightly he left marks in the fabric. But he couldn't sit still, and soon he was pacing the room again. "You got no idea what I've been dealing with here," he said bitterly. "I've been kissing up to the meanest bastard in the state of Kansas for twenty-nine years. I did every little task he ever asked me to do. I bided my time. *Go over them books again, boy,*" he spat, mocking his father's voice. *"Don't you never interrupt me in a business meeting. You come into the room behind me, and you talk when I ask you a question. You'll do what I say while I'm alive.* While you was alive!" Roger said derisively. "That's what you said! And now you're dead, and you still won't let me be a man! You still won't let me go!"

At this, Sarah came to life; transfixed by Roger's outburst, Henry had almost forgotten about her and Margaret. "That's enough," she said, her voice unsteady. "Daddy is only four hours in the ground, and this is still his house."

"What do you know about it?" Roger demanded, whirling toward her.

"There is nearly three million dollars involved, Roger," Henry intervened. "Sarah was certainly affected."

Roger ignored him and spoke directly to Sarah. Evidently this was a long-running conflict between brother and sister. "You're a woman," he said bitterly. "You don't know nothing about this, and you ain't gonna miss that money. You ain't the one that got screwed by that bastard."

Sarah was trembling with emotion. "There are some things you aren't going to say, not here, not now," she said. "He's barely in the ground, and it's a little early for you to disrespect him." She turned to Henry. "I'm sorry that you had to see all this," she said. "All this history. So now you know. Our family is a mess. Among other things, Daddy and Roger hated each other. One secret, at least, is out in the open." She returned to her mother, collecting her in her arms. Margaret stood shakily, no longer crying, fully retreated within her own mind.

"Look," Henry said, "I don't pretend to understand what's happened here. I'm not judging anyone. I just need some kind of order to move things forward."

"I'm ashamed for us all, of course," Sarah said, "but we are what we are." She took her mother by the arm once again and led her, shaking like an injured animal, from the room.

When Henry looked back across the room, Roger was laughing, a brittle, condescending sound. "Well, Henry," he said, "we've all shocked you, all us Crandalls."

Henry shook his head. "Get over that, Roger. My personal feelings about you aren't important here."

"I don't suppose anybody in Chicago can stand their father."

Henry had entered the Crandall home assuming his role would be as comforter, facilitator. Instead, he had found himself facing off with Roger. That was a role he had no desire to play. If things were going to get this far out of control he would head back to Chicago and let the courts work it out. "Look," he said, "let's get something out on the table. I don't pretend to know what you're thinking. I grew up here, but that was a long time ago, and we're not children anymore. I really don't know you at all. But it doesn't shock me to find out you're human, if that's what you're worried about."

"Is that some kind of pity?" Roger rasped. "Because pity is one thing no Crandall will ever need from a Mathews."

Henry's own emotions were strung tight by now, and he steadied himself with an effort. "When I said I don't understand what you feel, I meant that," he said. "But it's obvious you don't understand me either." He fixed Roger in a level gaze. "I'm going to tolerate some of this because you don't get out much, Roger. But evidently I need to explain some rules about how business is conducted outside of Council Grove. Rule number one is that you don't lay hands on lawyers."

Roger's eyes narrowed. "What the hell are you talking about?"

"The shove, Roger. I'm simply telling you that my professional courtesy doesn't extend that far."

Roger glared, obviously not accustomed to open opposition. "You're still pissed off because I whipped your ass in wrestling," he said.

Henry shook his head. He remembered Crandall's hostility on the mats, his willingness to hit opponents unfairly, to do anything to get the other player on his back. "We're not in that world anymore, Roger. Think of this as free legal advice. Or if you don't want my advice, be practical for your own benefit. Either way, it's not in your interest to create a serious legal problem with the executor of your father's estate."

Roger eyed him suspiciously, but Henry could feel him retreating. "You got damn touchy in Chicago," Roger said.

"Not touchy, Roger. But different."

Roger glared, saying nothing. Henry decided not to push it; it wasn't necessary to humiliate Roger, forcing an assent from his lips. It would be what it would be. If Roger could control himself, fine; if not, Henry would simply get on a plane and go back to Chicago. "Good," he said evenly. "If that's clear, then maybe we can get something done before we all get some rest, which I think everybody needs." Roger gave Henry an ugly look but sat obediently. "There are some things you need to understand about probate generally. First, your mother has some rights by law. The family home, that kind of thing. That appears to have been accomplished. You, as a child of a living spouse, aren't automatically entitled to anything, and therefore your father can more or less do what he wants as far as you and Sarah are concerned."

Roger cursed and said, "So you're actually saying this thing can be legal."

"Yes, it can. Unless, of course . . ." Henry trailed off, and Roger interrupted him eagerly.

"What is it?" Roger demanded. "You know something."

Henry sighed; the funeral already seemed like ages ago. "Look, Roger, the courts tend to take last wishes pretty seriously, but I'm not going to say people don't fight over estates. When they do it's invariably ugly. Things tend to boil down to two main arguments. Frankly, I can't believe I'm talking about this. It's the last thing I thought I'd be doing tonight."

"This whole thing ain't what I thought it would be."

"All right, Roger. I said there were two arguments. The first is that the will can be held invalid if your father was acting under duress. Compelled, in other words."

"You mean somebody forcin' him to do what he didn't want to do."

"Exactly. But the first question the judge is going to ask is who benefits from that duress. In this case that somebody would be Raymond Boyd, and nobody can seriously believe that he had the power to pressure your father into doing a thing. Your father was the most powerful man in this county, and Boyd is, well, the Birdman. You see my point."

Roger glared. "What's the other argument?"

"Uglier. The court can throw out a will if the deceased wasn't fully in command of his faculties when he wrote it. I mean insane, Roger."

Roger slammed his fist down on the table. "How else can you explain cuttin' your own flesh and blood out of a will? He must have been insane, out of his mind! You've got to *do* something, damn it. You got to talk to somebody and tell them that's what happened!"

"I take it you don't see the irony of this line of reasoning."

Roger stared. "What's that supposed to mean?"

"It's Boyd who's insane, Roger. Not your father."

Roger was stopped, but only for a moment. "What do you know about it?" he said at last. "You ain't seen my father in years."

"That's true," Henry said, "but I do know the man who drafted this will. I know he would never have had a part in it if Tyler hadn't been completely lucid when it was written."

Roger turned scarlet. "Yeah, I forgot that part," he said icily. "Your father did write up this piece of garbage. I'm sure he enjoyed that, seeing me around town, knowin' his little secret and not saying a thing. He knew the whole time. He spoke to me on the street, for God's sake."

"Your father was free to do anything he wanted with his money, and he simply exercised that option."

"I watch enough TV to know that I can contest this thing. And if that's what I want to do it ain't nobody's business but mine. And you're supposed to be helpin' me."

Henry sighed, worn down by Roger's open greed. It wasn't that there wasn't a genuine loss to be felt over the money; it was the simple hatred and lack of sorrow over anything else that Henry found so fatiguing. "You want my help?" he said. "All right, Roger. It's free legal advice day. So I'm going to lay this out for you very clearly so you know what the hell you're talking about." He picked up the papers. "Contesting this will on an insanity basis is going to involve public legal proceedings. Very public, in this case. Evidence would have to be introduced to prove that your father wasn't in control of himself at the time the will was written. Do you understand what that would mean?"

"Explain it."

"You'd have to talk to people in town to find evidence of your father's declining mental condition. Your testimony alone wouldn't be sufficient, for obvious reasons. You have far too much to gain. Witnesses would have to be called, people deposed. You'd have to find unsound business decisions, incoherent conversations. The entire town would become aware of what you were trying to do and how you were doing it. What you're talking about is humiliating your family in a public forum, and if by some chance you're successful, you will have destroyed the memory of your father. And all that's if it was true that your father was insane, which I don't believe for one second, and neither does anybody else in this town. To go through all that and lose would be a catastrophe."

"If you want to avoid all that, then give me an alternative."

"It's not me who should want to avoid it, Roger," Henry said flatly. "But there's something else." He stared down at the desk, wishing there were a way around what he had to say. "It's something you're going to find particularly unpleasant." Roger grunted something unintelligible, and Henry continued: "Do you remember asking me about what *in terrorem* meant?" Henry asked.

"Yeah."

"I'm sorry about this, Roger."

Roger got up and walked to the bar. He poured himself a tumbler of scotch, dispensing with the ice. He walked back to his chair and fell heavily into it. "Go on."

Henry spoke with studied calmness. "*In terrorem* is a very powerful legal concept. It has only one purpose, and that is to be a kind of lock on the will." Roger stared back at him blankly. "I'll give you this in plain English, Roger. The *in terrorem* clause provides that if anyone tries to contest the will—for any reason—they are completely excluded from the estate. Automatically and permanently. What I'm saying, Roger, is that if you contest this will you can never receive a penny from it for as long as you live. What you got may not seem like much, but you would be risking every cent of it to file against the will. But that's not the worst of it."

For the first time, Roger seemed to diminish. "What kind of law is that?" he asked. "How can there be such a law?"

"It doesn't come around much, obviously. Most family dynamics aren't as"—he sought for the word—"tortured as this," he said at last. "And look, I'm not going to lie to you, Roger. People have beat it in court."

"Then why can't I? And what do you mean by that not being the worst of it?"

"I think you'd lose, Roger."

"How can you be so sure?"

"Because any claim you have is after your mother's. A spouse might have a small chance. But a son, when the spouse isn't a complainant . . . the court isn't going to go against so much legal precedent for that. To have a chance, your mother would have to initiate the action. Risking your fifty grand is one thing. But if she contests, she's risking the money she needs to live on. Losing would mean that she would be penniless. She's too old to start over, Roger." Roger stared, ground to a halt, but Henry could see him working on things, trying to find a way through. "And even if you beat the *in terrorem*, that doesn't mean you get more money."

"What the hell are you talking about? This is why people hate lawyers. If I win, I win, ain't that right?"

Henry ignored the insult. "Winning just means that the court invalidates the clause itself. Then the judge redistributes the estate the way he sees fit. The judge isn't under any legal obligation to take things away from Boyd and give them to you. He might do that. He also might think you're a complete jerk and take away what you have."

"Laws on top of laws," Roger said, disgust on his face.

Henry turned away, tiredness giving way at last to exhaustion. What he wanted, he realized, was to be out of the Crandall house and back in his motel room, leaving the Crandalls behind. *No*, he thought, *what I want is to be back in Chicago, in a bathtub with Elaine, some nice music on, and a bar of soap*. "Let's take the night to think things over," he said. "We're not going to solve anything tonight."

Roger blocked his path to the doorway. "Look, Mathews, you said your piece a minute ago, and it's my turn now."

Henry sighed. "All right, Roger. What is it?"

"Fact is, I think I got a right to be upset. My own daddy has stabbed me in the back. You understand that? Not some stranger, my own daddy. And I'll tell you somethin' else, since we're bein' so damn honest. It pisses me off that you're the one I got to talk to about my family's business." Roger's anger was fueling him now, making him brave again. "You're supposed to be this hotshot lawyer, too big for Council Grove. You went to the same school as me and everybody else in this town, but you had to get your ass up to the big city and sue rich people. But you better know right now there's no way in hell I'm gonna take this lying down. That Birdman is not going to walk off with my money and he ain't gonna live my life. I ain't no fool. I know nothin' ain't final if you got the right lawyer. Ain't that right?"

Henry listened, not wanting what Roger said to be true. But his whole professional life was a testament to its accuracy. It was, in fact, the very truth that made his firm worth four hundred dollars an hour. "That's right, Roger," he said quietly. "Sometimes, anyway."

"Goddam right," Roger snapped. "People makin' millions of dollars off of hot coffee spillin' in their laps. Now you're supposed to be the real thing, ain't you? Up in Chicago? So I want you to show me why a big-city lawyer like you was too good for Council Grove. I want you here at eight o'clock tomorrow morning ready to *do* something about all this."

"I don't think you understand what I'm doing here, Roger," Henry stated calmly. "I'm not your lawyer."

"You was my father's lawyer, ain't that right? And ain't he dead now? So that makes you my lawyer."

"I'm still your father's lawyer, Roger. That's what an executor is. I'm trying to represent his wishes." He paused, knowing that his next words would be further lacerations for Roger's wounds. "And that's why I can't be here at eight o'clock tomorrow."

"Why the hell not?"

"Because the first thing in the morning I'm going to be trying to explain to Raymond Boyd that he has been named as the principal beneficiary of this will. I can't even imagine what that conversation will be like." Roger started to interrupt, but Henry stopped him. "I don't like what's happened here either, Roger. As far as I can see, it's a complete shame. On the other hand, I'm not going to get disbarred because of it. I have to see Boyd before any other action is taken. You've got to do what you've got to do, but so do I. I've got legal obligations, and I'm going to see Boyd."

Roger's eyes narrowed to tiny slits. He catapulted out of his seat, the self-control he had marshaled suddenly evaporating. "Get out!" he screamed. "Do you hear me? Get out of my house!"

Henry rose, Roger's outburst actually calming him, making him steady. "You know something, Roger?" he said. "I'm going to give you one last piece of advice, and it's not legal. It's the one thing you and I still have in common. What you're going to find out before this is all over is that the thing about a father is to have him, no matter how big an asshole he was."

Roger glared silently for a moment, then spun on his heel and strode out of the room. Henry found himself suddenly alone in Ty Crandall's study. He closed his briefcase deliberately, looking around at the awards and photographs on the wall, wondering what the man could have had in mind when he virtually cut his own family out of his estate. He would certainly have known how Roger would handle the decision. He wondered as well at his own father, who would also have anticipated this chaos, but chose to say nothing about it. *Client-attorney privilege, indeed*, Henry thought. He left the room and walked down the hallway to the front door, listening for the family; as he crossed the staircase leading upstairs, he could hear a woman weeping from above. He let himself quietly out, closing the door on a house full of misery.

Chapter Six

The Birdman looked up at the dry June sun and smiled. It was early morning but he could already tell the day would be hot, just the way he liked it. He had gradually acclimated to the heat, and he enjoyed seeing others suffer through it. If he suffered at all, he didn't show it; the wrinkled brown leather of his face didn't allow emotion to escape easily. He pulled his beat-up Stetson over his brow and hunched down in a crouch, knees bent like a baseball catcher's. He smiled again, squinting and tossing his head left and right in short, jabbing motions. The brow of his hat bobbed and danced in the air, kicking up like a bronco shedding a rider.

Council Grove was waking, but the Birdman had already been at his spot for over an hour. A car passed by, as it did at that time every day. The driver didn't wave.

The southeast corner of Custer's Elm was the Birdman's spot, five blocks off Chautauqua. There was little foot traffic there, which suited him—the heavy traffic near the courthouse and the bank made him uncomfortable. Not that he actually saw people much, or thought about their names. But the noise they made and the air they breathed intruded somehow, and he preferred to stay where the passersby were rare.

The Birdman had been at Custer's Elm for years—exactly how long nobody could be sure of, and in fact he had made it his spot by degrees, rather than in a moment. He had started by spending more and more time there one summer years earlier, sitting by himself for hours that eventually became endless. The little park had suited the Birdman perfectly even then, although in those days he still had a name. Raymond Boyd he had been called, although mostly that was forgotten now, even by the Birdman himself. It took hard thinking to recall it, and that was exactly what he didn't like doing.

As the Birdman settled into his morning routine, Henry sat in his car across town trying to organize his thoughts. If yesterday had been a debacle, he liked the job before him even less. *One case*, Henry thought as he started the car, seeing his father in his mind. *You died and left me one thing to handle. And now I have to try to explain to a lunatic that he's the richest man in town.* It was impossible to predict how Boyd would react to the news, or even if he could comprehend it. There was an excellent chance that he wouldn't allow Henry to get close enough to say a word. Worst of all, there was the bird—that creepy thing loomed over the whole enterprise—and

Henry had to forcibly remind himself that he wasn't the child who had been so unnerved by the creature years ago.

He pulled out and headed back toward town from the motel. As with every distasteful job, it was best to do it directly and without delay. What happened next would have to take care of itself. If the Birdman proved as mentally incompetent as Henry assumed, the court could appoint a guardian to act on his behalf and manage any assets that survived the legal wrangling. But if by chance the Birdman was judged merely eccentric and unsociable, then the county's most powerful man would be a mumbling old kook whose best friend was a large black vulture.

Henry drove west through town, turned off Chautauqua onto Owendale to pass by the Birdman's house. It hadn't changed appreciably, maintained just above the point at which the town could take action against it. The roof sagged a bit, the house needed paint, and the yard was high, but it was in no immediate danger of being condemned.

There was no one around, and Henry turned right off Owendale toward Custer's Elm Park. He slowed as he reached the south edge of the clearing and looked to his right across the grass; after yesterday, he wasn't sure if Boyd was still likely to be found in his usual place. But then he saw him, a large, lumpy shape on his usual concrete bench. The great bird, unfortunately, was beside him as well, walking back and forth like a sentry before a tiny jail. Henry rolled closer, and the bird jerked his head up and squawked, walking sideways and flapping a wing. The Birdman stirred on his bench, coming to life in sections. His feet moved, then a leg, then his torso straightened. At last he raised his head and looked straight at Henry's car. *So much for the element of surprise*, Henry thought.

Henry picked up his briefcase and got out of the car. Birdman and creature both watched, four eyes in one unbroken stare. Henry stood beside his car, looking back across the edge of the park at the Birdman. *Madness at twelve o'clock. God, I miss Chicago.* The bird looked ominous as it stared, a wild thing that should be out in distant fields hunting for the dead. Reluctantly, Henry willed his feet to walk. As he approached, the Birdman's features came into focus; the man looked a little more worn down, but with the same thin body, the same hat and leather face, the same brown eyes peering out from underneath the brim. His scraggly whiskers stuck out as before, but now more gray than brown. As Henry drew near, the bird's agitation increased until it was walking rapidly in tight circles, rising tall on its legs and stretching its neck.

Henry, determined not to show fear, walked steadily forward. Suddenly, the bird rose into the air and flapped away to the north, as if it had approved his presence. A hopeful thought formed in Henry's mind: *Maybe that thing isn't really a malignant beast after all. Maybe it's nothing but a big, ugly bird.*

Nevertheless, the sudden, noisy flapping of its wings was unnerving, and he stepped smartly back as the animal careened away. Henry was now about twenty feet away from the Birdman, trying not to look rattled. Boyd gazed up at him, his eyes barely visible under the shadow of the hat. He was whispering to himself, or to his ghosts. Henry could hear him but couldn't make out any words, just syllables rolling around and falling back onto themselves in the man's mouth. He was nothing like the winos and street people Henry had grown accustomed to in Chicago, rough-skinned men with the tough look of surviving downtown in a large city. There was nothing urban about Boyd. He was so covered with dust and grime that he looked perfectly at home in the park, almost like a kind of half-wild animal.

With the bird gone Henry made his way to a spot five feet away from Boyd and set down his briefcase on the sidewalk, just beyond the white spatters that made a broad semicircle around the bench. He decided to try his luck. He spoke the man's name quietly, looking for comprehension.

The Birdman whispered on, staring at his shoes, his expression unchanged. A disappointing, but hardly surprising beginning. Henry determined to press ahead. "I'm a lawyer, Mr. Boyd." Under normal circumstances, those were words of power, guaranteed to gain the attention of their target. But Boyd gave no sign that they had meant anything to him.

"I've got something important to talk over with you," Henry said. "I need you to pay attention very carefully. Do you think you could do that?" The Birdman whispered on, his head dancing slightly back and forth.

"Mr. Boyd, do you know who Tyler Crandall is?" At this, Boyd looked up, but not with any discernible expression of recognition. It was possible he understood; it was also possible that he was looking straight through Henry to a place that existed only in his own mind. Henry decided to interpret the glance as positive and press on until he had a reason to do otherwise.

"Tyler Crandall?" he repeated. "Does that name mean anything to you?" To Henry's consternation, Boyd's gaze slowly floated downward, and he began to scrape his left foot around in a small circle.

Apparently, the Birdman was as crazy as everyone thought after all. That meant that the legal proceedings would be much more complicated. It was a shame, Crandall leaving all that money to a person who couldn't even comprehend what it meant. It was an irony that would certainly not be lost on Roger, who had longed for that same money every day of his life. *It's over,* Henry thought. All that remained was to get a little due diligence off his chest, to get through the facts with Boyd whether the man was capable of understanding them or not. Then he could file to be excused and to have someone local appointed.

"Look, Mr. Boyd," Henry said, "I've got some very important information to pass on to you. What I'm trying to tell you, Mr. Boyd, is that Tyler Crandall is dead."

The whispering stopped. The wind blew several old leaves out past the Birdman's feet, and they tumbled over his filthy shoes, catching for a moment on the bench, then fluttering away into the grass beyond. Henry stood still, captivated in the new silence, pondering its meaning. The brim of Boyd's hat moved up and down a few times, but he still said nothing. "Did you understand me, Mr. Boyd?" Henry asked. "Do you know who Mr. Crandall is?"

The Birdman tilted his head slightly, peering up from the bench, revealing dry, cracked lips. They parted, dry skin pulling apart, and he spoke in a gravelly voice, metallic and cloudy from disuse. "Mathews?"

Henry stared at the man, surprised to hear his own name. "That's right. Henry Mathews."

Boyd scrunched up his face. "Law-yer," he said, stretching the word out.

Henry nodded. "Wilson, Lougherby and Mathers, in Chicago."

The Birdman smiled slightly, skin cracking softly back from his heavily chapped mouth. "*Law-yer,*" he repeated dreamily. Then, softly, even intimately, he whispered, "The day of the Lord is at hand." With this proclamation, he began mumbling again, picking at his dirty fingernails and cuticles. Henry gritted his teeth; in his newly urbane existence, he had become fastidious.

"I'd like to ask you a few questions, Mr. Boyd. And I want to start by asking what your relationship was to Tyler Crandall."

The Birdman fixed Henry in a sudden, intense gaze. Henry found himself drawn in, unable to look away. "The Lord speaks to me," Boyd said. "Right to me, like you and me are talkin' now. What he says is a secret. But I'll tell you if you want to know."

Henry searched Boyd's eyes, looking for coherence, for anything that said the man had some place of reality within him. But he couldn't ignore the invitation; he had watched, secreted behind a tree, too many times as a boy not to want to know the answer. He nodded yes.

The Birdman grinned up at him, a scarecrow with a brown-and-gray beard. "It is a terrible day when the Lord stretches out His hand in sulfur and towers of flame. When the day of the Lord comes, the truth will be let loose on every bastard who walks this town. Whatever is held in secret will be shouted from the rooftops. Be ye ready, for ye know not when comes the day of the Lord."

Henry watched silently. Suddenly the Birdman asked, "H.L.'s boy?"

"That's right," Henry answered, coming back to himself. "I'm his son, Henry Junior."

The Birdman bit a cuticle and a substantial piece of dirt came unstuck from his finger, drifting lazily down to the ground. "What he send a junior for?"

"My father's dead, Mr. Boyd. For several years now."

The Birdman continued biting at his fingernails, and then jerked his head up, squinting in the sun. "Guess that's why he didn't come then." Hearing his father's name in the Birdman's mouth gave Henry an uncomfortable feeling. Boyd stopped picking at himself and looked up intently once again. "You was around here, back in the day," he said. "Come to steal my sermons." He grinned. "I know you, boy. You came with them boys who threw rocks. You was gonna be a preacher, like me, ain't that right?"

Henry didn't like the Birdman knowing things about him, because there wasn't any explanation for how he could find them out. But his curiosity had been aroused. "How did you know that?" he asked. "I never said anything to you about that."

"I heard it," Boyd said, smiling his gap-toothed smile. "I ain't deaf. Just c-r-a-z-y." He whirled his finger around his ear. "But I don't see no preacher in front of me. I see a law-yer."

"I changed my mind."

Boyd squinted, regarding him closely. "I reckon my sermons is safe, then."

Henry shook himself loose from the Birdman's stare. He felt a sudden compulsion to press ahead with the will; there was no way of telling when he would be able to talk with Boyd again, especially without the bird around. It was now or never. The courts would have to sort it all out later. "Mr. Boyd," he said, "Tyler Crandall's death concerns you directly. Mr. Crandall has named you as a beneficiary in his will." Boyd said nothing. He scanned the sky, apparently looking for the vulture. Henry pressed on. "The fact is, Mr. Crandall has seen fit to leave you a substantial amount of money. A great deal of money. So I need to go over some things with you. I need to help you understand."

The Birdman now began to move. He lifted up a foot and scratched a leg with an old, worn-out shoe. The smell was assaulting Henry's nostrils, and it was all he could do to stand so close. Boyd rumbled up off the bench, the smell wafting off him as he moved. For the first time, the years that had added up on the man were apparent—as a boy, Henry had watched Boyd scoot across the park, lambasting kids intent on bothering him. But it was now obvious that his years of inactivity had taken their toll. "You're a liar, junior Henry," he said. "This must be a new game. Them kids used to throw rocks at me. Now dressed-up junior Henrys come to pester me. Go to hell, boy. Crandall didn't give me nothin'."

"I can tell you that he did, Mr. Boyd," Henry said levelly. Boyd had apparently understood, even though he didn't believe it. *And why should he?* Henry thought. In a way, Henry was relieved; that was, in its way, a sign of rationality. "Look, Mr. Boyd, I don't think you understand the dimensions of what I'm talking about here," he said. "Mr. Crandall has left you an estate worth over three million dollars. You may soon be the richest man in Cheney County, Mr. Boyd."

Boyd waved Henry off. "Bird?" he called testily, starting to shuffle away.

"You really should take a look at this." Henry searched quickly through his briefcase and pulled out the papers. A thought occurred to him: "You do read?" he asked. "I'll read it if you like."

Boyd whirled around angrily. "Who sent you, junior Henry?" he rasped. "Who sent you to pester? I'm gonna set my bird on you." He shuffled toward Henry, who stood his ground in the face of the smell by an act of will. When they were less than a foot apart, Boyd looked down at Henry's shoes, two cushions of soft, brown Italian leather. His eyes traveled upward, taking in every article of clothing. He seemed to be making an accounting of some kind. Suddenly, he reached up, and for a moment Henry thought he was going to strike him. But instead, Boyd made an exaggerated sign of the cross. His hands moved slowly, describing great lines two feet across. "All ye bastards who are heavy laden," he said, "ye of the talon and the claw, come unto me. I will give ye rest."

The two men were locked eye to eye for a long moment. Henry was irritated to find Boyd's words moving through him, hitting him in an irrational but exquisitely responsive place. *Rest*, he thought. *Whatever that means.* He shook himself free from Boyd's gaze. *God, I need to get back to Chicago.*

Boyd was speaking. "Give me them papers," he said. Henry cautiously handed over the white papers, and Boyd grasped them roughly with his dark, soiled fingers.

"Your name appears on page two," Henry said, pointing. The Birdman turned to the page and stared for some time, picking at his right ear, digging his fingernail far into the orifice. Eventually he looked up at Henry. He appeared, for the moment, surprisingly coherent. "This here says I own the granary," Boyd asked. "That right?"

That, indeed, is the question, Henry thought. For now, however, he simply nodded.

"And them rental houses. Them people livin' in my houses now, ain't that what this paper says?"

"The paper says that, Mr. Boyd."

"And the wells, how 'bout them?"

"The oil wells, yes. They're about played out, I'm afraid."

The Birdman looked up at Henry, his face tilted to the side. "And the *bank*." He said the word with emphasis, as though it were separate in his mind. "That mine, too?"

"Just the building, Mr. Boyd. Not the assets themselves. But everything on the list, Mr. Boyd. All the buildings, the land, the money, everything."

Boyd watched Henry for a while, obviously thinking. After a moment he said in a clear voice, "Let's go see my buildings."

The statement jarred Henry. "What do you mean?"

"Junior Henry don't hear too good, I guess."

"You're saying you want to leave the park?"

Boyd held up the papers. "See my buildings."

Henry pictured the Birdman strolling through one of the Crandall businesses proclaiming himself the new owner. It would certainly be the worst possible way to announce to the town the contents of the will. And Roger's reaction to an event like that was easy to predict: immediate, harsh, and ugly. "I'm not sure that would be in your best interest," he began. He was forced to stop; Boyd, bafflingly, had let the papers fall to the ground, and was now walking away. Henry was flooded with frustration. "Look, Mr. Boyd, I can't possibly help you if you don't pay attention."

Boyd turned back. "Junior Henry don't use rocks no more." He gestured to the scattered pages on the ground. "Got papers now."

"This isn't an attack, Mr. Boyd. What you're asking for is complicated."

Boyd shuffled away, mumbling softly to himself. He moved off the pavement toward the playground, his eyes scanning the skies. Henry watched him walk away, when a thought came to him. *He's testing you. If you don't give in, he'll never believe another word you say*. Henry shook his head, forced to make a snap decision. If he couldn't communicate with Boyd, legal forces would take their inevitable course. He didn't want that to happen, somehow. Boyd seemed different to him, meeting him again as an adult. He wasn't as frightening as he had remembered. His scowls were mostly bravura, the shell of a man living unprotected by shelter or sanity. And if Boyd needed a little protecting, Henry couldn't think of a reason why he shouldn't be the one to do it. So far in his career he had used his skills to peel back the protective covering of people and corporations for his firm, exposing them to the blistering attacks of Sheldon Parker. The chance to do the opposite, for once, was tantalizing to him, almost a kind of forbidden fruit. He toyed with the idea for a moment, drawn to it, but also aware of its implications. Then a thought came to him, magnificently clear, and once surfaced, unavoidable. *If you say no to this, you are Parker.* He repeated it to himself several times. *You are Parker. You are Parker.* If he had managed to avoid that conclusion, he might have been able to walk away.

But he had let his guard down, and the thought had come. Now it was too late, and his need to take risks overwhelmed him. Suddenly, almost palpably, it was essential not to be Parker, to prove it to himself, like the ability to leap across a deep canal. He was grateful, in a way; Boyd had presented him with a perfect, neatly packaged opportunity, one that wouldn't cost him more than he could pay: show the man the buildings. Enough to show he had played fair. Help the weak this one time, don't eat them. Then fly back to Chicago, secure in your goodness. Hold this memory like a battering ram when you needed it, when you feel yourself growing Parker skin. "Come back, Mr. Boyd," he said earnestly. Boyd was some distance away by now, and he looked around, half turning. "It's all right, Mr. Boyd," Henry said. "I'll take you to see the buildings."

Boyd stopped and looked back; Henry looked for gratitude in his eyes, or at least comprehension. But there was nothing. Henry stooped down and picked up the papers, reordering them and brushing them off. He held them up for Boyd, a gesture of reconciliation.

Boyd walked back and slowly took the stack from Henry, his grimy hands touching Henry's fingers as he did so. Boyd looked down at the papers, then squinted back up at Henry. He repeated this motion several times, his face scrunched up in dark wrinkles. There was a fleck of spittle on his lip, a white patch, which, in spite of his repugnance, Henry couldn't take his eyes off. At last a smile broke over the Birdman's face. "You know not when comes the day of the Lord," he said. "It's a terrible day if you ain't ready."

Chapter Seven

The lighting was notoriously poor in the large subcommittee chambers of the Kansas legislature, and in the gloom the thin wiggly lines that covered Amanda Ashton's prized chart had begun to converge, blurring and blending into black spaghetti on a rectangular paper plate. She stared at a three-foot-wide display, refocusing her eyes for the fortieth time, and adjusted her glasses for long-range squinting.

"What I *do* know, Senator," she said, "is that there are nearly two thousand aging oil wells across the state that are reaching the end of their structural lives. The wells and the pools around them contain thousands of pounds of highly poisonous chemicals, all surrounded by salt. So when I see the saline level in the subterranean aquifer rising sharply, that concerns me. It should concern all of us."

Senator Carl Durand, chairman of the oil and gas committee of the Kansas state senate, gazed at Amanda with a brittle, pasted-on movement of the lips that could be construed as a smile. He was a large, bull-like man with a rough, ruddy appearance: reddish, weathered skin, a fleshy, mottled nose, and thick eyebrows. He wore a light brown corduroy coat, a flannel shirt, and a bolo tie. "What concerns me, Miss Ashton," he replied icily, "is the fact that people have a right to be left alone from meddling bureaucrats. They don't need their fields dug up, and they don't need their business disturbed. What is the compelling interest here? The state's full of salt, Miss Ashton. There's a salt dome in Jefferson County big enough for all the french fries in Paris." The small crowd in the chamber, consisting mostly of oil company lobbyists, chuckled appreciatively.

Amanda glanced surreptitiously at her watch: she was now entering her third hour of testimony. Each loathsome minute had made her a wiser, albeit lonelier woman. She had begun the morning eagerly, determined to make a coherent case for the most comprehensive environmental action the state had ever undertaken. Now, embattled and frustrated, she counted her losses. Not that she had expected it to be easy; Durand was himself a retired oil wildcatter who had made millions in speculation across the Midwest. His drilling days were over, but he still ran an expansive energy distribution system in many rural areas throughout the Midwest. He was the oil industry's best friend in the senate, and his perspective on exploration was well known.

"The problem, as you know very well, Senator, isn't the salt itself. The salt is just a messenger. *The real problem,*" she said forcefully, *"is the ticking time bomb that comes later."*

A couple of reporters glanced up at Durand for a reaction, but the chairman had chosen this moment to turn his back and was speaking quietly to a young, athletic-looking aide. They conferred for some time, and Amanda felt the energy from her statement drain away into an awkward, waiting silence. After what seemed like an eternity, the assistant nodded silently and disappeared through a door behind black curtains. When Durand turned back, he was serene, even good humored. "You were saying, Miss Ashton?"

Amanda pushed the specter of the senator straddling an uncapped oil well out of her mind. "I was saying that there is a serious problem out there, Senator, something that the salt is, in effect, trying to tell us."

"I see. Talking salt." Durand smiled, condescension wafting from him across the chamber. "Well, let me guess what the salt says, Miss Ashton. The salt says that the sky is falling, as we've heard so many times before. The sky is always falling in the wacko environmental world which you inhabit. Yours is a world of talking salt and catastrophes around every corner, isn't it, Miss Ashton? But somehow we all keep getting up in the morning and breathing and drinking and living longer and longer. In spite of everything that you people keep saying, the sky doesn't fall at all."

Amanda was about to respond, but Durand interrupted with a raised forefinger. "Do you have an office, Miss Ashton?"

"I beg your pardon?"

"It's a straightforward question. Do you, or do you not, have an office?"

"It's on the fourth floor in this building, Senator."

"And in your office, I assume you have a desk?"

Amanda peered up at the speaker. "Yes, Senator, I have a desk."

"And on that desk you have a telephone?"

"That's correct."

Durand smiled broadly. "Excellent. Then what I suggest you do is to sit at your desk and use that telephone to get the county agent on the line. This is more in his line of work. Let him get out there and fine somebody for whatever the hell it is they're doing, and then let us get on with the business of governing this state. Could you do that for me, Miss Ashton?"

Amanda's face flushed scarlet. She knew she was being baited, and she was resolved not to give Durand any excuse to shut her down. "Senator, hundreds of aging wells are turning to corroded powder across this state. If it means what I think it does, a horror of acids and poisons will follow closely behind. Those wells were all made in the same way from the same materials. The same with the pools. If they have reached their life span, they could all collapse very rapidly. I admit that I'm not absolutely certain that this will happen. I've never claimed that I was. But if I'm right, we are looking at something truly catastrophic. So it's very simple. What I want, Senator, and what my agency desperately needs, is the money to find out."

The room grew silent, and Amanda leaned back in her chair, flushed by her own passion, and embarrassed to have had to take so much abuse from Durand simply because he controlled the purse strings to which she wanted access. Uncannily, as if reading her mind, Durand put his finger on her weak spot.

"Yes, Miss Ashton," he said dryly, "as usual, it all comes down to money. All this talk is another dreary plea for appropriations. Money that pays your salary."

Amanda grimaced. She had gotten into politics prepared to play hard-ball, eyes open. But the reality was nevertheless daunting. Durand had survived for seven terms in state politics, his power ever-growing. He had become wily and dangerous. He was eyeing a bid for governor, and the early money was betting he could win.

Sam Coulton, a quiet, introspective senator from western Kansas, had been listening intently. Suddenly, he came to life. "What kind of chemicals are we talking about, Ms. Ashton?" he interrupted. "If the senator will indulge me?"

Amanda smiled. It was the first question she had been asked all day that indicated an actual interest in what she was talking about. "Acids, mainly. Sulfuric, boric, hydrochloric. All used to break down rock and make the drilling easier. There's a good deal of formaldehyde down there as well. Most of it is thousands of feet down, right in the range of the aquifer. It's quite a brew."

Coulton jotted a note on a pad, nodding for Amanda to continue. "Of course," she went on, "these chemicals were nothing in quantity compared to the huge amount of salt that the wells produced when they were pumping, but this cocktail was, and in fact still is, stored in large, lined, man-made pools. The point is, gentlemen, that if salt is leaking, the chemicals can't be far behind."

Durand had heard enough, and he stopped her with pointed laughter. "If I can interrupt this fascinating doomsday scenario, Miss Ashton, you are entering into an area in which I have some expertise. I've drilled a well or two in my day. Fact is, some folks around here would consider me an expert on the subject. The pools and the wellheads are encased in concrete. The concrete is put down under four thousand pounds per square inch of pressure. If you'll pardon my French, you couldn't force a rat's behind through that concrete with a chisel and a fire hose." Durand excelled in colorful language, and he often used it to make his points.

"Nothing is coming out of those wellheads, Miss Ashton, and nothing is coming out of those pools. You may bank on that."

Amanda glanced at the faces of the committee members. She had sensed a subtle change in the room; a few of the senators had been actually listening. She needed to strike again quickly. "That's correct, Senator, for modern wells. But these wells are from another era, some as early as World War I. The techniques were very different. In some cases there was no concrete. In other cases the concrete wasn't poured under pressure. And in virtually all cases it only extends a short ways up from the bottom of the well."

Durand bristled. "I don't need a lecture from you about drilling, Miss Ashton. This is all the same old environmental poppycock we've been through before. It's nothing but another way to tell people what they can and can't do on their own land."

"With the senator's indulgence," Coulton interjected quietly, "I'd like to hear her out." Durand flashed back a dangerous look in response, but Coulton kept his eyes firmly on Amanda. "Let's get to the bottom of this, Ms. Ashton," he said. "These older wells can't still be pumping. They must have been inactive for years, even decades."

"That depends on how you define your terms, Senator. They aren't *chemically* inactive. They've been quite busy, actually, combining into some very nasty, highly abrasive compounds that have been gradually destroying the containers designed to house them. Picture these old casements, sixty, maybe seventy years old. They're interacting with the chemicals, with highly abrasive salt water. Eventually, even inevitably, they begin to leak. Once they begin to decompose, they will fall apart quite rapidly. In that case, the chemicals will certainly follow in a massive outflow. These compounds are toxic in parts per billion, gentlemen. And there are tons of it out there, hundreds of tons." At last she returned her gaze to Durand. "Think of it, Senator: hundreds of tons of chemicals that are toxic in parts per billion. What will we do if even small amounts of these poisons get into our underground water system? That water is connected beneath the surface of the earth to the major water systems of the Midwest, to the Missouri River itself. Thirty-six million people live along the Missouri and its tributaries. If these containers are melting down, the implications boggle the mind."

"Scare tactics," rumbled Durand. "You want this committee to wring its hands and interrupt the legitimate business of hundreds or even thousands of people. You haven't got a shred of hard data."

It was time for the hard pitch. "As you know, Senator, to get that data we need to actually go on the land. We need field agents, sophisticated equipment. We need this committee to recommend immediate funding for long-term research."

"Yes," Durand answered coolly. "Long-term. I'm glad you used that particular phrase. Government has a way of making everything long-term. First one year, then two, then five—and in the end all you've done is created a bunch of paperwork and intruded into the lives of a lot of hard-working people. That is exactly the kind of thing my constituents have sent me here to stop, Miss Ashton. Studies of monkeys and beetles and salt and God knows what else, all at the taxpayer's expense. I have no doubt that if the state's environmental agency had its way this program would be more than just long-term, Miss Ashton, it would be permanent. Then you and all your agency friends could celebrate getting cushy government jobs studying things nobody cares about!"

Amanda was poised to respond when the young aide once again materialized through the rear door and began whispering into the chairman's ear. Durand smiled as he listened. The aide finished speaking and took his seat behind the committee with a blank expression, and the senator tapped his microphone. "I understand that the highway appropriations bill has come up for a vote, gentlemen. It seems the agenda of the general assembly has abruptly cleared, and we're being called in. As you're all well aware, that is a bill that demands our full attention. The future of your districts rests on those highways. It appears that we will have to adjourn immediately to attend to some real problems." He smiled indulgently at Amanda. "Thank you for coming, Miss Ashton. You may consider your testimony concluded, with our deepest appreciation."

Amanda sat back, stunned. Durand's reputation as a calculating manipulator of procedure was deserved; when he couldn't shut people up, he simply scheduled them out of existence. The highway bill was the biggest thing on the legislative docket, and no senator could afford not to go on record on it. *Not just a waste of time*, she thought as she gathered her papers, *a colossal waste of time*. Anger and embarrassment pushed to the surface, and she tried to resist the impulse to protest. *Smile and live to fight another day*, she told herself. Nevertheless, an old habit came to the surface, a tendency that had made her a few enemies in her short career. For better or worse, she was determined to close with some dignity. "Thank you, Senator," she replied with steel-like calmness. "My agency is quite small, and very understaffed with what you call cushy jobs, as it happens. The entire environmental needs of this state are now being serviced by a total of four field agents." She looked directly into Durand's eyes, fixing him in a level stare. "But whether or not you approve increased funding, we will move forward with our limited resources. As the senator knows, our agency is empowered by *federal* law to fulfill its mission, with or without the approval of this committee."

Durand glared, stung by an unaccustomed strike. His face flushed red, and Amanda knew she had added another name to her list of adversaries. It hardly mattered; Durand had already made it clear that he would do everything in his power to make her life miserable. Staring coldly back into Amanda's eyes, Durand picked up a large wooden gavel and smacked a leather pad on the table. "Adjourn till Monday at three."

Chapter Eight

Henry opened the door of the Feed and Farm Supply Store and peered into the narrow register area, scouting for people. No one was about, and he murmured a silent blessing under his breath. Maybe they could slip in and out without being noticed. A display of American flags dominated the front of the building, the bright colors hanging from a long wire stretched the length of the store. To the left, a line of lawn mowers stood in formation. "All right, Mr. Boyd," he said, "let's get this over with."

The Birdman followed Henry in, humming softly to himself, a plaintive, unmusical sound. Henry stopped at the registers and said, "You wanted to come, and I've brought you."

"My buildings," Boyd said in a cracking voice. "Tell them."

Henry looked at him; a good bit of Boyd's anger had drained away, replaced with palpable discomfort. He was growing anxious, far from his park and in a public place. But in spite of his agitation, Boyd's eyes narrowed, and Henry could feel words forming in the man. It was evident that he was going to have to play the thing out. "All right," he said, "I'll say something to the manager. I don't know what, but something. Then we've got to leave."

The Birdman hacked up something from deep in his throat and swallowed it. "I own your store, Billy Payne," he said softly. "Them's my buildings."

"Who's Payne?" Henry asked. But Boyd didn't respond; he was mumbling softly to himself now, his speech turned inward once again. Henry stared at him a moment, then turned down the aisle to find the manager. His only goal was to get Raymond Boyd in and out of the store as quickly as possible.

Henry led Boyd down a long aisle and turned a corner. A dismal-looking man was stocking shelves two aisles away, and Henry motioned to him. "I'm looking for the manager," he said. Boyd stayed behind, hiding now behind Henry like a shy child. He made a clucking sound in his throat, nervous and guttural.

The man looked up from a box of insecticide bottles. He stared up at Henry with curiosity, then stood and dusted himself off at the knees. "I'm him," the man said. "I manage for Mr. Crandall. Name's Billy Payne." He set down his box cutter and stood silently, as if waiting for orders. Henry put on a businesslike, nonthreatening smile, but before he could speak the

Birdman rustled up against him from behind, knocking him forward several inches. The manager shifted to look over his shoulder, but Boyd was still concealed behind Henry's larger frame. A distinctly unsavory smell, however, was gaining ground on the bug killer and fertilizer surrounding them.

"Mr. Payne," Henry said, "my name is Henry Mathews, and I'm a lawyer. I'm here as executor of the late Mr. Tyler Crandall's estate. I've got . . ."

Suddenly, the Birdman reached a grimy hand around and pushed Henry to the side. Stepping forward, he bobbed in the aisle, smiling a yellowed smile. Then, without warning, he shrieked, "I own your store, Billy Payne! I come to see my buildings!"

Payne jerked reflexively backward, tipping a box of screws off a display. The parts scattered noisily, dancing and running along the floor. "Mother of God," the manager exclaimed. He froze, staring.

Henry closed his eyes and grimaced; the circus had begun. "I just need a second, Mr. Payne. Unless you're busy right now, in which case I'd be delighted to come back another time and explain this to you when we're alone. You have no idea how delighted."

"I got time," Payne said. He looked over at Boyd. "I got all the time in the world for this."

"I'm here to inform you that Mr. Boyd here . . ."

"Boyd?" Payne asked. "I thought he was just the damn Birdman."

"He's got a name, like everybody else. It's Boyd. And Tyler Crandall saw fit to leave Mr. Boyd certain properties in his estate. This store is one of them."

Boyd reached out and picked up a box of hinges, sniffed it cautiously and set it back down on a different shelf. Payne pointed at him. "You're sayin' that . . ."

"That's right, Mr. Payne."

Payne looked blankly back at him for some time. He appeared to be staring at an indecipherable mathematical equation. Then, in stages flickering and receding, a smile crept cautiously across his face. "To . . . him," he said slowly. "Joseph, Mary, and the baby Jesus."

A customer turned down the aisle, and Boyd made a low, guttural sound, not unlike a dog growling. The customer stared a moment, then retreated back out the door. "What I'm saying, Mr. Payne," Henry stated, anxious to finish, "is that it would appear you have a new boss."

Boyd rambled several feet down the aisle, his interest now occupied with some distant shelves. Payne, watching him, muttered, "The Birdman. The damn Birdman, in my store."

Henry was unwilling to let Boyd out of his sight. He nodded a perfunctory good-bye and said, "I appreciate your time, Mr. Payne. I'll be in touch." He started back down the aisle, ready to hustle Boyd out of the store. As he turned, Payne suddenly reached out a hand and grabbed him by the arm. The man's smile had vanished.

"What does Roger say about all this? About the Birdman owning the store?"

Something in the man's face made Henry pause; his expression looked like genuine fear. *I have the feeling you'll find out what Roger has to say*, he thought, *and you're going to wish you were someplace else when you do*. But he merely answered, "He's not pleased, Mr. Payne. He's not pleased at all."

Chapter Nine

*G*o *home.* That was the smart move. *Get on the plane, tell Sheldon all about it, about the freak and the greedy son and the whole idiotic mess. Have a good laugh over drinks with the boys, and fall into bed with Elaine.* But once again, he wasn't doing the smart move, the Sheldon Parker move. The edge beckoned, and more and more, he was answering. Henry had dialed Parker's direct line and explained that things had gotten complicated, carefully leaving out most of Roger's outburst, and all of Boyd's trip to the Crandall Feed and Farm Supply Store. He had started with some light humor, buttering Parker up, knowing that even though Parker saw through it he still couldn't resist it. And then the announcement, that the thing was a bit of a mess, that he needed some time to sort it out. Parker's response had been direct and to the point.

"So we got ourselves a little situation here."

"Yeah."

"Look, Henry," Parker had said, "it sounds to me like the family isn't thrilled with you anyway. Why roll a rock uphill? Write a letter requesting a release due to scheduling problems beyond your control. Come back to the real world, buddy."

Henry had heard himself say, "This is technically firm business, Sheldon. All my preexisting stuff got absorbed into the office. That was part of the deal."

"Of course it was, Henry. I *drafted* your deal. We can't have our new friends carrying on little probate cases behind our backs, can we? Of course not."

"It's a nice estate, Sheldon. Two and a half, three million. That makes our end, what, ninety grand?"

"Okay, Preacher," Parker had answered. "I don't know what the hell you're doing down there, but I'll throw you this bone. I have terms, of course. This wacko story stays plausible only if you tie the fruitcake directly to Crandall. *If.* Then things stay straightforward. But if there really is no connection between the two of them, you got nothing but a family drama and that's not our line of work. The kid . . . what's his name?"

"Roger."

"Right. Thing is, the kid's got a shot if there's no connection. Too good a shot to pass up. Not that I blame him. But there's no way in hell I'm letting you stick around for that melodrama. Too much time, not enough zeros."

"How long do I have to make the connection?"

"Till Monday."

"Sheldon . . ."

"Don't push me, Henry. Monday, and you can take the last flight out. But listen, don't get me wrong here. No matter what you find, I want your valuable butt back in the office next week. We got *real* problems back here. If Technology Enterprises' problems get into the papers, they'll lose three million in the market during lunch."

"Thanks, Sheldon."

"No tie-in between Crandall and the crazy guy, your ass is on the plane Monday night. That's the deal."

"Understood," Henry said with a grim smile. He had bought a fragment of time, but Sheldon's paybacks had a way of making a person wish he'd lost the argument in the first place.

He was about to hang up when Parker added, "Say, kid, I was just thinking."

"What's that?"

"Odd, isn't it? I mean about your father drafting the original will. It's a weird coincidence. What you wouldn't give to ask the old man now what was going on back then, huh?"

Henry paused. The thought had crossed his own mind more than once. "Yeah, no kidding. See you later, Sheldon."

Parker was right, Henry thought as he hung up the phone. It was strange, thinking about his father in the middle of all this craziness. The man was the straightest arrow in the world, the kind of man who never broke the speed limit. It was unsettling to think that he was somehow mixed up in an enigma like the Crandall will. And why the secrecy? Ty had insisted that the will be sealed and opened only in the presence of the family. Henry hoped that in the end there was nothing more involved than a disgruntled father and an angry son.

Henry flipped shut his cell phone and looked at his watch. It was nearly two. He hoped the rest of the day would be better than the morning; after the circus with Boyd he had gone to Roger's. Crandall had grilled him on what had happened with Boyd, and when Henry got to the part about taking Boyd to the Crandall store, Roger had hit the roof. Henry had told him flatly that Boyd had the right to go where he wanted, and he wasn't about to physically restrain the man. But Roger had refused to be placated. In the end, Henry had left, as much to get away from the chaos of Roger's outburst as to start his search into the Crandall estate.

At around two-fifteen Henry parked in front of the Cottonwood Valley Bank, anxious to check on Ty Crandall's bank records. If he was going to clear the mud a little, that was as good a place as any to start. He got out and walked toward the little bank, leaving his jacket behind. Summer had appeared from out of nowhere in the plains, and heat was crackling up off the sidewalks. But the worst was yet to come; by August the sun would be sucking water straight from the air, leaving a dusty film on the streets and the windshields of the cars and trucks.

The bank itself was a throwback to an earlier era: old, bordering on decrepit, and filled with heavy furniture that seemed to absorb the little light there was in the room. A few dilapidated ceiling fans whirred slowly overhead, and the handful of undersized light fixtures did little to scatter the gloom. Behind the reception area were three desks with women working at them, a large vault, and two modest, enclosed offices at the far end.

"Can I help you?" a voice asked. Henry turned toward the sound and saw a trim, middle-aged woman with heavy makeup seated behind one of the desks.

"Thanks," he answered. He gave her his card and said, "If the manager's around, I have some business to discuss with him."

"Mr. Walters isn't in at the moment," the woman answered. She had a smoker's voice, sexy, equal parts silk and leather. "Can I do something for you?"

"I'm the executor of the Ty Crandall estate. There are some details to work through." He held up a folder. "Just routine, power of attorney, things like that."

The woman looked Henry up and down, taking in his dark pants, matching shirt, and silk tie. "I can pass them along. Is there anything else?"

"There is, actually. But it's probably better handled with Mr. Walters. Will he be gone long?"

"He's in Kansas City until late tomorrow afternoon."

That was a blow; it had been hard enough to get the limited time he had from Sheldon. Waiting another day to even start digging through Ty's affairs was out of the question. "I'm his assistant," the woman said. "Maybe I can help."

That was hopeful. "I'm going to need to have a look at Mr. Crandall's accounts, his business with the bank." Henry smiled. "Would that be something you can arrange?"

"You mean his checking accounts, things like that?"

"Anything pertaining to his assets and liabilities. I really need to see his entire banking picture."

"On the basis of?"

"I can't disburse assets I don't know exist."

She looked at him a moment and said, "Well, let me see what I can do."

"Thanks. I appreciate it."

The woman returned after several minutes with three enormous folders, each stuffed with papers. She walked with a languid, swinging motion, obviously well practiced. As she approached, Henry looked at her left hand: no wedding ring. *Divorced,* he thought, *probably more than once.* Watching her, he thought briefly of Elaine back in Chicago, and suddenly missed her very much.

"Well, that's about everything," she said, "at least that I'm aware of. You're welcome to it, although it needs to stay in the bank." She nodded toward her desk. "You can take mine," she said. "I'm busy in Mr. Walters' office anyway."

"Thanks. I'll try to stay clear of things."

"Don't worry about it. If you need anything, let me know. I'm Ellen. Ellen Gaudet."

Henry dug in, spending the afternoon with the folders. The records were separated into sections: loans, active accounts, and financial statements. There was a massive amount of trivial information in the papers, and he combed through it all, looking for anything to connect Crandall to Boyd. The records covered only the past few years, too recent to learn anything about Crandall's early years in business. All the same, it was useful to get the actual numbers on everything, and he noted the totals in his laptop. Crandall's estate was cash-heavy, which wasn't a surprise; a lot of small-town high rollers never got much financial advice. Crandall had done well, but he would have been far richer if he had invested more outside Council Grove. There was nearly a million and a half dollars in cash, CDs, and low-interest bonds. The value of the real estate was difficult to gauge—current farming prospects cast a shadow on that part of the estate, and some property values in the area had actually declined over the past few years. But the granary and farm equipment businesses were solid. Together, they had cleared about three hundred thousand dollars the previous year. The oil wells were down to a dribble, however. Henry was surprised that the lot of them had brought in only around thirty-five thousand dollars the previous year. He worked through the records without a break until Ellen returned, interrupting his concentration. "We'll be closing soon," she said quietly.

Henry looked at his watch in surprise. "Sorry, I lost track of time. It's a bad habit."

"No problem," she answered. "Did you find what you need?"

"Not really. It's a start, though." Henry gathered the papers but stopped momentarily.

"Listen," he said, "I need to make you aware of something regarding the Crandall situation."

"All right."

There was no use trying to hide what would soon enough be all over town. "Let's say that everything didn't work out exactly as expected."

"What do you mean?"

"A pretty big slice of the estate wasn't left to a family member."

"I see."

"There's another person involved. I'm not breaking any confidences to tell you this. I have to do it for practical reasons. It isn't inconceivable this person could show up at the bank."

"And do what?"

Henry paused. *God knows*, he thought. *Preach a sermon. Take off his clothes. Maybe both.* "Well," he said, "he might want money. But I couldn't really predict. He's not particularly . . . sociable." Ellen raised a perfectly plucked eyebrow, but said nothing. "I just don't want you to be taken by surprise. He could be unpredictable, even hostile. I'm not saying he would be. I just don't know."

"I see. So who is this person?"

"Have you ever heard the name Raymond Boyd?"

What followed was one of those moments that makes a lawyer glad he has chosen his profession. Ellen's face formed an expression minutely too casual, as if it were being pushed through another, more immediate emotion. Ellen Gaudet, no matter what her next words were, knew exactly who Raymond Boyd was.

"No," she answered calmly, "I don't believe I've met anyone by that name."

Henry processed her answer instantly and invisibly. "It's more likely you know him by a different name, if I can call it a name," he said.

She looked at him blankly.

"I'm talking about the Birdman."

"The guy out in Custer's Elm? What about him?"

"Tyler Crandall left the bulk of his estate to him."

"My God." Henry watched her face carefully; her surprise, at least, seemed genuine. She may have known Boyd, but she hadn't anticipated Crandall making him the richest man in Cheney County.

"That is . . . a shock," she said.

"It's a mess, frankly," Henry said. "All of Ty Crandall's accounts are to be frozen as of today. No withdrawals from any of them, without my permission as executor. The money will go into escrow. I should be able to get some papers to you tomorrow."

"What about the accounts of other family members?" Ellen asked.

"This doesn't affect them. But any joint accounts—anything with Ty's name and anyone else's—they're frozen, too. No money can be transferred between them." *That'll keep Roger's nose clean, at least*, Henry thought.

"Whatever you say," Ellen muttered. The ripple of recognition that had been present at the mention of Boyd's name had now disappeared, leaving a remote, detached expression. Objectively, Henry was impressed: the fact that she could submerge her reactions so quickly indicated an almost professional level of self-control.

"Thanks for your help," he said. "Obviously, there's no telling what Mr. Boyd might do under these circumstances."

"No," she said softly, "no telling at all."

Henry smiled, radiating professional courtesy. "If you need me, here's the number of my cell phone. I'll have it with me at all times." He paused. "And naturally, if Mr. Boyd chooses to . . ."

"Of course," Ellen said. "I'll call you immediately."

"Thanks. Listen, would you mind if I came back first thing tomorrow morning? I haven't quite finished."

Ellen's face was blank. "Fine," she answered, turning to walk back into the manager's office.

Henry looked after her, wondering. She had certainly known Boyd, against all odds. But the important thing was that she was cooperating fully. He would take any break he could get, no matter how small. With a helpful Ellen Gaudet on the inside of the bank, maybe all he needed was time.

Chapter Ten

Roger Crandall could remember the exact moment he decided that he would be like his father. He was squatting on the steps of the Cheney County courthouse on a hot August afternoon, squinting through the sun at the heavy wooden doors before him. It wasn't any cooler inside, and he waited for his father out on the concrete. Sometimes he would climb up on the big cannon in the courtyard. He was thirteen years old, and his father had left him to rummage for himself while he took care of some pressing business inside. Roger was used to waiting for his father, even at such a young age. He waited for him at water commission meetings. He tagged along behind him while Ty stopped in the street every block or two to talk to people. He waited while his father went into the rental houses, and he sometimes heard him yelling inside. That day in August while Roger waited, Marty Roe, a farmer who was trying to develop some land on the outskirts of town, suddenly exploded out of the courthouse above him with an expression on his face somewhere between confusion and disgust. Roe practically ran over young Roger, who was crouched down around the man's knees. Roe jarred to a stop mere inches in front of the boy, his face a surprised scowl. Roger stared silently up at him, Roe's head backlit by the fierce summer sun.

Roe stared down at Roger a moment, then he growled, "Your father's done it again, you little runt," and, narrowly missing him, rapidly shoved off the steps and out into the street, leaving a hot vapor trail behind.

Roger didn't know what it was his father was doing, but it was obvious that he did it whenever he wanted, and it didn't matter that it made other people mad or that they wished with all their might that he didn't do it. He just *did* it. That was all his young mind needed to know; he longed for that freedom of action, for the power of unrestricted decision. Daddy had it: Roger would be like Daddy. Now that power that he had waited for so many years to possess was in danger of being taken away from him, and at the very moment it had come into his grasp. It was unthinkable.

Roger strode across his yard toward his car and swung himself into the big Eldorado. He slammed the door shut, being careful not to spill his drink. He sniffed cautiously; the car smelled of his father. He raced the engine and rammed it into reverse. Using the gears as a brake, he slipped the transmission into drive while he was still rolling backward. Tires spinning in a cloud of gravel, the car shot forward.

He wondered for a second how far the word had gotten out as he drove into town from the Crandall homestead, and realized that by now everyone surely knew. Humiliation burned red on his face. He took a drink, finishing the glass. He knew he had made enemies. He hadn't given a damn about that—he was a Crandall, and that came with the territory. But enemies when you didn't have power—that was something different. He imagined the people he had bullied all sitting around at the Trailside Diner, drinking coffee and laughing at jokes they wouldn't have dared tell two days earlier. Cursing, he turned right on Pawnee and gunned the engine. His first stop would be the Feed and Farm Supply.

Crandall blew into the store full of bluster and volume. He wasn't consciously choosing his methods—he was too angry for that, and the three drinks hadn't helped. It was as if there was a big hand in his back, and it pushed too hard for him to resist. He knew the hand well—this wasn't the first time he had wanted to slow down, to think things through. Sometimes he had seen the victims of his tirades and actually felt a tinge of regret. He had sometimes wished that he could handle things in a different way. But the hand was too big. It pushed him along, making him speak louder and faster than he wanted to. It made him angry, and if nothing else, the anger made him feel powerful. That feeling was a magic elixir, a drug too powerful to resist.

The words "Get out here, Payne" spat out of his mouth before the door had shut behind him. With the sound of Crandall's voice, Billy Payne looked over the shelves from the back of the store and felt the old, familiar fear come over him.

"Payne!" Roger shouted. "You taking the day off, or what?" Billy hustled around the corner and rapidly approached Roger.

"Right here, Mr. Crandall," he answered. His mind was racing. Maybe it had all been too strange after all. Maybe Crandall was here to tell him that the whole Birdman thing was some kind of bizarre joke. Maybe his life was going to continue being so deadly monotonous it would be boring if it didn't scared the crap out of him. "I'm sorry, sir," he ventured, "I was checking stock at the back."

"I gotta talk to you," Crandall growled. "I gotta talk to *everybody*. Any customers in the store?"

Payne looked around. "I don't think so."

"Then get everybody up here by the cash registers."

"Yes, sir." Billy trotted to the storeroom and rounded up the two employees there. There were three others, and they had already come to the front of the store, drawn by Crandall's voice.

Crandall scanned their faces, reading them. No one was smirking, at least. But he was no fool. He knew they had been laughing at him. He could feel it. He could smell it. He hated it. "Lock the front door, Billy," he said in a dry voice. "We're gonna be closed for a little while." Billy hurried to the door, locked it, and turned over the sign. He turned back to face Crandall, taking his place in the lineup.

Roger stood silently before the store employees, trying to calm himself and think. He needed to make this count. He needed to get control. He tasted scotch in the back of his mouth and blinked at the line of employees, steadying himself. The big hand pushed and pushed, and he narrowed his eyes. "Some of you probably seen a little circus in here yesterday," he began. It was all right; the words weren't slurring too badly. He would make it through this. "You seen that bird freak in here actin' like he owned this place. I'm sure it was real damn funny." He checked himself; he regretted the last statement—it sounded weak, defensive. But the big hand was in his back now, pushing.

"I'm here to tell you that whatever you think you saw, you can forget it. It never happened. Nothing is going to change around here. The bird freak ain't your boss, and he don't own this store." Crandall scanned the faces of the workers again; they looked confused, but he could also see fear. That was good.

"This here ain't nothin' but some legal screwup that's gonna get fixed right quick. This store's been Crandall since it opened, and it always will be. My daddy built it, and it's mine now. So if the goddam president of the United States or anybody else comes in here and tells you anything different, he's a liar and you're to throw him out on his bony ass. You got that?"

Only a few heads nodded up and down, and he threatened them, gravitating to that weapon effortlessly, through years of practice. "Let me put it to you this way. There ain't been a case decided against my family in the history of Cheney County law, and that ain't gonna change now. So one way or another, I'm gonna end up with this store. But what you do in the meantime is gonna affect you for the rest of your lives. If I hear that any one of you cooperates with the bird freak, I'll crush you like a fly. That clear enough?"

Heads nodded, but no one spoke. He wanted to hear their voices. "Do you got that?" he shrieked.

Several "Yes, sir"s filtered out, but in general the row of employees stared back at him blankly. He could see the fear in their eyes, but also the indecision. Having the lawyer with the Birdman had given the visit credibility. The big hand pushed. "This is my store, you hear me?" he yelled, and his voice trembled. He hated the big hand. It pushed again. "This here is my store, damn you, and you ain't gonna forget it! If you work with the bird freak, you're finished!"

Roger whirled around, the booze upsetting his sense of balance. He attempted to walk rapidly toward the door, but listed to the right just enough to bump into one of the cash registers. To his utter, hateful surprise, he heard a small chuckle; the stony silence enforced on his employees for so long had at last been broken, and by a laugh. He wanted to be out of there, someplace far away. He despised the store, despised everyone in it. He reached for the door and yanked on it. It banged against the lock. Another chuckle drifted up from behind him. "Open this door, Payne!" he yelled, and Billy lurched forward and fumbled with the keys. It took several seconds to select the right one, and Roger trembled with anger while he waited. When the key turned, he didn't wait for Billy to take his hand off it. He yanked the door open, and flew out the door. *The lawyer boy just ran out of time*, he thought to himself as he sped off in the big Cadillac. The big hand pushed and pushed. *If he don't come up with something soon, I'll solve this problem myself.*

Chapter Eleven

Amanda Ashton kicked off her black pumps and swung her legs out of the agency pickup, letting her stockinged feet dangle over the side. She dropped a pair of dirty hip waders onto the ground before her and gingerly stretched a foot down into the cold rubber. This was her third stop, and the insides of the boots were no longer entirely dry; she grimaced, paused a moment, and pushed her feet down into them. They weren't a great fit; the boots were made to wear shoes in, and her small feet slid around uncertainly in the unsupported rubber. She pulled the waders up over her slacks and slipped her arms under the suspenders. Stepping out of the truck carefully, she tested her weight on the muddy surface. The ground was unstable, but with a little care she could manage.

An all-night rain had left the conditions far from ideal for the tramping she needed to do. The agency truck had suddenly become available, however, and she didn't quibble. The garage had called with a miraculous, last-minute cancellation and given her exactly ten minutes to claim the vehicle before they went to the next name on the list. She was already walking toward the door before she hung up. Her clothes were another matter, however; had she known, she would have brought scrubs and boots. But she wasn't going to lose her morning driving in the opposite direction across Topeka to change clothes. She gazed down at herself ruefully; tailored blue business pantsuit, white blouse, silver brooch and earrings, Oriental scarf, nicely finished off with black rubber hip waders. She smiled, pushing a wisp of short auburn hair behind her ears. She liked incongruity, and government work gave her a never-ending supply of it.

Amanda fastened the waders and lifted a foot, the mud giving way with a sucking sound. Reaching into the truck bed, she pulled out a large canvas backpack and tossed it over her shoulder. This was followed by another, bulkier bundle bound together by more canvas and a rope. The thought crossed her mind that she could be in a corporate office somewhere making real money, and as always, it amused her. Money had never driven her. Unlike most of her friends in graduate school at Georgetown, she actually believed a government job could make a difference. Or at least some government jobs, and this was one of them. Grabbing the awkward bundle, she marched off into an unusually sodden bog just south of Matfield Green in the heart of the Flinthills.

The nasty weather was penance for the lucky stroke with the truck, and she accepted it good-naturedly. She trudged across a large easement off the highway, and twenty yards farther on came to a barbed-wire fence. The fence surrounded a wide, expansive field. Somewhere inside the Triple Z Ranch, she knew, there was a gate. It was useless to try to use it. Rory Zachariah owned the Triple Z, and he was as close to an honorary member of the Posse Comitatus as you could get. He hated government, government agents, government programs, and income tax all about equally, which is to say passionately, militantly, and dangerously. She had called him weeks earlier to explain that, pursuant to the Federal Land Stabilization Act of 1994, she had the authority to inspect his wells and to set up a time for that inspection. Zachariah's response had been utter simplicity, consisting of the words "You stay the hell off my land," followed by a dial tone. She looked sadly down the fence, connecting the horizon north and south. The wire was rusty, dangerous-looking, and five strands high. But in the absence of an enforcing militia, her legal authority to enter was purely academic; to get on the Triple Z, she would have to climb.

The day was hot, and whatever part of her that could feel feminine in hip waders recoiled at the task before her. She put on a pair of heavy canvas work gloves and reached out, pulling gently on the top strand of the wire; it snapped back with a taut *twang*, vibrating like a menacing guitar string. Zachariah maintained his place like a boot camp, and the fence was a perfect stretch of razor-sharp points. She hesitated a moment, casting out of her mind several ignoble scenarios resulting from a failed attempt to cross. At last, in an effort to force herself to act, she gently dropped her backpack over the side of the fence. It fell over and rolled two feet away from a post. The bundle followed. There was no going back; she would have to climb now.

The gloves protected her hands and she grabbed the top wire, stepping between barbs on the bottom strand as close as possible to the fence post. The wire sagged precipitously and began oscillating back and forth; for a moment she hung there, committed but afraid to continue. At last she stepped up two strands; she reached an arm over the wire, but her sleeve caught on a barb point, forcing her to stop. Carefully, she extricated it, continuing up. The top was the worst; her weight made the taut wire wiggle even faster, and she perched precariously, clinging to the post itself. Quickly she realized that waiting only increased her danger, so she slung a heavy rubber leg as high as possible over the fence. The other followed, and her bottom half was over, bending back over the fence at the waist. With some careful maneuvering she was able to finish the climb, hopping off the last two strands with a thud. Catching her breath, she grabbed her backpack and slung it over her shoulder. She peered out into a vast, wet expanse of tall bluestem grass. The first well was off to the east about three hundred yards.

Amanda picked up the other bundle and headed off toward the dead well, a rusting monument of black iron to the fading oil reserves of the central plains. To the north she could see two more wells, still clinging to life, slowly rocking. They dipped down, plunging spikes deep into the earth; tipping up, they extracted black blood like enormous, mechanical mosquitoes.

In spite of her federal authority, she didn't want to have to explain her current actions to a judge. In a cold legal light she supposed that what she was doing was nothing but trespassing. If the landowner denied access to the well, certain channels were prescribed to gain that access. One didn't just *walk on*. There was a protocol, and she was ignoring it. She readjusted her backpack and picked up her pace. It was done now. The sun beat down, and she mechanically pushed her hair away from the sweat gathering on her forehead. Getting on the Triple Z without owner approval would require a mountain of paperwork, not to mention the cooperation of at least three government departments who didn't speak much: Justice, EPA, and the local sheriff. She could imagine folders of forms, all meticulously filled out in the jargon of each separate agency. If everything went well, it could take six months. If feet were dragged, she could double that. In that year a hideous blend of acids and iron-rusted brine could enter the groundwater system of northeastern Kansas, flowing into irrigation systems, municipal water plants, artesian wells on private land.

The Triple Z was her best guess for a massive breakdown of drilling casings. It was closest to the pickup points that had showed elevated salt levels, and two of the wells were over sixty years old, long played out. In addition, they had been drilled by a small, private company, now defunct, wildcatting on low funds and quick scores. Companies like that worked quick and dirty, in and out. If her theory that shoddy wells were crumbling within themselves was true, the rusting hulk before her was a prime candidate to prove it.

She was making good time, and the well grew before her as she advanced. Fifty yards from the site she got a nasty suspicion, however; squinting at the base of the well, she thought she spied glints of more brown wire, obscured by bluestem stalks four feet high running and splitting in the breeze. She peered into the distance, focusing her eyes. Soon there could be no doubt: the well itself was surrounded by another fence, this one dilapidated and evil-looking. Climbing it would be truly dangerous; it could well collapse under her weight, casting her down onto the barbs. Disgusted, Amanda approached the well slowly. The posts leaned perilously out at lazy angles; the wire itself was covered in rust.

Amanda circled the well, carefully pushing bluestem away from the sagging arcs of wire, looking for a break. At last, she had an idea: if the wire was intact, perhaps the posts themselves would give way. She shook one; the loosely stretched wire offered no support, and the pole moved easily in her hands. As she rocked back and forth, the dirt at the base shifted and crumbled. The fence was literally ready to come down, and ten minutes' sweaty work pulled the post up and out of its hole entirely. Carefully lowering it to the ground, she stepped over the fence, tiptoeing between the wires. The ground around the well was a muddy, slippery slough, but more inconvenient than truly dangerous. The real hazard lurked in the casings three thousand feet down.

What looked from a distance like a simple black fulcrum revealed itself to be a maze of fittings, junctions, and valves. Amanda set her bundles down on the base of the well and stared up at the complex mass of pipes. Finding an inactive site was essential; a pumping well is a dangerous place, dangerous even to try to shut down for inspection. Even professionals can be confused by all the pipes, and more than one dead body had been hauled off a site because of a mistake. This well looked almost peaceful, as if it had never punctured the earth. Bird droppings ran down the sides, and an unused nest hung precariously off some upper junctions.

Amanda pulled a folded chart of thick paper out of her pack and spread it out before her on the wellhead. The paper was covered with colored symbols indicating porous rock formations in the area at depths down to thirteen thousand feet. She ran her finger down the page, every few inches another geological age: Jurassic, Triassic, Carboniferous. The map revealed an enormous salt dome a half mile wide and down three thousand feet; this was what the drillers in the 1930s must have been looking for. Oil loved to collect in salt domes, prehistoric plants and animals decomposing into millions of thick, black gallons that silently floated half a mile beneath the surface of the earth.

Amanda glanced at her watch; it was nearly eleven. The sun was growing strong and glared down brightly, heating the iron superstructure above her. She dropped to her knees, moving with some difficulty in the bulky waders. Quickly, she unloaded her pack, pulling out a laptop computer, a drum of cable, and two slender magnesium tubes eighteen inches long. She screwed the tubes together and attached one end of the cable to the base of the tubes. Then she plugged the other end of the cable into a port on her laptop. She powered up the computer and launched a program.

With the computer now on, she unscrewed the water-return flange on the wellhead. It was hard to move, and she had to kick it several times to get it started. Eventually the seal of rust and grime was broken, and after four or five threads she was able to pull open the flange and expose an eight-inch-wide tube that sank into the darkness of the well. She worked intently for a while, attempting to ignore the heat. After some time she relented, and peering up at the sun with annoyance, negotiated a bit of shade by moving a few feet around the wellhead. Another glance at her watch; nearly twenty minutes had passed at the wellhead. She looked nervously back at the road; she had been lucky so far. An encounter with Rory Zachariah was the last thing she needed. The road was quiet, and she returned to her work. Carefully, she lowered the magnesium tubes down by the cable into the shaft. Two handles flipped out from the sides of the cable drum, and she was able to rest the box securely against a couple of large gauges. Pushing a button, she heard the precision sound of two hundred feet per minute of digital cable spinning gently down into the gaseous darkness of the dead well.

A readout flickered on her laptop, and she monitored the sensor's descent: a thousand feet, two thousand, twenty-five hundred, three thousand. At thirty-one hundred feet she pressed another button, and the spinning smoothly slowed. The sensor stabilized at thirty-one hundred and sixty feet; just under two-thirds of a mile. Amanda hovered over the computer, then switched the motorized drum to a slow ascent. She stared at the computer as the cable rewound at seventy-five feet a minute. The readings were not good. Nothing would be definite without disassembling the well, but her concerns rose with every reading. She worked methodically, consulting her chart and rechecking her readings. The sun moved through the sky, heading west and casting shadows from the well across the field.

By noon the job was complete. Amanda closed the notebook and pressed a button on the cable drum. A whirring began, and the sensor ascended more quickly, and in a few minutes she was able to pull out the tubes by hand.

She quickly but carefully returned all the components to their containers and gathered her belongings. There was one more stop: the return pool for the brine. That would be a messy job; she would have to plod three or four feet directly into the mess, and a pool like that was pure muck after a rain.

Amanda crossed over the broken-down fence and headed for the pool. She had been spectacularly lucky so far, and her innate sense that bad luck followed good was worrying her. She once again glanced over at the road; a car speeding down the highway appeared to be slowing near her truck, and she froze. Instantly, she realized that there was nothing more suspicious than the sight of a person standing like a statue in the middle of a field, so she willed herself to resume walking. She headed as confidently as she could toward the pool, forcing herself not to look back at the car. By the time she had reached it she could resist no longer, but when she turned around the car had disappeared.

Amanda stepped tentatively into the brine pool, grasping a long tool. Immediately, her leg sank a foot into the slough. She would have to be cautious. It wasn't enough to scrape a sample from the top; the farther down, the better, because it represented the past. Her handheld tools would reach no more than six feet down, but it was better than nothing. If she could get some positive readings, she could force Durand's hand. What she needed was a smoking gun. She walked tentatively a few steps out into the pool, her footing shifting continuously under her weight. Suddenly, her left foot slid outward, and she lurched forward to keep her balance. She leaned forward, wavering unsteadily. The muck was well above her knees. *Far enough*, she thought. A reading deep from the center of the pool would have been ideal, but this would have to do.

Sweat poured from her face now, and she felt her clothes soaking against her skin. *No matter*, she thought. *If I get what I want, I'll send the dry-cleaning bill to Durand.* She held a long spike up with both hands and plunged it as hard as she could into the dark mess beneath her. It came slowly to a halt, as if in glue. Now came the real work; she began rotating the shaft, digging down into the sediment of the pool with every turn.

She was hard at work, focused completely on the muck when she heard it: a heavy footstep falling behind her, and then another. Instantly, her skin went cold and her breathing became shallow. She stood still for a moment, caught in the brine and her own vibrating nerves. It was quiet behind her now; for a moment, she played a game of deception with herself, letting herself think that if she didn't turn around whoever was behind her didn't exist. The sound was imagined; she could continue on, finish, and then slip away unseen back to her truck. But in the end she forced herself to turn slowly around, rotating the top half of her body while her legs stayed firmly planted in thick, briny mud. She was momentarily dazzled; the sun had crested bright and in her eyes. She could just make out the shape of a large figure on the edge of the pool. Squinting through the haze, she saw light glinting off the long barrel of a shotgun. The figure's face was still hidden in the sun's radiance.

"I thought I told you to stay the hell off my land," a voice said.

Chapter Twelve

The Birdman's brain hurt. He felt the blood pumping up through the veins in his skull, *pump pump*. He didn't like that feeling. Lately he had thought he could feel his organs working, his liver, kidneys, heart. There were times when he was sure he could feel his thoughts moving across the surface of his brain, crawling like little insects. That was the feeling he disliked the most; if the thoughts crawled across his brain, were they *his* thoughts? Why weren't they inside his brain, where they belonged? Or were they from somewhere else, sent to scratch a trail along his tissues? Perhaps they were even now burrowing, trying to enter him. In that case, he must keep them out. He must concentrate, make his brain hard and impenetrable. But what if the idea that he must keep his brain hard was one of the thoughts sent to burrow? What if he should just relax, let the thoughts crawl and crawl and fill him like little termites sent from God, little divine bugs that would consume him and then at last let him stop hurting? The Birdman scratched one leg with the other hard until it hurt, focusing on the pain. That seemed to help; the pain was real, the pain wasn't crawling. He could see his leg, he could make his foot move and scratch and scratch until it hurt. That was not sent from above. That thought was *his*. He pulled up the pant leg and stared; a black-and-blue splotch pulsed above the ankle where it had been habitually rubbed raw. He had been rubbing a lot lately. He smiled at the purple and red and black. He welcomed himself back to the park, to the grass and trees. He looked up at the sun, squinting, closing his eyes and feeling its heat on his face.

"Bird?" he asked. He turned his head rapidly to the right and opened his eyes. The vulture was ignoring him, intent on a crack in the concrete several feet away. He was jamming his beak into the crack, turning his head this way and that, rooting and digging. Suddenly, he snapped his head back and pulled out a writhing beetle. He tipped his head up and swallowed. The Birdman watched, wondering if the vulture was eating his thoughts when he ate those bugs.

"Bird?" he asked again. At that, the animal flapped one wing lamely and walked in a circle. "That's right, bird," the Birdman said. "Pluck, pluck, eat, eat. That's right. Eat them all."

Boyd wanted to get up. He had wanted to get up for about an hour now, but so far hadn't. He had been restless all morning, and now it was past one. He never knew what kind of day it would be: would the thoughts be burrowing thoughts, or his own thoughts? When the lawyer came it had been a good day, he had been peaceful and rested. But today wasn't so good, which was bad, because he needed to think. Lawyers and papers and Ty Crandall, all thoughts from somewhere. He needed to think from where. Were they burrowing thoughts? Or were they his? He looked over at his bird, who was scratching at the grass near the sidewalk with a black talon.

That day a restless feeling had been growing. All morning long it grew and grew. He was having a new thought, a strange and dangerous thought. Wherever it came from, the thought had been growing all day. There was nothing at all vague about it. It was very specific.

"Bird?" he murmured, and without looking, he leaned forward and tipped himself up off the park bench. He was standing; he looked around, mildly surprised. That was when things worked best, when they just happened, when he didn't think so hard and just tipped and he didn't have to *decide*. He stuck his hands in his pockets.

"Where's that damn junior Henry?" he asked the bird. "Where's the boy that don't live here no more?" He shuffled down the sidewalk toward town about ten feet, a worried look on his face. He scanned up and down the street, across the park. "Not here, no junior Henry today, no siree," he whispered. He stopped. The lawyer made him feel better. He could go into town with him. With the lawyer, he didn't have to explain anything. He could hide behind him, walk along and look at his buildings. The lawyer talked, and people couldn't hurt him. He kept the people away. But alone was different. Alone he might get the burrowing thoughts, and then he didn't know what would happen.

"Them's my buildings, ain't that right, junior Henry?" he asked the bird. He shuffled toward town again, moving a few feet before stopping. To avoid thinking the dangerous thought, he thought about the houses, the land. He started up again, moving at a good pace. He was nearly at the end of the block. He stopped and turned his head to the right and looked down Owendale away from his house. Four blocks away, he could see a stoplight. Cars were passing through the intersection. A few people stood and talked on Pawnee. They broke up into two smaller groups and headed in different directions. He thought about the grocery, the farm supply store.

"I own your store, Billy Payne," he whispered, and turned the corner. He was walking again, the stoplight growing as he moved toward it. *The granary. The two big silos full of grain.* He walked along. "Them's my buildings," he repeated. *The bank building*. He slowed. He didn't like to think about the bank. There were shadows there, shapes and memories that needed to be kept absolutely quiet. He ground to a halt, and looked back at his park bench; it was a hundred feet away. He could see the vulture staring after him, his head tilted and still. The Birdman stared back for a while, his face intense. He furrowed his brow and concentrated. It was okay. He would turn left at the light, away from the bank. He didn't need to pass by there to get where the dangerous thought was taking him.

The Birdman walked on toward the stoplight. He crossed the street at the edge of Custer's Elm. It had been four years since he had crossed that street; when Henry had taken him to the farm supply store, they had come up Hilldale, on the other side of the square. The Birdman walked, and the stoplight up at Pawnee grew. Two more blocks. He made his brain very hard, and concentrated. He made one more block.

Raymond Boyd stood at the corner of Pawnee and Owendale. Nobody was near, which comforted him, but there were people on the street farther up. He squinted his eyes and stared. To the north: the bank, which he didn't like; the square, with the courthouse; the café; and farther on, the Feed and Farm Supply. To the south: the grocery, post office, and Benton Street. His dangerous thought grew and grew. He turned south, walking up Pawnee with his head down. He watched his shoes moving back and forth. Eventually he passed the grocery store on the other side of the street. A few cars were parked in front, and a lady was pushing a cart from the store to her car. She saw him and stopped dead for a second. The Birdman didn't know her; he stared at her until she suddenly left her cart full of groceries and went back into the store. A few seconds later the Birdman could see several faces scrunched against the glass window of the store, talking animatedly. He looked at the window, but a car came between them, slowing markedly as it passed. The Birdman seemed to snap out of a daze, and without looking back he walked on toward Benton.

As he approached Benton, he slowed once again. The street was quiet. He stopped on the corner, facing straight ahead, Benton to his left. His dangerous thought was loud now, and it didn't matter if he made his brain hard or not. It pushed him left, turning him and propelling him down the gravel road. The Birdman thought he could feel clinging webs against his face as he walked, and he put his head down and leaned forward, as if walking against a wind. It took him nearly ten minutes to cross one block. Another ten, another block. The dangerous thought was all he could hear now. Halfway down the third block he stopped, facing straight ahead on the sidewalk. He turned his head to the side. He gazed silently at the little white frame house, at the curtained windows and white mailbox in front.

He looked at the mailbox. "Gaudet" was written on it, with the number "325." It was Ellen's house.

The Birdman stood without moving for a moment. Once more he looked to his right and left, mumbling softly to himself. He crossed the street rapidly, plunged into the brush to the left of the house, and vanished into the backyard.

Chapter Thirteen

"I'm not sure when I'll get home." There was a pointed silence on the other end of the phone. "Elaine?" Henry asked.

"Yes, Henry, I'm here. I suppose it can't be helped. But it's the last thing I expected, your being stuck for days on end in Kansas."

Her voice. It was her voice that had intrigued him from the beginning. He had been drawn to its polish, its conspicuous education and finesse. When Elaine talked, Brandeis and Junior League were all in the audible range, ready to be picked up by anybody trained to recognize the sound. It was the mating call of money, the firefly and pheromone of upward mobility. With their torrid work schedules they had seen so little of each other in the early days that he had, in effect, fallen for that voice, a tenuous telephone connection that had always aroused him.

"If Sheldon says let someone local handle it, why not go along?" she was saying. "You're letting yourself get personally involved, and that's always a mistake. Anyway, it's all from your past. It doesn't have anything to do with you now."

He hated to fight with her. Fighting with Elaine wasn't fair. She was logical, incisive, and determined—she would have been a good lawyer, in fact; but she wasn't above using her sexuality, which revealed his weakness to her power. Lately, their disagreements had gotten shorter and shorter. For one thing, he didn't want to lose valuable time on disputes when it was so hard to carve opportunities to be together. But also at stake was power; she gravitated toward it effortlessly, as a matter of course. Inevitably, she captured more and more of it, instinctively jockeying for position. The only way he knew to resist that movement was to argue, and he didn't want that. He didn't, he realized, want his love life to look like work. "If it's personal, that could be a good thing," he said. "I don't feel obligated to go through life never caring about a client."

"Of course not," she said. "But you have to remember that it's business. *Business*, Henry. I sell stocks, you sell legal expertise. But we're both selling our time. And I hate to see you waste it on that fruitcake."

"Try not to refer to him that way, Elaine. I admit I don't know exactly what he is, but that word doesn't describe it."

"How can you side with him? You can't mean you want the family cut out from the estate. I don't know these horrid people, but I do know that isn't fair."

He felt the drift from disagreement toward dispute and wanted to stop the inexorable slide. But he didn't know how to prevent it. She was so relentless, and he couldn't just cave in and pretend he didn't have opinions. "No," he said, "I don't like that part about it either. Although Roger's such a jerk it's easy to side against him. But that's the point, in a way. Roger can take care of himself. Boyd's different. He doesn't stand a chance, not in Council Grove."

"But isn't that *his* problem?" Elaine asked. "You can't take up every cause you run across. You don't have that kind of life. There's legal aid for that kind of thing, Henry. People like that don't *get* four-hundred-dollar-an-hour lawyers."

Exactly, Henry thought. "Look, Elaine, it's only a couple of days. You sound like I'm derailing a whole career."

There was silence on the phone. "It's not that," she said. "It's just a mistake. You haven't made any before. I don't understand why you would upset Sheldon. The thing I don't like about it is that you don't know what it will end up costing you."

"Sheldon's not upset, Elaine. He cleared me to do it."

There was a pause, and he knew what was coming. "We've been over this kind of thing before, darling," she said. "I love your compassionate side. It's what makes you adorable. But you're much too much like your father."

"I know."

"And I want to put this as delicately as I can . . ."

"You don't want me to duplicate his career."

More silence, tactful and effective. Then, in a more seductive voice, "Come home and let someone else handle it, darling. Sheldon needs you, he told you so. And I miss you."

She was magnetic, pulling him from both poles, physical and intellectual. He felt her body across the phone line, the memory coalescing in his mind. Of all the imperatives he had left behind in seminary, the one he enjoyed losing the most was celibacy. Elaine made love the way she made money, with total intensity. "All right, Elaine. It's late, and I don't want to argue. I'm not claiming to understand Boyd, anyway. But I do know that it wouldn't take much to snap him. Whatever twig he's hanging on to won't take much more weight. So maybe it's just that I don't want to be the last bit that crushes him. At least you can understand that."

There was a pause, and Henry listened to the silence. After a moment Elaine said, "I don't mean to sound cold, darling. And I'm sorry if this Boyd man is just a pawn in some game. But I would hate it if he got one cent of the money, and I'll tell you why. What on earth would he do with it? He would be a mess, and you know it. It would be a complete waste, and I don't think you'd be doing him any favors to get him any of it. Money is a *privilege*, Henry. You earn the right to have it by being the kind of person who understands and appreciates it."

God, she thinks like Parker. "Elaine, are you listening to yourself?"

Her voice turned brittle. "What does that mean?"

He sighed, a tired, spent sound. "Look, I'm going to stick around here and find out what I can. There's probably nothing to it. But my whole legal career doesn't have to be about dissecting corporations. I can actually protect somebody once."

"So you've decided."

"Yes, I have."

Her voice was instantly cold and impersonal. "What about the party at the Hargroves' on Sunday? *My* party?"

Elaine was receiving an award for outstanding junior broker at her firm, and the senior partner was giving her a reception at his home. It was all she had talked about for days, and he hadn't blamed her. She had worked incredibly hard, and the award was a terrific honor. "I don't know. If I can't crack this in a couple of days, Sheldon's going to pull the leash anyway."

He heard her exhale, a tortured but nevertheless sensuous sound. It would have been much easier for him if she hadn't been so sexy. But even when she was at her most irritating her erotic side hooked into him like fingernails into flesh. "All right, Henry," she said. "I think it's a mistake to use up favors with Sheldon, but that's your affair. In the meantime, keep your distance from that man Boyd. I'm not convinced he's safe."

"I'm not either, but I think that may be the point."

"What does that mean?"

"I don't know. I'm tired, and I'm hungry. Don't listen to me right now."

"I've already stopped listening. Good-bye."

Henry clicked off his cell phone and leaned back in his chair. She was utterly, profoundly under his skin, and when he thought of her his body had a mind of its own. Her high-maintenance side he had initially accepted as the cost of the package; Elaine had her own, highly successful life, and she would never be content to make cookies for a man in quiet acquiescence. But now he found himself wondering what there was, in the end, underneath her fantastic competence. What touched her and moved her? In the year they had been together, he had never seen her cry. There was something calculating about her that gave him an utterly surprising and fleeting sense of revulsion; he dismissed it instantly, unwilling to accept its implications. Being attracted to what you despised wasn't a new idea to him; he had read enough psychology to understand the phenomenon. But he had never considered himself a candidate for that particular neurosis. *No,* he thought, *she's probably right about all this. Keep a level head and don't get sucked into anything serious.*

A glance at his watch pushed all thoughts but digging into the remaining Crandall books from his mind. It was nearly nine-thirty on Friday morning, and he hadn't had breakfast. He decided to pick something up at the Trailside Diner, the one restaurant in town. He would be at the bank when it opened at ten, hoping to make progress. The manager would be back that afternoon, and he wanted to be through everything before he returned.

Henry drove over to the Trailside, shaking his head at the unchanged place. *The restaurant time forgot,* he thought. The diner faced the square, with an old-time western facade that looked like it had been taken off a movie lot. A sign swung from a bar above his head: AUTHENTIC NAVAJO KACHINA DOLLS. He walked in, taking in the checkerboard tablecloths, the row of ball caps hung neatly on nails in a line by the door. A handful of people were at the tables, farmers mostly, the men wiry and in need of a good washing, the women pools of defiant fat, settled in for a plate of biscuits and gravy. Henry got his breakfast to go, yielding to the temptation of a Danish and coffee to save time. He crossed Main, made his way down the square, and looked past the bank; his father's empty storefront office stood fifty yards beyond, looking like a forlorn relic of the past. *You're far too much like your father,* Elaine often said. That was her smart bomb, her weapon of mass destruction that ended all combat. But it was also a complex idea, more complex than she could have realized. In most ways, Henry admired his father as an idealist, a fighter for the rights of others. But what did those sacrifices mean in a world in which your life could end in the blink of an eye, and you vanished, barely remembered, underappreciated, having lost most of your battles? *Eat, drink, and be merry, for tomorrow you die.* And no one, he had to admit, knew more about being merry than the extraordinary band of overachievers at Wilson, Lougherby and Mathers.

Henry turned away from his father's office and walked to the bank. He entered and greeted Ellen at her desk, eager to put philosophical thoughts out of his mind. Nothing cleared his head like work. Ellen looked noticeably tired; she was showing her age today, with dark circles under her eyes. Henry found himself wondering if she were an insomniac.

"He didn't come in," she said. "I would have called if he had."

"I didn't think he would. The number was just in case."

"Well, he didn't." Her mood, along with her face, was dour, in contrast with the day before. She seemed preoccupied, as though she had been worrying about something.

"Well, I'm here to finish up on Mr. Crandall's records," Henry said. "Then I'll be out of your hair."

She looked at him, and for a moment he wondered if she might refuse him. But she dutifully rose and retrieved the folders of Crandall records.

She pointed to an empty desk at the back of the bank, and Henry carried his work over and started in.

He worked all morning, poring over the records meticulously, looking for some unknown clue to connect Ty and Boyd. It was tedious work, especially since he had no specific idea of the target. A single check stub could be the break he was looking for. He tried to formulate a theory in his head, some possible scenario to explain what had happened. He drew blanks: it was one thing to connect Crandall and Boyd, another to connect them in such a way that explained why Crandall left Boyd with most of what he owned. And why now? Crandall's will had been amended to include Boyd just before his own father's accident. It was, in fact, one of the last pieces of legal business he had conducted. What had happened to prompt Crandall to take such a measure?

Henry got hungry around noon but decided to work through. He had just glanced at his watch when he heard a chair push noisily back at the other end of the bank. He looked up and saw Ellen rise and walk the length of the floor over to his desk. She tiptoed on high heels across the dark hardwood floor until she stood directly in front of his desk.

"How's it coming?" she asked. She was smiling again, yesterday's mood apparently restored. "Getting anywhere?"

"All right," he answered. "One page at a time."

She nodded. "Tell me something, what exactly are you looking for?"

"I'm just trying to straighten out a confusing situation."

Ellen leaned over the desk, displaying her abundant cleavage through a low-cut blouse. She was well tanned, but her skin was permanently freckled from overexposure to the sun. "Well," she said in a low voice, "it's just as well you came now, when Mr. Walters isn't here."

"The manager? Why's that?"

Ellen ran her fingers along the edge of the desk. "He's by-the-book. A real company man. I doubt he would let you do much snooping."

"Is that what I'm doing?"

She smiled intimately. "I could be wrong."

Henry returned her gaze calmly. "I wouldn't want to put you in a compromising situation."

She leaned even closer. "Snoop all you want," she murmured, looking into his eyes.

Her pointed forwardness gave Henry a vaguely embarrassed feeling. *Early fifties and still working it*, he thought.

"Don't you need a break?" she asked. "Gonna work straight through?"

"Love one," Henry answered. "But I've got to get back to Chicago as soon as possible. Very soon, if I want to make my boss happy."

"At least you need some lunch. You can't work all day without eating."

Henry smiled and was about to dismiss her. Then he hesitated. *She lied about knowing Boyd.* He stared down at the stack of papers. There wasn't any particular reason to hope that the remaining few would be any more helpful than what he had already seen. At this point, a person might be a lot more help than more hours with canceled checks and loan statements. "I am a little hungry," he said, putting down his pen and folding up his notebook. "Maybe I'll just head over to the diner for a sandwich."

She smiled and leaned over the desk again. "I've got some fried chicken, if you don't mind sharing. The food at the Trailside'll kill you."

"I don't want to be a bother."

"Don't be silly." She laughed. "Come on over to my place. It's only a few blocks away." Without waiting for a reply she turned and walked toward her desk.

Henry watched her move away and packed up his things. *Her place*, he thought. She was already grabbing her purse, and there was nothing to do but follow her. She stopped at the door and turned to wait; he opened it for her. They stepped out onto the square and turned east, walking briskly.

"I have to get out of the bank for lunch," Ellen said. "It starts to feel like a prison sometimes." They walked up Pawnee toward Benton, her street. "Not that it does much good," she rattled on. "When I leave the bank I'm still in Council Grove. You could string a fence around this whole town and nobody would even notice."

Henry nodded. "I take it you don't get out in the world much?" he asked.

"*The world*," Ellen repeated dreamily. "Where there's more'n this trash around. People of quality." They reached Benton Street and turned east for the remaining block to the house. They walked up her gravel driveway and onto the porch; Ellen pulled a key off the ledge above the door, standing precariously on tiptoes to reach it. Her skirt lifted up her legs, and Henry caught a glance at her thighs. They were still trim, and he had to assume she had worked hard to stay in that kind of shape. *But to impress whom?* he couldn't help wondering. *If she hates it here so much, who's she dressing up for?*

Henry followed her inside, entering a kind of Wal-Mart tribute to Romanticism; heavy velvet curtains hung on the windows, and a strong scent of incense was in the air. The small living room contained a patterned love seat and a dark blue–covered chair, both arranged around a low coffee table strewn with fashion magazines. The walls were papered with a purple-and-white pattern, and several vaguely French prints of aristocratic couples in frilly clothes walking in a park. Beyond the living room he could see a small, circular dining table on one side of a combination kitchen and breakfast nook. Atop a window shelf was a vase full of inexpensive silk flowers. "Hope you're hungry," Ellen said, and she touched his shoulder as she passed by him to the kitchen.

He followed, and Ellen gestured to a chair. Henry sat and watched her pull some plates out of the cupboard. The plates were inexpensive, part of a set covered in lilacs and peonies. *It was*, Henry thought to himself, *a house of pure, seamless mediocrity*. But to his surprise he found it touching, in its way; the lack of taste was utterly exposed in its overwrought femininity, almost defiantly so. Ellen had never been anywhere, had lived on next to nothing for twenty years, and this was her best expression of living well. And he could see that she was proud of it. She was confident here, and seemed happy as she laid out a lunch of cold chicken, potato salad, and green beans. She set a pitcher of iced tea on the table and started to sit down opposite Henry. But she stopped herself, and carefully moved the flowers to the center of the table. Satisfied, she sat. "I remember you. You were just a kid. You came in with your father. Dig in," she said.

"Of course you would have known him."

"We're the only bank in town. I know everybody."

Henry smiled, taking a piece of chicken. "Valuable position to be in."

"Yeah, my desk is the CIA. Everybody who opens a bank account, I know how much, and from where. I know who pays their bills and who doesn't." She ate her chicken daintily, with a knife and fork. "So you were close to your father, then. I mean you got along okay."

"Mostly. We had our differences, like most fathers and sons."

"But you followed in his footsteps."

Depends on how you mean that, Henry thought. But out loud he merely answered, "Yes."

"I wasn't close to my father," Ellen said abruptly. "I sure as hell didn't want to *be* like him." She laughed, and Henry could hear the residue of liquor and cigarettes in her voice. "He drank. He came home dirty every night from work and watched TV until he passed out. He hit my mother. But he did one thing I can never thank him enough for."

"What was that?"

Ellen's mouth formed a thin, brittle smile. "He showed me exactly the kind of man I never wanted to be with." She paused a moment. "Which is funny, really."

"Why funny?"

"Because that's what I always end up doing anyway."

Her statement brought a pointed silence to the table. They ate quietly for a moment, her confession hanging awkwardly in the air. Henry rerouted the conversation back to Crandall and the will. "Tyler's death took me completely by surprise," he said. "Were there any clues about his health?"

"How do I know?" Ellen answered. "We didn't talk about his health."

"Of course. I thought you might have heard something, people talking. CIA, and all that."

"Nope," she answered. A note of sarcasm crept into her voice. "He wasn't exactly the friendly type, you know? But I guess he didn't have to be. He made a lot of money." She paused, and asked eagerly, "You ever meet any *really* rich people? I'm not talking about this little toilet bowl. Somebody gets a new truck around here and they think they're Rockefeller. I mean *rich*—like on *Dynasty* or something."

Henry smiled. "There's a lot of money in Chicago."

"How'd they get so rich, you figure?"

"Most of them inherited it."

"Daddy's money," Ellen said. "Like Roger wants."

Henry took a bite. "You know Roger well?"

"He likes to throw his weight around. You don't have to be a genius to see he's the one who loses if the Birdman gets the money." She pushed back from the table and crossed her legs.

Henry decided to come to the point. "Let me ask you something, Ellen," he said. "When you first heard about the Crandall will, what did you think?"

"I thought it was a damn shame," she said, making no effort to conceal her disgust. She frowned, and the lines around her eyes became clearly visible. "I thought the whole thing was a miserable cheat."

"Is that what you think Ty Crandall was?"

"Yeah, a cheat." But then she shook her head. "No, not Ty. The situation, you know, how it turned out. All the money going to . . ."

"To Raymond."

"Yeah."

"Can you think of any reason why Tyler would want to do something like that? Do you know of anything that could connect the two of them?"

Ellen gave Henry a level stare. "How should I know? All I do is open accounts and chase down bounced checks."

"I thought your desk was central intelligence. Into everything."

"And I didn't know this talk was a test. That's the kind of thing Tyler would do."

Henry smiled. "I thought you didn't have much of a relationship with him."

Ellen glanced at the clock above her stove and stood. "I *didn't*. Look, I got to get back to work. Can't afford to be gone if Mr. Walters comes back before schedule. You know how he is."

"Strictly by-the-book."

"Yeah."

Henry helped pick up the dishes, and they walked back to the bank without bringing up Crandall again. Henry spent the next two hours riffling through the Crandall accounts. As he feared, he found nothing unusual. He scanned the last few pages carefully, hoping for a miracle, but it was just another mundane transaction. He had worked for hours and not found a single link between Crandall and Boyd. He looked at his watch: it was nearly three. The bank was about to close, and Walters was due back in town any minute. He sighed and leaned back in his chair. Parker had made it clear; no connection, no more time. He didn't feel like explaining the pile of papers to Walters, so he quickly packed up and took the stack over to Ellen. "Thanks for the help," he said. "I appreciate it."

"Find what you were looking for?"

"Not really. I suppose Mr. Walters is on his way."

She glanced up at a big clock on an opposite wall. "Any second," she said. "He said he'd be back before close."

"Thanks again. For lunch, too."

She stood and stuck out her hand. "Say hello to Chicago," she said. "To all the rich people."

He smiled. "I'll do that."

Henry walked out of the bank convinced the Crandall situation was heading for certain, complicated litigation. He could file a petition to be removed from his position as executor as soon as the courthouse opened, and that night be in Elaine's arms. He could use the weekend to catch up on Parker's caseload.

He walked quickly toward his rental car, trying to remember what airlines went direct from Wichita to Chicago. He had nearly reached the car when he heard someone calling his name. He turned around and saw a middle-aged, slightly frumpy man gesturing from the other side of the bank, a good sixty feet down the sidewalk.

"You Henry Mathews?" the man shouted, walking toward him rapidly. He was puffing along as he walked, obviously out of shape. "Unless I miss my guess, I'd say you were. I figured you'd be back for the funeral."

Henry looked back quizzically. "That's right," he answered. "What can I do for you?"

"It's more what I can do for you, son," the man responded. Having reached Henry, he stuck out his hand. "I'm Frank Walters."

Got out just in time, Henry thought. "Nice meeting you. How did you know me?"

"Didn't," the man answered. He was seriously out of breath. "Good guess on my part. I saw you walking out of the bank, put two and two together. We've never met. I came to the bank after you left Council

Grove. But I've heard of you. Briefly knew your father, in fact. Couldn't miss the family resemblance."

"I see."

Walters smiled. "I'm more than half private investigator. Just a hobby. I made a bet with myself that if I had a chance, I'd recognize you before you could introduce yourself. Did it, too."

"Yes, you did," Henry answered, eager to detach.

"Get any help in there?" Walters asked. "Anything you need?"

"No problem."

"Well, that's good." Walters lowered his voice and added, "But listen, if there's one thing in the world you need, you just let me know." He glanced around conspiratorially. "I heard about Crandall's will," he said. "Shocker. Wife called me in Kansas City this morning with the news. Fell right out of my chair."

Henry hesitated; something in Walters' manner made Henry wonder if Ellen's description of the man was on the mark. If the manager was so buttoned-down and official, he certainly didn't appear it. Henry looked him over: a small man, mid-forties, not entirely put together, with brown hair in need of trimming. "I've gone over things with your bank staff," he said. "I've frozen the accounts until we sort this thing through."

"Of course you have." The manager's voice dropped lower. "Only thing *to* do."

Henry decided to string him along, see what he could find out. "I'm glad you agree. It seemed prudent."

"Right," Walters answered. "There's a lot of folks that would like to get their hands on that money."

Henry smiled inwardly; he could only be referring to Roger. "It's human nature," he said.

Walters sniffed. "Some are more human than others around here."

A Crandall enemy, Henry processed. *Which makes Ellen's description even more suspect.*

Walters had got his breath back, and was doing his own inspection of Henry. "What did you take a look for in there, if you don't mind my asking?"

Henry took a risk. "To be honest, a connection between Crandall and Raymond Boyd," Henry said. "I have to admit the thing's a mystery to me."

"Did you find out anything? Like I said, if you don't mind my asking."

"No," Henry answered. "Drew a blank."

Walters didn't say anything, but Henry could read his face. *He's disappointed. But why? Any bank would kill for a client who kept so much money liquid.* "It was a long shot to find out anything that way," he said. "If there is a connection, it would probably be years ago."

Walters gave a thoughtful look. "Probably right," he said. He brightened. "But if it's the old stuff you're interested in, did you get a look at the stuff downstairs?"

"Downstairs?" Ellen hadn't mentioned anything about that.

"Sure," Walters said. "There's piles of old stuff down there. Old records, boxes of it. You're welcome to take a look if you want."

Henry glanced at his watch. "Don't you close at three?"

"I wouldn't worry about that," Walters said. "I know the boss." He turned and reached for the door. It opened as he touched it, and Ellen stepped through.

"Mr. Walters," she said, "you're back."

"Hello, Ellen. Hold the door. We're going to pop in for a while."

"Of course," she answered. The two walked through, stepping in front of her. Henry felt her eyes on his back as he followed the manager inside. It was several seconds later that he heard the door to the street close behind them.

"How long do you keep files around?" Henry asked. "I've already gone back several years."

"The old stuff's in the basement. It all predates my time here, naturally. Back during Schiller's time."

"Schiller," Henry said. "Yes, I remember him. Dutch, studious type."

"Right. He would have been the manager here while you were growing up. Hell, he was here fifteen years or more." He walked to a door at the rear of the bank and Henry followed.

"Don't you put the old files on computer or something?" Henry asked.

Walters laughed. "It's the *new* ones we do that with. It would take years to key in all the ancient stuff. I think all the old Crandall files are sitting around in some big boxes, to tell you the truth."

"How far back do you suppose it goes?" Henry asked.

"Only one way to find out," Walters said.

Walters opened the door and flipped a light switch. He peered down a steep flight of stairs. "Be right back," he said, disappearing. "Oh," he added over his shoulder, "and don't rob us while I'm down here, okay? The cameras don't work."

Henry glanced up at two small video cameras aimed at the teller counter. "You're kidding," he said.

"Nope," Walters called back. "They broke a few days ago, and we haven't fixed 'em. Guy's coming tomorrow."

By-the-book my ass, Henry thought. Several minutes later Walters returned, his forehead glistening with sweat. *If you don't have a heart attack in the next ten minutes, maybe I can find something out.* Walters was holding three large, square boxes stuffed with papers and folders. "Hot down there?" Henry asked, taking one of the boxes.

"No wonder nobody goes down there anymore. They're all afraid somebody will think of asking them to clean it up." He dropped the other boxes onto Ellen's desk. "Lot more there than I expected," he said. "Piles of the stuff."

"Way more than I can begin to get through right now," Henry said.

"True," Walters answered. "But can't you go through it all tonight?"

"Of course. But it would take hours."

"You can't do it here. We've got to lock up. We do lock the place, you know. We might be a little lax in the video department, but we aren't nuts."

"Are you telling me you're prepared to just let me walk out of the bank with these records?"

Walters closed and locked the door to the basement. "Hell," he said, "that's no problem."

"It isn't?"

"Thing is, my wife will kill me if I stay around here while you worked. Been gone most of the week as it is." He glanced at the bulging boxes. "You can drop them by my house tomorrow. I live over on Brantley."

Walters was doing everything in his power to help. The question was why. Henry decided to try a small test. "I'm a little surprised to find you so accommodating," he said.

Walters looked up. "That so?"

"Ellen told me you ran a tight ship around here, which I interpreted as a compliment, by the way."

Walters looked genuinely surprised. "Me? A tight ship?" He laughed. "She must have been pulling your leg. If I played by the rules, you think I'd be in this godforsaken town? I'd be the damn vice president in charge of something or other somewhere, instead of just a branch manager in these boondocks. But I like it in these little places where things are looser." He paused a moment, giving Henry a penetrating look. "But look," he added, "don't get me wrong on this. You can see the records, but that doesn't mean I have any feelings for that kook out at the park."

"Mr. Boyd, you mean."

"That his name?"

"That's right. Raymond Boyd."

"He's just been 'the Birdman' as long as I've known about him. But whatever his name is, he doesn't mean anything to me."

"Given the size of Crandall's deposits, I figured you'd naturally be inclined in the family's direction."

Walters leaned against Ellen's desk, relaxing. "Son, we got somethin' in common, you and me. You know that?"

Henry smiled. "What would that be?"

"Bankers, lawyers, and preachers. We're all the same. We're in what's called the learned professions. We see everything and tell nobody. Preacher knows who's cheatin' on his wife, and he don't tell a soul. Lawyer knows who's about to get sued. Don't say a word. Banker knows who's about to go broke and drivin' a new car like they didn't have a care in the world. See, the first priority in the learned professions is discretion. You got to know how to keep a secret. You know how to keep a secret, don't you, boy?"

Henry nodded. "Certainly."

Walters gave him a final, appraising look. "Well then, I'll let you in on a little personal matter here. I'm not sayin' I'm for Boyd. Did I say I was?"

"You did not."

"Damn right I didn't. But I got a bone to pick with the Crandalls."

"I'd be curious to know what it is."

Walters ran a hand through already thinning hair. "I don't give a damn about his deposits. It ain't my money. Fact is, Crandall screwed up my plan for a life of ease in small-town America. Pissed me off. Fidelity Savings moved me here 'bout four years ago. They thought it was punishment, but I worked it that way from the start. Figured it'd be a sleepy town, loose, no one lookin' over your shoulder. Low corporate expectations." He flicked an errant scrap of paper off the top of one of the boxes. "But of course I hadn't heard the name of Ty Crandall at that point. It didn't take long to find out that the situation was a little different than I had hoped."

"In what way?"

"The man was a *leaner.*"

"A leaner?"

"Right," Walters said. "He *leaned.* He had a lotta plans, all of 'em good for Tyler Crandall. He had the idea you had to see things his way."

"And if you didn't?"

Walters shrugged. "He *leaned.*" His manner was increasingly confidential. "Like I say, I don't care nothin' for Boyd, if that's his name. But I figure it this way. If the crazy guy gets everything he'd be rich, so we couldn't have him livin' like an animal anymore. Hell, the world's full of poor crazy people, but get one rich and he's nothin' but a feed trough, money just sittin' there waitin' for hospitals and doctors and lawyers to feed on. Present company excepted." Henry nodded silently for him to continue. "So in two shakes the court's gonna appoint somebody to handle things," Walters went on. "A reasonable man, hell, maybe the man I'm talkin' to." He grinned. "Seems to me if that happened, then there's no more Birdman *and* no more Crandalls." Walters gave a wide, lazy smile. "Sounds good to me," he said. "I can finally get my town back, and settle down to the underachieving life I desire."

Henry shook his head; if the man had worked as hard at his job as he did scheming a life of leisure, he would probably be retired by now. But he had to admit the scenario Walters had painted wasn't entirely out of the realm of possibility. The main thing was that Walters was a pure busybody, something a lawyer can always use. He reached over and picked up the boxes from the desk. "Maybe things will work out that way," he said. "I'll see what I can find."

"You take the records, son. Good hunting."

Early that evening Henry called Elaine, studiously avoiding the subject of the will. For once, she let him off the hook, not pressing him. Instead, she described a dress that she had bought for the awards party at her boss's house.

"It's Badgley Mishka, Henry," she said. "I know it was too expensive, but I wanted to reward myself."

"Sleek?"

"Like a glove."

"Sexy?"

"Heart-stopping."

"How much?"

"Four thousand."

Henry whistled. "God, do they throw in the little Filipino family who sewed it?"

"Not funny. And anyway, quality always costs, Henry. And it's always worth it."

Henry thought of Ellen and wondered what she would do for a dress like the one Elaine was describing. Kill, probably. "Glad you told me what it costs," Henry said. "Now I'll know what I'm spending when I rip it off you."

She laughed, a light, relaxed sound. "You will be there, right, Henry?"

That was the question. He didn't want to leave, that was certain. Without his help, Henry gave Boyd's chances for a fair disposition of Crandell's assets as something less than zero. With so little time he could hardly lose the day and a half a quick flight back to Chicago would cost him. "I still don't know, Elaine," he answered cautiously. "I'm on a wicked time line here."

There was silence on the phone, broken by Elaine's suddenly detached voice.

"Oh, listen, that reminds me. I invited Sheldon Parker."

"I beg your pardon?"

"Sheldon. I invited him."

"Why were you even talking to him?"

"I didn't say he called me?"

"Sheldon? What for?"

She laughed again. "To invest money, of course. Thanks to you, he knows how good I am at it. God, Henry, I had no idea the kind of money he made."

"Don't tell me. I don't need any more reasons to detest him."

"I can't tell you, sweetheart. You know that. Anyway, I invited him to the party."

"I thought it was a private affair."

"Sort of. Nothing's really private, darling, not to the right people. But think of it, Henry. There I'll be, getting my award. It'll be a huge confidence booster for Sheldon. By the end of the night I'll have everything he owns."

Henry had no doubt she was right. But the idea of having his boss prowling the party without him there grated. On the other hand, Parker was no dummy. "How do you know he's not coming on his own fishing expedition?" he asked. "Maybe he's hoping to land a few clients of his own."

There was a silence, and Henry instantly regretted the statement. It was bad form, popping her little balloon. But he recognized the game she was playing, the little jealousy manipulations, and it was getting on his nerves. When she got like that, it was hard to resist sending out his own little reality check from time to time. But once again, he had underestimated her. "Let him," she said after a moment. "Why shouldn't it work both ways? Anyway, we got along famously. We were chatting like old friends in no time. Sheldon's such a sensible man. So focused."

"Make him a lot of money, because that way he'll be a lot more fun around the office."

"Since you won't be there Sunday, I'll have to tell you all about it. Or maybe I'll just let Sheldon do it."

Henry hung up the phone and pondered. *Parker called Elaine. And while I was out of town.* "*I always lose some fine muscle control when I think about that adorable creature,*" he had said. Of course, Elaine was a good broker, and Parker's enormous pay package needed somewhere to land. And he had told Parker about the party, in an offhanded way. But it wasn't, Henry decided, that Parker had called while he was gone that bothered him most. It was the sneaking realization that the two of them were made for each other, two clones in appetite and ambition. "*The thing I don't like about this trip is that you don't know where it will lead,*" Elaine had said. She had already been proved right about that; the will had actually turned into a rift between them, which he had certainly not anticipated. And it wasn't, he had to admit, a rift that would have happened if Sheldon were in his shoes. Parker would have taken one look at the situation and been on the next plane home, if he had bothered to come in the first place. Much more like Elaine. Of course, Elaine had never been unfaithful. She was merely working him over, making him pay. Henry looked across the room at the boxes sitting on the table. Maybe it was for the best if he didn't find anything in them. That way, he would be home sooner. A night in bed was what they needed, a night of more sweating and less analyzing. A night to make her forget about middle-aged partners with roving eyes.

Henry thought about room service, remembered it didn't exist, and started to rummage through the first box. He resolved to stay up all night, if necessary. It felt good, testing his endurance like he was back in law school. He had been broke then, barely scraping by. He looked around the sparse motel room; it could have passed for his old apartment.

As before, paper after mundane paper revealed itself, numbing him into a kind of trance. The records were disorganized, and it took considerable effort to create even an approximate chronology of the Crandall estate. Within the piles were the scattered remains of Crandall acquisitions going back over two decades. Henry pored over them, working backward, the story of Crandall's growing wealth revealing itself page by page. Crandall had apparently borrowed freely over the years, and loan after loan appeared in the records. Most bore the immaculate signature of Gustaf Schiller, Walters' predecessor. It was Schiller's name on the mortgages for the rental houses, and on a variety of property and business loans as well. Each acquisition was financed by the payments received by the previous property, so that Crandall had built an intricate house of debt. Some of the businesses had actually lost money, to Henry's surprise. But underneath the entire structure was the pillar of oil revenue, and that pillar had held firm. Each note was marked paid in full. The biggest notes were for the Feed and Farm Supply: in all, Crandall had borrowed almost six hundred thousand dollars to build the structure and finance the business. Inventory had taken the greatest share; the huge tractors and combines ate up large chunks of money just sitting on the lot. The recent declines in farm prices had slowed business, and the notes had been held over, in many cases, for a disturbingly long time. But like all the others, these short-term notes had been paid on time, as had a large balloon note in the tenth year.

Around two-thirty in the morning Henry turned on the little cof-feemaker in the room and made some coffee. Rubbing his eyes, he sat back down at the papers. He had nearly worked his way to the very beginning, but still wondered about something: how had Crandall managed to buy the very first piece of real estate, the one that oil was first discovered on? It was a large piece of ground, and it was the key to the entire financial puzzle. Crandall had opened his initial account with only thirteen hundred dollars; decent enough in 1973 for someone just getting started, but still a long way from what he needed to buy an entire section of prime farmland. The bank had gone out on a thin limb to loan that kind of money to a young GI just back from Vietnam. And what brilliant luck that oil was found on that land. Those first few years had been drought-stricken, and depending on crops alone would have put a quick end to Crandall's plans. The oil money had pushed him through.

Henry sorted through paper after paper, looking for the mortgage on the property. Time passed, and ultimately, he sensed a pale, growing light at the window; the sun would be up soon. He stretched and rubbed his eyes, a sinking feeling in his stomach. He was on the last box, and it was hard to go on with no sleep and little hope. He picked up a page and scanned down it—absently at first, then with more interest—and realized he had at last found the very document he needed. This was the beginning of the Crandall fortune; the loan was for a full section located at the corner of Route 12 and Council Grove Road. The oil land. Henry read slowly, a part of him not wanting to finish the page. If nothing unusual turned up he was back at square one, returning to Chicago with nothing. He spread the faded paper out on the table, carefully reading the standardized language of the loan, looking for anything out of the ordinary. But when he reached the bottom of the page, he stared blankly. Crandall's name was neatly signed, as always. But the name of the bank officer approving the loan wasn't Schiller.

It was Raymond Boyd.

Chapter Fourteen

Rory Zachariah did not shoot Amanda Ashton. He did not shoot because, as he stared down the perfectly oiled barrel of his twelve-gauge Remington, he knew several important things that Amanda did not: he knew, through Carl Durand, chairman of the oil and gas committee of the Kansas Senate and close personal friend, that his land was the center of her investigation. He knew, in fact, that she would be on his land before she had known it herself. A crack marksman, he also knew that she wouldn't be hit when he sent the buckshot into her vehicle as she drove off in embarrassment.

Amanda Ashton found a world of hurt began at the end of Rory Zachariah's shotgun. The recriminations had been immediate, bitter, and personal. Durand reconvened his committee the very next day with the idea of drafting legislation to defund the entire state department of environment immediately. Amanda was the government agent run amok; this was the kind of Gestapo tactic Durand had been sent to the capitol to stop. He failed by one vote, thanks to a heroic rally by Sam Coulton.

Amanda returned to work the next day to a reception of lethal coldness. The career bureaucrats at the agency did not, it appeared, appreciate hotshot antics that threatened the existence of their jobs. She spent the rest of the morning in isolation in her office. When she emerged for lunch the few people gathered in the break room rose together and walked out the door.

At three-thirty a memo appeared on Amanda's fax machine. When she read the cover page and learned that it had originated from within her own office, her sense of isolation was complete. The memo was from her department head, and rather than walk down the hall and speak to Amanda directly, she had elected to send her instructions with the utter impersonality of a machine. The message directed that, in view of her recent problems with agency procedure, Amanda was from now on under special instructions: not only must she elicit permission to enter any landowner's property, but said permission must be in writing and filed in the office before any trip commenced. Further, she must not enter any property without being accompanied at all times by the landowner himself. Finally, and most insultingly, she was not to use agency vehicles under any circumstances. In view of the damage incurred by buckshot to the truck, any request for an official vehicle would be refused.

Now the recriminations were her own. She had blown it. The biggest opportunity in her career and, more important, a chance to do what she had always dreamed of: make a difference. All lost, because of her own impatience and bravura. Amanda went home and spent the rest of the afternoon with a six-pack of beer, a blanket, and her dog, telling herself how stupid she was. She had ignored the rules once again, just as she had in graduate school, just as she had climbing the ranks of the agency. She had refused to learn; she was egotistical; she had delusions of grandeur. She flicked through TV stations aimlessly, feeling worthless. After the third beer she fell asleep.

The phone rang about six, jarring her back to reality. She licked her lips; her mouth felt like cotton. She picked up the receiver and muttered something barely intelligible into it. A voice answered, "Sam Coulton."

Amanda tried to fix on the sound through the beers and sleep. "Sam Coulton," she repeated numbly.

"No, Ms. Ashton. *I'm* Sam Coulton."

Amanda sat up, shaking off numbness. "*Senator* Sam Coulton?"

"That's right. That was some stunt you pulled."

Amanda forced her head to clear while her heart sank. Her only strong ally on the committee, now calling to heap more abuse. "I'm sorry, sir," she began softly. "I realize that . . ."

Coulton interrupted her with the last sound she expected: a deep, earthy laugh. "God, you won't believe what we had to go through to shut Durand up," he said. "What are you trying to do, get the guy elected governor?"

The sound of the voice on the phone made Amanda feel cautiously better. He sounded almost . . . friendly. Maybe she wasn't a complete outcast after all. "I'm terribly sorry to have put you in such an awful position, Senator," she offered. "I got ahead of myself a little bit."

"Ms. Ashton, does the word 'setup' mean anything to you?"

"What do you mean?"

"Let me ask you something first," Coulton said. "Where did you grow up?"

"Connecticut."

"Thought so. Northeasterner. Graduated from . . . ?"

"Georgetown."

Coulton laughed again. "Perfect. So you came to Kansas only for the job, obviously? I mean you weren't exactly drawn by the beauty of the plains?"

"I wanted to stay in Washington, but the EPA wasn't hiring. I went down the list of state jobs, and ended up here."

"And it's just possible that you grew up thinking that the people around here weren't too sophisticated, that they were a bunch of cow herders. Is that about right?" Coulton asked good-naturedly.

"Sir?" Amanda answered. That was, in fact, exactly what she, and most of her other friends, had thought. She had taken a fair amount of ribbing to that effect when she took the job in the first place. But she wasn't sure where Coulton was headed with this.

"It's all right," the senator said, as if reading her mind. "Don't sweat it, I've run into it before. College girl, liberal, activist comes down here thinking we're all a bunch of country bumpkins. Thinks we don't get out much, and she's lived up in Washington, where the big dogs play. Thinks there's a little Mickey Mouse show down here she can chew up and spit out."

Amanda swallowed, tasting her dry mouth once again. For once, however, she kept her mouth shut.

"Let me explain a couple of things to you, Ms. Ashton," Coulton went on. "First, I like you. You're a hell of a smart woman, and I admire that. Can't afford to lose you to one of your crazy indiscretions, though, so listen up. Politics down here is just as devious, just as calculating, and just as god-awful evil as anywhere else in this glorious country, the only difference being that we're fighting over a few less zeros. We just argue about millions instead of billions. You'll find, though, that millions seem to be enough to get in a snit over."

"Sir, I honestly never . . ."

"I know, honey. And don't give me any crap about calling you honey, 'cause that's what we do around here. In spite of what they told you in Washington, it doesn't mean we think you're stupid, it means we like you. So listen a second, and you'll learn something about that little pit of vipers we like to call the Kansas Senate."

Amanda sat still, saying nothing.

"Good girl. Here's the deal. Carl Durand saw you coming a mile away. He says to himself, 'Right, here's a clever little girl from D.C., and she could be trouble. Best thing about her, though, is that she thinks she's smarter than everybody else. That makes her vulnerable.' You following me so far?"

"Yes, sir."

"Good. So for starters, he submarines your testimony. Durand gets his buddy, the president pro tem of the senate, to call a vote on the one thing nobody who likes his job can possibly sit out on, the highway appropriations bill. So bang, you're out of the committee. I assume you picked up on that."

"Yes, sir, I caught that."

"So you thought, 'Great, that's over.' But it's not over. And do you know why it's not over, Ms. Ashton?"

"No, sir."

"Well, in a backhanded way, the buzzard paid you a compliment. He says, 'Right, this girl is a fighter, she doesn't give up so easy. She makes *noise*. She gets reporters to committee meetings that they haven't gone to in years. Things would be so much better for me and my oil company buddies if she could be out of the picture completely.' In his twisted world, this is taking you seriously, you see."

"You mean Durand was afraid of me?" Amanda asked cautiously.

"Damn right he was afraid of you," Coulton said. "There's nothing scarier in government than a smart, principled woman with a little bit of courage."

Amanda smiled in spite of herself. She suddenly felt better than she had all day.

"Also, you foolishly pissed him off with your last little remark."

"I had the feeling."

"So, Durand, who you think is nothing but a good old boy, calls your agency head, and the good senator sounds all concerned about the environment. He says, 'Look, send me over the info on these saline levels. I want to be aware of everything going on in the great state of Kansas.' And she does send them over. And he sees that the Triple Z is ground zero for your little experiment. And he thinks for a little while about Ms. Amanda Ashton, smart, gung-ho activist who's all worked up in a lather. And a little plan forms in his head. He calls his good buddy Rory Zachariah, who he knows hates government like a polecat hates dogs, and he says, 'Rory, how'd you like to chew on a pretty little government agent for a while?' And Rory says, 'Send her over, Carl, I'd like that fine. When she gonna get here?' Carl says, 'Oh, sometime tomorrow afternoon, I'd say.'"

"How on earth could he know that? I didn't even have the truck until . . ." Amanda slowed. "You mean . . . ?"

"That's right. He thinks about how damn eager you are, and he finds out who has that truck, and he finds something for him to do. And he makes sure that you get called offering it. Child's play."

"You're telling me this whole thing was set up from the beginning?"

"I am."

Amanda swallowed. She had never felt so stupid in her life. "But how could he know that I would go on Zachariah's land?"

Coulton laughed. "Don't take this the wrong way, Ms. Ashton, all right? But are you kidding?"

Amanda grimaced. "Is it that obvious?"

"You, Ms. Ashton, are as obvious as a tent preacher on the last day of a crusade. So you step into a big cow turd, I mean the full-sized model. And I had to fight like hell to keep the buzzard from legislating not only you but your entire agency out of existence."

"Sir, I'm deeply grateful . . ."

"You don't have to be grateful, Ms. Ashton. I didn't do it for you, I did it for my grandchildren. Just do me a favor."

"Anything."

"Well, two favors, actually. First, don't underestimate Carl Durand anymore just because he grew up in a house without plumbing. He was risking his fortune on wildcatting when you were watching cartoons."

"I can assure you that I will never make that mistake again."

"Good. And second, don't give up this fight."

"Sir?"

"Fight even harder. Take your lumps and get back in there."

Amanda listened, trying to let his words work in her. She was, she now realized, having a pity party of monumental proportions.

"You know why all us government types turn into hard-asses, Ms. Ashton?" Coulton asked.

"No, sir, I don't."

"Because we either turn into hard-asses or we quit. I'm hoping you've got some hard-ass in you, Ms. Ashton, because we need you around here. Now I'd like you to shake this off and get on the phone tomorrow morning and start working on getting on some of those properties. It won't be easy. No doubt Zachariah's put the word out on you, and the word will not be good."

"No doubt."

"But I have one bit of hope to offer, albeit a small bit."

Amanda perked up. Hope, even small hope, was exactly what she needed. "I'm listening."

"Good. The property adjacent to the Triple Z belongs, or rather belonged, to Tyler Crandall."

Amanda thought for a moment. "Crandall, that's right. I remember seeing the name on the plat. That property is nearly as important as the Triple Z."

"Crandall's dead, as it happens. Can't say as it's a tragedy. He made a few bucks, threw his money around the statehouse. Made him feel like a big shot. But here's my point: his estate's in probate, and it's a mess. There's a big blowup down there about it. Ordinarily, I'd say Crandall's boy wouldn't give you the time of day, but the whole thing's temporarily under the control of the executor. Maybe you can work something out."

Amanda grabbed a pencil. She was back in business. "Do you have a name?"

Coulton laughed again. "You want me to do *all* your work, don't you, Ms. Ashton?"

"I'm sorry, sir," Amanda answered quickly. "I didn't mean to imply . . ."

"That's all right. I had a feeling you'd be a little down in the dumps, so here's a present for you: the executor's name is Henry Mathews. Chicago lawyer, which should suit you. You two urbanites will have so much to talk about."

Amanda smiled, not minding the teasing. "I don't suppose you have . . ."

"Seven-three-one-oh-six hundred. Area code three-one-two."

"Senator, I can't tell you how much this means to me."

"Just get out there and kick some ass for truth, justice, and the American way, will you, Ms. Ashton?"

"I will do that, sir. And, sir?"

"Yes?"

"You can call me 'honey' anytime, sir."

Coulton laughed, and hung up the phone.

Chapter Fifteen

While Amanda leaned back on her couch and thanked God for Sam Coulton, Raymond Boyd moved slowly through the dusk toward Ellen's house, crawling on his hands and knees. It was his second consecutive night coming to Ellen's. The first night he had been content simply to watch. He had squinted up at the house from a great distance, catching glimpses of her form through half-open window shades. But tonight he had dragged several large sheets of cardboard with him into the scrub. His palms crushed the thick underbrush, opening tiny cuts on his skin. He smiled at the red slowly seeping from his fingers, watched the blood coagulate, combining with the caked dirt on his palms to make a burnt-reddish poultice. For a moment, the color filled his mind and he saw great licking flames scorching outward from his hands, burning the earth and sending thick black smoke climbing into the sky. *Not yet*, he thought. *The burning is later.* He shook his head, clearing his mind. Today had not been good; his thoughts were constantly changing, modifying before he could act. He grimaced and shook his head, reminding himself of his mission: *The virgin. She is untouched by the black sea. He will come for her, and she must be protected.* He resumed his crawl. Five feet closer to the house he peered through the tall bluestem grass that filtered through the bracken and scrub trees behind Ellen's backyard. The dense foliage created a natural hiding place about sixty feet behind the house, and Boyd had little difficulty concealing his motions. He stared across the lawn; no light shone from the windows.

Boyd leaned a large square of cardboard against a dead cottonwood, then tacked a nail into the middle of it, securing it to the tree. Repeating the process on another tree close by, he began to construct a makeshift shelter. Over the next several minutes he added another side and covered the lean-to with a cardboard ceiling held together with duct tape. He crawled back and examined the hut: a little less than four feet high, with three sides and a roof. Bracken, tall weeds, and bluestem obscured it from the house almost completely, and he could move within it without attracting attention. He reentered the lean-to, pulled out a long knife, and cut a slit into the wall facing Ellen's. Expanding the slit, he roughed out a three-inch circle as a kind of peephole at the right height to use when sitting. He blew the cardboard dust off the hole, feeling it with his fingers; a drop of his blood made a tiny stain on the edge. He stared at the drop a moment, then leaned back to wait.

Some time later, deep in the night, the lights flicked on in Ellen's house. Boyd stared as her blinds were pulled open, and he saw her moving through the rooms to her bedroom at the east side of the building. As he watched he began to chant softly. *"There shall be fire and sulfur. Torrents of rain. The Lord God brings the hidden things into judgment, ain't that right, bird?"* He smiled, his head bobbing its quirky motion, up and down, up and down. He sighed, settling himself onto the dirt floor, and his eyelids fluttered shut. His lips moved silently for some time. *"The virgin is untouched by the black sea,"* he whispered. He repeated the words several times, followed by a flow of apparent delirium. When he opened his eyes again, he was leaning forward, straining toward the yellow light that flowed from the house. *"He will come for her,"* he said. *"He will come."*

Chapter Sixteen

"Henry? What's going on down there in Podunkville, anyway?" It was nine-thirty Saturday morning, and Henry had left a voice mail for Parker to call the minute he got the message.

"You're up. Didn't expect that."

"Of course I'm up. I've got tennis in thirty minutes."

Henry fleetingly pictured Parker in absurdly expensive tennis clothes swinging a four-hundred-dollar racket, then discarded the image. "I've got something, Sheldon. I found a connection between Boyd and Crandall."

"So tell me."

"First off, this guy Crandall could have made a living pissing people off. But that ended up a good thing, as it turned out. The bank manager down here practically did somersaults trying to help me."

"The rich are rarely popular."

"With their bank managers?"

There was a momentary silence. "All right," Parker admitted, "I'll grant you that one. So what did you find out?"

"I got curious. How did everything start? Where did Crandall get his money in the very beginning, the jump start on his whole operation? I went through every bank record for the last twenty-five years on the family . . ."

"How the hell did you get access to all that? What did you do, hack into a computer?"

"I hacked into a bunch of dusty boxes. Anyway, this guy Walters, the bank manager, just gave them to me, if you can believe it. He had his own reasons."

"Glad you aren't in litigation. Inadmissible."

"The point is that Crandall needed some serious dollars to buy the land he found oil on. But he was just back from the service with a few bucks in combat pay and the shirt on his back. No job, no prospects. Approving that loan was a suicide move. But somebody at the bank did approve it, somebody was willing to risk his job to do it. And do you know who that person was?"

"Not a clue."

"Raymond Boyd."

There was a short silence while Parker processed Henry's words. "The crazy guy worked at the bank."

"Twenty-five years ago. But only for a few months, apparently. Right about the time he went insane."

Parker whistled. "So what are you saying, that this whole inheritance thing is some enormous act of gratitude? That Crandall was paying Boyd back for standing by him in the early days?"

"Gratitude wasn't one of Crandall's virtues."

"Maybe he surprised you. Guilt in his last hours."

"I don't think he was planning on such an early exit. He was only fifty-six."

"All right. Then what's your idea?"

Henry hesitated; the fact was, he didn't know what was going on, not yet. But Parker had promised more time if he could connect Boyd and Crandall, and he intended to collect on the promise. "Look, Sheldon, I've got a wedge in it now, something to go on. I want some time to play it out."

"Centel is what's playing out, buddy, more quickly every day," Parker answered. "Why does this have to be now?"

"You didn't hire me because I didn't give a damn, did you? This is part of the package."

"Keep your shirt on. Anyway, the fact is I *didn't* hire you because you gave a damn, at least not about bird lunatics and farmers. What you've got is this guy Boyd's name on a loan. But when you come down to it, what does it mean? Is that all you have?"

"I've got Ellen Gaudet."

"Who's she and what about her?"

"Early fifties, too much makeup, dresses one size too small. Works at the bank, opens accounts, mundane stuff. But she's been there forever, and her name's on some of the early papers, too. I'm pretty sure she was working at the bank when Boyd was there. So she knew the old Boyd before he went crazy. And she knew there was a positive connection between him and Crandall. Which is interesting, because when I asked her about it she denied it cold."

Parker paused, thinking. "I'll play along, for the purposes of conversation. You say the sexpot lied."

"Point-blank."

"You want to know why. Ask the obvious question."

Henry knew that in Parker's mind, there was, in the end, only one question. "What's in it for her?"

"Thank you for playing."

Henry paused. "There's always money."

"It tends to come up. But in her case I doubt it. She's a worker bee."

"Which means?"

Parker sighed. "The world is separated into two distinct classes,

Preacher. There's important people, people who run things and own things. *Us*, in other words. Then there's everybody else—worker bees. People who do what they're told. And little miss short-skirt-varicose-veins Ellen Gaudet is definitely worker bee."

"Charming analogy."

"She's a secretary, Preacher. She's never *done* anything. I doubt she's doing anything now." Parker paused. "Unless she was humping Crandall? That's doing something."

Henry shook his head silently; Parker was so sex-obsessed, it was the one topic where his normally crystalline vision was clouded. "Yeah, Sheldon," he said, "it's called getting used. And for what? If she's still a secretary she got nothing from it, and sugar daddy's dead and buried. He sure as hell didn't leave her anything." He paused, thinking. "Maybe it's pressure from the outside. Somebody leaning on her, forcing her silence."

"Makes sense. If it's not for money it has to be for something else. You just need to find out who she cares about. Who's not dead, I mean."

"Doesn't seem like she cares about anybody. She's the cold type. But what are you saying? That love is at the bottom of this?"

"I'm a lawyer, Preacher. What do I know about love?"

"Does this mean I get more time?"

There was a pause on the line, and Henry could almost hear Parker thinking. "If it goes to criminal it blows up in your face. We don't do small-town criminal. There's no money in it." Another pause; then: "Look, Henry, why don't we just drop this crap and talk about what's really pushing your buttons?"

"What would that be?"

"Just the fact that this screwy will was written by your father. That's the real reason you want to sort this out. And that's what's clouding your judgment. You've let this get way too personal."

Henry bristled; Elaine's words, almost exactly. "I'm not going to deny that's a factor," he said, "but it's a legitimate factor. It's natural to want to get to the bottom of it."

"Don't tell me you're worried about the old man's credibility."

Henry imagined his father toiling through his usual caseload of adoptions and bankruptcies. In every case, he had tried to put families back together, not tear them apart. "No, that's not it," he answered quietly. "It's more complicated than that, somehow. It has a lot more to do with Boyd, actually."

"The nutcase."

"I'm using his real name from now on."

"Please don't tell me you want to protect him."

Henry hesitated, saw the cliff, and stepped off it. "Yes, I do."

"Oh, God," Parker moaned. "Not that." Henry didn't respond; he could feel a lecture coming, and like clockwork, Parker delivered. "You know what my nickname was in law school, Preacher?"

"No, Sheldon, I don't."

"B.H."

"I see."

"Billable Hours."

"Very quaint."

"I was proud of it then and I'm proud of it now. I suggest you consider it a personal goal of your own. That's if you want to survive around here."

"As warnings go, that wasn't what I'd call veiled."

"It wasn't meant to be. Look, I've seen this whole thing before. Half the students in law school come up thinking they're going to be legal-aid heroes, protect the downtrodden, change the world. Then somebody waves an eighty-five-thousand-dollar paycheck in front of them, and they'd climb right over the backs of those inner-city blacks and Latinos trying to get to that cash. But once in a blue moon, somebody grows a conscience. They get a little crisis. It's called success guilt."

"You actually think this is just some pointless attempt to justify my good fortune."

"I know it is. I've seen it before. And believe it or not, I'm going to let you do it."

Henry spoke cautiously. "Why, may I ask?"

"Because I know you. I know that after you play out this little farce you'll be back in my office happy to be there. I'm not going to lose you, Henry. I've got too much invested. So take this little trip. Get it out of your system. Find out there's no Santa Claus or Mother Goose. There's just work and winning and losing."

"I'm not sure whether to thank you or not."

"It doesn't matter if you do or don't. I'm not doing it as a favor to you. The fact is that you're no good to this firm until you work this out."

Of everything Parker had said, those words were the most disturbing; they were completely true, which meant Parker was inside his head. He profoundly disliked that feeling. "How can we work it?" Henry asked.

"You've been at the firm a couple of years, right?"

"Twenty-six months."

"Which means technically we owe you fifteen, sixteen days of vacation. *Technically.* How many have you taken?"

"None."

"Exactly, because none of our junior associates take their vacation. So here's the deal. You're taking yours, as of now. I figure I can sell the idea around here that you're making us money on your own time. And I want every second you work on this case catalogued and billed to the estate. In quarter hours, and don't be afraid to round up. If you want to burn vacation time in Kansas instead of St. Bart's, that's your problem. Accept?"

"I accept."

"Remember, Henry, even this little scam has limits. If things get screwy, all bets are off. I don't want to hear about sheriffs getting involved. If this thing goes criminal, the state seizes the estate and the court has to approve the fees. I don't know what they pay lawyers down there, but it sure as hell isn't our rate. You follow me?"

"Yeah."

"Good. Meanwhile, I'm going to be spending my time up here thinking up exotic ways for you to make it up to me. They all involve picking up my laundry and other menial tasks you thought were beneath you."

Henry grimaced; he had won, but the payback would be enormous. "Thanks, Sheldon. I guess."

"Okay. Wait. Before you go, I got a message for you—some skirt named Amanda Ashton's looking for you. Kansas Department of Environment, which fascinated me, because I didn't know Kansas even had one."

"What's she want me for?"

"Some project she's working on. God help you if the EPA gets hold of you. Sexy voice, though. I told her you were a busy boy these days. Number's six-two-one-oh-four-four-nine, your area code."

Henry was about to hang up, but he casually added, "I hear Elaine's helping you with your portfolio. Pretty modern move for a guy like you. She's not exactly old boys' club."

"I don't care if she's from Mars if she can make me money. I saw her numbers and they were impressive. Met her for a drink at Romano's, and she laid it out for me. You were right, she picks stocks like Nolan Ryan threw fastballs. And looks a hell of a lot better. You don't have a problem with me sending her some business, do you?"

"I'd feel better if you weren't in acquisitions and mergers."

Parker laughed, an earthy, experienced sound. "She invited me to her big soiree. I guess I'll see you there. If you make it back, that is."

"Touch her and you're dead."

Parker laughed again. "I'm a hard man to kill," he said. "Stay in touch, Preacher."

If I were going to play by the rules, I'd go find Roger right now, Henry thought. Boyd's connection to Crandall was something he and the rest of the family deserved to know. But something had clearly happened to Ellen, and if it wasn't Tyler, he wanted to find out what it was. Something terrible was etched on her face in tired lines, like her innocence had been drained from her soul. More and more he was convinced she was the hinge that moved the locked door he faced. He had rattled her at lunch, he had felt that. But he would have to be careful; she was no pushover. Roger would have to wait; he picked up the phone and dialed her house.

"Ellen," he said. "Henry Mathews. From yesterday, at the bank."

There was a momentary silence. "How are you?"

"I need a minute of your time."

Her voice was cautious. "Why don't you drop by the bank later? We open at ten on Saturdays."

"It's a personal matter," Henry said. "I'd like to come by now, if that's okay."

He could feel her thinking. "Is this a social call?"

God, she doesn't let up. "I'm afraid not," Henry said. "It's about the Crandall estate."

"All right. I'm putting on my makeup. We'll have to talk while I finish."

"That's fine. I'll be there in five minutes."

Henry made the short drive over to Ellen's, pulled into the gravel drive, and walked onto her porch. He didn't have to knock.

The door swung open, and Ellen, her makeup half applied, stood before him. The difference in her appearance was striking; without eyeliner and mascara she looked like the woman she was: someone twice his age. She nodded for him to come in and said, "Whatever it is, I don't want to be late to work for it." She motioned for him to sit and took her place in front of a mirror. With her back to him she picked lipstick out of a small bag and began applying it carefully. Henry disliked the arrangement; from the seated angle he could only see her face in the reflection, which placed him at a disadvantage. Ellen looked over at him briefly in the mirror, then began running lipstick along her bottom lip. "So you're here," she said. "So talk."

Henry opened his briefcase and pulled out some aging, rumpled papers. He held them up, but Ellen's gaze remained fixed on her mouth. "What's that?" she asked, her voice casual.

"A loan agreement between the Cottonwood Valley Bank and Ty Crandall."

"What of it? Tyler had a lot of loans with the bank."

"This is the loan that set Tyler up in business back in seventy-three. It's for a great deal of money, money that Crandall was in a dubious position to ever repay. Without these papers, there is no Tyler Crandall. No king of Cheney County, no ruler of Council Grove. Just another mustered-out soldier with not much more than the shirt on his back. Whoever signed this loan was making a fool's gamble, unless he knew something that isn't in the documentation." He held out the paper. "I'm going to come straight to the point, Ellen. The name at the bottom of this page is Raymond Boyd." Ellen looked up at Henry, but she said nothing. "I checked, Ellen. You were working at the bank at the time of this loan."

"How did you know that?"

I know it because the ever-helpful Frank Walters went to the bank at eight o'clock this morning to dig up your employment records. "I just know," he said. "So therefore you know that Raymond Boyd preceded Schiller at the bank."

Ellen stared back into Henry's eyes a moment, then broke off and began rummaging in her makeup bag. She began applying eyeliner in quick, professional strokes. "I don't follow you, Henry," she said. "What's this about?"

"It's about why you felt the need to lie."

Ellen looked at him with a hurt expression. "Is that why you came over here, Henry, to call me a liar?"

Henry leaned forward in his chair. She would have to do a lot better than that to deflect him. "I'm going to lay this out for you very clearly, so we don't misunderstand each other," he said. "There's nothing personal here. I'm just trying to fill in some blanks. The fact is that you've known Boyd all this time. Obviously, you knew Crandall as well. You also knew that they had business dealings together at one time. It seems to me that you are the missing link, Ellen, and I want to know why you wanted to keep that a secret."

Ellen set down her makeup. "I don't know what you think you found out, but I can't see what difference any of it makes now," she said. "That paper, if it's real, is from a very long time ago."

"The papers prove that Boyd once held a position in this town. I don't know what happened to him back then, but I do know that with Tyler Crandall dead, you're the only witness to it that I've got."

"Everybody knows what happened to him," she answered. "He went crazy."

"I think you know why. I want you to tell me."

Ellen swiveled around on her chair, meeting Henry's eyes. "Bang, I'm dead," she said darkly. "You got me." She crossed her legs and blotted her lips on a tissue; her makeup finished, the transformation was complete. She looked once again like the woman Henry had encountered at the bank. "All right," she admitted, her voice calm. "I knew Raymond. It was twenty-five years ago. Big deal."

Henry watched her face carefully; finally, there had been a break in her armor. It might lead to more, if he could keep her talking. But Ellen regarded her admission as insignificant. "Look, I knew him. It doesn't matter. It doesn't change anything."

"Let's start with why you lied to me. If this is no big deal, then why not just tell me about it?"

Ellen gave him another reproachful look. "You're still a boy, Henry," she said. "There's a lot you don't know about things."

"Enlighten me."

"You know why I lied to you?" She laughed, a cool, detached sound. "I did it because that's what Raymond would have wanted."

Which means you knew Boyd well enough to know his inner desires. "What makes you say that?" he asked.

"Look, I knew him. But he went crazy. He's not the person he was. That person died twenty-five years ago. I felt bad for him, so I left him alone. It doesn't make any sense to make things worse for anybody now. I don't know what Ty was trying to do with that will."

"Did Crandall pressure Boyd to help him? Those early loans were way out of scale for somebody in Crandall's position."

"Look, I was just working my desk. If Ty weren't dead and Raymond weren't crazy, you could ask them."

"If Boyd was a bank officer twenty-five years ago, why doesn't anybody remember him? Why didn't anybody contact his family or something?"

"He only worked at the bank for a few months. He got sent here by the main branch. I suppose they could have helped him, but it was his first position with the bank. I imagine they just chalked him up as a flake and went on about their business."

"But the people here," Henry insisted. "How about them?"

Ellen's face was implacable. "It didn't take that long to forget him. He was always private anyway, shy. He wasn't from around here. No family connection, nothing. He was at the bank such a short time a lot of people never met him in the first place. So one day he's been fired, and a while later he shows up out at the park, not talking to a soul. You know how people are. They don't like talking to somebody when they've been fired, and they don't like talking to crazy people. After a while he just faded out of their minds. People die, people move away, people forget. But just to make sure, I started some of the rumors about him—you know, the stories about him being a gangster and all."

"Those came from you?"

"All I had to do was start it. Once they got rolling they had a life of their own. Gangster, crazy man. It didn't matter. I just wanted the name Raymond Boyd forgotten."

"Why was that so important?"

She looked at him, and for a moment he could see a younger woman within her, a woman who would be humiliated to see what she had become. "Look, I wasn't always like this," she said, compressing a lifetime of disappointment into a single sentence.

"You mean you cared."

"Not like you mean. I worked beside him. I knew him better than anybody else, so I did what I thought he would want. Or would have, if he could still think straight."

"Why didn't anybody help him? Why didn't anybody get him some treatment or something?"

"Takes money," Ellen said, standing and picking up her bag. "Like everything else in this damn life. You know, Henry, *money*?"

Henry calculated a moment, then decided to take a risk. "Look, I'm going to level with you. We both know Roger. There's no way he's going to roll over and play dead. But if I can find a meaningful connection from Raymond to Crandall, the will could be found valid. If it is, Boyd will have all the money he'll ever need."

"Do you think the money would make any difference to somebody who spends all day sitting on a park bench? *Money!*" she spat bitterly.

"It's not only about money, Ellen," he said.

"Oh really?" She gave him a mocking look. "All right then, where have you been the past twenty years? Why didn't you help him yourself? How come the only time you or anybody else started trying to help him is when he got in Crandall's will? You don't work free, do you?"

Her words momentarily derailed him; she was right, of course. Boyd had mostly been a mere object of fascination to him, not a real person with needs and a future. In all those years the simple idea of helping the man had never occurred to him. Boyd's gruff exterior and bizarre habits were sufficient to render him an outcast, and no one had possessed enough grit or plain compassion to push through that fact. After a moment he said, "None of us helped him. Not me, not anybody. I'll take my blame. But you still haven't answered my question. I want to know why you lied."

"To protect him," Ellen answered. "To protect him from people like you." She pulled her little bag together and pushed by him. "I don't have any more answers for you. I'm sorry. I've got to go. I'm gonna be late." She stepped quickly through the door and stood on the porch. Henry followed her outside.

"One last thing," he said. "You're asking me to believe that you lied to me to protect him," he said. "All right. That means you cared about him, Ellen. You cared more than anyone did."

Ellen walked off the porch and got in her car and rolled down the window. "I'm not asking you to believe anything, Henry," she said, starting the engine. She put the car in gear and drove off spinning her wheels, filling the air with a shower of dust.

Chapter Seventeen

*F*irst to Roger—*I can't put that off anymore. But then over to Boyd.* He fingered a leather valise. *If I show him the bank papers, maybe it'll jog him into talking, remembering.* He had parked and was walking toward the square, deep in thought, when his cell phone went off in his jacket. "What?" he barked into the receiver.

A female voice gave a shocked "Beg your pardon?"

"Sorry, sorry. You just surprised me. Henry Mathews here."

"This is Amanda Ashton. I'm with the state department of environment. I'm going to be in Council Grove today, and I wonder if we could get together briefly."

"Right, Sheldon Parker told me you'd be calling. Look, things are a little hectic around here. What's it all about?"

"It's nothing serious, but since I'm going to be there anyway I thought we could meet for a few minutes. It'll be easier to explain in person."

"All right. I'll be busy most of the day. What time will you be here?"

The voice gave a short, slightly embarrassed laugh. "I'm at a pay phone in front of some cafe at the moment."

"You mean you're already here?"

"Well, yes."

"You work fast."

"Try to. So can we meet?"

"Look, I don't really have an office down here. The building you're in front of is the Trailside Diner. It's as good a place as any. I haven't had breakfast, come to think of it. I can be there in two minutes."

"Wonderful. Shall I describe myself?"

"Just a guess, but I imagine you'll be the one in the dark pants, white shirt, and dark green vest."

"Excuse me?"

"The one with the short brown hair, wearing flats, and carrying a black government-issue briefcase. Oh yeah, and a puzzled expression."

There was a pause, and then: "Where are you?"

"About a hundred feet away from you. Now it's ninety-five."

She turned, and saw him walking toward her. "How will I know *you?*" she asked into the phone, laughing.

"Six-one, slightly wrinkled khakis, dark green shirt. We both like green, apparently." He reached her, took the phone from her hand, and hung it up. "Impressed?"

"For a minute I thought you were clairvoyant."

"Watch what you think."

She smiled and stuck out her hand. "Amanda Ashton. Are you always this efficient?"

"Absolutely." They walked the few steps to the diner, and Henry said, "Listen, can you go on in? I've got to make a quick phone call. Just take a second."

"Sure. I'll get a table."

"Thanks." Amanda disappeared into the diner, and Henry called the Crandall house. Sarah answered. "Hey there," he said quietly. "How you holding up?"

To his relief, she sounded better than he had thought. Some life had come back into her, from the sound of it. "All right," she said. "Mother's better. She's eating, and we actually talked a little this morning."

"Listen, Sarah, is Roger around?" he asked. "I'd like to come out and fill all of you in on a few things."

"He's not, Henry. I think he went to Topeka for the day."

That was a disappointment; he had wanted to get the family together as soon as possible. "I didn't know he was heading out of town," Henry said.

"He didn't either, really. He left early. I think it came up suddenly."

"Do you know when he'll be home?"

"He didn't say. Is it important? Have you found out anything?"

"Nothing to worry about. Just have Roger call me when he gets back. You have my number there, right?"

"It's right here by the phone. Is everything all right, Henry?"

"Everything's fine, Sarah. Just have Roger call me."

The time pressure off, Henry walked back into the Trailside. He glanced around the place; there was the usual collection of middle-aged farmers in the Naugahyde booths. Then he saw Amanda smiling at him from a table near the back.

Henry took his seat, considering his caller. She was a pleasant change from his recent engagements; she looked pretty and smart, and above all, not from Council Grove. "Sorry for the informal meeting place," he said. "But I was starving anyway."

"What do you recommend?"

"How's your cholesterol?"

"I've got a little room to maneuver."

"Consider it sacrificed."

"That's fine. I haven't got time to be fussy."

Gladys Neumann, the enormous waitress at the diner, took their order. Amanda, to Henry's surprise, ordered eggs, hash browns, toast, and coffee.

"You don't eat like a girl," Henry said, smiling.

She gave him a surprised look. "Whatever that means."

"It's a compliment, actually. I'm always fascinated when a woman orders water and a piece of lettuce." Elaine, he had to admit, had that kind of eating down to a science.

"I work too hard not to eat like a real person."

"Apparently. Working Saturday's pretty gung-ho for the government."

"Sometimes it's the only time I can get things done. If they paid me by the hour I'd be a millionaire."

Henry smiled. "You said this has something to do with the state department of environment. Rarely the bearers of good news."

She raised an eyebrow. "Another stereotype."

"I never claimed to be progressive."

"It's okay. I just need some information, and maybe a favor."

"I ought to warn you I don't really practice law in this state. I'm a little lax on the regs around here."

"What kind of practice are you in?"

Henry considered several phrases and said, "Carnage, mostly."

She laughed. "What does that mean?"

"Dismantling things."

"Pretty grim job description."

"Well, sometimes we put new things together out of the parts."

She looked at him, trying to decide if he was being serious. "Are you dangerous?" she asked.

"Yes," he said simply. He smiled. "But don't worry, it's my day off for corporate raiding. I find myself being a Good Samaritan lately."

"So maybe I've come at a good time."

"Maybe."

"This is a pretty simple matter, actually. I'm trying to find out the condition of some of the older oil wells in this part of the state for the agency. I'd like to go out and take a look at the wells on the Crandall property."

"Sounds reasonable. What do you need my help for?"

Amanda hesitated. "Rumor has it Crandall's heir is belligerently opposed to my agency's looking around," she said. "So I'm needing a little help with getting on the property. I don't want a scene."

Henry shrugged. "I doubt that he comprehends the notion of a state department of environment in the first place."

"Excuse me?"

"I think I see the problem here. Your rumor mill assumes Crandall's son Roger is the heir."

"I wasn't told the name. I just assumed a Crandall would be involved."

"Not exactly true." Henry took a minute to explain the circumstances of the will to Amanda, including Raymond Boyd's condition. "Of course," he finished, "he might not be any friendlier to the idea than Roger. If it is his land, in the end. Things are in suspended animation around here."

She looked at him thoughtfully. "So is that what you meant about being the Good Samaritan? Are you defending this man Boyd?"

"I didn't say that."

"You didn't have to," she said. "It's obviously the thing to do. But of course I'm a civil servant."

"Liberal?"

"Passionately." She smiled. "You?"

"Politics? I don't know. Republican, when I think about it."

"You obviously need to think about it a little bit harder."

He smiled; it had been a while since he had talked with someone who believed in . . . well, in anything, he supposed. "My boss would call you naive," he said. She frowned, obviously displeased. "Don't worry about it," he said. "Parker calling someone naive just means they're a decent human being."

She laughed. "And now a Chicago lawyer ends up sorting through a local mess. How did that happen?"

"Like Raymond, I inherited it. My father drafted the will."

"So he's a lawyer as well."

"Was," Henry said. "He passed away, with my mother. I grew up here, actually. This journey into the past is in my hometown. Graduated from KU, took the bar to get state-certified, and hauled out."

"I'm sorry about your parents. I didn't realize."

"No problem."

She smiled, pushing her hair back behind her ears. Henry found himself admiring the line of her jaw, the way the hair traced down her neck. She was no model, but she was definitely attractive, in a flawed, comfortable way. "I love Chicago," she said. "Don't get there much anymore."

"You know it?"

"I dated a boy at Northwestern. I was at Georgetown at the time, so it was the typical long-distance thing. Phone bills from hell. Had a heck of a summer, though."

Their food came, and between bites Henry asked, "I still don't understand what I have to do with this. Surely you've got all the authority you need without my help."

Amanda hesitated, obviously uneasy. "I made the mistake of getting on the wrong side of somebody powerful," she said, "somebody who tends to make my job as difficult as possible anyway. It's a special pleasure for him. So unless I'm willing to fight a bureaucratic nightmare, it would be better to do things this way."

"And what exactly is 'this way'?"

"I need the property owner present at the test." She sighed. "I was hoping you could grease the rails a little. I realize now how difficult that would be. The last thing I expected was this insanity curveball."

"So this isn't the normal policy, then?"

"No. Like I said, I got on the wrong side of the wrong person."

"And who is this protector of the earth that you ticked off?"

Amanda paused, as though having the name in her mouth made her queasy. "Carl Durand," she said tersely. "*Senator* Carl Durand."

"Well, that explains everything."

She looked up, surprised. "You know him?"

"I know of him. Durand's been selling oil and natural gas around here since I was a kid. He runs a tight ship, and nobody's been able to cut into his little pie. And I've just seen his name again anyway. I've been going over all the Crandall business records, and he's bought every drop of oil off the Crandall property since day one. Still does, although there's not much left."

"I'm not surprised. He tends to be everywhere I don't want him."

"All right. Suppose I can get you on the property. What is it you want to look at?"

Amanda launched into her concerns about the leaching chemicals, the remains of her breakfast growing cold, unheeded. Henry smiled, then smiled wider, finally laughing out loud.

She ground to a halt. "What?" she demanded.

"Take a breath," Henry said. "The oil isn't going anywhere during breakfast." It felt good to let his smile surface; he had always been a sucker for intelligent flirtation, and the girl sitting across from him was good at it, even better than Elaine. Just as tough, but without the venom.

"So what about it?" Amanda said. "Can you borrow my crusade for a day?"

He paused. "Didn't a lot of people get killed in the Crusades?"

"They believed in the cause."

"Still dead, though." Henry pushed back from the table. "Look, you're only needing temporary access. Go out there and do your test. If you get any flak, just blame me. I could care less what Carl Durand thinks. This time next week I'll be back in Chicago reading briefs."

"But I'll still be here, dealing with the mess. Although I appreciate your sense of adventure."

"Then I'm not sure what I can do for you. The thing is, I can't really imagine Boyd going with you."

"But he has to go. He's my only chance. No offense, but if you won't help me, I'll find him and ask him myself."

The waitress brought the bill, and Henry reflexively picked it up. After a moment, however, he pushed it across the table to Amanda. "Take me to breakfast," he said simply. Amanda picked up the bill with a raised eyebrow. "It's only fair, considering how much you're going to owe me," Henry said.

"For what?"

"Trust me, you'd never get Boyd to go anywhere with you. And if you did I'm not sure it would be entirely safe. But I'll take you both—if I can get him to agree. No promises, but I'll give it a shot. Like you said, I've borrowed your crusade."

"Why would you do that?"

"Maybe I want to see what it feels like for a while. Anyway, I've got my own reasons to get Boyd onto the Crandall ranch."

She smiled broadly. "I ought to warn you, not everyone wants a crusader around. They ask for favors a lot."

"I'll let you know if you start to wear thin."

She stood, dropping some money onto the table. "You do that."

The capitol building was nearly deserted on Saturday morning, and the long corridor on the third floor leading to Carl Durand's office was empty. Roger walked down it, scanning nameplates on the doors. He found Durand's and walked in at ten-fifty, ten minutes early. No one was in the outer waiting area, and he opened the door to Durand's private chambers without knocking. "I'm here," he said, crossing the room and flopping into a chair opposite Durand's desk.

"So I see," Durand replied. "Tell me something, Roger, did you grow up in a barn? Sorry, stupid question."

Roger stared back at Durand blankly; the senator shrugged and said, "Let's go over here. More comfortable." He led Roger into a sitting area off to one side of the office, where a couch, a low table, and a couple of wing chairs were situated. Against a wall was a wet bar. "Since you're early," he continued with a sarcasm lost on his visitor, "we can talk privately a few minutes. I've gone ahead and invited Frank Hesston to meet with us, just to fill you in from that angle."

"The lawyer."

"That's right. It's time we got you your own representation, Roger. Someone on *your* side. Frank's an old friend. He'll look out for your interests."

Roger grunted an assent and leaned back in his chair. He had driven hard that morning, the big hand pushing him and his yellow Cadillac fast up I-75 through the Flinthills to the state capital. He knew showing up early for the meeting was a sign of weakness, something his father would never have done. But it had been pure torture waiting until eleven. For starters, he had got his fill of Henry Mathews, and he wanted to put into motion as quickly as possible a way to punish him, make him regret taking a tone of equality, even superiority. But there was more—new information that made even his feud with Henry seem insignificant. *Small-time's over,* he thought, focusing unsteadily on Durand's face across the table. It had taken a few shots of whiskey to steady his nerves, and they had hit his empty stomach with destabilizing force. He had been drinking harder lately, partly because it would have annoyed his father and partly because the ordeal over the will had made him jumpy. But soon all that would be over. *The balance of power around here is about to get seriously fucked up.*

Durand carefully took Roger in for a moment, scanning him up and down. "Jesus, Roger, are you drinking already?" he said with irritation. "It's not even noon."

Roger looked shocked. "Hell, no," he lied. "Never touch it before lunch. You know me."

Durand muttered something unintelligible under his breath. When he spoke, however, his tone was one of concern. "We've got to settle this estate once and for all," he said. "I was too close to your father to see this thing handled this way. That's why I've called in Frank."

Roger eyed Durand. *You're breakin' my heart,* he thought. *Now that Daddy's dead, you're real interested in me. And now I know why.*

A door opened behind them, and Durand said, "Frank's here. He can fill you in."

Roger turned his head quickly to see Hesston enter, and the sudden motion sent the office spinning past him for a moment. Durand and Hesston exchanged a look, the lawyer taking in the situation in a moment. "Don't get up, Roger," Hesston said, passing quickly by him and taking a seat. "You look perfectly comfortable where you are."

Frank Hesston was a short man, stocky, but not soft. His face was full and round, the face of substance and affluence. His intense, pale blue eyes revealed a robust, incisive mind and a keen interest in detail. He was about fifty years old; his brownish hair was thinning, and a bald spot crept outward from the crown of his skull. He wore a dark blue business suit and a tasteful, conservative tie, the clothes of a successful lobbyist. He turned to Durand. "I assume you've brought Roger up to date?"

"Not yet," Durand said. He looked at Roger and said, "I invited Frank to meet with us because he's the finest attorney in this state, and that's the kind of legal representation I want you to have. We've got to get you back in the saddle, Roger. Sitting tall, like you deserve."

Damn right, Roger thought. *But with what I know, I won't need either one of you to do that.*

"What Carl's saying, Roger, is that I'm here to handle this situation from a legal standpoint. This *in terrorem* clause can be beat. I've beat it myself. With the right judge . . ."

"So you're real interested in my welfare, that's what you're saying."

Hesston looked quizzically at Durand. "That's why we're here, Roger."

Roger looked at Hesston, then at Durand, fixing each with a level smile. "So you're both my friends. I can trust you."

"Your father and I went back a long time," Hesston said. "I figure I owe him this."

"You owe him!" Roger sneered. The hand pushed, and he couldn't wait another second. *Showtime*, he thought. *Time to turn some tables.* He rose from his chair and walked slowly past Durand and Hesston, forcing them to turn completely around, a move he had often watched his father use. "Well, I'm glad we got those little speeches taken care of," he said lightly, "because you can both kiss my ass."

Durand's face reddened instantly and he started to get up; Hesston put up his hand, watching Roger closely. "We're all friends here, Roger," he said quietly. "That's why we're here to help you. I can't think why you would want to test that friendship with such . . . unwise words."

Roger walked to the bar, pulled out a tumbler, and filled it with scotch. He tossed back the drink and said, "I don't give a damn what you think." His words were starting to slur, and he spoke deliberately, which only served to emphasize his growing inebriation. "And I don't care what you think either, *Carl*," he added, saying the name with insolent familiarity. He stared at both of them. "The game's up. I know what the hell's been going on around here. I know the whole story, and I've decided that there's gonna be some new rules."

Hesston's friendly politeness promptly vanished. Durand fixed Roger with a level, malign stare. Roger, in spite of his confidence, blinked; even his father's rages seemed less dangerous than what he saw in Durand's face. Hesston said, "You have a lot of problems already, Roger, and I don't think making enemies out of us helps you out any. But if you want to take us on, put your cards on the table. You got something to say, let's hear it."

Roger's head was singing with fear, booze, and adrenaline now, the combination rushing through him with crackling energy. He reached into his coat pocket and pulled out a sheaf of tightly bound papers, forcing his hand steady. "It's funny what you find when people die," he growled. "Things that other people thought were hidden forever."

Durand stood, a menacing expression on his face. "What do you think you have there, Roger?" he asked through clenched teeth.

"It's what I *know* I have." Roger stepped toward Durand, determined to face him down. "These are the accounts between my father, Carl Durand"— he turned to face Hesston—"and the supposedly honorable attorney-at-law Frank Hesston. It's real interesting reading."

Durand crossed the space between himself and Roger in three steps and ripped the papers from Crandall's hand. He flipped through the pages in quick succession, and to Roger's satisfaction, a trace of fear could be seen through the anger. "That son of a bitch," Durand snarled. "That little son of a bitch." He took the pages, crumpled them, walked to his desk, and calmly set them on fire with a lighter. They burned orange and red as he dropped them into a metal wastebasket. He sat down, still visibly enraged but in control. "Well, Roger, what do you think about that?"

Roger walked as casually as he could up to Durand. "I think you'll have to burn a lot more of those before I give a damn about that." He laughed. "You don't think I'm stupid enough to bring the only copy here, do you?"

Durand was about to reply when Frank Hesston spoke. He had retained his composure from the beginning, his face clouding over into intense thought. "No, of course not, Roger," he said calmly. "No one thinks you're stupid. Naturally you made copies, probably on the way here. Is that what you did, Roger? Did you stop and make copies along the way?"

Roger turned to Hesston. "What difference does it make?" he said angrily. "I made the copies. That's all you need to know."

Hesston's face remained calm, even sympathetic. "It might make a difference," he said. "And of course Carl here would be more likely to believe that you actually had these copies if you told us where you made them."

"I made them at the damn copy store!" Roger yelled. "I don't know, Kinko's or something."

Hesston turned to say something to Durand, but Carl had already had enough. "So you walked into a public place and made God knows how many copies of fifteen pages each. You're a fool, Roger. A fool."

"What's got you?" Roger said, confusion creeping into his voice. "They didn't know what the hell I was copying."

"For twenty-five years nobody knows about the business we've been doing," Durand said. "And Crandall told me there were no records at his place. Now, a week after he dies, his son is making copies of the books at goddam Kinko's!"

Hesston stood and walked over to Roger. "What's done is done, Carl," he said quietly. "But tell me, Roger, what do you think these so-called books mean?"

"They're not so-called books, Frank. They're the *real* books. And they show that the Crandall ranch wasn't a bunch of burnt-out oil wells hanging on for dear life. I don't know how it works. Hell, those wells only pump a few hours every day. But somehow you two and my father were making millions of dollars that nobody knows anything about." He stopped, a far-away look in his eyes. "*Millions*," he repeated.

"He doesn't know anything," Durand said. "He's got nothing but numbers on a page."

"Just a minute, Carl," Hesston said. He turned back to Roger. "Supposing, just for the purpose of discussion, that this were true. What do you suppose you would do with that information?"

"Get in on the goddam action!" Roger exclaimed. "Take my share! Just like my father did." He blinked. "With some changes."

"I see," Hesston said. "What kind of changes, Roger? Again, just for the purposes of discussion."

Roger eyed the man narrowly. "For starters, you can kiss that even split good-bye. My share is going to be sixty percent. Sixty for me, twenty each for you two."

At this Durand lunged at Roger, but Hesston, in a surprisingly quick move, came between them and restrained him. His small but bulky frame proved remarkably tough, and he handled the much larger Durand with relative ease. "Sit down, Carl," he said. "Putting marks on him won't help matters."

"You heard that little punk!" Durand protested, but Hesston pushed him down into his chair.

"Let me handle this," he said. He turned to Roger, his voice absolutely level. "Don't misunderstand me, Roger," he said. "Stopping Durand from taking you apart doesn't mean I'm opposed to it in principle. It just means I want to find out how stupid you are first. Then the appropriate pain can be applied."

Roger looked at Hesston cautiously. The lawyer's physical prowess had proved a surprise, but his relative calm when applying it had been more unnerving. There was a quiet menace to the man, a casual disinterest in the way he talked about Durand hurting him that made Roger's skin crawl. But it was too late to reconsider; if he were ever going to get the power, he couldn't back down now. He heard his father's voice: *You got to have the will to act, boy. You got to have the will.* He had seen his father stare down adversaries, taking control of them with a word or a look. He would push through. "I'm not gonna argue about this, 'cause it's a waste of my time," he said. "It's real simple. There's new rules, and I'm telling you what they are. First, you bring me completely up to date on this little scam of yours. Second, I'm in for sixty percent." He turned to Durand. "You can understand that, can't you, little man?"

This time Durand was too quick for Hesston. He ducked under him and hit Roger with a roundhouse to the jaw, knocking Roger backward several feet. Roger's lip exploded in pain, and between the force of the blow and the booze he found himself toppling backward, sprawled on the carpeted floor. Now his athletic competitiveness came to the surface, and he struggled to his feet, determined to repay Durand with everything he had. But the drinking had diminished his balance, and he ended up teetering back and forth a moment before falling sideways against a chair. The chair broke under his sudden weight, a leg snapping cleanly off and dumping him once again on the floor. Durand cursed and walked away. "He had that coming, Frank."

"And now you have a split lip and a broken chair to explain," Hesston said with irritation. "For God's sake, I can't stand either one of you right now. At the rate we're going we might as well just invite the police in for coffee. Carl, sit down and let me sort this out."

Durand held up his hand and said, "Then get on with it, damn it, because if that idiot mouths off again I'm not going to be responsible for what happens."

Roger sat slumped in his chair, watching Durand and Hesston and feeling his isolation growing like a hideous cancer. Durand and his father had worked together for twenty-five years, their strength increasing with each other's help. If Durand and Hesston really were going to be his enemies, he had no plan of attack save one: to threaten them into cooperation. But he didn't feel very threatening at the moment. Nothing had gone according to plan. But he had one card left to play, and he could think of nothing else to do but play it. "If you don't like my terms you can both go to hell. I'll shut the wells down tomorrow and go straight to the police. You'll both fry." He looked at Durand. "You, especially."

Hesston stopped Durand with a look. "So that's your big plan, Roger?" he said sarcastically. "You'll run to the police?" He smiled, a relaxed look on his face. "You wasted your punch, Carl," he said casually, and pulled another chair out and sat. He looked at Roger placidly, saying nothing.

"Do you hear me?" Roger demanded. "If I don't get what I want, I'm going to the police! I'll tell them I had no idea that this was going on, but like a good little citizen I'm turning you bastards in." He pointed to the burnt fragments of paper in the wastebasket. "I have everything I need to put you both in jail for the rest of your lives."

Hesston smiled and crossed his legs. "Go ahead, Roger," he said. "Do it."

Roger blinked, frustration and rage filling his mind. "What?" he stammered. "What are you saying? You want me to turn you in?"

Hesston's face showed an infuriating lack of concern. "You see why I told you to wait, Carl," he said. "I wanted to see how stupid he was. Unbelievably stupid, it turns out." He laughed. "Go on, Roger. Go to the police. Turn us in." He picked up the receiver of Durand's phone. "Here, I'll dial it for you." He dialed a number and held the phone out to Roger. "Go ahead. They'll be on the line any second."

Roger trembled in his chair, unable to move. Several seconds passed silently, and Hesston hung up the phone. "Congratulations, Roger," he said. "You're stupid, but there's at least some instinct for self-preservation in your small mind. I'm so pleased."

"What's this game?" Durand said uneasily. "Why toy with him? Just let me kill him, okay?"

Hesston gave Durand an annoyed look. "Killing isn't the answer to everything, Carl," he said. "Anyway, that won't be necessary." He smiled once again at Roger. "You see, Roger here is a mean-spirited little man, weak and greedy. And he knows that if he turns us in, the IRS will come to his little farm and take every bit of it away. The penalties and back taxes that his father accrued will be in the millions. His family will have nothing, which doesn't give a damn about, but more important, *he* will have nothing, the thought of which he can't stand. He'll be nothing but the penniless son of a felon." He laughed. "Maybe you can get a job in the hardware store, Roger, after the government auctions it off. Of course you won't be able to buy it yourself, because you won't have a dime. You'll be homeless, because your house will be sold with everything else. You know who you'll be, Roger? You'll be the fucking Birdman." His laughter grew louder. "Now, Roger, I hope you feel better for having got this off your chest. But the fact is I'm going to represent you in a legal action. You're going to contest the will, because I can't have things screwed up by the land getting outside our control. I need unrestricted access, and if it goes out of your family I can't have that guarantee. Your father was pretty damn smart, thinking he was sending our little scam south."

"Damn ironic, too, giving the land to Boyd," Durand said. "But that doesn't matter now. You see, Roger, Frank here's the best lawyer in this state. You're going to do what he says, and he's going to get things back to normal. In the meantime, you'll live with *ten* percent, plus you get to walk around that little shithole of a town and act like you own it." He stretched, and to Roger's horror he actually yawned. "I think I'll have a drink," he said, walking to the bar. "Can I get you anything, Roger?" he asked. "A little shot for your nerves?"

Henry pulled his car over at the edge of Custer's Elm Park and asked Amanda to stay put. She nodded, and he detected a bit of apprehension on her face. "We'll see how he is," he said. "I'm not making any promises. But if he's calm, I'll ask him." She blinked and smiled.

Henry got out and spotted Boyd across the park. It didn't look hopeful. The man was in one of his fits of sermonizing, gesturing to the sky.

Henry stopped and watched for a moment, transfixed as usual. Boyd's thin frame seemed as fragile as his mind; he looked as though a stiff wind might suck him up and carry him away like a scarecrow in the breeze. *But my God, he believes*, Henry thought. *Total faith. No doubts, no questions. He could do anything.*

Henry walked across the grass and heard the man's voice carried back to him in the wind. "I will free the slaves from the yoke of the black sea, the black ocean! I will redeem them with my mighty arm, says the Lord!" Boyd strode back and forth in front of his bench in full cry, passionate and fiery. The great bird was squawking and flapping, his wings beating the air. Henry watched in horrified fascination; the two seemed connected somehow, as if the bird were some kind of animal extension of the man's madness.

Henry stepped softly forward, and the bird whirled to face him, rising and hovering two feet in the air. Boyd turned as well, his face agitated. With the sight of Henry, however, he calmed, and lowered his arms. The bird flapped down to the ground and stared with yellow eyes. "The virgin awaits. She is untouched by the black sea. She is undefiled."

"Hello, Mr. Boyd."

"Have you seen the virgin?" Boyd asked eagerly. His eyes were shining. "She is untouched by the black ocean. Pure and without stain." He sat down on his bench. "Do you have more papers, junior Henry? More papers about my buildings?"

Henry radiated calmness. "No, Raymond. I've come to ask you a question. Try to answer as honestly as you can." Boyd sat quietly, apparently waiting. "I have a friend," Henry went on, "who needs to go on the Crandall property. A part of the property that was willed to you."

Boyd looked steadily back at him, and Henry almost felt that they were communicating in a normal way. He wondered how long it would last. "The thing is, Raymond, this person would like for you to come along."

Boyd's face grew troubled. "Go see my buildings?" he asked.

"Not the buildings this time, Mr. Boyd. She wants to see the wells."

At the mention of the wells Boyd diminished before Henry's eyes, retreating into a small space on the park bench. He withdrew, beginning his singsong of unintelligible muttering.

"Mr. Boyd?" Henry moved toward him, but with the first step, Boyd's agitation seemed to increase. Henry stopped. He had known it was a long shot, but Boyd's emotional response to going out to the wells was still a surprise. "We don't have to go," he said quietly. "If it upsets you we can forget about it."

Boyd suddenly reached up and rubbed his head with startling ferocity, and for a moment Henry was afraid that the man would do damage to himself. He was on the verge of reaching out to stop him when Boyd looked up suddenly and said, "*I will spread my net for him*, says the Lord. *I will execute my judgment*."

"It's all right, Mr. Boyd. Just stay right here and take it easy, okay? It was just an idea."

But Boyd stood up from the bench and looked across the park at the car. "Absolution," he said. "Let there be absolution."

Boyd headed resolutely past Henry across the park, forcing him to follow. Henry looked past Boyd and could see Amanda watching them with a nervous expression. But to his surprise, she got out of the car while they were still some yards away. He could see she was anxious, but she was controlling it beautifully. "Hello, Mr. Boyd," she said calmly. "This is a lovely place. However, you spend a lot of time here."

Boyd looked at her intently a moment, then continued forward. "Apparently Raymond's decided to go," Henry said. "So let's get out there before he changes his mind." Amanda nodded, and Henry put Boyd into the back seat of the car.

"Government work is getting more interesting," Amanda said, walking around to her door.

"If somebody had told me two weeks ago I'd be driving across the prairie in a rented car with an insane millionaire to see some dead oil wells, it's vaguely possible I wouldn't have believed them."

To Henry's relief, Boyd was relatively quiet as they rolled down Route 12, content in his subdued singsong. It was a fifteen-minute drive to the Crandall land with the wells, a large section of range about three miles away from the main house. Henry pulled off the highway, opened the big gate, and drove his car through. He closed the gate behind them and started slowly across the bumpy field, glad to be in a rental. "A truck wouldn't hurt right now," he said.

"It still beats climbing fences."

He looked at her. "There's a story there."

She nodded. "Another time."

As they approached the well, Boyd's singsong message steadily grew in intensity. Amanda turned to listen; Henry was impressed with how quickly she came to terms with the man, and Boyd, in turn, seemed not to be disturbed by her presence. After a moment she asked, "What's he saying?"

Henry glanced at Boyd in the rearview mirror. "I've picked up bits and pieces. It's all religious stuff. He goes back and forth between judgment and absolution. When he's on the judgment thing it gets nasty, real serious hellfire."

She turned to look at Boyd again with curiosity. "He doesn't look mean to me."

"He scared the hell out of me as a kid."

"Really? So you've known him for a long time, then."

"I wouldn't say I've known him. But I've known of him, yeah. I used to go out to the park and hear him preach."

"What do you suppose he means by absolution?"

Henry shook his head. "I don't know. Absolution from what? From past sins?" He turned left to avoid a big gully, then let the car roll to a stop. The closest well was a hundred yards away. "That's it by car," he said. "We'll have to walk from here." He nodded toward Boyd. "Let's just leave him where he is. I don't want to push things. He's on the land, and that's what you wanted." He turned to Raymond. "Just stay here, okay, Mr. Boyd? We'll be back in a few minutes."

Henry and Amanda got out and Henry opened the trunk. He grabbed the parcels and the two of them set off toward the well. They had gone less than twenty yards when they heard the car door open.

Henry turned and saw Boyd standing in the field, the open door forgotten. Never was the man's inner turmoil more apparent; his face was contorted into a kind of anguish, and he was shaking. "Plague and bloodshed," he cried, "burning sulfur and hailstones! There will be judgment, judgment by my mighty hand!"

While Henry and Amanda stared, Boyd headed off briskly toward the dead well, walking directly past them without a word.

"This is not good," Henry said. "I don't know what this is, but it's definitely not good."

"I didn't realize what I was asking when I wanted him out here," Amanda said quietly. "Henry, we should just take him back."

Boyd was approaching the first well, and he stood erect, lifting his arms into the air. "I will pour down torrents of rain," he shrieked, "hailstones and burning sulfur!" He threw his fists at the well in anguish. "The hidden things will be brought into judgment! The wicked will not hide from my arm!"

"What is this?" Henry asked, watching Boyd. "Is it just this well, or wells in general? Or is he just having some kind of episode?"

They walked quickly toward the well, covering the distance in a few seconds. Boyd turned toward them, passion blazing in his face. When he spoke, his voice had become a hoarse, dangerous-sounding whisper. "*This is what the Lord says,*" he breathed. "*Thoughts will come into your mind. You will devise an evil scheme.*"

"My God," Amanda said softly, "he's completely insane."

Henry watched Boyd's face closely, drawn in as so often before with a sense of the overwhelming pain there. In his seminary days he had volunteered in the psychiatric ward of a hospital, and he had seen the truly lost there, the irreparable damage of brain chemistry gone permanently awry. Boyd seemed different, although he couldn't place just why. "I don't know," he said slowly as he stared at Boyd. "I think something or someone has damaged him. I wish I knew the whole story. But this is pretty damn creepy."

"Riding in the car, I thought he was crazy and sweet. But if there is somebody out there who hurt him, God help them if he ever gets hold of them."

Henry nodded. "I'm just trying to figure out what to do now." But even as they watched, Boyd began to calm; whether his rage was spent, or simply because his mind was unable to hold its passion for very long, he eventually slumped down, sitting like a child on the ground with his back to the well. He stared out into the vast expanse of Kansas, the anguish on his face slowly draining away.

"Ever see anything like that before?" Amanda asked.

"No," Henry answered. "Nothing like that. I've seen his anger. But this is new." He stared up at the well. "He genuinely seemed tortured by the sight of this thing. 'Hailstones and burning sulfur,' that I've heard. It's a big part of the judgment theme. I never thought it meant anything." He looked up at the well. "But oil burns."

"And there's always sulfur around wells. It's the most dangerous thing about them, actually."

Henry studied Boyd a moment. Boyd was mumbling to himself again, but quietly now, his voice a low, tremulous vibration. "Look, how long will this take?" Henry asked. "He's calm now, but I don't think this place is healthy for him, although I don't know why." Henry walked slowly over to him; Boyd looked up, the horror temporarily banished.

"Let your pain be washed in the sea of black, junior Henry," Boyd said. Henry reached a hand down to him, but Boyd ignored it. Instead, he made a grandiose sign of the cross and said, "Fools and whores, I absolve thee."

"That's the second time he's done that," Henry said to Amanda. "It's unnerving, to tell you the truth."

"The sign of the cross?"

"When he plays priest like that. It's like he's forgiving me for something. I never did him any harm."

"Absolution," Amanda said. "You said that was the other theme."

"Not for me, for God's sake," Henry said. He glanced back at Boyd, who was staring at him intently.

"Henry," she said, "I think I can compress the whole test into thirty minutes or so. It's obvious I'll never get another chance. What do you think?"

Boyd was running his finger in the dirt, making circles and obscure, apparently meaningless figures. "Okay," Henry said after a moment. "But if there's another scene we'll have to pack up immediately. Or I can take Boyd and leave you to finish."

"Understood. Help me with this stuff for a second, and I'll get through it as fast as I can."

Henry picked up the packs and hauled them over to the well. Amanda began quickly organizing her tools, nodding for Henry to look after Boyd. Henry walked back over and squatted down about four feet away from him. It was enough, apparently, to be near; Boyd looked up at him with what could pass for gratitude. The minutes passed, Amanda rushing through her tests. After about twenty minutes, Henry heard Amanda call out.

"What's up?" he said, turning toward her.

"Just something weird," she said over her shoulder. "Can you get free for a second?"

Boyd was sitting quietly for the moment, his eyes closed. "All right," he said. "Hang on." He crossed over to the well and saw Amanda crouched down, adjusting a complicated instrument. "What's that?"

"Gamma ray and microelectric sondes." She smiled. But you knew that, of course."

He liked her smile; it was warm, and he couldn't find any hidden agenda behind it. "I despise women who are smarter than me," he said. "What's going on?"

"I just finished my neutron and gamma ray tests."

"I was going to suggest those."

"Listen, Henry, when I said weird I meant it. Unless I miss my guess, this well is . . . I was going to say unusual, but that kind of understates it." She looked up at the steel fittings, wonder on her face. "I'd say it's something of a geological miracle."

Henry followed her gaze up the rusting metal. "What makes you say that?"

Amanda scanned her readings again, her expression serious. "I keep thinking there's got to be some mistake. I must be doing something wrong, unless the laws of geology have been temporarily suspended." She fiddled with the controls for a moment, then looked back up. "Nope," she said, "the thing's working, and I've checked the nominal settings twice." She stood up from her cramped position and rubbed her neck. "Well," she said, "I'm not a geologist. I just picked up bits and pieces in my research on this project. But I do know there shouldn't be oil in extruded limestone, which this"—she pointed downward—"is." She picked up the tester. "See?" she asked, pointing to a digital readout. "This thing detects rock type with gamma rays. And it says that the rock down there is almost exclusively limestone. There's a little clay, but not enough of that to speak of. Anyway, you don't find oil in either one of them."

"Considering we're standing in front of an oil well, I think you need new instruments."

"The instruments are perfect. This kind of rock isn't porous, which oil needs. The liquid hides in the porosity of the rock. If rock is sufficiently dense, like this, no oil."

"I refer you once again to the well."

Amanda shook her head. "Let me show you something," she said. She led him five yards uphill to a small, elevated patch of earth covered with reddish-brown exposed rock. Reaching down, she smacked a piece of the rock smartly a few times with the palm of her hand. The formation split easily into several pieces. Picking up a handful, she crumbled it in her hand. "Chalk," she said, looking up at Henry. "Extruded limestone, in other words. That's what chalk is. So the bottom line is there's no reason why oil was ever discovered here in the first place."

"Some of these wells have been dead for some time. Would that make a difference?"

"Not unless they've been dead for about six million years."

"I see."

"The rock is the rock, Henry. But if by some miracle oil ever was found here, it couldn't have amounted to anything. They might have found some freak, anomalous pool, but it would have gone bust quick. No legs."

"Actually, I think that's what happened. My understanding is that the income was pretty significant early on, but it's dwindled in recent years."

Amanda looked across the field at a slowly pumping well. "Look, I've been researching this area for more than two years, and state records say these wells are among the oldest producing sites in this part of the United States. They're record setters, almost legends. That's why I wanted to be here so badly, testing for long-term leakage. They're perfect for my purposes. I had never heard of such a shallow well lasting ten years, much less more than twenty. But after this test I can't picture a well here lasting six months."

"Maybe this one burnt out early. Could the other wells be in a different kind of rock?"

"No," Amanda said, "not at such close range." She waved out across the field. "This whole area was a sea bottom a few million years ago. That's what gives it the gentle rolling, the hills. It was all underwater, shaped by tides."

Henry looked across the sloping grassland; it was easy to imagine an ocean covering an expanse of earth so immense, so gently and enormously shaped.

"Mind if I think out loud a second?" Amanda asked. She was staring intently at a pumping well a hundred and fifty yards away. "Say somehow they did find oil."

"They obviously did."

"The real question is why anybody would drill here in the first place. No wildcatter worth his salt would ever have bet on this site. The risks are great enough even when everything looks perfect. But to drill extruded limestone . . ." She paused, considering. "I don't suppose you know who the drilling company was, by any chance?"

Henry thought for a moment, then suddenly laughed out loud. "I do, actually. You'll be so pleased."

"Don't tell me."

"Yeah. It's your old buddy Durand. He drilled a lot in the early days. Now the easy oil's gone, and he's shut that part of the business down. Can't compete with the bigger companies, I guess."

Amanda groaned. "Durand. You've got to be kidding."

Henry shrugged. "I still don't see where you are heading with this. Things were less sophisticated back then. Maybe they just got lucky."

"Maybe," Amanda answered slowly. Then she shook her head emphatically. "No, I'm not going down that road. Let's get past the drilling itself for a second. I can't tell you why anybody would do it, but I agree that it's a moot question at this point. But the fact remains that there just isn't twenty-five years of oil under our feet. It would be like going to the Mojave Desert and finding a lake. It's simply impossible."

"I don't see how all this matters to your tests. I thought this was about decaying wells. Whatever happened, it was over twenty-five years ago. You may think the wells are a miracle, but they don't produce much. About thirty-five thousand dollars a year altogether."

"Then call it professional curiosity. I can feel there's something wrong here."

Henry nodded. "I believe in hunches. But I don't follow them down blind alleys. You're missing some piece of the puzzle. Oil wells don't pump oil that doesn't exist. Anyway, if you're trying to imply some impropriety, thirty-five thousand a year isn't much to scheme over."

Amanda had stopped listening; she was staring out across the field. "You would have been just a kid when these wells were drilled," she said quietly.

"That's right. All that's in a kind of childhood haze. I do remember one thing, though. A guy got killed during the drilling."

Amanda looked up. "Really? What happened?"

Henry thought. "I don't remember the details. It was a low-level guy, a roustabout, they called him. But it was big news at the time."

"Someone was killed here," she mused. "I didn't know that. Look, I have to follow this up, if only to find out why I'm wrong." She hesitated a moment, and moaned, "But why does it have to be Durand?"

"Is it that bad between you two?"

"I loathe him, whereas he merely detests me. He almost got me fired last week. So I can't let my curiosity about this look like I'm trying to drag something up on him." She paused, and her mouth crinkled into a demure smile. "On the other hand, it wouldn't break my heart to nail him if there is something going on here. Is that wrong?"

Henry laughed. "Lawyers never blame people for wanting a little revenge. It's the basis of our careers. Good luck, as far as I'm concerned. Unless it's something else."

"Something else?"

"Driving you. I've seen the symptoms before. This could be a Joan of Arc complex."

"What's that?"

"A destructive desire to die for a good cause."

Her smile faded. "That's the downside, I admit that." She picked up her tools and began filling her knapsack. "The fact that Durand knows the oil business so well makes me wonder about this place even more," she said. "Okay, I'm no fan of his, I admit that. But he knows the oil business inside and out. Nobody is going to tell me that he would drill in rock like this."

"He *did* drill here," Henry said. "That much we do know." He took the heavy pack from her and hoisted it to his own shoulder. She gave him a reproachful look, and he muttered, "Sorry. Midwestern Protestant upbringing. Can't help myself."

"It's okay. I don't mind chivalry as long as it doesn't ask me to make it coffee or wear short skirts."

Henry nodded. "That shouldn't be a problem."

The two walked side by side toward Boyd. "You of all people should understand this," she said. "You can't tell me this is any stranger than Crandall leaving his money to our friend over there. And you're pursuing that."

Henry looked over at Boyd. "All right," he said. "I didn't want to say this, but the truth is your suspicions about the drilling make me wonder more about my own problem. It kind of fits the pattern of weirdness." He kicked a small stone out of their way, and it scuttled away, rolling down a gradually sloping hill. "But let's get practical. I can't just have people digging around indiscriminately. Roger's already about to blow. And Durand's an old family friend of the Crandalls. So if Roger finds out you're out here,

Durand will know ten minutes later. I can easily see this thing blowing up in both our faces, and I don't like that."

Amanda nodded. "There's some work I can do at the capitol, some discreet sniffing around into records. I don't have to bring you or Crandall into that. This whole area has been geologically surveyed, and I want to make sure I have my facts right. If anything's going to blow up, I want at least to know what I'm talking about. The last thing I need right now is more egg on my face." She looked across the field toward the wells with a concerned expression. "But that's only going to take me so far. Assuming everything checks out, ultimately I'm going to need to get back on the property, Henry. And I'll have to bring someone with me, someone more experienced. A real geologist."

Henry frowned. "Which means Boyd has to come back too, then."

Amanda nodded. "If I'm going to do this, I can't give Durand any excuses to have my head. I need Boyd."

"I wish there were another way," Henry said quietly. "Bringing him out here was hard enough to justify once. I don't want to expose him to any more torture, which this place seems to be for him. It passed quickly, but next time we might not be so lucky."

"So where do we go from here?"

Henry paused, thinking. "I should say forget it."

"But you aren't going to, are you?"

He looked at her, surprised that she could read him so well so quickly. "All right," he said slowly. "Raymond's reaction to this place makes me want to follow up for my own reasons. I hate how disconnected all these pieces seem right now—your hunch about the wells, the will itself, Boyd's outburst. So many things look slightly wrong, you know, just wrong enough to make me wonder. And there's Boyd's condition—I've never accepted the idea that he just went crazy."

"It happens."

Henry looked out into the horizon. "You have your intuitions, I have mine." He turned to her and said, "I've seen some crazy people. I'm not pretending to be an expert, but I think Boyd's different. I think he was pushed. If somehow it's all connected, maybe we could find the answer to his life along with everything else. That's something I would be willing to take a risk to do." He hesitated, looking over at the car. "He's lost now, adrift in his own mind. But being here obviously disturbed him. That must mean something." He turned to her. "So I guess I'm saying I have no objection to your digging in, as long as you keep me in the loop."

They had reached the car. Boyd was quiet, obediently taking his place in the back seat. "Let's go," Henry said after a moment. "Let's get the richest man in town back to his park bench."

Chapter Eighteen

It was nearly two by the time they got back to Council Grove. Boyd returned to Custer's Elm without incident, apparently none the worse for the trip. But the episode at the wells had left a mark on Henry; he had forgotten how agitated the man could become. Boyd had actually looked dangerous for a moment at the wells, flailing his arms about and crying to the sky.

Amanda headed off to Topeka, anxious to check into the geological surveys for the land. Henry was suddenly on his own, and his mind went to the Crandall place; if Roger was back from Topeka, giving him some kind of update couldn't be reasonably delayed any longer. Amanda's interest in the wells, however, he would keep to himself.

By the time Henry pulled into the U-shaped Crandall driveway the sun was just beginning to cast short shadows from behind the house, shooting light and dark across the eaves of the building into the front yard. Henry knocked on the door and Sarah answered it, dressed in black jeans and a pale yellow cotton blouse.

"Henry," she said, "Roger's out back. But come in for a second." Sarah led him to a breakfast table that looked out through a window onto the back side of the Crandall property. Henry could see Roger some distance away on horseback, working cattle with several ranch hands. Sarah offered him a cup of coffee, then poured one of her own.

"It's been a long time," she said, taking the seat across the table from him.

"Seven years."

"You don't get back much, Henry."

"I guess when I left it was final." He tried the coffee; it was black and hot, and he took another sip. "I wasn't the only one who shook the dust of this town off his feet. There's hardly a soul left from our class."

"It's been hard to watch. People move to the jobs."

"But not you. Didn't you ever want to leave?" It had always surprised Henry that Sarah hadn't got as far away from her controlling father and brother as possible. For one thing, it would have done her social life good; the assumption, mostly perpetrated by Roger, was that the Crandalls were too good for Council Grove. It had been especially hard for Sarah, because asking her out meant facing Tyler. Few in Council Grove had felt up to that task.

"It's not that I thought I couldn't leave," she answered. "I'm not my mother, you know."

"I wasn't implying anything."

She softened. "All right. I just didn't want you to think I was the helpless little farm girl. It was just different with me. I didn't need the work, but that wasn't it either. For some reason I keep on choosing to try and fix this life."

"What do you mean by that?"

He could feel her weighing the consequences of opening up. After a moment she said, "It comes down to getting a new life or staying to fix this one. I keep staying." She smiled softly. "You might have noticed my family isn't exactly in the best of shape."

"Go easy on yourself," Henry said. "I'm not sure one person can make a whole family right."

"All the same, I never stop thinking we could live together in peace somehow. It's been my little pipe dream. Of course, now it's too late, really." Her eyes moved past him, out through the window. "You know something I've never admitted to a soul?"

Henry's eyes followed hers, not sure he wanted to be Sarah's confessor. But he didn't doubt she needed someone; she could hardly take her feelings to Roger, and her mother was barely hanging on. "What's that?" he asked quietly.

"It's horrible, but the truth is I've tried to kill that feeling of believing sometimes, kill it dead."

"Why?"

She shrugged. "It must be easier to live without always thinking about how things could be better. You get tired of hoping, of wanting some image of how a family should be. You start wanting to give up."

"Maybe you were just trying to survive."

Sarah shook her head. "Everyone thinks I'm brave. No matter how bad things got, I always smiled and kept on going. Year after year, I was the rock. Both Daddy and Roger counted on me, you know."

Henry was genuinely surprised. "For what?"

Sarah looked down. "I've only just been able to admit this to myself. But I realize now I gave them the space to hate each other."

Henry fell silent; the stark intimacy of Sarah's confession was disconcerting. But whether because Tyler's controlling hand was gone or simply because her father's death had brought her emotions to the surface, she seemed determined to unload. "I would always intervene," she said. "I'd plead with them to stop fighting. I really believe they let their rage vent knowing that I would keep them from killing each other. Not literally, maybe. But things were said in this house . . ." She looked up. "Believe me, there were times I wanted to let them tear each other to pieces and be done with it. I wanted them to leave Mother and me in peace." She sighed. "There was worse than that in me, Henry. There were times I even wanted to turn rotten inside, like my father. I know what he was. But I couldn't do it. Believing is just a part of me."

Henry set down his cup. "Look, I really don't want to ask this, but I'm glad you brought up your mother." He paused, feeling the weight of the question. "Were there problems between your parents? Marriage problems?"

Sarah accepted the question without surprise. "Not like you mean," she said, staring into her coffee. "Their whole relationship fits into one sentence: She was the obedient wife."

"So nothing rocked the boat between them."

"Everything revolved around Daddy. He was the great provider, the lord of everything. You live with a strong man like that, after a while your life doesn't make sense without him." She frowned. "Of course, it didn't make sense with him either. She just shut down, bit by bit. She was so different when I was a girl, so much brighter. But Daddy changed during that time, too."

"How?"

"Something was on his mind a lot near the end," she replied. "His shell was cracking a little."

"What do you mean?"

"Less confident, I guess. You won't believe this, but there were times I think he almost looked scared. But only to us. I don't think anybody around town could have noticed it."

Henry paused, thinking. "Any idea what was behind it?"

She shook her head. "You couldn't talk to him about it, of course. He would have just turned on that stone face and made you feel like a fool." She smiled. "He was so hard on Mother. It's ironic that losing him has finally done her in."

"I know," Henry said quietly. "She doesn't look good."

"She's fifty-six, Henry. And helpless." She turned her face away. "And if Roger contests the will . . ."

"Maybe he won't," Henry said.

She smiled sadly. "Can we change the subject?"

"Of course."

"It's not just Daddy who's changed, you know. Look at you." She poured him more coffee, a thoughtful look on her face. "You know," she said, "I gave you quite a lot of thought back then, when we were in school. You probably had no idea."

"We didn't talk much that last year."

"I even kept up with you when you left. I was impressed when you went to seminary."

Henry suppressed a frown; Council Grove was the one place on earth where what had happened during that time was common knowledge. "It didn't end very impressively," he said.

Sarah nodded. "You know, Henry, all this talk makes me feel old. It started at the funeral. Lately I feel like I've been alive a million years."

"It's grief," Henry said. "It ages you."

She looked up at him and said, "I'm only twenty-seven, Henry. How can I not be young?"

Henry greeted territory with which he was painfully familiar. "When a parent dies your youth dies with them. It doesn't matter if you're twelve when it happens. You see your own mortality, and the second you see that, you're not a child anymore."

"Pastor Chambers came by after Daddy died. I thought what he said would help, but it hasn't."

Henry shrugged. "Does that surprise you?"

"No. But I could use some comfort." She smiled. "I still think you would have made a good preacher, Henry."

Henry looked down at his coffee, dark and impenetrable. "I lacked the essential ingredient."

"What's that?"

"Faith," he said simply. "The one thing a preacher can't do without."

"You just need to find it again."

"I don't want to find it again."

Sarah shook her head. "If you ever had any, you still do. It's not something you put on and take off like a coat. I already told you I tried to kill my own, and I couldn't do it. It just stayed in me, still believing."

"Maybe I'm the exception."

She regarded him silently a moment, then took a deep breath. "And now, my final act of believing. Just as futile as the others, but as usual, I can't help it."

"What's that?"

"Henry, I'm glad about the will."

Henry set down his coffee. "You can't be serious."

Sarah nodded. "If the will had gone as planned, wouldn't everything be the same, only worse? Roger would take Daddy's place. And would we ever figure out how to love one another, how to take care of each other? And we're all we have, Henry. I'm not kidding myself about that. I told you that Pastor Chambers came out here after Daddy died. I didn't tell you that he was the only one who came."

"I'm sorry, Sarah. My God, after all these years."

"It's all right," she said quietly. "I'm not surprised. I know we're hated. But it makes Roger's big act so horrible. We're completely alone. That's the unspoken truth that hangs over our heads here."

Henry hesitated, trying to process her words. "Do you actually believe this was some desperate gamble by your father to bring you all together?"

Sarah shook her head. "No," she said doubtfully. "If Daddy had wanted that, he could have started it a long time ago. I only know that if that will had been what everybody expected, it would have been the death of this family."

"You have a gift to see any good in this."

She smiled grimly. "Or maybe it's a curse, the curse of not knowing when to give up." She laughed, and a trace of bitterness filtered through her voice. "It's like Daddy always told Roger. *I guess there's a lot of things you'd change if you was king of the world.* He was right about that, wasn't he? In spite of how he meant it?" She let her fingers entwine in the fabric of her collar. "But we're not kings of this world. It was just a saying." She stood, forcing herself to brighten. Her face had colored, and Henry wondered if she was suddenly embarrassed to have shared so much. "Now go see Roger," she said. "It looks like he's wrapping up out there." She smiled her melancholy smile again, and looking at her, Henry could hardly believe she was Roger's sister. Living in that house had left its inevitable marks on her, but she had somehow managed to hang on to some genuine grace. To have done so in the face of those two men was a brave accomplishment.

Sarah led him out through the back door, squeezing his hand good-bye. Henry walked toward the cattle pens some distance away, admiring the rolling expanse of land that stretched out from the back fence to the horizon; it was prime cattle land, capable of sustaining one head every two acres. The land fell gently away from the homestead, making a huge, shallow cup a mile and a half across. Sixty yards from the house was a series of working pens, the grass pounded into dirt from the constant traffic of cattle and cowboys. Crandall and his hands were running young bulls—Angus yearlings, dark red like Oklahoma clay. Their commotion raised a small whirlwind of dust and dirt. Henry could see Roger on horseback herding a group of ten or so into one of the pens, a system designed to trap cattle one at a time for polling, castration, or any examinations by the vet. The pen was built in a V shape, wide at the entrance and increasingly narrow at the back. The narrow part of the pen led into the trap, a set of restraints that held a single animal firmly in place, locking onto its head and collapsing down onto its sides. Roger pushed the little herd toward the narrow end, until at last one young bull turned into the trap, and three ranch hands immediately clamped the metal pipes hard around his neck and body. The bull bellowed wildly, struggling uselessly against the bars.

Roger saw Henry as he approached, nodded, but didn't speak. He walked casually up to the yearling in the trap and picked up a huge set of shears built like the tools firemen use to cut through door handles. Taking his place near the head of the bull, he placed the cutting edge of the shears on one of the bull's small horns and, pulling the handles together, sliced through the horn just above the hairline. The bull called out, a voice full of dull resentment and unfocused anger at the intrusion. He began bucking, actually knocking a ranch hand off his perch above the trap. As he bucked, the animal got a front leg caught in between the bars of the side restraints, agitating him further. One of the ranch hands said, "Mr. Crandall, we better let him out. We leave him in there and he's gonna break a leg."

A hand moved toward the handles to release the chute, but Crandall, looking straight at Henry, said, "We'll never get him back in the trap now. He'll be wary. Hold your ground." Roger moved to the other side of the bull and attempted to position the shears on the remaining horn. This proved difficult, as the bull was now fully enraged, and even with the restraints was moving violently. Henry held his breath; it was obvious that the bull's leg would be broken at any second. Roger grappled with the shears, his own face red with effort and irritation. "Stand still, damn you," he yelled, and at that moment he pulled the shears together with all his might. Henry blanched; the shears partially missed their mark, cutting cleanly through half the horn but tearing through the remainder, creating a gash on the animal that immediately began bleeding profusely. Roger cursed loudly and barked instructions to the hands, all of whom were older and clearly more experienced in handling cattle. "Let the son of a bitch out," he yelled at last, and with a violent struggle the bull freed himself, miraculously keeping his legs intact. With a final, enraged bellow he ran through the herd with blood and sweat flying from his head, dispersing it back to the far end of the pen.

"We'll have to paint that cut, Mr. Crandall," one of the hands said. "It'll infect without it."

"I know that," Crandall said harshly, turning toward Henry and heading back to the house. "You catch him," he added over his shoulder. "I got a meeting."

Henry walked with Roger to the house, mounting the stairs to the back porch. He was appalled at the episode with the bull. He wasn't squeamish; he had been present at everything from artificial insemination to breech births. But those procedures should be handled professionally, minimizing the pain to the animal. It was pure ego that had driven Roger to handle the delicate polling process, and that ego had caused the young bull a great deal of agony. More important, it had cost Roger the respect of his ranch crew. Henry frowned; that process was likely to continue. In Roger's vain, desperate attempts to project his authority, he was likely to cause a great deal of havoc all over Cheney County, and not just on animals.

Roger led Henry through the back door of the house into the mud-room, a utility area at the back of the house. Henry stood a distance away as Roger sat on a low bench and pulled his boots off. Crandall's arms were spattered with blood from the bull, and he washed it off in a big metal sink at one end of the room.

"What happened to your lip?" Henry asked. "You got quite a pop there."

"Bull ran me into a fence," Roger said over his shoulder. "Right before you got here. But I got him for it." He rubbed a towel over his face and the back of his neck. Turning, he looked at Henry stoically, ignoring the ugly scene of the past several minutes. "I'm going back to Topeka tomorrow late. Got business up there. Be back Monday, maybe Tuesday."

"I'm sorry to hear that. We may need to talk."

"Don't see as there's much to talk about," Roger stated. "Look, Math-ews, I'm not going to drag this out. The truth is I went to Topeka this morning to get myself a lawyer. I gotta look after my own interests."

Roger's words were no surprise; Henry had been expecting this. If Amanda's vague suspicions panned into something real, it would certainly be better that way, in the end. But for another reason, he deeply regretted hearing Roger's words; Sheldon Parker had made it clear that any more complications spelled the end of his own time on the case. Roger's decision would probably bring that ending about, which frustrated Henry immensely. He had played a complicated game of controlling information, gaining time, and hoping for answers before Parker pulled the plug. That game was now probably obsolete. "All right, Roger," he said, hiding his disappointment. "I hope you got yourself a good one, because I have the feeling you're going to need it."

"It's Frank Hesston. Carl Durand set it up."

"Durand?" *The ghost in the machine.*

"Durand's been a friend to this family for more than twenty-five years, which is more than I can say for you. Whoever he recommends is fine by me. He's got no feelings for Boyd, that's for damn sure."

"Are you saying Durand knows Boyd, Roger?"

"I didn't say that," Roger snapped. "I'm just sayin' Durand is for me. And he says go with Hesston, and that's good enough. Anyway, it's all set. We met in Durand's office this morning. Hesston says I should contest. He says I can win."

Hearing Durand's name again so soon after his talk with Amanda lit up

Henry's brain. He looked at Roger's split lip, examining it more closely. *He's lying about that. It's several hours old.* "Have Hesston call me," he said. "I'm still the executor of the estate."

"For now," Roger said darkly. "One thing I've already learned, executors can be removed. I've got a feeling you'll be back in Chicago to stay, Mathews. Your time down here is short."

Probably right, and Sheldon Parker will save you the trouble of petitioning the court. Henry rose, but felt little anger toward Roger for his insult; Roger Crandall, he decided, was nothing but a small-town bully in a tight spot, and he didn't have time to worry about people like that. Things would work out however they did, that was all. And if Amanda's vague suspicions turned out to bear fruit, nobody could predict how things would change. "I'll expect Hesston's call," he said. "We'll proceed from there." He turned and walked out of the room.

Henry knew his obligation to call Parker was absolute. Sheldon had demanded instant updates whenever his situation changed substantively, and Roger's obtaining legal counsel, however inevitable, certainly represented such a change. But still he hesitated. He had driven back over to the motel in two minds, fatigued with his indecision. He looked at his watch: it was Saturday, and he would have to catch Parker at home. But it was likely that his next conversation with Parker about the Crandall will would be his last. The situation had deteriorated from day one, devolving by stages into what would shortly be a frozen legal muddle. Now, with Roger's decision, the chaos was complete. There was no longer any real way to justify his continuing involvement in so messy and time-consuming a case. He would call. He would explain everything, Parker would lower the boom, and he would be on a plane, back to his real life. On Monday he would be filing briefs for Technologies Enterprises.

And where does that leave Boyd? The words formed in his brain, unbidden. Henry knew of Hesston; well known in the state, he had actually come as a guest speaker to law school while Henry was attending. He was superbly connected in state politics and on intimate terms with every district judge in the state. *Against whom,* Henry imagined, *some hapless, court-appointed legal hack will be sacrificially pitted on behalf of one Raymond Boyd. It shouldn't take long. A day, maybe two. The strong will eat the weak, because the strong have better lawyers. Raymond will be off to the funny farm, and Roger can take over Council Grove like everyone expects. The order of the universe will be restored.*

Henry opened his suitcase and threw a shirt into it. *And after a year or so, nobody will remember who Raymond Boyd was. No one will care about what really happened to him, or whether or not he was entitled to that money. Whatever secrets lay behind that will will go with him to be locked into a state mental health truck, transported to some godforsaken ward of a godforsaken mental hospital.*

Henry sat on the bed and stared at the bedstand. He opened the drawer and pulled out a Gideon Bible, a graceless, cardboard-covered black lump. *And no more shrill sermons, no passionate, exquisite prophecies. No more visions of divine justice. Twenty-four hours after they take him, the fire that burned so brightly in Raymond Boyd's belly and brain will be extinguished, dulled to sleep by drugs and endless boredom. Just the silence of the injection, the nurse-enforced stillness. Just the dark of a tiny hospital room, possibly for the rest of his life.*

He opened the book, letting his gaze fall on the pages. He hadn't read a verse since the day he left seminary. Joshua. Ruth. Hosea. Ezekiel. He began to read absently, flipping pages; the words comforted him, their liturgical formality settling his mind. He read for a few minutes, using the pages as an excuse to avoid calling Parker. *This is what the Lord says: On that day thoughts will come into your mind and you will devise an evil scheme.* He stopped; *an evil scheme.* Those were Boyd's exact words at the well. *So it wasn't just babbling,* he thought. He read on, but for some time nothing else connected. Then, several verses later, he saw, *I will execute judgment upon him with plague and bloodshed; I will pour down torrents of rain, hailstones, and burning sulfur.* Henry sat up on the bed. Had Boyd simply chosen the verses at random, attracted by their apocalyptic nature? *Torrents of rain, hailstones, and burning sulfur.* Amanda had said that sulfur was the most dangerous thing about a well. Was it possible that Boyd had something truly destructive within him?

Henry stared at the phone, letting the cost of answering that question settle into him. Parker wouldn't give a damn about obscure Scripture references. He wouldn't give a damn about intuitions. What Parker gave a damn about was his own ass and his own remarkable bonus checks, the maintenance of which required Henry's presence. He would demand Henry's return, and the inevitable result of disobeying that command would be Henry's career. That was the choice. He could forget about Raymond Boyd, or he could write off two years' work at the firm. Henry picked up the phone in his room, looking blankly at the numbers. *No one to remember,* he thought. Out loud, to the empty room, he said, "I'll remember you, Raymond Boyd. I'll remember your fire and brimstone to my dying day."

Henry mechanically filled Sheldon in on what had happened in the case, including Amanda's suspicions about the Crandall wells. He had no doubt as to the eventual outcome. Parker listened attentively, asking questions and making sure he had all the facts. Then, in one short, dispassionate statement, he said the inevitable.

"You're out, Preacher," he said simply. Henry listened to the silence that followed on the phone; Parker, having made his proclamation, evidently felt nothing more was left to be said.

"Sheldon, I don't need to remind you that I'm on my own vacation time."

Parker's voice was unconcerned. "Nope, you don't. Got a great memory. Came in handy in law school."

"And you're saying your decision's final."

"Of course." He paused. "Look, to humor you, it wouldn't have mattered what you said happened. I was going to call you anyway. As of late yesterday afternoon, the whole Centel Technologies thing has officially blown up. As in *boom*."

"What happened?"

"You remember the nature of the takeover—it was hostile, in every sense of the word. Well, now it's turned into an SEC thing. The original owners smell a rat, and they're calling out the rat catchers."

"Is there anything to it?"

Henry could almost hear Sheldon's smile. "What difference does it make?" Parker answered lightly. "We have our client, the rats. They're paying us four hundred bucks an hour to see things their way. I personally have no problem with that." There was a pause, and then he asked, "Tell me, Henry, do you have a problem with that?"

Henry held the phone quietly, understanding perfectly the significance of Parker's question. It went to the heart of his job, and in reality his future with the firm. Every man for himself, and let the courts decide. If your client's guilty, make sure he doesn't tell you about it, then defend him to the death. If you're on the other side, well, in the end it didn't really matter what side you were on. The fees were the same.

Parker's voice broke into his thoughts. "Preacher, I like you. So I'll tell you something. It's like I learned in church . . . how's it go? 'It's not my will that any should be lost,' something like that, right?"

Henry, still holding the Bible, was surprised by Parker's words. "Didn't picture you a churchgoing man, Sheldon."

"Altar boy," Parker said. "Long time ago. But like I said, I got a good memory. And right now I'm Jesus H. Christ Himself, with a message from on high. And I'm telling you to be careful, 'cause I don't want you to be lost, understand? And lost you will be if you don't haul your ass back to Chicago tomorrow."

Henry paused, feeling every second passing as a dangerous eternity. "I see," he said quietly.

"There's nothing personal here, Preacher. This is fifteen years of legal experience talking. If your friend Amanda is right about some small-town oil scandal, and I'll just add here that I personally think it's a crock of shit and you're letting your Johnson do your thinking for you, you're entering deep into criminal territory. In that case the best thing for you to do is contact the district attorney on your way out of town, protecting the valuable name of Wilson, Lougherby and Mathers as you go. Meantime, whatever few dollars that estate was worth are going to go up in smoke, courtesy of back taxes and penalties to our friends at the IRS. We'll be lucky to get our current fees out of it. Meanwhile I have real problems back here, and I can't spare you another day. Hell, I can't spare you another hour, but I can't figure out how to get you out of there before morning. Now, Suzie's going to book you on the twelve-fifteen tomorrow from Kansas City. That'll give you plenty of time to drive in and make the plane. You'll be in the office by three, and I have the rest of the afternoon cleared for you." He stopped for a moment, and added, "I know it'll be Sunday, but we billed a half million in legal fees on the Centel sale, for which the buyers expect to be bulletproof. For that kind of money we don't have days of the week. I don't intend to disappoint them. You don't have any option, Henry. I'm ordering you to come back. Now."

With his instructions given, Parker's voice lightened. "Gotta go, Preacher. The new board of Centel Technologies is in the conference room looking at Suzie's ass until I get there. I figure her ass is worth about ten minutes, tops. So I'm outta here. She'll pick you up at the airport."

"I'll be there," Henry said dully.

"Good," Parker answered. "Don't miss the plane, Henry. You've had a nice little vacation, but your grace is all used up."

Henry didn't have to reply; a dial tone followed Sheldon's statement, leaving Henry holding a dead phone.

Henry looked out the large picture window of his motel room. *So Elaine will get her wish. I'll see her moment of triumph after all.* He would have to call Amanda, but resisted it for the moment; hearing her voice would just make it worse. In spite of how short a time they had known each other, he thought he knew what she would say. She would understand, and she would be grateful for the help he had managed to give. His leaving would complicate things for her enormously, but he had no doubt she would do everything she could to keep going. Life was different for her, a battle between good and evil that she fought with everything in her. But it was already too late for him; twenty-eight years old, already entrenched in a life that seemed beyond changing. He would go back to Chicago. He would make partner in six or seven grueling years, senior partner in five more, and then get fat and rich. He stared out the window; the sun was setting across the big back field, dropping into the nothingness below a large, open alfalfa field. It looked so quiet through the glass, so thoroughly peaceful. The tips of the alfalfa breathed back and forth in the breeze, and a part of him wanted to sit quietly there forever, decisions permanently suspended, nothing good or bad happening, just quiet uneventfulness. He wanted the country life to sink back into him, the simplicity, the slow turning of days. Chicago suddenly seemed to him unnatural, a blur of motion. The energy of the place, which he normally loved, seemed oppressive to him in that moment, and he found he was reluctant to return. This time would be over, and the fury and pace of the place would take him over again, maybe not immediately, but soon. A month from now he wouldn't even remember the differences. He would have been assimilated once again, taken up by a power bigger than himself that pushed and shoved and brainwashed and never stopped to rest, even in the dark of night. He wanted to push that time away. But instead, he turned his back to the window and began to pack.

Chapter Nineteen

The phone rang an hour later. Henry recognized Amanda's voice at once.

"I've got news," she was saying, "and I wanted to fill you in as soon as possible."

"All right."

"I've found a geologist who's interested in the Crandall ranch. He knows the area inside out, and when I told him about the extruded limestone he agreed to come out and examine the well sites."

"Wonderful."

"So all I need is to set it up with you and Raymond."

"I see."

Amanda's excited voice ground to a stop, dragged down by Henry's flat responses. "You don't sound very pleased."

"I'm going back to Chicago, Amanda. I've been called back to the firm. There's nothing I can do about it."

There was a moment's silence, and Henry could almost feel Amanda's enthusiasm draining away. "When do you leave?" she asked quietly.

"First thing in the morning. I'm sorry about it. Very sorry."

"What happened?"

"Another case has gone critical, something with a lot more zeros involved. The Crandall case is a luxury the firm can't afford any longer."

There was a silence, and Amanda said, "I was just getting used to the idea of having someone on my side for a change."

"If it helps any, I'm as disappointed as you are. The idea of leaving Raymond to the wolves is killing me. I pushed as hard as I could, but things were made pretty clear. If I'm not on the plane to Chicago tomorrow, it's my job."

"It's so ironic," Amanda said, and there was real disappointment in her voice.

"Why do you say that?"

"You were the break I needed on my case. But I got the feeling you were hoping I was the break you needed on yours, too. It fit so perfectly."

"I know. So what are you going to do? Roger will never let you bring a geologist on the land."

"I don't know. Find some other way. Or not. Stay home and drink. Something. Anything."

Henry paused, and said, "You know, I have the feeling you wouldn't have made my choice."

"Between staying to protect Boyd and your job?"

"That's right."

"I don't know what I would do. I can't be in your shoes."

"I know what you would have done. And it disappoints me that I'm not doing the same thing."

"It's all right. Protecting Raymond's not worth your job."

"You don't believe that."

There was a silence, and after a moment she said, "No, I don't." Before Henry could speak she added, "But look, Henry, you've already described my problem. Fatal desire to save somebody. Joan of Arc complex, remember? You're lucky you don't have it."

"I remember." Henry paused, and said, "I had the feeling we were becoming friends. I'm sorry we won't have the chance to do that now."

The silence after his statement lasted a long time. "Me, too."

The flight back to O'Hare ran ahead of schedule, a stiff tailwind defying Henry's longing to delay the moment he would be thrust back into his Chicago life. He had tried to sleep, seeking an escape from his ambivalence. But closing his eyes only brought the characters in Council Grove forward in his mind, highlighting them in his inner darkness. He saw Boyd, grizzled and fractured; Roger, so ready to take matters into his own hands; Sarah, desperately trying to keep her family intact; Ellen, bitter and concupiscent, a keeper of secrets. Behind them all floated Tyler Crandall, unreachable and silent. And now the possibility of Carl Durand's involvement, although that was little more than Amanda's premonition. He wanted to discount that, if for no other reason than her understandable dislike of the man. But when he thought of Amanda he didn't see an overly emotional woman on a vendetta; instead he saw a kind of crusader, relentlessly believing in her causes.

They had spent only a brief time together, but her image came to him easily, with surprising clarity. He was jealous of her, in a way; she had what he himself had possessed and then lost: real passion for battle, and the belief that somehow one had to fight even if there was no winning. And not blind passion; she felt her defeats to the core, their last conversation had shown that. But even after defeat there would always be another battle, and another, and another, and for people like her, that was the glory and the power of the thing.

Thoughts of Amanda led him inevitably to Elaine. He fought off a moment of self-revulsion at his own inconstancy. He ordered a drink and sipped it thoughtfully, feeling his dilemma. He couldn't go around falling for women wherever he went. *Falling for women.* Was that what he had done? He hadn't put it that way to himself before that moment. *Yes. Falling. Or would have, if I had spent much more time with her.* For whatever reason, he was vulnerable. He wasn't the playboy type; monogamy wasn't the huge stretch it seemed to be for the other young lawyers at the firm. The surprising, painful reality was that it was possible he didn't love Elaine. *Not love the most beautiful, ambitious woman I have ever known?* He let the thought surface, assuming it would vanish as quickly as it came. But minutes passed, and it gained strength, refusing to release him. *If not love, then what?* The question deserved an answer; he couldn't cast away a year-and-a-half investment on a whim. He leaned back in his seat, letting the first word he thought about Elaine materialize. It was disappointingly clinical: admiration. *Yes,* he thought. *Admiration.* She had succeeded in a world just as competitive as his, and he knew what that took. *Is that all? A year and a half, just to admire her?* He closed his eyes again. *Lust, absolutely. From the first second, lust.* That was better; at least it was human and romantic. Her naked form took shape in his mind, and he felt the familiar stirring. But as quickly as she appeared, the insufficiency of the thing pressed in on him. Before Amanda, admiration and lust could have passed quite easily for love—he was certain it was doing so with half the people he knew. But the idea of something more was alive now, glimmering with possibility. To love a woman's core, not for what she had accomplished or her sexual appetite but just for *her,* that was what he wanted now. He knew his picture of Amanda was idealized, but wasn't that the fuel of every new relationship? Given the chance, he couldn't promise not to rush headlong into what he suspected was deeper than what he could ever have with Elaine. And if that was true, Elaine deserved to know it. Their plans for each other were too far along to ignore a self-discovery like that.

Resolved, he began to form the words in his mind, searching for a way to explain what had happened. He was surprised to find he wasn't emotional about it, and then, with a shock, he realized that he didn't expect Elaine to be either. In that moment what there really was between them coalesced in his mind with perfect, sudden clarity; they had been so objectively right for each other, neither of them had actually stopped to fall in love. They hadn't stopped for anything, when he thought about it. There was always a pressure to be more, to race with and against each other up a ladder of success that he was already suspecting had no end. Their relationship had been just one more piece of a comprehensive plan for success for both of them. Sooner or later, someone would touch Elaine in the way that Amanda had touched him, and when he did, she was sure to respond.

It was strange, seeing it all so clearly, so instantly, without the typical scenes and breakdowns a relationship normally went through in its devolution. The idea that he would part from Elaine came to his mind fully formed, inevitable and uncontestable.

The plane landed with a harsh jolt. Henry pulled himself together and entered the terminal, instantly submerged in an ocean of frenetic noise. After the decompression of Council Grove the chaos surprised him; he looked around, expecting to see a throng in some dispute. But the terminal was no more crowded than usual on Sundays. The typical thrumming sound of humanity had simply grown louder to him after a week in the plains. Around him Spanish, Japanese, and English swirled, converging in his ear into one unintelligible babble. He grasped his briefcase and headed toward the moving sidewalk that led to the baggage claim area. As he approached it, he found himself suddenly enthralled by its monotonous, circular motion. Somehow, he didn't want to get on; its motorized, unthinking obedience repulsed him. He turned to step away, but a group of loud teenagers brushed by him, four boys dressed in urban uniforms, their baseball caps turned backward, wearing untucked T-shirts, their out-sized pants slung low over slim hips. Henry stepped back quickly to avoid being run over. One of the group, a boy of about sixteen, turned and looked directly at Henry as he pushed brusquely past. The boy was brown and muscular, hard and streetwise. He was laughing, a razor-edged accent that cut across the minute space between them. Then he was gone, receding into the distance with his friends. Henry watched the boys vanish into the crowded terminal, feeling inconsolably like a stranger. At the boy's age Henry was playing Babe Ruth League baseball and riding the Millers' tractor across enormous, empty fields. Seeing the boy made Henry realize something that had never occurred to him before that moment: he was a stranger in this town, nothing but a visitor looking across a chasm that no law degree or job could bridge. *Preacher* they called him at the firm, and that was a lie, because he couldn't preach what he didn't believe anymore. But they were right to call him a name from the past; they knew him to be an outsider, and the name branded him as such.

Henry closed his eyes and stepped onto the moving sidewalk. He was halfway down it when a female voice shattered his thoughts. "Mr. Math-ews," it said, the voice impossibly close. He opened his eyes; Suzie was walking briskly beside him on the main hallway, puffing to keep up.

"Mr. Mathews," she repeated. "Are you dreaming? You went right past me. I had to race to catch up to you."

"What?" he asked, surprised. "I didn't hear you."

"You were in another world."

"Sorry," Henry said quickly. "I forgot Sheldon sent you."

"Mr. Parker wanted me to deliver you personally. He didn't want you waiting."

Henry frowned and instinctively began walking, speeding up the motorized pace. "I take it Sheldon's stressing."

Suzie made a face. "Like you wouldn't believe," she said. "It's Centel. He's called everybody in, even though it's Sunday. I heard Mr. Parker talking to some of the other staff attorneys, and it was pretty ugly. I'm kind of worried about him, to tell you the truth."

"Good old B.H.," Henry said. "Nobody with a trust fund his size can ever really worry, Suzie."

"So he told you the B.H. story at last? Well, you set a record."

"What do you mean?"

Suzie shrugged. "Mr. Parker always gives his young attorneys the B.H. lecture sooner or later. The ones that don't stick around get it sooner. The hard workers get it later."

"It's very motivational," Henry said. "I certainly got the message."

Henry had carried his baggage on, and Suzie led the way to her car. They pulled out onto the loop for the trip downtown. There was a huge legal brief waiting for him in the car, and Henry reviewed the last week's events silently while Suzie drove. Sheldon was right to be concerned; the original owners of the company were threatening a formal complaint with the SEC, and the mere rumor of that action had sent the stock down 7 percent in a single day. TE representatives had put a bold face on it, making a categorical denial of any wrongdoing. Nevertheless, they had been forced to suspend trading on their stock after the free fall. If the company were to survive, it was essential that good news precede the reopening. Centel, the object of the takeover, was only a two-hundred-and-fifty-million-dollar company, tiny by Wall Street standards. But the Street had seen much smaller companies grow into billion-dollar giants in a matter of a few months. There was a lot riding on the case, and Wilson, Lougherby and Mathers was entrusted to make things right.

Henry walked into the firm conference room without knocking, Suzie pushing him along. He was dropped into a near-shouting match between Parker and a man Henry didn't recognize. Henry blinked and looked around; about fifteen people were sitting around the big walnut table, all in expensive suits and looking extremely serious.

"Henry," Parker said, seeing him enter. "Sit down and we'll catch you up." He glanced at the others. "This is Henry Mathews," he said, "young, but the brightest kid on the team." Henry walked along the table to an empty chair, feeling hostility from the other, highly competitive attorneys lining the table.

"Gentlemen," he said, taking his seat and opening his briefcase. "I read the brief on the way in, Sheldon. But I still don't understand the basis for the complaint."

"That's because there is no goddam basis for the complaint!" an extravagantly dressed man across the table shouted. "And the reason there's no basis for a complaint is that we paid you people a hell of a lot of money to make sure of it." He stared at Henry as if he were looking at a spoiled piece of meat.

Henry smiled his most calming, nonthreatening smile. "Sheldon," he said carefully, "would you like to bring me up to speed?"

"Henry Mathews, meet Bob Kramp," Sheldon said. "President of Technology Enterprises, the entity we constructed to buy Centel. You'll meet the others as we go along. Here's the short version. We put together a contract for Bob and TE to buy Centel from its founders, as you know. The deal was complex; options, performance equations, cash, stock, you know the drill. There's always the potential for problems, but the contract specifically indemnifies our clients from any legal recourse on the matter."

"So what's the problem?"

"For starters, the original owners expected to be kept on in their management positions," Sheldon said. "After the sale, however, Bob and his partners felt the company would be better served with new leadership. So they let them go."

Henry paused; the contract was vast, but he had seen the provision for the owners to keep their positions and yearly salaries. But he could think of no tactful way to bring the fact up. Instead he asked, "Why not buy them out of their contracts? It would be pennies compared to what's happening on the Street."

Kramp mumbled something unintelligible, but Henry could hardly have missed its hostile tone. Parker said, "That's not an option, Henry. We have to come up with something else."

Henry paused; his solution was so sensible he couldn't understand why it wasn't immediately received. In fact, it seemed impossible that it wouldn't have already occurred to everyone in the room. The twenty or thirty million it would take to buy the executives out of their contracts was cheap compared with the bloodletting that was happening to the stock. "I'm not sure I understand," he said cautiously. "It seems like a logical solution."

Across the desk, Bob Kramp was beginning to tremble. At first, Henry thought he was seeing simple anger. But as the man slowly lost control, he saw something else: fear. *Something's going on here*, Henry thought, *something everyone's dancing around.* At last Kramp could take it no longer. He blurted, "It's not a logical solution because we've already tried buying them out and they won't accept."

Henry was genuinely surprised. "All right, but I can't see how they have a legal basis to refuse. If they want to take us to court over that, they're dead in the water. There are hundreds of precedents to voiding employment contracts with buyouts. We would win in a walk. At any rate, even a courtroom is better than an SEC investigation."

Parker and Kramp exchanged glances, Kramp at last nodding his head with irritation for Parker to speak. "The thing is," Sheldon said quietly, "getting canned isn't the only issue."

Henry perked up; Parker was finally getting to the real heart of the matter. He waited for more, but Parker was hesitating. Henry watched him carefully; Sheldon was rarely at a loss for words. The silence in the room was stifling. After a moment Henry asked, "I take it there's a difficult issue here?"

Parker smiled. "Just a little touchy. Technology Enterprises wasn't the first group to try to buy Centel. Orion tried a hostile takeover a year earlier and failed."

"I know Orion," Henry said. "Four-billion-dollar-a-year hard-drive company. They've got the OEM contracts for three of the largest computer companies in the world. Stock's getting hammered lately, for some reason."

"Right," Parker said. "It was messy, but Centel paid dearly, fought it out and turned them away. Lots of blood on the tracks. TE made a similar offer that was accepted, mainly because the owners didn't perceive it as a consolidation of the industry. They're fanatical about their little company, and they didn't want to be swallowed by a giant. Well, it turns out that Bob and his partners are in the process of selling Centel's core technology to Orion at this moment. It contains some rather revolutionary ways of storing data that have the potential to turn the hard-drive industry upside down. You can imagine that the original owners aren't very happy."

Henry considered; if Centel posessed a breakthrough like Sheldon was describing, the value to a company like Orion would be immense. It would also, however, destroy the company. It was an undeniably quick turn-around, but not unheard of; in the 1980s companies were routinely bought and dismantled if the buyers could turn a quick profit on the individual parts. The original company inevitably suffered, and the tactic had always seemed morally repugnant to Henry. But it wasn't illegal. And it didn't explain why Bob Kramp was sweating bullets across the table from him. Looking around the room, he could see that there was something more to come. "I can see why they're upset," he said, "but I think we're on firm footing. Let them take us to court. You're the owners of the company now, and if you want to sell to Orion, I don't see what they can do about it. A company like that obviously has the money."

Parker shifted uncomfortably in his seat. "Tiny problem is, there appears to be something of an overlap."

"Overlap?" Henry had never seen Sheldon so uncomfortable.

"In the timing. It seems that a sort of document has surfaced."

"A document that we dispute utterly," Kramp said intently. He was really sweating now; Henry could hardly keep his eyes off the moisture beading up on his forehead.

"Of course, Bob," Sheldon said calmly. "We all know it's a fake. But the thing is, this document dates talks about Centel between TE and Orion precedent to the sale. It calls into question, in fact, whether or not TE and Orion aren't connected in some way."

"An outright forgery," Kramp growled, openly hostile. "Goddam liars."

"What do you mean, 'connected'?" Henry asked.

"A construct of Orion's in the first place," Parker said limply. "A way to hide its identity."

Henry looked at Kramp, then back at Parker. If the document was true, Technology Enterprises would be nothing but a front for the much larger and more public Orion, an elaborate means of reattacking the company without revealing the real buyers. It meant that Kramp and his partners were possibly guilty of fraud. "Before?" he asked quietly.

"Nothing's proved, of course," Parker said. "But it does create a situation."

"Who's seen the document?" Henry asked.

"Nobody, yet," Parker answered. "It came as a fax. An Orion number, so it's internal."

Which gives it validity, Henry thought. Aloud he said, "I see your problem."

"A problem with a time bomb attached," Kramp said.

Henry turned. "How so?"

Parker coughed softly and said, "We received another fax today. A different Orion number, but obviously the same leak. It says that the documents are going to *The Wall Street Journal* in ten days unless we give them their company back."

"And when that happens nobody's going to give a damn about Centel's stock," Kramp exploded, "because they'll be too busy watching Orion's vanish. And that's over sixteen billion worldwide, so . . . Jesus . . ."

Henry stared hard at Kramp; he saw the picture clearly now. The real issue was that if Orion were found to have fraudulently obtained Centel, Orion's own stock would be decimated. And the level of concern that Kramp was showing over Orion's stock price meant that his interest was more than just passing; it was intensely personal. He had no doubt that Kramp held a substantial amount of Orion, which pushed him further over the legal edge. "I see," Henry said quietly. He looked at Sheldon, waiting for his partner to say the obvious. If the document was a lie, then there was only one course of action: face it down. Once the facts came out the situation would right itself. If the document was true, however, the men sitting opposite them had violated dozens of securities regulations and were common criminals. At a minimum they would be fined millions, and could possibly serve time. Henry had to assume that Wilson, Lougherby and Mathers couldn't possibly represent them knowing that fact. He sneaked a glance at Parker; his partner was certainly an enterprising man, but he had to assume that willingly representing crooks was beyond even his ambition. He needed to believe it, because, having worked on the original sale, the firm could well have been dragged into the crime itself. Technology Enterprises wasn't a real company in the traditional sense; it existed only on paper, a legal construction of the law firm so that the sale could be made. Any improprieties meant that the firm itself was in up to its neck. Parker didn't look as surprised by things as Henry would have preferred. "Do they want something?" Henry asked. "I mean, this is a kind of blackmail, right?" Parker leaned back in his chair and refused to look at him. "What are the terms?" Henry asked, pressing. "What do they want to go away?"

"There aren't any terms," Parker said at last. "Just give them back the company. That's it."

Henry looked at Kramp; the man's face was an utter stone wall now, implacable. "Then there's only one thing to do," Henry said. "Face down whoever this guy is. Call his bluff. Since it's a lie, he can't prove it's true." He smiled hopefully. "You'll probably end up making a pile of money."

Kramp leaned forward. "What are you talking about?"

"Simple. First you go public with the accusation. The stock will fall on the speculation. It's inevitable, and it will be painful in the short-term. But it's also an opportunity. You buy in at the low, demonstrating your confidence in the eventual outcome. You're telling the truth, and you're backing it with your own money. The Street will watch, and when the truth comes out the stock will rocket back up. You could turn twenty, thirty percent in a few weeks. It'll be like stealing, only legal." He watched Kramp, hoping for a smile. Instead, the man's face was flushed, and he was rising from his chair. Instantly his companions rose with him.

"Parker," he growled, "I want some answers on this thing, and I want them soon." He pointed at Henry. "And I don't want to see him again."

Henry stood, and Parker walked Kramp to the door. "All right, Bob," he said, "we'll pull out our bag of tricks. Don't panic yet."

Kramp turned at the door and faced Parker. "I don't have to panic," he said in a voice of ice, "because that's what I pay you to do." He strode out the door, the other men trailing behind.

Parker turned to Henry and waved him over, ignoring the others. "In my office, Preacher," he said. "Now."

* * *

"What the hell was that about?" Parker demanded.

Henry sat down opposite Parker's desk. "My idea seemed reasonable."

"Were you listening in there?" Sheldon retorted. "How could you have been so naive?"

"Hammering me without telling me where I went wrong doesn't help, Sheldon."

Parker's voice took on an edgy hostility. "We're adults. Don't make me spell it out."

Henry sat silently, not wanting to reach the conclusion inexorably moving through his mind. But he could reach no other. He felt a gnawing in the pit of his stomach. Softly he said, "He's guilty, isn't he? The whole bunch of them."

Parker didn't answer. Instead, he opened a drawer and pulled out a flask and a couple of tumblers. "Secret stash," he said, pouring himself a drink. He looked at Henry, his expression a bit softer. "You want one?"

Henry shook his head no. "He couldn't take my obvious solution," he said. "The last thing in the world he wants is for the real facts to come out."

"How did you get through law school, Einstein?" Parker said, tossing back a shot.

Henry looked at his managing partner. Sheldon was nervous, almost furtive. It was shocking, given his normally effusive confidence. But Henry took it as a hopeful sign. Parker's discomfort meant that some inner decency remained in the man; maybe there was still time to avoid crossing an ethical line of no return.

"So what do you propose to do?" Henry asked quietly. "I mean, we obviously can't go forward on this thing."

"Everybody gets their day in court, Preacher. That's the law."

"Theoretically, yes. But it's one thing to represent someone you later find out was guilty. It's something else if you're positive your client is guilty, guilty in this case of securities fraud on a massive, elaborate scale . . . I mean, Sheldon, we're possibly complicit in it. We wrote the original deal. We could be subpoenaed, have to prove what we knew when. We would certainly be deposed."

Parker, who had been leaning back in his chair breathing shallowly, opened his eyes. "How big are your balls, Preacher?" he asked.

"I beg your pardon?"

"You heard me. See, this is a balls issue. That's the one thing law school doesn't cover. Balls."

"It's an ethical issue, Sheldon. It's not being complicit in a crime."

Parker, in an uncharacteristic burst of anger, slammed his hand down on the table. "Don't give me that sanctimonious crap," he said, his voice betraying his nerves. "Look, I hate this as much as you do, okay? But this is where the rubber meets the road. We billed over five hundred thousand dollars on this takeover package. *Half a million*, Henry. And there's that much again in front of us. So we're at a million right there. But Kramp can deliver . . ." He paused for another swallow. "Look, Henry, this is totally in confidence, okay? Kramp is giving us Orion once the smoke clears if we handle this. Orion, Henry. We're looking at a million-dollar retainer, year in, year out. And bringing that kind of business in changes lives, Henry. Not just mine. Yours. I don't know how you feel about making partner, but what we do seems pretty goddam clear to me."

Henry saw the edge; he felt the now familiar destabilizing rush, longing to step over it. Nevertheless, the size of this leap was unprecedented, a dance with career death. He paused, leaned, and stepped into space. "How can Kramp deliver Orion, Sheldon?" he asked quietly.

"What?"

"I asked you how Kramp can deliver Orion. I thought Kramp didn't work for Orion."

Parker stared back at his protégé blankly. He had been working hard lately. It wasn't like him to make a slip like this. "Orion's not the point."

"You *knew*, Sheldon," Henry said. He felt himself falling, vertigo taking him over. "You knew because Kramp said he could hand you Orion, and he couldn't have done that unless talks were under way from the beginning. God, Sheldon, you knew about this from day one."

"The thing to do is stay calm," Parker said. "Things like this blow over if everyone keeps their head."

"What does that mean? Lie to a grand jury?"

"It means thinking long-term. It means being realistic and doing what it takes to win. It means staying loyal."

"And if you knew . . . Jesus, Sheldon, have you been buying Orion stock?" Dark clouds were gathering in Henry's mind. "Orion's a hell of a bargain right now, isn't it? And what did you say about the Centel thing— they have some new technology in data storage, right? So once Orion assimilates Centel, it will be a whole new company. Somebody on the inside could make a fortune."

Parker's face became a mask. "I assume that's true, if someone were to do what you're suggesting."

"It's insider trading, Sheldon. On top of everything else."

"In no way do I confirm your implication. I will state that it happens every day. It's something that, for example, you have the opportunity to make a personal decision about."

"What does that mean?"

"You've already stated that Orion's stock is in the toilet. I assume you own a calculator. The math for someone aware of the . . . let's say the *circumstances*, is compelling."

Henry was surprised by how calm he felt, how clear things looked to him. Falling in space, he found, was more comfortable than trying to balance the life he had been leading. He had pushed with Parker from day one, taking risk after risk. Staying in Council Grove so long in the first place showed that. But this line was terminal, and he recognized it as such at once. The clear-cut nature of what had happened made his choice remarkably easy. He was his father's son, and that meant that he would not work another day for Sheldon Parker. There was no mistaking what that meant for his future with the firm: it was over. He had crossed a lot of lines to be a success, little compromises not with the law but with his nature. To compensate, he had developed the nervous tic of outrageous banter with Parker, pushing him, almost daring him to unload. But this line he would never cross. There was no reason to extend the conversation a minute longer, no reason to see Sheldon embarrass himself further. "I won't do it, Sheldon," he said simply. "You can forget it."

Parker eyed him warily. When he spoke, his voice was calm, but there was venom just below the surface.

"We're clear that I have admitted nothing to you."

Henry suddenly felt tired. "Yes, Sheldon. Nothing at all."

Parker regarded him for a moment, and his face softened slightly. "Let me explain something. Every year over six thousand people graduate from law school. They come rooting around for jobs like little hogs. We don't bother interviewing anybody but the top one percent. You know why?"

Henry said nothing; he was already detached, listening to Sheldon only in objective fascination. He was watching the way a man morally deconstructs himself. He was seeing what, perhaps, in time he would have become.

"We don't waste our time with second best because we know it's a damn tough world out there. What the hell do you think business is? It's Darwinian, Preacher. It's kill or be killed. This firm is made up of survivors." He finished off his second tumbler. "We eat the weak, Henry. From the day I entered law school I knew one thing: I'll never be the weak."

Henry watched, feeling something he had never felt for the man before: simple pity. "I won't do it, Sheldon."

"Take twenty-four hours, Preacher. This is a big decision. It's hard to get back on the fast track when you've been bumped off."

"It won't matter, Sheldon. I won't do it."

"Go to your party, Henry. Talk to Elaine."

Elaine. He hadn't thought about her in the tension of the moment. It was miserable timing, coming on the night of her triumph.

"Talk to her, Henry. She's a smart woman. Don't make any final decisions without her." Henry glanced quickly at his watch; it was nearly five-
fifteen. The party started at seven. He would barely have time to drive
home, change clothes, and make it all the way across town to the Hargroves'. He rose and headed for the door. "You could have been a hell of a
lawyer, Preacher," Parker said. "You still can be, if you stay calm."

"Are you still coming tonight, Sheldon?"

"I'll be there. Talk to her."

Henry stopped by his office briefly before leaving; he looked blankly at
the stack of files that cluttered its surface, realizing that none of the papers
had meaning for him now. Nothing at Wilson, Lougherby and Mathers
had meaning after his talk with Parker. Out of habit he reached toward a
stack to put in his briefcase; stopping himself, he sat down, momentarily
paralyzed.

Talk to her, Henry. She's a smart woman. Parker's words were true, but
what had been growing in Henry ever since going to Council Grove now
catapulted to the forefront of his mind, impossible to ignore. In the midst
of Elaine's fabulous capability there was something lacking, a human, nur-
turing quality that he realized he wanted. She would interpret his feelings
as a weakness, he knew; he knew he was supposed to meet her halfway, two
independent equals coming together out of mutual desire and benefit. But
he realized now he needed something more from a woman: understanding, at a minimum, and ultimately faith. He wanted to be believed in, supported in such a difficult decision. In his heart he knew that Elaine would
take what had happened as a crushing defeat in his life, and she was not tol-
erant of defeats. The thought of disappointing her was bad enough; the
knowledge that her response would certainly disappoint him filled him
with melancholy.

He reached down and opened a drawer on his right; it bulged with
papers, on the top of which was his appointment book. None of those
appointments would be kept by him. Into his place would slide another
eager, young lawyer anxious to prove his loyalty and expertise in the art of
power. Henry began to empty his desk into a large cardboard box he had
retrieved from the file room. Pens, legal pads, pictures of Elaine, a bulky
laptop due for replacing. Then a picture of his father, which stopped him.
The photo showed his father sitting in his office back in Council Grove,
his perpetually tired smile on his face. A stack of papers teetered behind
him, a disorganized filing cabinet was stuck half open in the background.
Henry looked at the picture, and felt a tingling crawling up his back.

With the sense of awkwardness that comes from being where you no
longer belong, Henry packed quickly and efficiently. It took a surprisingly

short time to erase himself from the place; the offices at the firm were notoriously small for the younger lawyers, and his personal effects had been kept to a minimum. In less than twenty minutes there was no visible trace of his life at Wilson, Lougherby and Mathers.

He sat at his desk, empty now except for a computer. Quickly, he wrote an E-mail to all the staff explaining that he would no longer be working at the firm and expressing his gratitude for the time he had spent there.

He spoke to no one on the way out. What it meant to leave the firm, he wanted to keep at bay, and talking about it would make that impossible. For now, he resolved simply to take the elevator as inconspicuously as possible and let himself feel it all later. The elevator door glided shut behind him, closing with a solid, final thud.

Charles Hargrove's home loomed before Henry like a luxurious, sybaritic hotel. Henry stepped through double doors ten feet high and entered a huge foyer. Above him hung an enormous cut-glass chandelier; Henry overheard someone say it had been brought from a country estate in Italy. He stared at it a moment, wondering how all its perfectly shiny pieces were kept so impeccably clean. The entryway beckoned visitors into a great hall, exquisitely paneled in light ash with dark walnut accents. The floor was light-colored marble, and it shone like glass. Almost instantly he was presented with champagne and hors d'oeuvres.

The party was a bustling, noisy affair that at first appeared to be nothing more than a throng of superbly dressed people chatting amiably and drinking. But as he moved through the crowd, his practiced eye noticed the office hierarchy that was perpetually, invisibly in force at such affairs. The main room was full of younger people, up-and-comers laughing and talking with exaggerated, almost fierce good nature. In an antechamber to the right a smaller, more subdued group mingled; their pretty wives wore expensive jewelry, and a couple of the men were smoking cigars. *Executives*, Henry thought with a smile. *But not the top echelon, not yet.* He moved through the party, passing one exquisitely decorated room after another. He passed a formal dining room with seating for twelve, then a study with a wet bar and sitting area. He turned down a short hallway and saw a group gathered in a large media room; the stereo was blaring dance music, although no one was dancing. Eventually he passed a dimly lit billiards room in which seven or eight older men were talking quietly. They were drinking what looked like brandy, a dark, liquid shine in large snifters. Their wives were congregated at the opposite end of the room, talking separately. *Here they are*, Henry thought, *seeking refuge from the ass-kissers. The partners.*

He walked past the room, following the flow of the house toward the pool area. Here the heavy architecture gave way, softening into an immense Italian courtyard. The entryway led to a great covered patio with bleached-oak floors, the center of which contained a large bar. Island music came from hidden loudspeakers, and two tuxedoed bartenders smiled blandly as they mixed drinks. Little groups of people milled around the edge of the pool, their laughter filtering across the water. Then he heard her.

He looked to his left. There, surrounded by a small group of young, absurdly eager men, was Elaine. She was laughing with them, but her refined pleasure floated to him separately from all others, his ears attuned to her sound. Seeing her from a distance, he saw her objectively, almost as if they had never met. She was startlingly attractive, one of the most impressive women he had ever seen. Tall, with high cheekbones, short but feminine hair, and every inch emanating a sense of refined grace and power. She was wearing the dress she had described, the one she had called an investment. Seeing her now, on the eve of her success, he had to agree. She resonated with private clubs, tennis courts, and generations of uninterrupted success. He was a fool, he knew. She was a ticket to everything he had thought he wanted, a business and social asset he would never be able to equal. But where he most needed to be touched, she lacked the simple capacity to find him. More, he doubted whether she regarded those areas as important in the first place. And he had this comfort: if he left her, she wouldn't be alone one second longer than she wanted to be.

He looked a long moment, and as if by telepathy, she turned and met his eyes. She smiled, and for a moment, he wavered. She was flawless. Her dark magenta dress came tight at the waist, her white bosom lifted, her long legs tapered to high heels. He moved toward her. He had crossed half the distance when her glance looked past him, and she waved.

"Sheldon," she cried, "you came!" She beamed. "Look, Henry, Sheldon's here. How wonderful." Henry turned and saw Parker striding toward them, a drink in each hand. Parker nodded to Henry and stared rapaciously at Elaine.

"You look lovely, my dear," he said, handing her a glass of champagne. "You must try this. Cristal Roederer, '85."

"My goodness, for a party this size," Elaine said, smiling.

"*Not* for a party this size," Parker said. "I've been chatting with Chuck . . ."

"Mr. Hargrove? I didn't even know you were acquainted."

"We weren't. But we're both Exeter," Parker said casually. "Bond of brothers, all that. Anyway, he insisted I get the good stuff, and he took me down to his cellar. I brought you back a glass. Exquisite." He turned and said, "Hello, Henry. Remind me to give you something before I leave." His tone was completely neutral; no trace remained of their earlier argument.

Henry turned to Elaine and said, "How are you, darling?" He kissed her on the cheek. "Congratulations. You look fantastic."

Elaine twirled. "It does work, doesn't it?" she said. "I'm never wearing *prêt-à-porter* again."

Parker laughed. "It's the woman who makes the dress, my dear."

"When's the award ceremony?" Henry asked, stepping intuitively between them.

"In about thirty minutes," she answered. "I'm on pins and needles."

Parker leaned forward and gave her a faux buss on the cheek. "Enjoy it," he said, grinning. "And get used to it." Turning to Henry, he said, "I'm sure you'll get out of your little mess, Henry. Just talk things over with this very sensible woman. Five minutes with her and things will seem so much clearer." He stepped back, consuming her, his eyes full of unashamed avarice. "Remarkable," he said. "Simply remarkable." Parker backed away and then was gone, vanishing into a crowd of evening wear.

When Henry looked back at Elaine, her face had clouded. "What was that all about?" she asked.

"It can wait. There's no reason to darken a perfect evening with my problems."

"What kind of problems? Don't tell me it has anything to do with that absurd will."

"Not really. Or I suppose, in a way, it does. But anyway, it's not going to change in the next few hours, so let's just have a wonderful night."

She looked at him, an incisive, penetrating look. He felt, for the moment, like an equity she was evaluating. She took him by the arm and led him to a small study nearby and closed the door. "Tell me what's going on between you and Sheldon, Henry."

Henry exhaled. "I'd rather not, for your sake. It's going to be a long talk, and this isn't the place or the time. You look marvelous, and you're going to get your award in a half hour. Trust me, Elaine, we don't want to do this right now."

Concern grew on Elaine's face. "What have you done, Henry? Sheldon wouldn't have said what he did if you hadn't *done* something."

Henry looked at her. "Why are you assuming I'm in the wrong? The fact is, I didn't do anything."

"Then why did he say that?"

"We'll talk, Elaine. But later."

She fixed him in her gaze. "If you're having trouble with Sheldon, tonight is the perfect chance to patch it up. You're both here, and it's a casual environment. You'll both be more reasonable."

He sighed; she was a better, more persistent fighter than he was. He could never fully turn on his lawyer mode in a debate with her; somehow it had always felt unseemly, and she had exploited that compunction often. Not that she was cruel, he admitted; it was just that she was a winner, always and in every possible circumstance. "I can't do that," he said. "And I'm not sure I want to, anyway."

Shock covered her face. "That kind of statement is exactly why you need me. You constantly lose perspective."

Her persistence annoyed him. "Perspective is just what I think I found."

"If it involves damaging your relationship with Sheldon, I'd say you're terribly wrong. Did you see him tonight, Henry? Sheldon Parker was drinking champagne with Charles Hargrove in fifteen minutes. Mr. Hargrove took him to his wine cellar. There are people who have worked at our firm for twenty years and never got that invitation. Sheldon Parker's charming, he's witty, and he's incredibly successful. He's also a big supporter of yours. Arguing with him is certainly a mistake."

All right, Henry thought. *You have to win, even when it costs you. Then here it is.* "Sheldon is the best lawyer I've ever seen," Henry said evenly. "He's also an utterly corrupt man."

She pulled away, startled by his blunt statement. "I will never believe that, Henry. And I hate that kind of sanctimonious talk. It's not your place to judge another person."

"Then let's call it something else. Say that something came between us that can't be fixed."

"Don't scare me like this, Henry. It has to be fixed. I don't want this tonight."

"I don't want it tonight either," Henry said, his sense of exasperation growing. He grabbed her hand, starting to lead her back toward the door. "For once let it go. For once. For me. Come on, you'll be missed."

She pulled her hand back. "Don't patronize me, Henry," she said. "I'm not some little girl to be led away. It's my life, too."

Henry stopped. "What does that mean?"

She softened for a moment. "Everything's working out so well, darling," she said. "My award, Sheldon taking you under his wing. It's all just like we planned. Don't mess up everything. It's ridiculous."

"Like *we* planned."

"Of course. I always pictured us together." She paused, and added, "I know you did, too."

She was right; he had pictured them together, right from the beginning.

At first it had been merely a hope. Then, to his utter surprise, she had wanted him in the way he wanted her. It had never dawned on him that he would be the one to leave. "I never wanted to create any problems," he said. "Things are changing too fast lately. I can't keep up."

"Then let me, darling. Let me fix everything. I'm sure this is all a misunderstanding with Sheldon. Now promise me before you leave tonight you'll patch everything up."

He looked at her, radiant and purposeful. She was more than he deserved, in every objective sense. But he had never lied to her before, and he wasn't going to start now. "I can't promise that, because we aren't going to patch things up. I've already resigned from the firm, Elaine. It's effective immediately."

Anger and disbelief spread over her face. "You will not do this to me," she said sternly, pulling away. "You will not do this on my night. You will not ruin what I've worked to achieve for three solid years with some stupid argument with Sheldon. You simply won't."

"Then why did you push me?" Henry said bitterly. "I didn't want to talk about it in the first place. I wanted your night to be perfect as much as you did."

"It is going to be perfect, Henry. It has to be. I've earned it."

He looked at her, feeling, for the moment, surprise that he had ever thought he might love her. But he knew now that it had never been love, only intense, consuming desire. "Yes, Elaine, you have. In every way."

She gathered herself together, rebounding from the surprise of Henry's statements. Composing herself, she stood up tall, almost imperious. "I will give you ten seconds to tell me what this is about. Then maybe I can salvage something out of the mess you've made."

"I can't do that." She began to speak, but he stopped her. "Believe me, I want to. I want to tell you every unethical, grimy detail. Some of why I want you to know is for good reasons, some of it not so noble. But I can't violate my fiduciary responsibility, Elaine. If I breathe a word of what I know, I could be disbarred."

"Don't be so dramatic, Henry," Elaine interjected. "It's me. We don't have secrets."

Not in words, he thought. *But in places we can never understand about each other. You were simply so beautiful, I never saw it before.* "I've been asked to do something I know is wrong. Sheldon gave me an ultimatum, and I won't do it. I may have already been unwittingly exposed to something questionable. I know it's hard, and I know it's unfair not to say more. But you'll have to trust me on this." Suddenly, even though he knew their relationship was ending, it was important to him to have that trust from her. It might validate the time they had spent together, at least. "Can you do that, Elaine?" he asked earnestly. "Can you believe in me that way?"

"Sheldon is asking for your support, Henry. The bigger the request, the bigger the payback. Things get sticky sometimes in the real world, and people like Sheldon take care of their own."

"You didn't answer my question."

"You didn't answer mine."

Henry looked at her; she would never lose. Giving in simply wasn't a part of her nature. He looked at his watch. "You have to go," he said. "Hargrove will be looking for you about now."

"This isn't Kansas, Henry," she said, fixing her hair. "This is real, this is our life. Business isn't always black and white. Your small-town morality is going to ruin your career."

More and more, she reminded him of Parker. "I didn't know morality changed with the size of the town."

She stared at him a moment and said, "I won't go down with you, Henry. If you screw things up at the firm, you do it for one." She turned crisply on her heel and walked to the door. As she was about to leave, she hesitated; turning back briefly, she whispered, "I hope you'll change your mind. I do love you, of course."

The door closed behind her, and Henry stood in the empty room, suddenly reverberant with her absence. He walked numbly to a chair and sat, leaning back and closing his eyes. She had never told him that before. He had longed to hear it, unwilling to reveal his own feelings until he was sure. And now, in the midst of destruction, her beautiful mouth moved and those words came out. But it was too late, and in his deepest self he knew it. He would never be sure if the words were nothing more than a carrot, a dangling jewel to make him grasp. In that insecurity the power of the phrase was drained, and in a matter of seconds he had regained his equilibrium. The room was cool, and in the dim lighting he felt almost peaceful. He wanted that feeling to stay; he had meant it when he said that things were happening too fast. He needed a time-out, a chance to think without a timetable. But he had not constructed a life like that. His life had transpired in broad stages of ever-increasing pressure: college, and the rush into law school after the accident; the competitiveness there, clerking and law review; and then the firm, clawing his way to the best position under Sheldon's personal care. And then, magnificently, Elaine had entered his life, and with her had come one more layer of pressure to do more. Now, with transcendent suddenness, all the layers were removed. He felt light—so light, in fact, he thought he might float from the chair. The future and its inevitable concerns had not yet descended; now, all he felt was the relief of not having to accomplish more than he had ever dreamed possible.

He actually thought he might sleep, smiling at the irony of dozing in Charles Hargrove's mansion, Elaine getting her award a few feet away. Noise was filtering through the door; there was a cheering, followed by quiet. It was time; Hargrove was calling the troops.

Henry rose, left the room, and walked to the entryway of the great hall. It was crammed with bodies, a remarkably homogeneous group of lovely, successful people. Six weeks ago he would have craved entrance to their innermost sanctum. Now, the sight of them nearly made his skin crawl. At the front stood Hargrove, a distinguished man of about sixty, with silver hair and an intelligent, highly acquisitive face.

"I love rewarding hard work," the man said. "And this little lady has worked as hard as anybody I've seen around here. But that's not why she's getting this award. She's getting this award for results. She doesn't just talk about it, she brings it home. And over the past twelve months she's brought more of it home to Hargrove and Leach than any other broker. We like that." Chuckles filtered through the room. "Elaine, come up here, please."

Elaine floated up from the side of the crowd, her steps elegant and contained. Hargrove put his arm around her, and she drew close to him, willing to be engulfed. "Elaine, I'm proud of you. Damn proud. And I can't think of a more deserving person to receive this award." He held up a large plaque. "Ladies and gentlemen, I present to you the outstanding broker of the year."

Applause broke out across the room as Elaine took the plaque. She looked, Henry had to admit, absolutely, triumphantly happy. *It's what you want*, he thought. *It's what makes you happy.* It was, he realized, what he had always assumed would make him happy as well, and he was utterly surprised by the realization that it wouldn't. Somehow, without being aware of it, he had changed. He drifted through the crowd, staying to the back as he made his way toward the front door. It was time to leave, in every sense of the word. He turned, and suddenly he found himself face-to-face with Sheldon Parker.

"Quite a woman," Parker said, his face serious. "Remarkable."

"Yes," Henry said. "She really is quite wonderful."

Parker looked at him sideways a moment, reading him. He shook his head and said, "Like I said, you could have been a hell of a lawyer, kid."

"Be good to her, Sheldon. She likes flowers and jewelry."

Parker stared back at him a moment, then turned away toward the stage without answering. Henry moved on through the crowd, eventually making it to the great front doors. Before he left, he turned back and looked; he could just see Elaine in a crowd of people at the front. Sheldon was with her, and she looked happy, almost euphoric. Henry opened the door, and a valet in a tuxedo looked at him expectantly.

"BMW," he said, handing him a ticket. "Dark green two-door."

Chapter Twenty

Henry hit the couch fully clothed, taking off only his tie, and slept a shallow sleep for two or three hours. When he woke it was nearly one. He pulled off his pants and fumbled his way to the bedroom, flipping on a bathroom light. They had kept separate apartments, but there were still some of Elaine's things casually tossed about, artifacts of womanness: a nightgown, a pair of silk panties, a sheer black slip. His apartment he had kept, if not scrupulously clean, at least orderly. But these mysterious objects he had felt a kind of elation at allowing to fall where they would, settling like exotic strangers in his masculine world. They were signs of intimacy, reminders of sweat and warmth and her soft hair falling down on his face as she lowered herself onto him. He stared at the slip, following its shape as it spilled down off the edge of the bathtub onto the tile floor. He had watched her step out of it the last night they had made love, and the sight of it brought all of that back with a rush.

He had walked into the bathroom feeling disastrously tired; the emotions of the last several days had finally broken through his determined, law-school endurance. In that exhaustion, surrounded by remembrances of her, he felt her absence more strongly. Her femaleness, the comfort of her weight lightly against him in sleep, the presence of her sensual beauty—to lose all of that left him feeling hollow, as if, having been with her, he was less than complete alone.

He stripped, preparing for bed. Naked, he stood before the mirror, his shoulders tired, the determined posture momentarily gone. The sight of his exhausted eyes disturbed him, and he flicked off the light to brush his teeth in the light from his bedroom. He crossed to his bed and fell upon it, thinking. He felt terribly alone, and missed his father very much; it would have been good to talk about things with him at such a time. But both father and mother were gone. None of his friends at the firm would understand; besides, there were ethical constraints on even discussing his problem. But the need to unload was palpable, and he searched his mind for someone who would listen and reach back. He closed his eyes and saw a face: an unlikely surrogate, but the only man still living who had ever touched him in a truly fatherly way.

Samuel Baxter spent half his day on the campus of Trinity Seminary in ancient Greece and the other half working in the projects of Louisville. Of all his teachers, Baxter had seemed the most real, the most unafraid to get his hands dirty. He dug in, rattling cages and spending his life for the underclass of society. Samuel Baxter. *God, he must be in his sixties by now. Maybe retired.* The man saw ghosts, Henry remembered; not literal ghosts but the Hand of God behind innocuous, apparently unrelated events. Someone died; Baxter saw God. Another lived; God again, Baxter proclaimed. No matter what result, no matter what the circumstances, God was at work. Henry worked at Wilson, Lougherby and Mathers; God had brought him there. He was quitting; God again, moving behind the shadows for His own, inscrutable purposes.

Henry turned and stared at the wall. Sarah had hinted at it. Where was God when you needed Him? For everyone in Henry's current world He was invisible, unthreaded into life, rarely discussed and mostly unlamented. And then came moments when you needed meaning, needed design so badly you couldn't face the grotesque possibility that life just was, that every choice you made was neutral and, in the end, void.

But he couldn't deny the tingling, the sense of awe building in his brain. There was nothing that anybody would describe as a miracle in what had happened to him. There was instead a sense of connectedness, willowy and indistinct, but nevertheless discernible. His life was spinning—not out of control, but as if in someone else's control. And if this extravagant set of circumstances were built for him, why not for the others? Why not for Ellen, for Roger? Even for Amanda and Elaine? Somehow Ty Crandall's will had picked up all their lives and spun them like tops, flinging off nonessentials, forcing them into unfamiliar territory. It was, if not God, a brilliant opportunity, a set of circumstances so interconnected that its happening accidentally required its own leap of faith. But it all depended upon the perspective; from the outside, looking at each individual piece, it seemed only like life happening one person at a time. Ty Crandall died. He left a will. People reacted. Things happened.

He turned over. What, in the end, was there to depend upon besides Baxter's Hand? It was one thing to walk away from Elaine and the firm. But the idea of living without some animating idea filled him with a sense of dread. What if he had exhaled one life only to find that there was nothing at all to inhale, that he lived in a vacuum? What if all there was to breathe in was just some other work, a few years of eating and sleeping, some moments of the chemical confusion of love, certain to fade, and then a final, infinite darkness?

He could hear, through the double-paned glass of his downtown seventh-floor apartment, the faint, diffuse blare of car horns and traffic. Without Baxter's Hand his building, the entire city—the whole earth—was nothing but a kind of ant farm, countless millions burrowing through life, heads down, mindless, pointless, a flickering struggle ending in nothing.

The finality of that thought turned through his mind for several minutes in the quiet of his bedroom. Then, with deliberation, he turned over and picked up the phone. He stared at it awhile, then pushed the numbers of Louisville Information. "Samuel Baxter," he said quietly. He listened, clicked the phone off, and sat up in the dark, not moving for some time. At last he pushed the buttons once again, and after a moment heard a voice, full of sleep, answer. He didn't speak. The voice came through again, this time more distinct, with concern. At last, Henry spoke. "Dr. Baxter? This is Henry Mathews. I quit my job today."

"Let me get to my study. Niva's asleep. Go ahead, I'm taking you with me."

"I'm sorry to wake you. I didn't know what else to do."

"It's all right. Tell me what's happened."

"I quit my job. I left my girlfriend. I went home."

There was a pause on the line. Baxter said, "Which came first?"

"I don't know. I went home."

"I see. That makes sense."

"Why do you say that?"

"Home can be a dangerous place."

"Look, I don't even know why I'm calling you. What time is it anyway?"

"I don't know. It's about two."

"I'm sorry."

"You already said that."

"I went home on a case. I had to handle a legal matter."

"I had heard you were a lawyer."

"Who from? I haven't kept in touch with anybody from those days."

"Career services. Your firm called for a reference. I was quite surprised. But then I remembered your father had been a lawyer."

"Yes, he was."

"I checked up on the firm, out of curiosity. Quite an industrious organization."

"You could say that."

"But now you've quit."

"That's right."

"And you wanted to call me in the middle of the night and tell me."

"It doesn't make sense, I realize that. I'm not sure anything makes sense anymore, to be honest."

Neither spoke for some time, and Henry began to wonder if the call was a mistake. Then Baxter said, "I think it makes perfect sense."

"Why?"

"Listen, Henry, since you woke me up, I'm going to be blunt and tell you some things you probably won't like. But at this point I figure you owe me a favor."

Henry closed his eyes. "Go ahead."

"First off, I thought this might happen, to tell you the truth. Not the call, but the meltdown. I'm actually surprised it took this long."

"That's fairly presumptuous."

"I suppose. But seminary is a magnet for the damaged. In thirty years of teaching I've become an unwilling expert on pain."

"Not exactly a ringing endorsement for the clergy."

"On the contrary. I don't want a doctor who's never been sick."

Henry paused. "All right. So you think you understand my pain."

"No. I only recognize it."

"And what would you call it?"

"A simple word that carries a world of meaning. It's anger, Henry. Consuming and all-encompassing, but only anger. And that's why I thought you would come apart. I couldn't believe that kind of anger would last. Not in you anyway."

"So it's my anger I'm losing. I thought it was my reason for living."

"The thing is, Henry, for you I'm not sure there's that much of a difference between the two."

"I have a right to that anger," Henry said tersely. "But you're wrong if you think I live for it."

"I agree you have the right," Baxter said quietly. "But I'm not so sure about the rest of it. Look, when your folks died I bled for you. The shock wave went through the whole school. You didn't see that, first because you were suffering, and then because you left before we could show you. And I watched you shake your fist and create a kind of anti-life. I'm going to be completely honest with you, because I can tell you're finally through with anything else. Like a lot of people, you thought you had finally cut through the great religious fantasy to live life on your own terms. But all you were really doing was saying no."

"No to what?"

"Not to the ministry, if that's what you're thinking. I never pegged you for that. That didn't bother me, in itself. A lot of people pass through here on their way somewhere else. But you were saying no to the life you were supposed to lead, wherever and whatever that life is. You were saying no to a life that includes death. To the dangerous and unpredictable. To the Mystery."

"I've worked too hard to hear that all I've done since I left school is encased in some negative," Henry said with irritation. "There's a yes in every decision I've made."

"I had you in my office for hours at a time, Henry, before the accident. I know where you come from. I know what's in you. This isn't it."

"You're saying I should be back in seminary. That's impossible. Maybe I shook my fist at God. But I'm not prepared to shake hands again."

There was a pause, and Baxter said, "No, to be honest, I don't think you should come back. Every choice has a consequence, and doors close. But that doesn't make the life you've lived the right one."

"Why didn't you try to stop me if you felt that way?"

"Would you have heard a word I said?"

Henry thought. "No."

"Exactly. I wasn't willing to waste this talk when it didn't have a chance of making any difference. So I prayed you over to God, and hoped for the best."

"Pretty weak."

"I suppose." Baxter paused a moment and added, "And yet here you are."

Henry leaned back against the headboard. "And you place great meaning in that."

"I place enormous meaning in that."

Henry sat quietly for a moment and said, "So you trusted your God I'd come back around."

"No. I just trusted God. I had no idea if you'd come around. I pray for everybody, Henry. Some get better. Some don't. God's not on the end of my chain."

"But surely you can see how thin it is. And we're supposed to live like it was everything we needed. It's absurd."

"It's all we get. Anything else is just mumbo-jumbo to make us feel better about the unknown. I won't do that. Look, Henry, the only difference between you and me is what we see when we look into the dark. That's it. You look into the dark, and you see nothing. I look, and I see a light. Distant, maybe, and not always very clear. But we both see the dark. Everyone awake sees the dark."

"And what is this dark? Surely you don't believe in some Satan."

"The dark is the thing that makes the light utterly precious. I hang on to the light. That's all prayer is, Henry. It's nothing more than deciding to hang on to the light. And it doesn't bother me as much as it used to that I can't know beforehand what God is going to do about my prayers. It wouldn't be much of a story if I knew the ending before it began."

"And on this thread you base your life."

"You call God unreliable. I call Him the Mystery. But even a mysterious God is better than no God at all. If I really believed we were alone in the universe I wouldn't hesitate to kill myself. You would call that cowardice, probably. But I would call it a heroic act of disdain for the meaninglessness of life." He laughed softly. "Of course what either one of us thought about it wouldn't make any difference. Nothing would matter."

"So you refuse to believe in that nothing."

"You refuse to believe in my God."

"It's paper thin."

"I suppose. And yet here you are."

Henry paused. "So you keep saying."

"Sorry," Baxter said, and he laughed again. "If you believe in the good ending, it's possible to smile without disregarding the pain of today."

"The good ending."

"You can call it grace, if you like."

"If this is grace, it hurts like hell. I thought it was supposed to take away pain."

"If you thought that, you've forgotten how grace entered this world."

"That's the big story, isn't it? The cross. But hope is all you have on that. You don't *know* anything."

"That's perfectly true. But if it's not real, they're going to have to pry it out of my cold, dead hands."

The two sat in silence a moment. At last Baxter said, "Get some sleep, Henry. I can't fix this. It may not get fixed. There aren't any guarantees. But calling me was the right thing to do. I don't know what will happen next. I think you're in the grip of the Hand, but that's looking at it from my point of view. From where you sit . . . well, I wouldn't want to be where you sit."

"If I am in some grip, I want out."

"You have that right. Sleep now. And call me when you want to. It might help."

Henry hung up the phone and lay back on the bed in the dark. He could hear the traffic again now, the sounds of life filtering up from the streets below. For some time he didn't move. Then, because there was nothing else to do, he opened his mouth and inhaled deeply, feeling the air rush back into him.

Chapter Twenty-one

The next day passed slowly. Henry awoke early, habit enforcing its will. His first, automatic thought was to go to the office. Then, with the thudding realization that he had nowhere to go, he got up, made himself breakfast, and sat down to look over his accounts. If he was out of work, he needed to know his precise financial condition. It wasn't as bad as it could have been; his spending had loosened up considerably since meeting Elaine, but his relatively poor upbringing had kept him from doing anything truly irresponsible. But Chicago was an expensive city, and he estimated about four months was all he had before things became serious.

He dressed, ate an early lunch at home to save money, and spent the afternoon near the lake. Growing up on the plains had left him with an innate wonder at anything having to do with water, and Lake Michigan had always held him spellbound. He prowled the dock area, watching men loading the outsized cargo vessels. He felt a wave of romanticism for a life of simple physical labor; the easy camaraderie of the longshoremen seemed enormously appealing, watching them cuss and talk trash to one another. But he moved on downtown, wandering through the little shops and restaurants by the water. Office buildings towered behind him, and he looked at them for a long time, thinking about the stupendous amount of living that went on within their glass-and-steel frames. He bought a beer at a little place off Carter Street, nursing it for a long time. At last, when dusk began to form out on the water, he took a last look at the lake and drove home.

It was early evening but he had already drifted off to sleep when he heard a distant ringing. He opened his eyes, trying to pinpoint the sound. It was his cell phone, and he was hearing it through his briefcase. He leaped to open the case, flipped open the phone, and said, "Hello?"

"Billy Payne, sir," the voice on the line said. "The manager down at the Feed and Farm Supply. There's been a little trouble, and I thought you'd want to know."

Payne, Henry thought. *He probably doesn't even know I'm in Chicago yet.* "What kind of trouble?" he said. "What's happened?"

"It's that Birdman," Payne said. "He's gone crazy."

Henry came instantly to attention. "Tell me what you know, and start at the beginning."

"All I know is that the alarm went off at the store," Payne said, "and it's my number at the alarm company, so I got called. I got there about the same time Collier did."

"Who's Collier?"

"Sheriff Collier. He was just gettin' out of his car when I pulled up."

"What happened? What does Boyd have to do with it?"

"I guess he went crazy, like I said. It was a real mess we found. The glass was broken out all along the front of the store. He'd been throwin' rocks, big ones. Busted out the picture windows, every one of 'em. Then he come in and went through the stock, and left quite a trail. When that old man gets angry he's got some energy."

"Is he all right? Did anything happen to him?"

"Yeah, the old man's all right," Payne said. "It's Collier's the one that's hurt."

Henry's stomach tightened. "How bad?"

"Not bad, but he's mad as hell. That Birdman bit him, bit him hard, too, right on the arm. Doc's on his way over here."

"God, what a mess. Where's Boyd now?"

"Collier's got him locked up. Got him in a straitjacket. Took three of us to hold him down."

Henry imagined Boyd, anguished and uncomprehending, being man-handled into submission. Tumblers clicked in Henry's mind, expensive, life-changing thoughts that he wished he could avoid. "Listen, Billy, I hear a lot of noise in the background. What's going on over there now?"

"Whole damn town's out here. Must be forty, fifty people milling around."

"All right, Billy, listen to me carefully. I'm in Chicago right now."

"Huh? Didn't know that."

"The number rings me wherever I am. Now tell me what kind of man this Collier is."

"He's all right, I guess. Hates trouble. Mad as a rattlesnake right now."

"Okay. Then I need you to do me a favor."

"Whatever I can."

"Good man. Tell Sheriff Collier that Boyd isn't for public display. Tell him that I said to take him over to his office and keep people away from him. There's a ten-fifteen from O'Hare to Kansas City. If I make it, I'll be at Collier's office in about five hours."

"I'm sorry to bother you about this. Like I say, I didn't know you had left."

"Just tell Collier to go easy on Boyd."

"I'm not sure he's in a listening mood."

"Just tell him."

* * *

Henry changed clothes quickly. *It may not get fixed*, Baxter had said. *There aren't any guarantees.* He might find a destiny behind Boyd. He might find nothing but a lunatic and a plane ride home. But for now, what mattered was getting to Boyd. It was the right thing to do, and improbably, he was free to do it. To have a purpose again was enough. His bag was still packed; in the rush to make Elaine's party there hadn't been time to unpack, and he had ignored the job in the malaise of the previous day. He looked around his apartment for a moment before leaving. Thoughtfully, he walked to a drawer in a chest in his bedroom. He opened it, stared at a somewhat yellowed envelope, and put the envelope in his pocket. He drove straight to O'Hare, parked in long-term, and took the tram to the ticket counter. There were plenty of seats available, and he got a row to himself for the seventy-five-minute flight.

When Henry pulled his car up at the sheriff's office it was just after two in the morning. The crowd had dwindled, but the headlights of three or four latecomers with nothing better to do shot through the night across the parking lot, sending streaks of luminescence through the limbs of the people still standing around outside the office. Henry screeched to a halt and had the door open before the car stopped. He entered the sheriff's office at a trot.

Sheriff Collier was about forty-five, with a dark, sunburnt face, short-cropped hair, and sallow gray eyes. His weight had settled comfortably in his stomach, which protruded from an otherwise slender frame with spindly legs and an arched back. When Henry saw him he was standing by his desk, adjusting a bandage on his wrist and hand.

"Sheriff, I'm Henry Mathews. I'm the one who asked you to get Boyd out of there."

Collier turned toward the voice without actually acknowledging it. "Didn't do it for you," he said. "Don't need any scenes around the Crandall store, that's all. Roger wouldn't like that. Best to bring the nutcase in here, till we can get him out in the morning. Already got a call in to the state hospital up in Larned. Night nurse in the psychiatric ward said they'd come over first thing in the morning, pick him up."

"I want to see Boyd," Henry said. "Immediately."

Collier tucked in his shirt, walked around behind his desk, and sat down. "I could've called out to the Crandall place, but no need. I happen to know Roger's in Topeka."

"I'm glad to know that. I'd like to see Boyd, now."

"He's gettin' himself another lawyer, what he told me before he left. Told me you're out. So I'm just tryin' to figure out why I should give a damn about you seein' Boyd."

Henry walked to the desk. "I never worked for Roger Crandall. He's been free to get any representation he wanted from the day I first got here." Collier rose and walked to a coffeemaker, pouring himself a cup. He looked Henry over, weighing the size of the threat. "Don't make me no difference anyway." He gestured toward the door leading into the small cellblock. "See, I got myself a lunatic in there. The man just destroyed a lot of valuable property. *Crandall* property, not that I give a damn."

"You're above all that, then? The Crandall name strikes no fear in your heart?"

Collier gave Henry a dark look. "I don't take my orders from Roger," he said in a low voice. "No, thing is, the whole town's in an uproar. So like I said, I don't believe we're gonna have any visitors tonight."

Henry thought, *If not from Crandall, then whom?* "I have no idea what happened tonight," he said, "but I do know that Boyd is obviously extremely upset about something. I want to know what that thing is. This kind of action isn't in his history at all."

Collier sat back down and pushed back his chair. "See this?" he said. He shook his bandaged forearm. "The little rat bit me. Bit me, like a damn animal. Now, I got a responsibility to keep order in this town, Mathews, and I'm gonna do just that." He looked out the window at the crowd milling around in front of the office. "I got a situation here," he said. "There isn't a hell of a lot to do on a Monday night in Council Grove. Folks got a lotta time on their hands. So like I said, no visitors tonight. We got us a criminal matter now. Destruction of property. Disturbin' the peace. Criminal trespass. So I'd say you can get on home now and leave this matter to me."

Henry looked Collier directly in the eyes. *Maybe there was a reason I became a lawyer after all,* he thought. *It's not much, but it's something. At least I can put the fear of God into small-town punks like this.* He leaned over Collier's desk. "I'm going to explain something to you now, Sheriff," he said, "and I'm going to use small words, so you don't miss anything. I'm not some podunk legal-aid attorney from one of the little insect-infested towns around here. I've been paid a lot of money to destroy people, and I haven't forgotten how to do it. I say this without the slightest hostility— simply to inform you—that I am a legal nightmare beyond your limited comprehension. It would mean nothing to me to bury you in actions you lack the simple capacity to read. Understand me, Sheriff. I don't mean burying your department, insignificant as it is. I mean burying you, personally. By the time I'm finished, for the rest of your small, insignificant life, your pathetic little salary will go entirely to Mr. Raymond Boyd, in compensation for the gross violation of his civil and medical rights you are now foolish enough to imagine perpetrating." He leaned even closer, and felt Collier retreat in the face of his energy. "It might have crept into your minuscule brain that I'm bullshitting you. Look at me, Sheriff. Do I look like I'm bullshitting you?" Collier didn't speak. "I don't ever bullshit about destroying people. Given Mr. Boyd's extremely tentative mental condition and your lack of medical expertise, I would say that your ruthless restraint of him in a straitjacket is tantamount to psychiatric murder. I'm confident that a number of psychiatrists can be found to testify to that fact. You will be held liable for any harm that comes to him as a result of your impulsive action, and I will see that you are found negligent because you didn't seek expert psychiatric and medical opinions regarding that restraint. Of course, if he has any type of seizure or suffers any physical harm in attempting to free himself, those damages will be added to the total. The violation of his civil rights, which are grotesque, are an entirely different matter, but we're already somewhere in the millions. That's off the top of my head, Sheriff. I can sit down and really start to work on making you miserable, if you like. Or you can find some keys. It's entirely up to you."

Collier stared for a full half minute, and Henry didn't allow himself even to blink. He merely bored a hole into Collier's skull with his eyes, and watched the sheriff levitate off his chair and fumble nervously for the cell keys.

"Shit," Collier said, "if you're gonna throw that legal crap around you can go see him. If this'll get you out of my hair, go on. But hurry up. I don't want you in there all night."

"I'll let you know when I'm done," Henry answered dismissively.

"Just watch his teeth, damn it. Doc's gone home, and I ain't in the mood to patch anybody up tonight."

Collier led Henry through a heavy steel door with a single, barred window. The door opened into a narrow hallway with four cells arranged in a row on one side. Boyd was the only prisoner. Henry walked down the hallway, looking in each cell, until he got to the third; there, he saw Boyd sitting on the edge of a bare metal cot. He was hugging himself tightly, his arms pulled back by the tight cords of the straitjacket. Henry walked in front of Collier to the cell door and placed his hand on it; Boyd didn't look up.

"There's no reason for the personal restraint," Henry said sternly. "He's incarcerated as it is."

"He's still got to be handled," Collier answered. "I don't want any more incidents. Easier this way." He looked at Henry. "I like things easy."

"The man can't even go to the bathroom, did you ever think about that? We're getting him out of that thing."

Boyd was still for the moment, slumped over and breathing quietly. His eyes were open but he stared into space, apparently unseeing. His hair and beard were streaked with sweat and dirt. After a few seconds Collier pulled a wooden nightstick from his belt and gripped it firmly. "Tell you what," he said. "You take it off him. But if he so much as peeps, the jacket's goin' back on, and he can go in his pants for all I care."

Collier unlocked the door of the cell, his eyes on Boyd. The door swung open, but Boyd didn't move. Henry walked into the cell, passing Collier, who stayed in the hall. Boyd was trembling slightly within the straitjacket, tiny shudders erupting as if he were freezing. Henry looked at him searchingly, wondering if he should continue forward. "This man has been minding his own business for a very long time," he said. "It must have taken something severe to drive him to this. A man doesn't sit on a park bench for twenty-five years and suddenly attack a building."

"Don't mean nothing to me."

"Aren't you interested at all in what the thing that pushed him over the edge might be?"

"How should I know?" He waved his nightstick. "The man's a nut, Mathews. Who knows why he does anything? Maybe he thinks God told him to do it."

"This didn't just happen. There has to be a reason." Henry turned back to Boyd, approaching slowly. Boyd was calm for the moment, and Henry helped him up off the metal bed. He removed the jacket, Boyd looking sullenly downward, his thoughts apparently far away. As Henry let the jacket fall at last to the floor, Boyd looked up into his eyes. There was a longing and hurting there that overwhelmed. But even as Henry looked, the face quickly clouded over again into oblivion, shutting him out. Henry turned and looked at the sheriff, seeing the habitual, lazy disinterest in the man. It wasn't hard to imagine what would happen if the situation was left unchecked: criminal prosecution for Boyd, public humiliation, eventual committal to a psychiatric ward, possibly indefinitely. He turned back to Boyd, catching his gaze once again. "Absolution," Henry whispered. "Absolution, old man."

Boyd looked up briefly, giving Henry the feeling of a moment's connection. But as before, it passed quickly into an impenetrable void. "We've got to check out what's happened here," Henry said sharply, "and right away."

Collier shrugged. "Say you're right, say somethin' pushed him. What do you expect me to do about it?"

"I expect you to do your job, damn it. In fact, I'm going with you to make sure you do it. One thing I'm positive of—Boyd's not dangerous. For all his bluster, he's perfectly harmless, and you know it. Something, or someone, got to him."

"I don't know nothin' about that."

"That's why you're going to check it out right now, Sheriff, because the first thing in the morning you have the funny farm lined up to take him to a psychiatric hospital. I want to know what's happened before then, because once they get hold of him I have no doubt he'll be so drugged the person you see in that cell will no longer exist."

"You're actin' like the man's lawyer. Which you ain't."

Henry looked at Boyd, and saw him looking searchingly into his eyes. "Sheriff," he said, "I'm going to find out what happened here if it's the last thing I do. As of this moment I'm representing Raymond Boyd."

Collier smiled and ran his hand through his thinning hair. "Then I take it you ain't representin' the estate no more. Can't be both, son. I know that much about the law. Conflict of interest. I'll scc to that, since we're flingin' threats around here. You'll be just some low-paid flunky representing an indigent fruitcake. That'd be new territory for you, I imagine. I'd think that over pretty carefully."

Henry stepped out of the cell and pulled the door shut. "I resigned that position two days ago, Sheriff. You're behind the times. Now go start your car."

Collier stared back, a bemused expression on his face. Twenty years of Crandalls had taught him to look after himself. There were forces at work here that the kid knew nothing about, forces that could crush both of them without a thought. But the boy had stuck his oar in things, and set into motion a legal chain of events that followed one another like night followed day. It was goddam annoying. If he didn't investigate the case properly, the punk would turn it on him and burn him. On the other hand, if he did investigate, his bosses wouldn't like that. *Why*, he thought, *did Tyler Crandall have to go and die?* He picked up his gun and holster, slinging it around his waist. "Hell, let's go," he said. "Lemme see if I can get what's left of this little audience to go home first."

Collier talked the crowd home, and by waiting a few minutes he and Henry were able to ride out to Custer's Elm without a public escort of hangers-on. The trip across town was brief, and Henry found himself exhilarated as they drove. He smiled, the first really free smile he had experienced in a long time. Ten minutes later the police cruiser swung into a parking space on the street opposite Boyd's bench, and the two of them got out and looked around for twenty minutes or so with a couple of Collier's big police flashlights. Nothing appeared unusual or out of the ordinary, and Collier said at last, "Well, I hope you're happy. All you're doin' is costing me sleep. I'm startin' to hate this case already, and it's only the first day."

Henry, ignoring Collier, stood quietly by the bench, staring into the night. The park was dead quiet, which disturbed Henry, although he wasn't sure why for a moment. Suddenly he asked, "Where's the bird?"

"The vulture? How should I know? Asleep, I hope. Or maybe carryin' babies off into the night."

Henry gave the sheriff a look of profound irritation. "Are they nocturnal? Do they sleep nights, or what?"

Collier, feeling he had exhausted his expertise on the subject, said nothing. Henry turned suddenly and said, "Come on."

"I ain't no taxi service, boy," Collier replied. "Where you headin'?"

"We're going to Boyd's house," Henry said. "Right now."

Collier sighed and walked to the car, getting in after Henry. It was only about ten blocks to Boyd's place, and soon the cruiser's headlights streaked across the run-down home, settling on the porch. Henry looked at the house, gasped out a low moaning sound, and turned his face.

Collier, hearing Henry, peered up through the harsh light of the headlights at the house. What he saw made him catch his breath; there, nailed to Boyd's front door, was the bird. The head had been wrenched horribly, twisted into a disfiguring angle. Each wing was fully extended and a long nail held it in place, hammered into the splintering wood. A large iron spike was run through the center of the bird's body, pinning it to the door. A pool of blood and body fluids lay collected on the porch below the animal. Henry retched, and Collier whistled. "Shit," he said quietly, "now that is truly sick."

Henry closed his eyes and leaned back in the car seat. "Truly personal," he whispered. "Truly designed to do exactly what it did."

Collier looked at him. "What does that mean?"

"This was a calculated move, something intended to push Boyd over an already very fragile edge."

"I don't like this any better than you do, but if you're tryin' to tell me that this is some excuse for what happened tonight, you can kiss my ass, boy. The law's the law. Boyd's goin' up on charges, period."

Henry took a deep breath and forced his eyes away from the door. There was something transfixing and horrifying about the sight of the bird, once a tyrannical legend in his own life, now so evidently, manifestly dead. It was, in a bizarre way, like Ty; both characters, once so frightening, suddenly finished. "Look, Sheriff," he said, "that bird was the only thing Raymond Boyd cared about. It was like a child to him. Killing it was an act of inhumane cruelty. You ought to be asking yourself who did this and make finding them your first priority."

"You're takin' me the wrong way, son. I told you I don't like this, and I meant it. Like I said, I like a quiet town, which is what this place was until that damn will screwed everything up." He pushed his hat back. "I'll handle this like any other case. But you're as crazy as Boyd if you think this means I'm easin' up on him. And you can forget what you're thinkin'."

"And what's that?" Henry's irritation was turning into profound dislike.

"You're thinkin' it's Roger Crandall did this, and you're dead wrong."

"I wasn't thinking that. But since you bring it up, what makes you so sure?"

"For starters, because he's in Topeka, like I already told you. Point is, Roger's no fool, and everybody in town knows how he feels about the Birdman. Too damn obvious."

"Everything Roger Crandall does is obvious," Henry said. "He wouldn't have given that a thought." He paused a long moment, and added quietly, "But that doesn't mean I think he did it. The fact is, it's not his style."

"What the hell does that mean?"

"It means that when Roger's pissed off he's more likely to just haul off and hit somebody. There's a finesse to this cruelty, something truly diabolical that's beyond his limited mental faculties. If nothing else, he lacks the imagination to think of it." He turned to the sheriff. "If, after seeing this, you're still bringing charges against Boyd, I want you to remand him to my custody. There's no need for the hospital."

"If I ever saw somebody who does need a hospital, it's him," Collier replied flatly.

"I don't think so," Henry said. "Twenty minutes ago you thought you had a dangerous man going off for no reason, a loaded gun. It's obvious now that Boyd was more than just pushed. He was shoved."

Collier looked at Henry. "Shoved is still shoved. I don't give a damn why he's dangerous. I just care that he is dangerous."

"Not dangerous," Henry said, "just crushed inside. Just because he's a little crazy doesn't mean he can't feel pain. Maybe he feels it even more deeply than we do."

"What do you expect me to do? Just let him go? I can't do that and you know it. After what happened tonight, if I just let Boyd go I might as well hand in my badge."

"I want Boyd to get help. I just want it to happen without his being committed."

"What about the medical care? You expect them to come out here?"

"Yes, I do," Henry said firmly. "Look, Sheriff, what I want is merely a change of venue. Let your hospital people come here in the morning. Let them do an initial workup on him. But guarantee me that unless it's absolutely necessary, he won't be committed. This man lived peacefully for over twenty-five years, not bothering a soul. What he did tonight is completely understandable. I won't have him locked up in the state hospital. I've seen it. It's whitewashed hell."

"That's a hell of a big request, boy. It ain't psychiatrists gonna be comin' out in the morning. It's just the lockups they send in the van."

"Then we get a psychiatrist to come. Use your head, damn it. For some reason Boyd has found it absolutely essential to spend the past twenty-five years away from people, out in the least congested place in this whole town. Forcing him into a tiny room for the next few years is probably enough to snap whatever cord he has left. If they do that, it won't make a bit of difference what kind of treatment they give him, because there won't be anyone left to save. Somewhere there's a doctor who understands that. Besides, if there is someone else behind this, committing Boyd just gets him out of the way. I don't want that. I want him very much in the way."

Collier watched him narrowly, his mind in an unaccustomed effort of concentration. The lawyer was dangerous, and it didn't look like he was going away. He hated this whole night, and it wasn't over yet. Neither spoke for a long time. Finally Collier released a short, sardonic burst of laughter. "Hell, you can have him," he said in a gritty voice. "I'll let you step in it. But I've got a condition—you get nothin' unless you can get a board-certified doctor out here tomorrow by noon to sign off on it. I gotta have the paperwork or it's my ass. Till then he stays where he is. But if he does get released to you, that don't mean I can't change my mind. If I hear one thing out of that nut, I'm sending him away to the padded room, and I don't give a damn what anybody says."

"He'll be fine."

The sheriff gave him a sideways glance. "Ain't *his* safety I'm worried about," he said dryly. "But that's your problem. You wake up with an ax in your back, I'll be glad to handle your funeral arrangements."

"Thanks, that's a real comfort."

Collier started the engine. "Let's go," he said. "If we're lucky, maybe Boyd will have killed himself while we were gone. Then I can get some sleep."

Chapter Twenty-two

Henry drove to the Flinthills Motel, woke up the owner, and checked in. There were only two other cars, and the parking lot looked forlorn under the glare of harsh streetlamps. He dropped his bag on the bed and looked out the picture window of his motel room. A shallow haze of orange was just forming to the east, coalescing into light. He stared at his watch; it was after five. He would need to sleep, if only for an hour or two. He pulled out a travel alarm, put it on the nightstand near his ear, and lay down, fully clothed, on top of the bed. At six-thirty it went off, and he rose, surprisingly alert. He was hungry, and rummaging through his briefcase yielded a bag of peanuts and a granola bar. He devoured them and calculated when he could call Amanda. He showered, and at seven he dialed her number. The instant she answered he could feel her still sleeping.

"Amanda, this is Henry."

"Mmm."

"Henry Mathews. Sorry to wake you."

A pause, and her voice was more alert. "Henry? It's okay, my alarm was just about to go off. Where are you?"

"I'm in Council Grove. I've got news." There was a rustling of sheets; he could hear her sitting up in bed.

"You're supposed to be in Chicago."

"Raymond's in jail."

He could feel her catch her breath. "What happened?"

"It's a long story, and we don't have time to go into that right now."

"We?"

"Look, I know this is a presumption, but I could really use some help."

"You helped me. Seems fair."

"Helped you, then left town."

"You couldn't help that. Or maybe you could, since you're back. I don't know what's happened to you or Raymond. Neither one of you is where you're supposed to be."

"I'll fill you in on both of us when I see you. Can you get away today?"

"I can get away for the week. My office would probably pay you to get me out of their hair."

"All right. Then do you feel like a new cause?"

There was still a trace of early-morning husk in her voice. "I love causes."

"Then meet me at the sheriff's office at about ten."

"No problem."

"And I need you to do something in the meantime. Unless I can get a psychiatrist out here to declare Raymond safe for polite society, the sheriff is going to have him carted off to the state hospital and nothing much will matter after that. I need a sympathetic man, not a government robot, and I need him by noon. Can you help?"

"Do I *seem* like I'd know a lot of psychiatrists?"

Henry smiled. "Well, you don't appear to play well with your class-mates. It was just a guess."

"Hate to disappoint you. But I have a friend who's a nurse. I can ask her."

"That will have to do. Just tell her we need somebody with some humanity, will you?"

"All right. I can't make any promises, but we'll see. And, Henry . . ."

"Yeah?"

"I don't know what's happened, but I'm glad you're back."

"I'm glad, too. And I don't know what's happened, either."

To pray seemed unlikely, at a minimum. He hadn't prayed in . . . well, not much since his parents' accident, and not at all since law school. There had been the railing against God for a short time, the angry, Job-like questions that turned quickly into stilted recriminations. Then, like the quiet after a storm, his soul had settled into a silent disbelief. The bomb had been dropped, and the patient was terminal. Now, against all odds, there were signs of life once again.

It could never be like it had been, that he realized absolutely. It could never be the kind of faith that asked no questions and believed blindly. He could never take his requests to the God of his childhood, that imaginary beast, half ogre, half heavenly honey bear. He never knew whether to be terrified of that God or to beg Him for treats, like a puppy. That was gone forever. But a tremor of something else moved very quietly within, a vibration that he was tempted to quell before it developed pitch and voice.

To open that door again. To believe . . . if not in the earlier God, then in what or in whom? In an amorphous God, a blind force of nature? In a karmic accountant who dealt benevolently or harshly based on a scale of worthiness? None seemed alive to him, none worthy of taking the enormous personal risk of believing again. Behind them all, there was a suspect, however; moving still in shadows, not of evil but of stupendous, incomprehensible politeness, a God who could somehow wait in utter silence—as if dead or never having lived—and then, in a web of events so complex and interconnected they were beyond comprehension, begin to move, to gently push and prod and unveil Himself. This God could, perhaps, be prayed to. A God not on the end of a chain but on and in the synapses of his very brain, behind everything and in everything and more enormous than he had ever imagined.

It was short, in the end, this reopening of communication. There was no ritual, no bowing of the head, no bending of knee. After five years of silence, Henry's first utterance into the invisible space surrounding him was little more than a Morse code of a prayer, a short collection of letters that spelled out only two words: "Help Raymond."

Chapter Twenty-three

Seeing her was different from hearing her. He watched her come across the street from her car and once again liked her walk: it was strong, but feminine, with a subdued, comfortable sexuality. She was dressed casually, in pants and a collared shirt that merely hinted at her figure. She smiled, the sweetly crooked line of her mouth curving upward, a welcome flaw in an otherwise charming face. He bussed her cheek, feeling the warmth of her skin against his own. There was a flush of attraction, but he pushed it away. "Right where I left you," he said.

"I think you have that backward. I have news."

"It's good, obviously. The smile doesn't go with disappointment."

She nodded. "Dr. T. R. Harris. Shrink to the downtrodden, apparently. My friend says he's wonderful, and he's on his way." She grasped his hand momentarily, then let go. He took her fingers back into his own.

"There's a lot to tell you," he said. "But at least the part about me can wait, if you can."

"After we see Raymond. Then tell me everything."

The two crossed Chautauqua, passed by the Trailside Diner, and walked into Sheriff Collier's office. Collier glanced up at Amanda, and Henry pointedly declined to introduce her. "How's my client?" he asked. "Anything happen while I was gone?"

Collier put down his cup of coffee with languorous deliberation, as if thinking over an important crime strategy. He pulled on a chain that snaked from his right front pocket, and a huge set of keys popped out. "Birdman's had a quiet morning," he said. "He paced for the first few hours, which didn't bother me none."

"Did he eat?"

"I pushed some food in there a couple of hours ago. What he did after I left I couldn't tell you."

Collier pushed a key into the heavy metal door that led into the cell-block, turned it, and opened the door. "She stays," he said. "You got fifteen minutes."

Amanda sat down while Henry followed Collier through the door and down the narrow hallway. The sheriff unlocked Boyd's cell and said, "Yell if you need help. I can hear through the door grates." Henry walked quietly inside. He heard the barred door swing shut behind him, clanging locked with a solid, metallic clank. He was locked in. "See ya, kid," Collier said. He walked down the hall and closed the door behind him.

Boyd's face was gray and gaunt. He was sitting, rocking back and forth in an endless, repeated motion. He looked like he hadn't slept, and the plate of food was untouched.

Henry walked up to him and sat down on the cot. "How are you, Raymond?" he asked quietly.

The nodding and rocking continued, but he finally spoke. His voice was trembling, fractured. "There's gold in my blood."

"What are you talking about, Raymond?"

"They're tryin' to poison me. I need to get my blood cleaned, get the gold out of it."

Henry stared at him. "Who's trying to poison you, Raymond?"

"Always the same, always the same. Always tryin' to fill my blood with gold."

Henry paused, unsure of how to respond. After a moment he said, "I don't blame you for being angry about what happened to the bird, Raymond. Before anything else happens, I want you to know that." At this Boyd looked away, locking his eyes on the opposite wall. Henry pressed on, determined to continue his own stream of logic. "You're still in trouble over breaking up the store. We have to do something about that."

Boyd hugged his knees as he rocked. "Bird," he said quietly.

"I'm going to find out who did that, and I'm going to do everything in my power to make them pay," Henry said. "You can count on that." Henry turned and kneeled down in front of Boyd, bringing him face-to-face. "I need to explain something important to you, Raymond. Because of what you did at the store, a doctor is coming. He's going to talk to you. I don't know him personally, so I can't vouch for him. I think he's a good man. I hope he is."

"Doctor. Get the gold out of my blood."

"I don't know, Raymond. Maybe."

Boyd made a guttural sound low in his throat. It contained, without words, utter contempt. Henry looked at his watch; Harris would arrive soon. "Raymond, a lot depends on what you say to this man." He felt flooded with emotion. He wanted to protect Boyd, but he didn't know how. "Just be yourself," he said at last. "I'm just going to trust that everything will work out."

"Everything will work out," Boyd said.

Henry stared a moment, and asked, "What do you mean, Raymond? Why do you think that?"

"The terrible arm of the Lord," Boyd said, rocking vigorously. "Trust in the terrible arm of the Lord."

Henry sat on his heels looking at Boyd a long moment, then called through the grate to Collier, who, in typical extended fashion, took several minutes to unlock the cell and let Henry out. By the time they had returned to the main office, a short, plump man in khaki pants and an open-collared white shirt was coming in the front door.

Collier took his seat behind his desk and put his feet up. The man walked to the desk and introduced himself. "T. R. Harris," he said. "Evidently there's a Mr. Raymond Boyd here for me to examine."

Collier looked up dispassionately. "You the shrink?" he asked.

The man smiled. "Depends. You Raymond Boyd?"

Collier's face betrayed his irritation. "Hell, no," he barked. "See this uniform? The nut's in a cell."

"The last guy I talked to thought he was the Emperor of Mexico, so a sheriff's uniform doesn't impress me too much."

Amanda laughed out loud, and the doctor turned to her with an intelligent smile. "You're not Boyd," he said easily. "At least you're not a Raymond."

"No," Amanda said. "I'm a friend of Susan's, the nurse who called you. Thanks for coming."

"T. R. Harris," the man said, reaching out and shaking her hand. "Beats talking to housewives about their credit card bills."

Henry, watching from the doorway, liked the man immediately. He didn't seem like a doctor, exactly—more like somebody it would be good to simply sit down with and just talk. He stuck out his hand and introduced himself. "I know it was short notice," he said. "We were really in a bind."

The sheriff broke in. "I ain't got all day for this, Doc. Let's get it over with." He nodded toward the cellblock. "Prisoner's in there."

"I'd rather not conduct the examination in a cell," Harris said. "Got a break room, maybe a little coffee?"

"Yeah, right through there," Collier answered, pointing toward a painted metal door. "But I'd advise against it. Prisoner's shown to be violent." He held up his bandaged arm and grimaced.

The doctor looked at Collier's arm, and Henry noticed a tiny smile flicker briefly on his face. "Well," Harris said, "I'll holler if there's a problem. That okay?"

"Up to you," Collier said. He walked to a cabinet near his desk, unlocked it, and took out a small stun gun. He took off the safety and looked at the doctor. "Two thousand volts, but real low amps. Kinda like electroshock treatment. I'll be right outside the door."

Henry stood and said, "I'd like to come along," fully aware that the request would be denied.

"Not this time, Counselor," Harris answered with a smile. "But nice try."

Harris disappeared behind the metal door, taking a seat in the coffee room while the sheriff got Boyd. In a couple of minutes Collier led in his prisoner, firmly pushing him from behind by his cuffed hands. Harris pointed to the restraints and said, "Those won't be necessary, Sheriff." Collier shrugged and unlocked Boyd, pushing him down into a chair near the doctor. He looked at Harris, patted his stun gun, and walked out.

Harris sat quietly, apparently in no hurry to begin the examination. For a long time the low murmur of Boyd's self-talk was the only sound in the room. Several minutes passed, the doctor smiling good-naturedly but not speaking. After some time, Boyd's self-talk began to slowly subside. Eventually, he was barely whispering. Boyd looked up, and when their eyes met, Harris spoke.

"Hello, Raymond," he said. "My name is Tom Harris. I'm a psychiatrist."

Boyd didn't answer out loud; his lips continued to move, silently now.

"I'm going to explain a couple of things before we get started," Harris said. "You can just listen for now, unless you feel like saying anything." He pulled a notebook and pen out of a leather valise and situated the pad on his knee. "I hope you don't mind my calling you Raymond, by the way. I don't mean to imply we're friends at this point. Somebody I don't know acts like my friend, it usually means they're selling something. So if you prefer I use Mr. Boyd, I can understand that." Boyd stared back silently.

"Some folks around here are pretty interested in what's going on inside your head, Raymond. I'm supposed to find out and tell them. I'm going to ask you some questions and see what I can make of your answers. If I think that you can handle things on your own after our talk, the sheriff will release you to the lawyer for the time being. If I think you're dangerous to yourself or anyone else, he's going to begin a proceeding to have you hospitalized until I think you're better. I'll be the first to admit that it's not fair. You don't know any of the people who are deciding. But so far nobody has been able to figure out a better way to do this, so we all have to live with it." Harris smiled softly. "If it helps any, I hate that part of the job myself." He flicked on a tape recorder. "I'm going to record this, Raymond. That way nobody can argue later on about what we said. I can't make you answer the questions, and I won't try. I'm a doctor, not a policeman, so it's up to you. But it's only fair to tell you that not answering leaves things up to my imagination, and if you're sane you might not want to do that." Harris picked up his notepad. "Ready?"

Boyd had looked away, his expression disinterested.

"Raymond, have you ever been admitted to a hospital? A long time ago, perhaps?" Boyd said nothing. "Have you ever been prescribed any medications? Has a doctor ever given you any pills to take?"

Harris watched Boyd, who said nothing. The two sat silently again for a while, until the doctor said, "I understand you had a bad day yesterday, Raymond. Apparently you did some pretty considerable damage to a store, broke out some windows. Do you remember doing that?" Raymond looked up at the doctor, and a shallow smile slowly spread across his face. "I'll take that as a yes," the doctor said. "What were you thinking about when you broke the windows, Raymond? Can you remember how you felt while you were doing that?"

Boyd, instead of answering, stood straight up out of his chair with surprising suddenness. In standing he hit a small table, knocking an empty coffee cup to the floor. The plastic cup didn't break but rolled noisily across the tile. The doctor momentarily flinched in surprise, but held his position, arms tense. Almost instantly the door opened and Collier rushed into the room, his stun gun raised.

"What the hell's going on in here?" the sheriff demanded, moving quickly toward Boyd. Boyd made no movement to defend himself; he stared blankly at the sheriff as he approached, but Harris quickly rose. "That's all right," he said, stopping Collier. "Mr. Boyd was just feeling a little crowded."

Collier glared. "I'm tryin' to keep you alive, if you'd get your head out of your ass," he muttered harshly. Boyd, ignoring them both, turned and walked to the opposite wall, separating himself from the others by the maximum possible distance the room would allow. He stood with his back to the men, a good fifteen feet away.

"I said I'd call out if there was a problem, and I meant it," Harris said. "Now let me get on with this, please."

Collier shoved his stun gun into his belt. "I'll come when I feel like it. I ain't on call, not to you." The door shut behind him with a metallic clang.

Harris sat down again, composing himself. He was formulating another question when he was surprised to hear Boyd's voice. He looked up and saw Boyd staring at him. Boyd repeated himself in a low, gravelly voice. "Custer's Elm," he said.

The doctor smiled. "What about Custer's Elm?"

"Spent the night there on the way to gettin' killed."

"You don't look dead to me, Raymond."

"Seventh Calvary, United States Army. They came in September. Early cold that year, yessiree."

"Ah. I see. You mean Custer and his men. What year was that, Raymond? I was never too good in history."

Boyd smiled, a thin, humorless expression. "Last Indian victory," he said.

"Little Bighorn. I remember now. I haven't thought about that since high school."

"That's right, that's right. Them men was goin' up to Montana."

"To fight Indians."

Boyd's smile evaporated. "Min-er-al rights," he said, stretching out the word. "That was sacred burial ground. Reservation land. Indians wouldn't let nobody dig up there, 'cause they didn't much care about gold. That's what the killin' was for."

"I wasn't aware of that."

Boyd's head bobbed, his speech coming more easily. "That's right, that's right," he said. "They was gonna get the money in the ground. Only thing was, the Indians killed every last one of 'em. Cut their ears off 'em. Hair, too. Cut their hearts out of 'em, a few. Just goes to show ya, don't it?"

"What does it show, Raymond?"

"When the bloody hand of the Lord comes down, man's plans don't mean shit."

Harris set down his pen. "Why do you call it the hand of the Lord, Raymond? It was Indians who killed the soldiers."

"Northern Pacific Railroad."

"I don't follow you again."

Boyd grinned, his horrific teeth showing. "Custer wasn't no soldier, not for years. He was workin' for the Northern Pacific Railroad. Hired to clean out them Indians."

Harris looked at Boyd a long time. "Why do you live at the park, Raymond?"

Boyd glanced up with a sharp look. "No doctors," he said.

Harris smiled. "There's nobody at all there, Raymond. Is that what you like about it?"

Boyd's expression changed with startling rapidity, sadness covering him. "Bird," he whispered.

Harris paused. "I heard about that," he said. "Whoever did that needs me a lot more than you do, Raymond."

With his memory of the bird, Boyd seemed to diminish; his shoulders slumped forward and he lowered his head, staring at the floor. Harris set his notebook down, rose, and slowly walked to a coffeemaker near where Boyd was sitting; as he approached, Boyd stood nervously and began edging away, keeping the distance constant. Harris ignored this and held up the coffeepot. "Want some?" he asked. He poured himself a cup and tasted it. "Jail coffee," he said, smiling. Boyd made no response, and he walked back to his seat, Raymond circling him like a boxer.

"Raymond, when I came out here I had a lot of things I wanted to ask you. But it's pretty obvious you'd rather just be left alone. That doesn't make you crazy. I don't pretend to understand how you felt about the bird, but I believe it was precious to you. I also believe that you deserve a chance to mourn that loss, and getting interrogated right now must be very painful. We're going to have a lot of talks in the future. So right now I'm going to ask you just one more question, and if you feel like answering it, we'll end there. If you don't, I'll have the sheriff take you back to your cell and think things over for a while. That sound okay?" Boyd remained silent. "I'll take that as a yes, too," Harris said. "I'm interested in the story you told me, Raymond, the one about General Custer getting killed. I want to ask you something about it. I want you to tell me who did wrong in the story. Tell me who did wrong, Raymond, the Indians or the soldiers?"

Boyd looked carefully at the doctor a moment; he twisted his hands together, his head bobbing back and forth. Harris, sensing his anguish, leaned forward, his eyes locked on Boyd. The two men stared at each other, neither blinking. Harris asked again, his voice no more than a whisper. "Who was the wicked in the story, Raymond? Who deserved to be punished?"

Boyd licked his lips and rubbed his hands together vigorously, his face contorted in anxiety. At last, he stood and walked to the center of the room. Harris gripped his chair, but didn't flinch. Slowly, Raymond began to unbutton his shirt. One button after another was carefully unfastened; when they were all opened, he pulled the shirt apart. There, five inches tall in the center of his chest, was a reddish, raised scar, the ruins of a wound obviously self-inflicted, in the rough shape of a cross. Boyd lifted his arms to the ceiling and spoke a single word: "Me."

The door to the break room opened and Harris appeared. "We're finished for now, Sheriff," the doctor said. "You can take Mr. Boyd back to his cell."

Collier grunted and walked past the man, forcing the doctor to make way. Harris let him by and came into the front room of the office. "Well," he said, "that was interesting."

"I had a feeling you might think so," Henry said.

"First, I want to say that it's appalling that this man wasn't treated a long time ago. Fifteen minutes with any qualified psychiatrist, or even an M.D., for God's sake, would have made the need for that abundantly clear."

"In a little town like this he could lay low and not be bothered," Henry said.

"And the state medical system isn't exactly set up for indigent health care." Harris nodded, irritation on his face. "Apparently this man has dropped twenty-plus years, and I'd like to get him through it as quickly as possible."

"Good," Henry said. "Tell us what you know at this point."

"With someone so delusional it would be easy to say that he's a schizophrenic. But I would be using the term less professionally than I prefer. He does exhibit some obvious schizophrenic behaviors: religious ideation, dropping in and out of conversation, even the self-molestation."

"Self-molestation?" Amanda whispered. "What are you talking about?"

"Were either of you aware that Raymond has carved a cross on his chest?" Harris asked, his voice level.

"My God," Henry said, "I had no idea things had gone that far."

"It's obviously from some time ago, if that gives you any comfort. But there's no question it was done by Raymond himself. Probably a pocket-knife." Henry leaned against a table, fighting back a sudden wave of nausea. He steadied himself and asked, "What are your reservations with calling him schizophrenic?"

"It's strange, but the kinds of things you normally see accompanying those types of symptoms aren't present."

"For example?" Henry asked.

"Inappropriate affect, for one. Giggling when something bad happens, that kind of thing. Inappropriate moods. Raymond is nothing like that. He's obviously deeply, horribly wounded, and he acts like it. He's in touch with his emotions in a way that schizophrenics normally aren't. To tell you the truth, I had the feeling that he understood exactly what was going on during our talk. I don't think he would have tolerated the least condescension or manipulation from me."

"What did he say?" Henry asked. "Did you find out anything about his past we didn't know?"

"We talked about General Custer," Harris answered. "And mineral rights. Raymond gave me a very coherent history of Little Bighorn."

"Mineral rights," Amanda said. "That's very odd."

"I thought so."

"No," Amanda interjected, "there's a battle going on around here on that subject. The Crandall land is in the middle of it."

Harris looked concerned. "I'm going to need you to fill me in on that," he said. "It was obvious to me that he had identified very deeply with Custer's story. Our conversation ended on a very disturbing note."

The door from the cellblock grated noisily open. Collier shoved his keys back into his pocket as he entered the room. He looked disappointed and said, "Well, Doc, he went in like a lamb."

Henry stepped between them and quietly asked the doctor, "Can we finish talking outside?"

Harris nodded, and the three of them walked out onto the sidewalk in front of Collier's office.

"I take it you and the sheriff aren't exactly friends," Harris said.

"He's just wondering where the power is right now," Henry said. "That makes him pliable, for the time being. If he ever takes a side, he'll be impossible."

"I see."

"Look, Doctor, what I want to find out right now is the course of action you're going to recommend."

Harris sighed. "Everything in me would normally say hospitalization. But it's obvious that Raymond has a major problem with confined spaces, and from what I've heard, he's been living out at the park quietly for more than twenty-five years."

"I'm going to level with you, Doctor," Henry said. "It's a huge request I'm making, and I realize that fact. I've got two requests, really. The first is for you to recommend that Raymond be remanded to my custody. The second is for you to agree to treat him here, in Council Grove."

"You're right. Those are huge requests. Why should I agree?"

"Because I think it would be a serious mistake to confine him and because I need him here."

"I'm not particularly worried about your needs at the moment," Harris said, but his voice wasn't hostile. "I agree that confining him might do him more harm than good. On the other hand, it might save his life."

"But you've seen how territorial he is," Amanda interrupted. "I can't stand to think about him in a cell."

"What about the sheriff?" Harris asked. "Raymond's up on charges."

"He's got nothing. I could argue Raymond was breaking into his own property, if it came to that. Nobody's used to real opposition around here. I'd have Boyd out in two hours. The only basis for holding him this long is his psychiatric evaluation. So it's really back in your court."

Harris regarded Henry thoughtfully. "Look, are you really sure you understand what it means to take responsibility for somebody like that? We're talking about a very unpredictable situation."

"Both choices have risk," Henry said. "But if the will goes against him, Raymond has no money we know of. We both know what we're talking about, Doctor. We're talking about the state mental hospital, rubber rooms, guards with truncheons, the whole thing. That place would drive a healthy person insane."

Harris fixed him in a level gaze. "I work at that hospital," he said. "Frankly, I don't think spending time with me would drive him crazy."

"Sorry," Henry said, "and I agree with you on that—I am hoping you will spend time with him. I'm just hoping you'll do it here."

Harris stood thinking a moment. "It's up to him," he said at last.

"Him?" Amanda asked. "Then it's all settled. Raymond will never voluntarily go to any hospital."

"I'm not going to ask him permission," Harris said. "I'm still the doctor, and as of now he's still under arrest. But no matter where he is, he has to be medicated. I'm going to jump-start him with an injection of Ativan and Navane, then he can get started on some oral medications. If he agrees to take his medicine voluntarily, I'll let him stay. If he refuses, I have no choice but to send the suits. I will not allow one more day to pass without treatment for him."

Henry looked at the doctor a long moment. "That's exactly the kind of attitude I hoped to find," he said at last, "and I accept your terms."

"All right. Then you need to know what you're in for. Neuro-drugs like the ones I'm going to put Raymond on are powerful, and he's going to get a large dose. Even so, it will take time to see any results, months for the full effect. I'll sedate him mildly to get him across the first stages, but in the meantime you can get some unpleasant side effects."

"Such as?"

"Look, I won't play any games with you. I believe in these drugs, but they're not a panacea. For one thing they're fat-soluble, so you basically have to drug the entire body just to get them to the sixty square inches of brain you want. By then you can have Parkinsonian symptoms, facial tics, nausea, mood swings, a bunch of stuff. I can tinker with things to try to even that out, but I make no promises. Some people are susceptible, others aren't. As far as his schizophrenia is concerned, the drugs may help a lot. They may not make any difference at all. They can actually make things worse. Obviously, in that case, he's got to be hospitalized."

"They might bring Raymond Boyd back to life," Henry said.

"They might," Harris said cautiously. "But they won't solve whatever happened to him that started all this."

Henry leaned forward, his face alive with interest. "You see it, don't you?" he asked. "That something happened to him to begin all this."

"I see it," the doctor answered. "And that will still be there waiting for him when he gets back. These drugs won't change any of that. He's going to need long-term help."

"We still have to go forward," Amanda said. "Anything is better than what he's facing now."

"I'm glad Raymond has you two looking after him," Harris said. "It's the only reason I'm going along with this scheme. Now let me go do my job."

"You won," Amanda said, looking up at Henry. "Raymond's sleeping quietly in his cell, and we can get him back home by tomorrow afternoon." The two stood at the corner of Chautauqua and Main. The sun had crested above them two hours earlier, and the air was hot, dry, and dusty.

"It went well," Henry answered, feeling lighter than he had in some time. "You scored on Harris. Good man." He chuckled. "I loved how he handled Collier."

"You're welcome," Amanda said, smiling. "Where to now?"

"I think celebrations are in order," Henry answered, returning her smile. "Great, massive, probably premature celebrations."

Amanda looked down Chautauqua. Not a single car was moving. "This really is the perfect place for it, don't you think?"

"Do you think they keep any champagne at the Trailside?" Henry asked thoughtfully. "Preferably Cristal Roederer."

She laughed out loud. "Doubtful. Why that kind?"

"You'd think less of me if I explained. Let's just say it would put a nice period on a former relationship."

Amanda's expression showed that her curiosity was piqued. "I take it you left more than your job behind in Chicago?"

"You could say that," Henry said, leading her toward his car. "And I really don't mean to make light of it. But I love irony, and there it is."

"Apparently I'll have to be content without the details."

"But you must not be content without Cristal. One thing I learned from my buddies at Wilson, Lougherby and Mathers: drink your champagne now, because you're only one meeting away from bad news."

"I don't know if that's cynical or merely practical."

"Doesn't matter. The point is, you get to drink a lot of champagne that way."

"You're right, it doesn't matter."

"Then let's go."

They arrived at the car, and Henry opened the passenger door for her. He felt her brush close by him as she got in, and he felt a dizzy, acquiring sensation in his chest. She slid across the bench seat toward his side; not enough to be forward, but enough to create a pleasant sense of proximity. He got in and they drove north out of town.

"Where are we going?" Amanda asked after several miles had passed, obviously content to be surprised.

"To the only restaurant with a wine list between here and Kansas City," Henry answered. "I ate there my graduation day from law school, and I haven't been back since. If there is a God, the place is still there."

Amanda leaned back in the seat, and Henry drove northeast toward

Lawrence. He pointed out the landmarks of his youth with pleasure as the miles rolled by. "See that windmill at the horizon?" he asked, pointing over her shoulder. "I saw my first birth up there."

She looked at him, surprised. "Of what?"

"Calf," he said, laughing. "That's Clara Littlewater's place. Her husband's long gone, but his widow still runs the place. She's tough as a boot. In calving season most of the men around go up and help her. My father took me up there when I was a kid."

"And you watched a calf being born?"

"Very messy. But worth it when the little guy stood up on those spindly legs." They drove on, Henry pointing out a line of geese far to the east, flying high toward the road. Beyond them, ephemeral in the haze of distance, cattle were scattered like dots on the yellowish-green range grass.

"This is nothing like Connecticut," Amanda said, staring out the window. "You'd have hated us, Henry. We were all terminally bored, little spoiled kids with nice cars."

"Maybe. But you wouldn't have given that up to come here."

"No, not at that point. But I still can't help despising how stuck-up we were."

"When I think about you, that's not the phrase that comes to mind."

She smiled. "What does come to mind?"

Henry laughed, unwilling to be baited. Before she could press him, he turned the car into a gravel driveway. "What's on my mind right now is a good steak."

"Where are we?"

"Skunk Pepper's."

"I am not eating at a place called Skunk Pepper's."

"It's not *named* Skunk Pepper's, it belongs to Skunk Pepper. You are in the middle of the most productive cattle land in the world, and you are going to eat steak."

She stared up at the sign dubiously. FLINTHILLS STEAK HOUSE flickered in neon above them. "God, Henry, how do you find these places?"

"Law school," he said, opening his door. "We'd make runs down here whenever we could afford it. Which in my case was exactly twice in three years."

Henry led her into the restaurant. The dining room consisted of nine or ten tables pressed close together in a small room, but the decor was surprisingly tasteful. The waiter, a short, well-dressed man, greeted them with a gratitude that said customers were rare and appreciated.

When they were seated, Amanda looked around the restaurant with approval. "Not bad," she said, pulling a brass ring off her cloth napkin. "How do they stay in business?"

"Exorbitant prices, and by growing his own beef. Skunk's a Charolais rancher from way back. French cattle, pure white." A waiter approached and Henry asked for Cristal Roederer, '85, savoring the words. The waiter nodded demurely and drifted away.

"I'm stunned," Amanda said.

"It was inevitable, actually. Leave it to a bunch of law students to discover the one civilized place within two hours' driving distance of Wertner Residence Hall."

They both ordered steaks, and when the champagne came Henry waved off the waiter's attempt to open it. He took the bottle in his hand and stared at the label. "We who are about to receive, thank Thee." He covered the cork with a white cloth napkin and popped open the bottle. "To one tiny victory in a war I really want to win," he said, pouring Amanda a glass. "Bad."

Over dinner Amanda asked what Henry had known was inevitable. "I've let you slide about why you're back in Council Grove," she said, "but no more. When you called to say you were here I nearly fainted."

"You weren't as surprised as I was."

"I'll give you a starting point. The guy I talked to . . . the guy who gave me your number?"

"My managing partner."

"That's right, Sheldon something. I remember he said something very odd. I let it go. I guess I was just preoccupied with getting on that land."

"What was that?"

"It's what he called you." She changed voices, doing a fairly convincing impression of Parker. "'Preacher's in Kansas somewhere. God knows the name of the town. He's picking me up some chickens.'" She smiled, returning to her normal voice. "He called you Preacher."

"You want to know why."

"It's the kind of thing that gets your attention."

Henry took a swallow and set down his glass. He had kept this part of his life locked away from everyone in his new life, consciously, scrupulously. But that life was over, and maintaining that privacy had taken a great deal of energy. He wouldn't resist this conversation, for once. Suddenly, he wanted her to know. "Sheldon—and everybody else in that godforsaken firm—called me Preacher because for seven glorious months I was a seminary student."

She looked up, surprised. "I wouldn't have pictured that."

"Me neither."

"Seven months isn't very long. What happened?"

Henry hesitated, knowing she didn't understand the meaning of her question, the fact that the answer went to the center of everything important in him. But at length he said, "A drunk in a pickup happened. He came over a hill at high speed on Highway 12 and introduced himself to my parents."

"My God, Henry, I'm sorry."

"It was a random . . . what do you call it? Things with position and direction? *Vortex.* Two vortices in a random world, colliding. A few seconds sooner, nothing. A minute later, nothing. They would be sitting here with us. Or they wouldn't, because I would never have come back to Council Grove. Crandall's will would have been handled by my father."

He could see her embarrassment and regret at asking her question, and he wanted her to know it was all right. "It's okay," he said. "You didn't know. So I came back here and buried them. The gods of chaos and indifference had spoken, and my seminary days were over." He picked up his glass, rubbing it between his hands. "It's all ancient history now. Life goes on."

"So why law school? Is this following in your father's footsteps, like a tribute?"

"I wouldn't say that."

She smiled sympathetically. "I'm sure he was a great lawyer."

"He was a lousy lawyer," Henry said. "I know that sounds harsh. If it helps, I never told anybody that before. But it's the truth. He worked as hard as anybody I've ever seen, but he didn't know how to finish, how to bring it home. He let a lot of victories slip away." He paused, and added, "Lousy lawyer, good man."

"That's a lot more important, isn't it?"

Henry shrugged. "At Wilson, Lougherby and Mathers you could get a difference of opinion on that."

"Which brings us back to why you're here." She leaned forward. "What happened in Chicago, Henry?"

Henry exhaled. "Being back here is Boyd, pure and simple. But leaving Chicago . . . I didn't plan that part. There was a difference of opinion, the kind that doesn't get talked out. I was asked to do something I couldn't do. So that was it."

"An ethical issue?"

"Yeah, although God knows I don't want to come off as holier-than-thou."

"I wouldn't worry about that." Amanda smiled, lifting the glass of champagne to her lips. She sipped it, letting the liquid settle in her mouth. "Look," she said, "I have something I need to say right now. I don't exactly have the right, but it's going to drive me crazy if I don't."

"Then go ahead. I've already got Boyd, so you need to stay sane."

"It's serious."

"I'm listening."

She sat back. "What I want to say is that I don't believe in random."

"That's because random didn't kill your parents."

She stopped, obviously hurt by his statement. He wanted to bail her out, but she was treading on places that had no reserve capacity for pain. She looked at him, regarding him differently for a moment; he could see it in her eyes: *He's not harmless. He can strike.* "Don't presume my story," she said more quietly. "I'm only saying that I think things happen for a reason."

"Where'd you get this cosmic sense of meaning?"

"Lapsed Catholic," Amanda said. "I learned two things at Catholic school: my catechism and the facts of life."

"How lapsed?"

Amanda gave a languid smile. "Appallingly. But you can never get that stuff completely out of your system. It's burned into you. I remember once . . . God, it was seventh grade. There was a hurricane. It came up north, bounced off North Carolina and was coming back inland near the school. The nuns got all the classes together in this long, narrow room. We all said our Hail Mary's together until the storm passed. Three hundred kids sitting on the floor, back-to-back in the center of the room, facing the walls. We chanted in the dark for nearly an hour. *Hail Mary, full of grace. The Lord is with Thee. Blessed art Thou among women and blessed is the fruit of Thy womb, Jesus.* You could see the storm gather through the open windows. The sky got blacker and blacker, and after a while you could see trees starting to bend over from the wind. The sound was terrific."

"What happened?"

"Nothing," she said. "Nothing at all. The wind howled for a while, and gradually it began to clear up. The sun came out, and we stopped chanting. The nuns almost looked disappointed."

"You're kidding."

"Not at all. I really think they wanted something bad to happen. They wanted to test their faith. They wanted everything to be important. They wanted to suffer for God. I think they felt cheated. Anyway, they weren't smiling."

Henry leaned back in his chair. "And the moral of the story?"

"All I know is that when I get up against it I still say my Hail Mary's."

Henry smiled, admiring the way the champagne flute looked in her fingers, the simple, graceful curve of her hand. "That storm," he said, "did it just blow back out to sea?"

Amanda thought for a moment. "It did come in, four or five miles north of us. Did quite a bit of damage. Killed three or four people, I think."

Henry's smile faded. "And how about them?" he asked. "Didn't God hear their prayers?"

"I don't know. Maybe we prayed harder."

Henry picked up the bottle and tipped it over Amanda's glass; the last few drops dribbled out, making tiny splashes in her champagne. "I'd love another bottle, but now that I only have one client I can't afford it," he said.

"So where do we go with Boyd?" Amanda asked. "What are you planning on doing about the will?"

"Maybe I'll say a few Hail Mary's."

"You're not Catholic."

"I'll take whatever help I can get."

"You can joke if you like. But I'm going to light a candle for Raymond tomorrow morning at the cathedral in Topeka."

"And will that keep the hurricane from coming in?"

"I don't know," Amanda said, looking into his eyes. "Maybe the wind will bounce off our prayers."

Chapter Twenty-four

"They have Boyd under medical care."

"What?" Frank Hesston eyed Carl Durand uneasily. The news was not good, and he wanted to make sure he had got it right. "*Who* has him under medical care?"

"Mathews. Collier says he got a doctor to sign Boyd off to his custody."

"What do they have him on?"

"Shit, Frank, I can't get the medical files. I'm not the CIA."

Hesston rubbed his temples. He was starting to hate Henry Mathews. "I thought we were done with Mathews problems when his old man died," he said after a moment. "He was always filing pointless motions over foreclosures and getting in the way. Now the son is back here, just as bad as the father. This is turning into a mess."

"So? What about your plans now? If you had let me kill Boyd in the first place, we wouldn't have this situation."

"We can't just kill everybody, Carl," Hesston said with exasperation. "You're too indiscriminate." His partner had every asset necessary for a profitable relationship except the most important: self-restraint. "Tell me what else Collier said."

"One more thing. I don't know what the hell it means, though. Mathews has hooked up with somebody. A woman."

"Who is she?"

Durand gave a malevolent expression of loathing. "Amanda Ashton," he said with disgust. "A real pain-in-the-ass, save-the-whales type. I've run into her before. Works in the state department of environment. She's snooping around the wells in Cheney County. I thought I had her taken care of, but thanks to Tyler's will, she's back, like a bad disease."

"What do you mean, snooping?"

"She's got some idea about the old wells falling apart. Thinks chemicals are leaching into the groundwater."

"Are they?"

"How the hell do I know? The main thing is she wants access to the wells for tests."

"Could she find out anything?"

Durand thought. "I doubt it. She could take her little samples for days and never find out what we're doing. On the other hand, she's not stupid, and she's curious as hell. Either way, I hate the idea of anybody near those wells, Frank. It makes things unpredictable. I don't like that."

"What's she doing with Mathews?"

"Collier doesn't know yet. But Mathews connects her to Boyd. I don't like that either. You got a wacko environmentalist and a hotshot lawyer hanging around asking a lot of questions."

Hesston leaned back in his chair, his eyes closed. "Where's Boyd now?" he asked.

"He's back at his own place, if you can believe that. Or will be soon. Collier says Mathews and his new girlfriend are gonna clean up his place and try to get him back over there. The doctor's overseeing the deal. Collier thinks Boyd will do whatever they want. Apparently the little freak feels safe around the two of them." Durand ground out his cigarette. "Look, Frank, this is getting serious. Maybe you think doing Boyd is messy, but it's not any messier than this. We can't have a convention around Boyd and expect nothing to happen."

Hesston opened his eyes and looked intently at his partner. "This little machine has been running for more than twenty-five years because of my careful planning, Carl, and I'm not going to let it blow up now. Of course we have to get rid of Boyd. But it has to be smart. Just killing him would put a spotlight on things. Roger would get tagged, and he would turn us over without a thought. The whole thing would be over in forty-eight hours."

"Are we overestimating this kid Mathews? His father wasn't much of a problem."

"His father didn't make it to Wilson, Lougherby and Mathers."

"Never heard of 'em."

"They've never heard of you, more accurately. They're big, they're mean, and they're nasty. If the boy ended up there, he's not his father."

"Then what?"

Hesston paused, concentrating hard. "Things aren't that bad, not yet. They don't really know anything, not even Roger. Anyway, greed can control him. There's still only two people who know enough to pose a genuine threat."

"Boyd and Ellen."

Hesston nodded. "If they stay contained, we can ride this out."

"Boyd isn't going to stay contained. He's going to get treatment, and he's going to start making sense."

"Then we can't let him improve. It's as simple as that."

"He knows everything about the scam. He knows about Ellen. And he obviously knows about the field hand. Your trick with the bird bought us some time, but it got him arrested, and that got him a doctor. A few weeks from now he could be reciting the whole story in a coherent state of mind."

Hesston shook his head. "I'm not going to second-guess killing the bird, Carl. When you hit a man that hard, you can't predict where he'll fall within an inch. The important thing was to keep him under pressure. But I agree that we need a long-term solution." He paused. "I don't like Mathews hanging around. We have to keep him occupied. He's not afraid of anybody in the equation, and that makes him dangerous. But there's an easy solution to that situation, fortunately."

"Which is?"

"We start proceedings contesting the will. I'll file this afternoon, and by dinner Collier serves Mathews with papers."

"How fast can you turn it around?"

Hesston smiled. "Judge Brackman's a friend, and his clerk is in my pocket. By tomorrow afternoon Mathews will be up to his neck in briefs."

"All right. What about Boyd?"

Hesston mused for a moment, deep in thought. After some time, his face cleared, and he poured himself a glass of bourbon. "Let me ask you something, Carl," he said, leaning back in his chair. "What does Ellen Gaudet want more than anything else in the world?"

"To be Mrs. Tyler William Crandall. I have a feeling that's not going to happen now."

"Other than that."

"Other than that, I'd say a truckload of money might ease her pain. To never work in that two-bit bank again."

"Money we might be willing to pay her, in return for services rendered."

"What kind of services? And what kind of money?"

"She has no concept of real wealth. A couple hundred grand at the most. Money to get her to do something . . ." He paused, lingering over his choice of words. "Final," he said at last.

Durand stared at his partner, comprehension coming into his eyes. "Do you think it would work?"

"It worked before. She got Boyd involved in the first place. Now that Ty's dead, she'll be anxious, vulnerable."

"But she's got a soft spot for the fruitcake."

"I didn't say she'd take a gun and pull the trigger. She doesn't even need to know what we have in mind. She'll just bring him to us where we can take care of things."

"So when do we talk to her?"

"*We* don't talk to her, not yet." Hesston sighed and said, "Efficiency, Carl. Neither one of us can go to Council Grove, obviously. Roger can do that."

"And get him in deeper."

"I thought you'd like that."

Durand looked at his watch. "He'll be here in three hours for instructions about the will."

Hesston smiled. "Leave him to me."

Chapter Twenty-five

Henry, Amanda, and Dr. Harris walked into the Trailside Diner dog tired; it had been a long day cleaning up Raymond's house, and it had gone well. At least Collier had removed the bird from the door. The inside of the house hadn't been the nightmare it could have been as well; there was nothing really frightening inside, just a startling accumulation of dirt and the mild chaos that comes from almost complete neglect. But the payoff had been substantial: Boyd had gone in easily, if only to look around the place and then to retreat back to the park and his worn bench.

They found a booth near the back and ordered coffee. Harris took off his glasses, rubbed his temples, and sighed. "I don't know whether to be happy or sad," he said. "All that work, and he wasn't in the place ten minutes."

"And you don't see a problem with him going back to the park?" Amanda asked, sounding concerned.

"The park is the one thing I don't worry about," Harris replied. "He's obviously comfortable there. There's really nothing we can do until we have him regulated medically, anyway. You saw him take his medication this morning, right, Henry?"

"Every morning at nine, that's our deal," Henry answered. "I give him the pills, and I watch him take them."

"Then that's all right. If we can get the delusions to fade, we can get down to the real work."

"You deserve to be in some psychiatrist hall of fame for helping with the house," Henry said.

"I had my reasons," Harris answered matter-of-factly. "The way a schizophrenic lives is a major source of information about him. I was hoping to find some window into Raymond at the house."

"Did you?" Amanda asked.

"What I got was confirmation, I suppose. There wasn't the kind of disorder I would have expected in that place if his was a true, deep schizophrenia. At this point I'm convinced he's simply been decompensated."

Henry and Amanda settled in for the explanation. The coffee came, and Harris stirred sugar into his cup, staring into the dark liquid. "A lot of people have latent brain pathologies, but they compensate for it. They find ways to manage. You could work right beside one of them and never know it." He nodded at Henry. "You, for example."

Henry looked up, surprised, and Harris smiled, releasing him. "It was just an example. But people can quietly live for years on the edge of coming unglued."

"How is that possible?" Henry asked.

"They develop strategies to stay ahead of their illness. Maybe they self-medicate with booze or drugs. Maybe they have a secret compulsion they indulge. They stack matchbooks or they clean floors. They rearrange socks. These strategies can get incredibly elaborate, but they're hidden from public view. They can actually get through life that way, if they're lucky."

"What about the decompensation?" Amanda asked.

"An emotional trauma of sufficient power destroys their ability to mask the illness. The energy used to manage the trauma can't be spared from the pathology. They break, and the illness emerges. Decompensation."

"Could a person in that condition hold a position of some responsibility?" Henry asked. "Say, manage a bank?"

"Until the decompensation, he could function at a tolerable level. But there would be subtle signs, if you could find them." Harris stared past Henry and Amanda, his eyes focusing on the space beyond them. "The important thing now is what caused it," he said. "Something has obviously hurt him, and I'm not talking about the bird. This is something from his past, something never resolved."

"We do know one thing," Amanda said. "Raymond is terribly disturbed by the wells on Crandall's land."

"Tell me about the wells," Harris said, putting on his glasses and pulling out a notebook. "Tell me everything."

"We took Raymond out there about a week ago and he went into an apocalyptic tirade about plague and bloodshed," Henry answered. "Something about burning sulfur and hailstones."

"And there was something else," Amanda broke in, "something about hidden things being brought into judgment."

Harris' face clouded over. "I don't like that," he said quietly. He looked at Henry. "I remember your saying at the jail that the wells were in some dispute."

Henry nodded. "To put it mildly."

"Raymond has an obsession with General Custer," Harris said. "He said the whole Custer thing was about mineral rights. He had completely identified with Custer himself. What do you two know about the story?"

"Just the schoolboy version," Henry said. "But obviously Custer gets it in the end. That's not very hopeful."

Harris nodded. "There's something else that bothers me. What Custer is getting is really a kind of justice, depending on which side of the story you're on. He was ambushed, but on the other hand he was going up there to kill a bunch of Indians minding their own business on reservation land. From that perspective, he was nothing but a common criminal."

"You're inferring a lot from this story," Henry ventured doubtfully. "What if this is just a part of his delusion? After all, Custer's Elm is where he's spent the past twenty-five years. Custer's the main character. It's a natural connection to make."

"He definitely *is* delusional," Harris said, "but that doesn't mean his delusions don't have meaning. They certainly do."

"Custer wanted to go up and strip all the money off that reservation land," Amanda said. "And that's what Crandall has been doing for the past twenty-five years with those wells. Isn't Raymond's association with Custer a way of saying he had something to do with that?"

"Drilling for oil doesn't make someone a criminal," Harris replied.

"It might in this case."

"What does that mean?"

"It's a long story," Amanda answered. "But leave that for a second. The wells connect Raymond to Crandall. Based on his reaction to them, they also connect him with his illness."

"They also connect *you* to Carl Durand," Henry said. "Are you sure you're not confusing your personal feelings here?"

"I don't pretend to be objective. But the wells don't just connect me to Durand. If there's really something funny going on out there, they might connect Raymond to him as well."

"Who's Durand?" Harris asked.

"Satan," Amanda answered simply.

Henry held up his hand. "A wildcatter from around here who's up in state government now."

Amanda cleared her throat softly. "That's the longer description. But listen, I can help on all this. Henry, I told you I wanted another look at those wells, this time with a real geologist. I've found one."

"Is he any good?"

"He can be here tomorrow."

"Not exactly compelling qualifications."

"It's the same way I picked Dr. Harris."

Henry looked at the doctor. "Maybe we were lucky."

"I asked him to come just before the pumps run, in the early evening. We'll have just enough daylight."

At that moment the door to the Trailside opened. Henry glanced over Amanda's shoulder to see Sheriff Collier coming in the restaurant with his lazy gait. The sheriff glanced around the place, strolled through the mostly empty diner, and walked up to the table. "Look what we got here," he said, scratching himself. "It's the fucking dream team."

"Sheriff Collier," Henry answered lightly, "no dogs to catch today?"

Collier shot Henry back an indifferent look. "I had to take your shit the other day," he said, "but you're gonna be kinda busy from now on. If you got any left, better shovel it now." He threw an envelope down on the table.

Henry looked at the envelope and instantly understood its meaning. "I'm impressed that you were able to take time off from writing parking tickets to deliver this," he said. "What an exciting life you lead."

"What's going on?" Amanda asked.

"This," Henry said, keeping his eyes on Collier, "is a court date for one Roger Crandall and one Raymond Boyd to meet at the Cheney County courthouse for a legal tango. I will be representing Mr. Boyd. Roger will be dancing with Frank Hesston, I believe."

"That's right," Collier said, staring back at Henry.

"Amanda, you'd just love Hesston," Henry said, smiling grimly. "Always defending the downtrodden, wherever he may find them."

"I hope he cleans your clock," Collier said, his sallow grin gone.

"It's been a pleasure, Sheriff," Henry stated, looking unconcerned. "With you on patrol, let no man live in fear."

Collier stood before the table, attempting to formulate an answer. At last he muttered, "I gotta go," and spun on his heel.

When he had left, Amanda said, "My God, Henry. You've got a mean streak."

Henry's expression was implacable. "None of that was meant for Collier."

"Excuse me?"

"Our sheriff has picked sides," he replied calmly. "I don't know if something's changed, but he's obviously made his decision, for whatever reason. He thinks we're going to lose, and he's acting accordingly. I wanted him to let his bosses know that I'm not afraid of them."

"You mean Crandall?" Amanda asked.

Henry shook his head. "Durand. And Hesston, by the looks of it."

"You might just make them angrier."

"I hope so," Henry answered. "Angry people make mistakes."

"So what does this mean?" Harris asked. "How does it affect our plans?"

"This was inevitable," Henry stated. "Roger was never going to let the will go uncontested anyway. But with Durand and Hesston, he might actually pull it off." He fingered the envelope a moment thoughtfully, then ran his thumb through the flap and tore it open. He pulled out several pages stapled together, flipped to the end, and read for a moment. "His mother's name is on the petition as well, the bastard."

Amanda frowned. "And Sarah's?"

"No," Henry answered. "I knew she wouldn't have anything to do with this."

"So what happens now?" Amanda asked.

"Court happens. We have three days."

Chapter Twenty-six

The geologist was not what Henry had expected. When the man's hat appeared over a ridge close by on the north, it was topped with a long, somewhat weathered feather—eagle, by the look of it. Eagles were protected, and the adornment raised certain legal issues: the fine for killing one of the birds was twenty-five thousand dollars and a year in jail. The hat and feather were followed by an equally weathered face, darkened by the sun but still, unmistakably, red in color. "What's his name?" Henry asked.

"John Brown."

"An Indian named John Brown?" Henry asked. "You mean like the abolitionist?"

"I didn't know. I only talked to him on the phone."

Henry watched the man come over the ridge, taking him in: he was tall, and quite lean; Henry guessed about forty-five, but the red-tinged face hid years in sun-beaten lines and it was hard to be sure. His jet-black hair was interspersed with thin streaks of gray and was pulled back in a long pony-tail between his shoulders. A turquoise earring hung from his left ear. He wore black work boots, faded blue jeans, and in spite of the day's growing heat, a rough-cut leather vest over a white cotton shirt. A bulky canvas bag was slung over his shoulder, and he carried a small shovel. Henry and Amanda walked toward the approaching figure, and Henry stuck out his hand to introduce himself. The man shook it rather formally. "Thanks for coming," Henry said. "Glad you could make it."

"Thing got my curiosity up," Brown answered. He looked at Amanda. "And I knew about you anyway. I heard about what you're trying to do, checking up on the old wells. It's a good idea."

"Really?" Amanda looked surprised. "I didn't know anyone else was thinking the same thing."

"It makes sense," Brown replied. "I think everybody knows it does, but folks don't like to think long-range."

"Are your people from around here, Mr. Brown?" Henry asked.

Brown looked up, but his face remained implacable. "Now or then?"

Henry nodded, understanding the meaning of the question; every Native American tribe, without exception, had been relocated during the years following the Civil War, sometimes more than once. "Originally," he said.

Brown waved to the east. "We stretched from Pennsylvania to Ohio in the twenties," he said. "But the Indian wars drove us west, here to the Kansas territories." He took his shovel and drew a circle in the dirt at his feet. He pointed toward the top of the circle and said, "Northern rim of Colby County. The other side is a hundred forty, hundred fifty miles south. Inside the circle was all that was left by the start of the war."

"You're Shawnee," Henry said, pleased with himself.

For the first time Brown's face flickered with interest, but he merely nodded.

"I was interested in that stuff as a kid," Henry said. "My father took me to see the old ruts of the wagon trains ten miles from where we're standing. They run right through the buffalo wallers."

"Shawnee hunted them here," Brown said. "With antelope, and bear, and everything else that's gone now. The only thing left is jackrabbits and coyotes."

"Henry's surprised by your name," Amanda said, smiling.

Henry shrugged and said, "I can't be the first."

"Shawnee don't hand down names like whites," Brown answered. "We change them from time to time, to commemorate a big event. My grandfather was the first in my family to be educated in a white school, and he admired John Brown. He took his name."

"I've seen him," Amanda said. "His painting's up in the mural on the capitol rotunda. He looks possessed. He's standing in front of a burning building, with an enormous beard and long wild hair in the wind."

"He set the fire," Brown said. "Burned out some settlers, and when they came out he hacked them to pieces with a saber. Called himself the Hand of God."

"John Brown killed Indians, too," Henry said.

"Just Iroquois," the man answered stoically. "We were hunting them ourselves. Shawnee hid Brown sometimes when the government hunted him." The geologist glanced across the field at Boyd, who was sitting quietly in the car.

"Who's that?" he asked.

"Raymond Boyd," Henry answered. "He's just inherited this land. He'll be staying in the car."

Brown stared at the car a moment, then shrugged. "His life. Now let's see this so-called oil field."

The three figures climbed up a sloping hill toward the closest well. After some time they crossed a shallow but treacherous gully; the sides of the depression were crumbling pebbles, shifting under their feet.

Amanda pointed. "Limestone," she said. "And clearly extruded."

"We'll see what we see," Brown answered.

When they arrived at the first well, Brown stared at the hulking, rusted tower. "This still pumps?" he asked skeptically.

"About two hours a day," Amanda said. She looked at her watch. "Three barrels a week, roughly. It's timed to start in about fifteen minutes."

"Twelve barrels a month," Brown mused. "For a well this age, that's pretty good. Most of them that are still alive at all only pump every other day."

"It's a miracle, considering the fact that we're standing on pure chalk," Amanda said. She pulled out a geological survey and spread it on the ground. Brown knelt down beside her, scanning the page.

"I checked into this site at the statehouse," Amanda said. "It's been spot-checked by field agents six times since it was drilled. Came back legit every time. Flow at the pump checked out, everything. This one peaked at twenty-eight barrels a day, then went shallow in the third year. Now that's where it gets weird. It's been running about two, two and a half a day for years. No drop-off, no increase. It never changes. Ever hear of a well like that?"

Brown didn't answer. He had already turned and was cleaning the face of a pressure gauge with a bandanna. Black grime and oil streaked away. He peered at the gauge and said, "Six pounds of pressure. A little high for such small production, but within reason." He turned to Amanda. "How deep is the well?"

She looked at her chart. "Thirty-six hundred feet," she said. "And the pay zone is pretty thin—no more than forty feet."

"Okay," Brown said, "so they drilled three-quarters of a mile down, and they found forty feet of oil." A disbelieving smile spread across his face, the sunburned lines creasing back around his eyes. "They've been pumping it for more than twenty years, and they've been doing it in pure chalk."

"Then I'm not crazy," Amanda said, her face flushed. "I knew there was something wrong here."

"The pump is due to start in ten minutes," Brown said, glancing at his watch. "We'll see what we see."

The three waited in silence as the minutes ticked slowly by. Then, at 7 P.M., a subterranean, graunching sound creaked from the base of the wellhead. The rusting hulk came slowly, painfully to life. In the next minute or so it rumbled into the monotony of another day's pumping. Brown leaned over to the pressure gauge and squinted through its grimy cover. "That's strange. It didn't move," he said.

"Why strange?" Henry asked.

"The pumps build up pressure at rest. When they start, the pressure is released and the gauges should go down. This one started at six psi; it shouldn't read more than two or three when pumping. But nothing changed."

"Can you explain it?" Amanda asked.

"It usually means that there's still a lot of oil down there, so much that even when the well pumps the back-pressure remains constant," Brown said. He shook his head. "But even the wells in the Gulf drop pressure after this many years." He stared up at the well a moment and picked up his bag. "All right, let's find out what's going on here."

Brown led the others to a large collector tank thirty yards down a gentle hill behind the well. "They store the oil here," he said. "Pick it up by truck every couple of months. There'll be a flow gauge measuring what's coming in from the well. They can monkey with the gauges, of course, but at least it's something." Brown dropped his bag and looked through a tight maze of iron pipes and fittings. Eventually he got down on his knees and peered underneath a large pipe. "Got it," he said after a few moments. "Gauge says seven cubic feet per hour. And you said, what, two barrels a day? So that's about right." He got up and dusted off his pants. "Checks out so far," he said. A low metallic scream to the west cut across the field; another well was starting. "They all run about the same time?" Brown asked.

"That's right," Amanda said. "The difference must just be the internal clocks."

The light was fading; the sun was slowly drifting downward toward the horizon. In another thirty minutes, it would be dark. Brown stared across the range grass at the first well. "What are you hiding, princess?" he asked. "What's your little secret?"

"It's bad timing with the sun setting," Henry said. "Doesn't give us much time."

"The darkness can help," Brown answered. He turned to Henry, an odd smile playing on his lips. "Are you feeling brave today, city lawyer?" he asked.

"Depends."

Brown picked up his shovel. "The lady says in two hours the pumping will stop on its own. But I can stop it anytime. Then I can open this pipe and see what's really going on inside."

"And what should we see?"

"Pure black crude," Brown said, "running from the well to the holding tank. That's what the gauges say. But gauges lie."

"I see you're not above bending a few rules."

"Main reason I never took an oil company job. I like the flexibility."

"So what do you think, Henry?" Amanda asked. "Any problem with stopping the well?"

"Probably," Henry said. "But why did I leave Wilson, Lougherby and Mathers if I can't break a few rules?"

"I thought it was because you *wouldn't* break rules you left."

"Different rules," Henry replied. "Go ahead, Mr. Brown. Stop the well."

Brown nodded and opened his leather bag. He pulled out a large wrench and walked to the wellhead. "This will take a few minutes," he said. He examined the well for a long time, walking completely around the structure twice and poking his head underneath pipes. At last, he switched off the motor to the pump and it ground to a halt.

"That's it?" Henry asked.

"Shutting off the pump doesn't shut down the well. It's still active." Brown methodically turned a metal wheel, shutting off a pipe. He stood staring at it silently for a full two minutes.

Henry watched, finally blurting, "And what are we doing now?"

"Got to let the pressure equalize," Brown said. "Course, if you want me to hurry you might want to back up a half mile or so." Brown reapproached the well. He turned several more wheels, watching and listening carefully. Finally, he picked up a large wrench. "All right," he said. "Let's see what's coming out of this thing." He placed the wrench around the fitting and pulled down with all his might; the bolt didn't budge. He rummaged through his bag and retrieved a spray lubricant, liberally applying it to the metal. When he pulled again, it jarred loose and began to slowly move. As contact between the pipe and the fitting became looser, black oil began leaking through the threads, further lubricating the nut. It began to spin easily; suddenly, the connection was broken and a half gallon of crude splashed out of the pipe. The oil pooled on the grass below and began running farther downhill in thick rivulets. "The oil's flowing, just like it should," Brown said. "The back-pressure looks about right, too." He placed his hands on his hips. "Whatever this is, it's clever," he said. "I don't see it yet."

Amanda picked up the shovel and absentmindedly pushed dirt around near her feet. Brown watched her with an occupied, distant expression. Suddenly, however, he came to life. "Forget geology for a minute," he said. "Let's try archeology. If there's nothing aboveground, we go down."

"That will leave more signs that we were here," Amanda said, looking at Henry.

"I'll handle that," Henry said. "In fact, I'll dig." He reached over and took the shovel from Amanda. Since coming back to Council Grove, he had found himself longing for physical exertion. Growing up he had loved outside work, and the health club workouts in Chicago had never been a good substitute for him. "Just point," he said to Brown.

Brown indicated an area just below the aboveground pipes and said, "Go slow. Don't blow us up. Test, then dig. Metal on metal makes sparks."

"That oil can't possibly burn."

"Oil won't. Fumes will."

"I understand." Henry pushed the spade point in cautiously; satisfied, he pulled several shovelfuls of dirt from the site. Soon he hit rock, but it crumbled easily under his effort.

"Chalk," Brown said, nodding to Amanda. "Like you said, all the way to the surface."

Henry worked carefully but doggedly, sweat building on his muscles in spite of the cooling temperature. The sun was dying now, a rim fragment sliding into the edge of the fields. "Dark soon," he said, breathing heavily. "Do we have lights?" Brown opened his bag and pulled out a couple of powerful flashlights, handing one to Amanda.

"Ready for a rest?" Brown asked.

Henry stood a moment, resting an arm on the shovel handle. He hadn't built up a real sweat outside of a racquetball court in more than three years. It was a loss he hadn't truly appreciated until this moment. "Nope," he said with a smile. "I wouldn't trade this, frankly. Now if you'll get out of my way, I have some earth to move." Brown stepped back, and Henry dug back in with vigor, welcoming his second wind. The dirt was flying off his shovel as he dug.

"Careful," Brown said. "If there's anything there, it can't be much farther down."

"But what are we looking for?" Amanda asked. "Are we just digging with no idea?"

Brown was silent, concentrating on the digging. He pointed his flashlight down and a pool of white light appeared at Henry's feet. "Hang on," he said softly. "Everybody be quiet. Henry, pick up your left shoe."

Henry looked down and slowly raised his foot; to his surprise, it made a sucking sound. "Let me see the flashlight," he said. He bent his knees and played the light around his feet from close range. The dirt appeared to be slightly wet, although from what he couldn't tell. He reached down and dipped his finger in the moist earth and shone the light directly on it.

"Oil," Brown said. "Not a lot, just normal leakage."

"Leakage from what?" Amanda asked.

"From another set of pipes," Brown answered. "Come out, Henry. I better take over."

Henry took Brown's hand and pulled himself out of the hole. Brown stepped away, carefully removed his vest, and set his hat on the ground a good distance from the hole. He stepped nimbly down into the hole and began gently prodding the ground with the spade. He continued digging and searching for several minutes, when a soft thrust downward yielded a clanking, metallic sound. "That's it," he said, looking up at Henry and Amanda.

Now Brown dug earnestly, clearing the ground from around a steel pipe about four feet below ground level. It was dark now, and Henry and Amanda kept their lights on his work. After twenty minutes he had managed to make several feet of pipe visible. "Another pipe, hidden from view," he said at last. "It runs underground, but to the same collecting tank."

"What's it for?" Henry asked.

"I've seen this kind of thing before and it works pretty simply," Brown answered. "If you're a driller, you tell the farmer that you're pumping out so much oil from the land. You meter it aboveground, like normal, where everybody can see. But you put another set of pipes underground and pump more oil, unmetered oil that nobody knows about."

"And steal from the farmer," Henry concluded.

"Sometimes the farmer is in on it," Brown said. "They both steal from the government. But to make it work you need an inside man, somebody at the refinery or in distribution."

"Durand," Amanda said quietly.

Brown shrugged. "Except that it's impossible in this case. More and more oil where there shouldn't be any in the first place."

"You say there's oil in the underground pipe," Amanda said, "but we don't really know. All we can see is a pipe. It could have played out years ago."

"I was standing in leakage when I was digging," Henry said. "That couldn't be twenty-five years old."

"No," Brown said, "it would have been absorbed long ago. Whatever's here has to be fairly recent." He tapped the pipe with the flat side of the shovel. "There's nothing to do but open this."

"Is there a visible fitting?" Henry asked.

"Right before it turns upward there's a fitted sleeve," Brown answered. "I can unscrew it there."

In five minutes Brown had cleared the dirt away from the fitting and was working hard with his wrench. This connection was tougher, and even after a good deal of grunting the pipe held fast. At last he stood precariously on the wrench and bounced, balancing his weight unsteadily with his hands on the side of the hole. After several tries there was a sudden jerk and Brown disappeared into the darkness with a thud. The fitting had come loose all at once, unsettling Brown from his perch on the wrench and tumbling him into the oily dirt.

"John!" Amanda called, scrambling to the edge of the hole and pointing her flashlight downward. She could see him crumpled up at the bottom. A flow of black oil spilled out of the opened pipe and was collecting over his legs.

"I'm okay," he called out. He came unsteadily to his feet and tested his weight on his left leg. The spilling oil was filling the small hole, and had already climbed halfway to his knees. He was covered in black fluid. "God, what a mess."

Henry shone his light on Brown's face. He appeared unhurt, and Henry said, "I guess we owe you for some clothes."

Brown bent over, disappearing again into the hole. "Hand me a flashlight," he called. Henry handed his flashlight carefully down into Brown's hand.

"What's it look like?" he asked.

"Like oil. But there's no doubt about it. This pipe has crude running through it. The back-pressure alone tells me that it's not just sitting in the pipe." He handed the light back to Henry, and reached up for a hand. "Coming up," he said. Henry took the hand, and black goo squeezed between their fingers. With a hard pull Brown scrambled out of the hole. Amanda shone her light on him; he was covered with streaks of oil from head to toe.

"Damnedest thing I've ever seen," Brown muttered. He sat on the ground, breathing heavily, oblivious to the dirt.

"I've got a suggestion," Henry said after a moment. "It's weak, probably, but it's the only thing I can think of."

Brown looked up. "I'm listening."

"You say the pump can't be doing what it's doing, because there shouldn't be any oil in this rock to pump. But the truth is, it only *seems* impossible. There is a clear test to end this once and for all."

"I'd like to know what it is," Brown said with irritation.

"It's going to sound obvious, I suppose. But my idea is to open one side of the pipes and start the well again."

There was a short silence, which Amanda broke. "Exactly! We turn it on and *watch* it do the impossible. Whatever it's doing, we'll have to see it."

"Such is my plan," Henry said with a soft smile. "What do you think, John?"

Brown was already on his feet and walking back to the containing tank. "If you want one side open, I'll close the one aboveground." He nodded toward the hole. "Whatever the secret is must be in the buried pipe."

"Right," Henry said. He helped Brown pull the pipes back together, and John tightened the fitting once again.

"Okay," Brown said. "So the system is intact, except the underground pipe is open. Let's do it." He walked back to the wellhead. After a couple of minutes, the well rumbled back to life. The huge arms began plunging up and down, gradually picking up speed. Brown moved back over to the open hole; Amanda and Henry were training their flashlights into the darkness.

Nothing happened for a long moment. Suddenly, however, oil sprayed through one side of the pipes. "Well, now," Brown said, blinking.

Henry stared at the spurting oil. "Am I seeing what I think I'm seeing?"

"Yeah," Brown said. "It's oil, and it's flowing in the wrong direction."

"Explain," Amanda demanded.

"The oil should flow from the well to the tank, obviously," Brown answered. "But unfortunately, it doesn't."

Amanda stared. "My God, you're right. It's flowing from the tank to the well. But why? Why would anybody pump oil *into* a well?"

Brown stared at the flowing oil for a long time. Nobody spoke. Suddenly, his face cleared. "I see it now," he said. "It's a closed system. This isn't different oil at all, not fresh from underground. They're just pumping the same oil in a circle over and over again." He gestured toward the well. "Aboveground the oil flows to the holding tank, and on the way it gets metered. That's why when we checked the flow it looked correct. But the same oil is going back to the well in the underground pipe. This well has been pumping the same oil for twenty-five years. It leaks a little, but they could just top it off. No problem."

"So the production never drops," Henry said. "It's the same oil, year after year. But anybody can come out here and check production to his heart's content and it will always look right."

"Yeah," Brown said. "The one thing they couldn't control was the wellhead pressure gauge. Since the system's closed, the pressure can't drop when the pump starts."

"Couldn't they just remove it?" Henry asked.

"The gauge is required by law. Removing it would have attracted too much attention. No, this was the lower risk. Very few people would check the pressure change like we just did. Nobody would unless he already suspected a problem."

The three watched the oil for a few moments, and Amanda said, "We've got to shut it off, John. Any more and we won't be able to reattach the fitting."

"Right," Brown answered, jogging to the wellhead. He got the pump stopped as quickly as possible, returned to the hole, and muttered, "I guess I'm elected to get back down there. No sense in either one of you doing it."

Neither Henry nor Amanda protested; seeing John's clothes drip black onto the ground was more than enough reason to let him have his way. Brown clambered back down into the hole. The oil was over the pipe now, and he had to work blind in the crude. But he got the pipe reconnected quickly, and soon he had climbed out of the hole. The wet oil had collected a layer of dirt and he was even filthier, if possible.

"The real question is why?" Amanda said after a moment. "Why would anybody pump the same oil to themselves for twenty-five years?"

"Look, I know nothing about oil, but I know a lot about money," Henry said. "In theory this could be a pretty good money-laundering setup. You pump oil, it shows up in your books, you pretend to sell it to a distributor. You say the government checks your pumps from time to time. Everything looks fine, so the system keeps right on working. Money changes hands, but there's no product. You could wash dollar for dollar for every drop of oil you pumped. It's beautiful. But in this case it doesn't make sense, naturally."

"What's the problem?" Amanda asked.

"Why would Crandall or Durand need to wash money?" Henry answered. "That's urban crime. What are we saying, that they were running drugs? Anyway, there's not enough dollars to make it worth the trouble. I've seen Ty Crandall's bank records going back for years. Depending on the price of crude, these wells only bring in about thirty-five thousand dollars a year total. It's an absurdly elaborate setup for that kind of money, especially if this underground arrangement is duplicated on all the working wells."

"It has to be," Brown stated. "If those wells are pumping anything, it has to be like this."

"Okay," Henry said. "Then we're still missing something." As they stood thinking, the moon appeared, rising from the west and casting a pale, yellowish-white light over the range. The breeze had cooled with the evening, and it spoke quietly, rustling the high grass around their legs.

"Something tragic did happen, at least," Amanda said, suddenly thoughtful. "Someone died here."

Sweat shone in the moonlight off Brown's face. "I didn't know that," he said.

"It was an accident," Henry said, nodding. "A field hand bought it when this place was first drilled." He was about to continue, but the evening's silence was broken by the sound of an opening car door. "Raymond," he said, spinning around. "He's been so quiet, I forgot all about him."

Raymond Boyd stepped out of the car into the night air about thirty yards away from the well. He moved briskly away from the vehicle, his eyes on the sky. He opened his mouth, and called out to the Alpha and the Omega in a loud, anguished voice.

Chapter Twenty-seven

"He had another episode." Henry had returned to Council Grove, and was speaking into his cell phone. It was nearly ten o'clock at night, but Harris had given him his home phone number. Henry filled in Harris on what they had discovered at the well, and winced when he got to the part where Boyd came unglued. "I got him back into the car okay, but it wasn't as easy as last time. For a second I thought he was going to really resist me."

Harris' voice was full of concern. "Where is he now?" he asked.

"At the park," Henry answered. "He bolted back to his bench when we got back. I didn't have a chance to explain anything to him."

"Explain what?"

"Raymond doesn't know about the trial yet. I need time to sit down with him and try to get him to understand what's going to happen."

"It would have been better to have tried that before hauling him out to those oil wells," Harris said. "I'm beginning to wonder about this whole arrangement. If he were in the hospital we could control things so much better."

"It doesn't do any good to second-guess now," Henry said. "Amanda can't go on the Crandall property without him, and I made the decision it was worth the risk."

"I'm not sure you're in a position to do that."

"It paid off. Thanks to her and Brown, we know those wells are about as normal as Raymond is. And there was another reason to bring Raymond. Seeing his reaction to them confirms that they're the center of the storm."

There was a pause, and Harris said, "My concern is Raymond, not oil wells. Look, I'm not going to rake you over the coals. But that doesn't make me less concerned about his condition. He should have leveled off a little by now. He's still taking his medication?"

"No problem."

"You're watching him swallow it?"

"Yes."

"All right. Look, I'm going to come out there in the morning and have another talk with him. In the meantime, let's give him some air. Don't talk to him about the trial until after I examine him. I want to let him recover from the trip out to the wells."

"All right. Can you meet us at the Trailside tomorrow afternoon?"

"Make it sooner. I'll be there by noon."

Early the next morning Henry and Amanda walked down Pawnee, heading toward the square. "I need a place to work," Henry said. "And it's not just space I need. I can't even make copies right now."

Amanda nodded. "You can't do business at the Trailside."

"And the motel doesn't even have a fax. Hard beds and four television channels for forty-seven bucks a night."

"So what are you going to do?"

"I'm thinking of something, and it's either completely brilliant or the worst idea I ever had in my life." They turned the corner onto Chautauqua and Henry pulled Amanda to a stop. The square opened before them, a collection of storefronts surrounding the courthouse. Wooden doors opened onto the streets: Jenny's Quilts and Things, Melba's Shoe Center, the bank, the diner, a barbershop. Henry pointed across the square at an empty office with large picture windows. "My father's old office."

"And you're thinking of reopening it?" she asked soberly.

"Just for the trial," he answered. "Definitely not long-term. But it makes sense, in a way. He drafted the original will, you know."

"Yes. And you love irony."

"Opening up that place would be one of the hardest things I've ever done."

"Is there anything inside?"

"Empty filing cabinets, a couple of desks. I could have had them hauled off, but the agency thought it would be easier to rent if it wasn't so empty-looking. They were wrong, apparently." They stepped off the curb and crossed the street, dodging a couple of trucks that were circling the square.

As they approached the office, Amanda asked, "Who owns it now?"

"I'm not sure, at this point," Henry replied. "I heard it was sold, but I didn't follow up to whom. It wasn't worth coming all the way back for the cabinets. Besides, I wasn't sure I wanted to go back in there."

He reached into his pocket and pulled out the yellowed envelope he had retrieved before leaving Chicago. "I don't know why I've kept this," he said quietly. "It should have been sent back long ago. Bringing it was just an impulse. Lately I find I don't resist that kind of thing in my life too well. And now here I am, standing in front of this door."

Amanda looked at the envelope. "What is it?"

Henry tore open the envelope and pulled out a key. "I'm betting these locks were never changed," he said. "Strictly speaking, I suppose we're trespassing. But what the hell."

Henry put the key in the lock and turned it; the door popped open slightly as the lock released. He pushed the door open, and it creaked from disuse. Light from the street fell into the large front room through the open door and the large picture windows.

Henry walked slowly into the office, Amanda following behind. The front room was twenty-five by twenty, and, as Henry had described, nearly empty. A single desk was parked at an odd angle against a wall, and a couple of tall wooden file cabinets were pushed off to the other side. "Slightly creepy," Amanda said softly.

Henry walked past her, crazy rectangles of light from the windows glancing across his legs. "This is all that's left of twenty years of legal practice," he said. "A couple of empty rooms. Every day he came in here and worked, and look at this place. It's like none of it ever happened." He walked over to a light switch and absently flicked it. To his surprise, he heard a humming above him. A scattering of long fluorescent lights above him came to life, eventually bathing the room in an uneven white glare. "Two of the four lights work," Henry said. "That seems appropriate."

Amanda walked to the desk and pulled on the center drawer. It slid open easily, and she looked inside. "There's still some pens and stuff in here," she said with surprise. "These are from your father's days?"

"A lot happens when you lose both your parents at one time," Henry said. "There was no one to go through anything. His secretary moved out of state after the accident. She refused to ever come in here again. I was no better, frankly. I had someone come in and clean up as best they could."

"So you haven't been through that door since then."

"No."

Henry looked at her, pausing momentarily on the edge of an emotional scar. "It's a symbol of the futility of my father's life, and that makes me angry," he said. "It also makes me miss him like hell." He looked around the gloom. "Who knows, maybe I could redeem this place by coming in and kicking Durand's and Hesston's ass."

"You've got my full support on that. I know it's not my business, but maybe you should do this. It feels right."

"All right. If I can figure out who owns this dump, we'll reopen tomorrow. If they're not afraid of Crandalls, that is."

"Need any help?" Amanda asked, and he saw a trace of red suffuse through her cheeks. He liked it; she was so competent, he found her capacity for shyness an attractive surprise.

"Yes, and you can give yourself any title you like."

"Queen of the world will do."

"What about your job?"

She raised an eyebrow. "There's rejoicing in the office when I don't show up."

Henry nodded. "I still need some equipment. Any ideas?"

"You can use my fax and printer."

"Can you get me a small copy machine?"

"Not from my office, but I can do that."

"Thanks," he said gratefully. "Meanwhile I'm going over to the bank and see if I can find out who owns this place."

The discovery that Henry's father's office was the property of the Cottonwood Valley Bank gave Henry a momentary sense of awe; if his destiny was finding him, it was running, for the moment, on rails. He had bumped into Frank Walters coming out of the bank and asked him if he had any information on the place, and Walters had lit up like a headlight. "I own it," he said, "or rather the bank does. And if you know a buyer I'll pay you a nice finder's fee."

"I had something more temporary in mind," Henry said. "I'd like to use the office for a while."

Walters gave him an interested look. "That so?" he asked. "What you got in mind?"

"Bringing the dead back to life," Henry said. "At least the office anyway. I need a place to set up shop for a while."

"I heard you left town in a hurry."

"I'm back. Roger Crandall's contesting the will, and it goes to court Thursday. I'm representing Raymond."

"I'll be damned."

"Roger was never going to be satisfied with anything less."

Walters nodded. "Well, you can have the office. It's been empty for so long I'd like to see somebody in it. Anyway, I already told you how I feel about Crandalls."

"I'm not sure it's Crandalls I'm fighting."

Walters' face lit up. "Who, then?"

"Another level up the food chain, I think. I'll be moving some stuff in there in the morning."

Walters smiled. "You let me know if I can help. Anything at all."

Henry's second prayer was as short as his first. He turned to cross Main and slowed, spontaneously, at the curb. He didn't close his eyes or even look down. He merely paused between steps and said, "Thank you."

Setting up the office was an exercise in emotional self-restraint. Henry came to terms with the place in stages, pushing through barriers of nostalgia. He arranged the sparse furniture, turned to pick up a box, and caught his breath; he had, unconsciously, put each piece exactly where it had been in his father's day. It was as though the first pieces of a jigsaw puzzle had been placed, and if a cutout of his father and the remaining file cabinets and pictures could be pressed into the scene, time would have been stopped six years earlier.

Unnerved, he scattered the furniture with an almost manic energy, eventually moving the main desk to the center of the room, just under one of the working light fixtures. Satisfied, he settled in to work, opening up the folder of Crandall assets and looking once again for connecting points between Crandall and Raymond. The only solid lead he had was Raymond's job at the bank, and he felt certain Hesston and Durand knew about that as well. But the only person who could actually unravel what had happened during that time was Ellen, and she wasn't talking. He needed a lever on her, but she was tough, hardened by years of living alone. Worse, she had in those years clearly learned to despise men. Walters had been no help with her; she'd been a good employee, according to him, and if her skirts were a little short, well, he didn't mind that either. She kept her nose clean, did her job, and left at the end of the day.

All of which left Henry exactly where he had started. If nothing in the conspiracy broke down, he would have little on which to proceed. On a whim, he flipped open his phone and called a Chicago exchange.

"Matt?" he said into the phone. "Matt Phillips?"

"Yeah."

"It's Henry, Matt."

"Mathews!" the voice retorted. "What you go and get your ass canned for, you crazy son of a bitch? And you didn't come by and say good-bye, you bastard."

"Which is it, Matt? Son of a bitch or bastard?"

"Hell, I don't know. But it pissed me off."

"I know. Things were . . . awkward. It was better that way. Sorry I didn't get by."

"I thought you were Sheldon's golden boy. Anyway, the shots you gave him in meetings sure fooled the rest of us."

"We melted down. I can't go into it."

"You don't have to. I already heard. You did the right thing."

"Thanks. Would you have done the same thing?"

"No fuckin' way."

Henry smiled. That was, in its simplest form, the prevailing philosophy at the firm. Work hard, cover your ass, and don't let your convictions get in the way. "Care to salve your guilty conscience with a good deed?" he asked. "I've got a situation I could use some research on."

"Sure. The interns don't have anything better to do."

"Good. I've got a name I need you to check on. Ellen Gaudet."

"Details?"

"Early fifties, bit of a tart, residence in Council Grove, Kansas. Works at the Cottonwood Valley Bank, same town."

"What am I looking for?"

"Anything."

"Pretty vague."

"Thanks, I'm desperate."

There was laughter on the phone, a sound highly communicative of the distance Henry had moved down the career chain since leaving the firm. His problems were minuscule compared with the cases the firm was handling. "I'll see what I can do," Matt said. "No promises. But I'll put somebody on it. Maybe something will shake loose."

"Thanks."

"No problem. Hey, you know about Sheldon banging your girlfriend?"

"Yes, Matt. I see your legendary tact is unchanged."

"Sorry, man. I just thought you should know."

"I wish them each other, which is the cruelest thing I can do."

There was more laughter, and then a dial tone.

Chapter Twenty-eight

Roger Crandall walked into the Cottonwood Valley Bank just before closing. He saw Frank Walters through a half-closed door, and moved quickly past the line of sight. He wasn't there to see Walters. Instead, he approached Ellen, feeling the big hand in his back pushing hard. It would have been better, he supposed, to have waited until the bank closed for this talk. But he had been reduced to Carl Durand's and Frank Hesston's errand boy, and that brought up a set of emotions he couldn't easily control. Being an errand boy was something he had his fill of, and the idea of playing that role with no end in sight was utterly intolerable. He wanted to slow his pulse, to think. But all he could do was ride and feel the big hand. He ground to a halt before Ellen's desk, and forced his voice to a low whisper. "We need to talk."

Ellen looked at him placidly, as if by perfect stillness she could negate his agitation. "Have a seat," she said softly, in a bank teller's voice. "How can I help?"

"Not that kind of talk," Roger growled. His eyes seemed stuck open, staring. But he couldn't do anything about it. "We have to talk alone. Right now."

"I'm working, Roger," Ellen answered. She glanced at the clock on the opposite wall. "I can't just pick up and leave. I get off in about ten minutes. Wait till then."

Roger stood brusquely and turned on his heel. "Make it five," he spat over his shoulder. He left the bank and got into the Cadillac. A few passersby on the street looked into the car; their stares invaded him and he glared back, locking eyes on a man standing a few yards away. *This would never have happened before*, he thought. *One look would have sent them running like rats*. He started the engine and pulled away to a gravel clearing a half block away. From there, he could look across the street and watch the front door of the bank.

Work on her, Hesston had said. *Don't spell things out, that's my job. Just plant the seed*. Once again, Roger felt power drifting away from him, floating beyond his reach. Hesston had given orders but had not explained the game. *But the game's not over yet*, he thought. *I'll do Hesston's errand but anything else I can pry out of her is mine*. Durand had said it was ironic that his father gave the money to Boyd, and that had troubled him. *I just have to work out what Boyd has to do with everything. Find a card to play. Then squeeze.*

Four minutes. He fiddled with the radio, banging the buttons from station to station. *Two minutes.* The big hand pushed. He watched the bank door eagerly. *She's late, damn it.* Just before he was sure he would explode, the door opened and Ellen emerged.

Roger put the car in gear and drove slowly down the street. Ellen was walking rapidly toward Benton when Roger pulled alongside. He pushed open the door, still rolling. "Get in."

Ellen glanced up and down the street and stopped. Roger braked and she slipped into the car. He was gunning the engine before she had the door closed. The force of the acceleration pushed her awkwardly back in the seat. "For God's sake, Roger," she said, "what's got into you? What's all this about?"

Roger gripped the wheel silently and drove. After a quick U-turn he turned off Main onto Owendale and headed toward Custer's Elm. "I don't like this," Ellen said. "Either tell me what's going on or let me out right now."

Roger shot her a glance, but said nothing. He drove silently the seven blocks to Custer's Elm, and pulled the Cadillac to the edge of the park. He stopped and looked down the wide clearing; the Birdman sat at its opposite end, loosely hunched over and staring at the ground. "That is what's going on," Roger said, pointing at Boyd. "I want to know what the hell he and my father had to do with each other."

"Your father didn't share his secrets with bank employees, Roger."

Roger stared back at her. "You don't really expect me to buy that, do you?" he asked. "Look, I know about you and Daddy. Not everything. But enough."

Ellen blanched. "What do you think you know, Roger?"

"I know you and Daddy didn't get together to talk about the bank," Roger said bitterly. "I know you were his little *whore.*"

With that word Ellen felt her soul catch in a vise; part of her wanted to weep, while the rest of her wanted to strike Roger's face in fury. Between those two forces she found herself unable to speak or move. She merely sat in misery, breathing in unsteady gulps.

"Did you really think I didn't know about that?" Roger demanded. "Don't be crazy. Of course, I didn't know it was you at first. Just that it was *someone.* When he told me to stay away from certain meetings. When he took his drives at night. I found out it was you later."

Ellen found a small voice in the midst of her shock and horror. She used it to throw up a last, pathetic denial. "Your daddy and I didn't do anything. You can't prove a single thing you're saying."

Roger laughed bitterly. "Daddy had a big appetite. He ate big. He bought big and he sold big. And I know he picked you up along the way, too, like some kind of trophy fish. He would have mounted you on his wall, if he could have got away with it." He grimaced. "Anyway, in the end I *saw* you together. And it didn't surprise me none it was you. You were the logical choice."

"What does that mean?"

Roger gave Ellen a withering stare. "Why, Ellen, you're the town tramp. Didn't nobody ever tell you that?"

With those words, Ellen found her strength. She reached out to strike, but Roger caught her wrist inches from his face. Her hand trembled in his powerful grip. She tried to wrench her arm back in frustration, but he held it, immovable. She struggled against him for a moment, but eventually slumped down, beaten. She looked out at Boyd. He was standing now, his back to them. He raised his hands into the air and made the sign of the cross. *Poor beautiful fool,* she thought. *The poor beautiful fool and the whore. Council Grove has more than one walking dead, now.* For a moment, she wanted to let everything unravel, to let the whole story roll out of her. She couldn't take much more of this inner leaking, the gradual erosion of her resolve. When she spoke, it was in a whisper. "Your father and I were once very much in love," she breathed. "I don't say he loved me at the end, all right? But in the beginning. In the beginning he cared for me."

"I suppose you think that makes a difference to me."

"I say that for me. It means I'm not . . . that word you called me." She pushed her hair back. Grayish-brown roots were beginning to fleck once again into the bottle blonde. She looked tired. "That was all before he was married."

"If he loved you, then why didn't he marry you? Maybe it was you who was in love. Not him."

Whore. Tramp. The words hung in the air like floating skeletons. Ellen exhaled bleakly, fighting back tears. She battled with her emotions awhile, eventually recovering herself. "Your daddy had just got back from the service. That was what, seventy-three? He was beautiful. Of course I loved him. I knew he was selfish. That didn't bother me. I liked that he knew what he wanted and how to get it." She shifted in her seat. "It's so hot in here. It's stifling."

Roger clicked the key over and lowered the windows. "I want the straight story. I want it now."

Ellen looked into Roger's face a moment. "So similar," she murmured, "but different." She peered back across the park. Boyd had noticed the car, but she doubted he could make out who was in it. Nevertheless, she hunched down, turning her back to the door. "*He* happened," she said, closing her eyes.

"What does that mean?"

"Raymond wasn't always like this. Something happened to him, something horrible. I can't say anything else."

Roger grabbed her arm once again and squeezed. "I'm gonna find out one way or another. Either you tell me everything or . . ."

Ellen, holding her arm stiff against his grip, looked him in the eye. "Don't threaten me, Roger. You're just another man. Do you think you're more powerful than your daddy was?"

Roger's anger poured through him. "I'm twice the man Daddy was," he snarled. "But that don't matter anymore. I got friends now, powerful friends."

Ellen eyed him cautiously. "What friends?"

Roger's face bloated with self-importance. "I told Carl Durand . . ."

With the mention of Durand's name, Ellen stiffened. "Durand? Why are you talking to Durand?"

"What crawled up your skirt?" Roger laughed. "I ain't afraid of him."

Ellen looked away. "You shouldn't have talked to Carl Durand, Roger. Stay away from him. *Stay away from Durand.*"

Roger studied Ellen's face. After a moment, his mouth made a thin smile. "Hesston said you'd do something like that," he said. "You look like you seen a ghost."

"You mean he sent you here?" Ellen's voice was edgy, unsteady. "You don't know what you're dealing with," she said. "You don't know . . ."

"Hesston says he wants to talk," Roger interrupted. "He says it's something you'll be interested in."

Ellen looked at Roger intently. "He's wrong if he told you that. Now take me home."

"You haven't told me what I want to know."

"I've told you more than I've told anyone for more than twenty-five years."

"Hesston said there was a lot of money involved. Enough . . ." Roger paused, thinking. *Enough for her to get the hell out of Council Grove forever.*

For a moment it appeared as though Ellen might begin to cry. But she merely whispered, "Either you drive or I walk."

Roger shrugged and started the engine. "I don't think Hesston's gonna like this." He put the car in gear and backed away from the park. Ellen shot a look back at Raymond as they sped away; the bench was empty. Boyd was gone.

"So how'd it go?"

"She turned white when I said your name."

Hesston smiled and sat back in his leather chair. "Good. You keep on playing ball. Everything's all right."

"She said she wouldn't come. She sounded like she meant it."

"She'll come."

"I still don't understand the game you're playing with her."

Hesston looked at Roger with disregard. "You don't have to understand. You have to do what you're told, and you'll get your share; ten percent."

"Daddy got a third."

"You're not your father."

"It's not fair. I want more."

Hesston laughed. "We've been through this, Roger. You want more. Or you'll what? Turn me in? You're along for the ride and you earn your money one way: by keeping your mouth shut. That's your total responsibility. Not to think. And sure as hell not to complain."

Roger paced the office, swirling ice cubes in his glass. "I need another drink."

"Yes, have a drink, Roger. Have a lot of drinks."

Roger poured whiskey into a glass and fell into a chair. "I did your job. So what now?"

Hesston smiled. "It's very simple. This whole mess has one obvious, tidy solution. Get rid of Boyd." Roger stared, but said nothing. "Without Boyd everything reverts to your family. Your mother, in fact, which is perfect. She doesn't know about the real money, and the land would still be in our control. Business as usual. You can handle dear old Mom, can't you?"

"Daddy did, didn't he?"

"I already told you, you're not your father."

"I can handle her," he said grimly.

"All right. So Boyd has to go."

Roger hammered down his drink. "How gone?"

Hesston shrugged.

Roger's expression hardened. "You're talking about murder."

"I'm talking about money, Roger. And nerve."

Roger felt his own inner unease and the booze swirling together in his mind. *Murder. To kill a man.* He was rattled by the words, but Hesston was disturbingly calm. Roger pushed down his fear, attempting to control his emotions. Gradually, the idea of killing Boyd took shape in his mind, and he was simultaneously repulsed and fascinated. It would solve everything, and it risked everything. Then his blood suddenly ran cold. "If anything happens to Boyd I wouldn't be able to get out of Council Grove before the shit hit the fan. It ain't exactly a secret I hate the little freak. The whole town would point their stubby fingers at me, and I'm not going down for it just so you can make all the real money."

"What's this, another push for more? That conversation's over."

"For a start. God, let me think." He rose and walked across the room, picking up the whiskey bottle as he went. Hesston watched him carefully, not speaking. "You serious about this?" Roger asked. "Actually kill him?"

Hesston pulled a pack of cigarettes out of his jacket and lit one. "Not a joking matter," he said calmly. "But neither is twelve million dollars."

"Your twelve million. You keep forgetting that." The booze burned in the back of Roger's throat. He was tired of getting ordered around. If Hesston meant what he was talking about, the equation was changed. "You're raising the stakes for all of us," he said, "you, me, Durand. If you're serious about this I have to have a bigger cut. I mean it, Frank. I don't care what your plan is, I'm going to take most of the heat. You know it."

Hesston sat back in the chair, pleased with himself. The more Roger melted down, the easier it was to play him. The boy's buttons were so big he barely needed to think about pushing them. "If you want more, you have to earn it."

"What does that mean?"

"It means nothing is free. Your father was man enough to do what needed doing when the time came." He looked at Roger a moment and said, "Did you ever wonder why he never brought you into our little scheme?" Roger stared back; he hated being left out, and despised his father for not confiding in him. "He told me why he kept you in the dark, Roger. He said you couldn't handle it."

"That's a damn lie," Roger spat. "I can handle anything he did."

Hesston smiled. It was like playing poker with a child. "All right, Roger," he said, "I believe you. You handle Boyd, and you get another five percent. Not of the back money, but from here on out. That's fifteen total. No more, and don't piss me off by bringing this up again."

Roger took a drink. The word "murder" rattled in his brain, careering through his synapses. He felt vaguely nauseous. "Not enough."

Hesston's face was set in stone. "Fourteen percent."

"What the hell is that?" Roger snapped. "You're going the wrong way."

"Thirteen percent."

Roger looked at Hesston but kept his mouth shut.

"Good boy. And don't worry about Boyd. Nobody is going to suspect you. Nobody is going to suspect anybody. It's wired."

Roger swallowed another gulp of whiskey to cover his humiliation and fear. He tried to tell himself he had won; he had pried out another three percent. "But what do you expect me to do? I can't just walk up and kill the guy."

"Of course not, Roger. That would endanger all of us, and I can't have that. Raymond is going to die the only death with no suspects. Suicide."

"You mean for Boyd to kill himself?" Roger asked incredulously. "Why would he kill himself right after finding out he's rich?"

"Money doesn't mean anything to Boyd, Roger."

Roger tried to think, but his emotions and the booze made it hard to focus. "I don't know about that," he said. "Daddy always said everybody has a price."

Hesston looked bored. "There's only one thing in this world that matters to Boyd. You're forgetting where we started today, Roger."

Roger's eyes opened wide. "You mean Ellen?"

Hesston smiled. "Ellen."

Chapter Twenty-nine

T. R. Harris walked into the law office of Henry's father shortly before noon the next morning, his face a scowl. He fixed Henry with a level gaze and said, "This was a setback."

Henry stood up and shook his hand. "Tell me."

"He's more distant now. I tried to talk to him, but he was gone, retreated in his own world. We've got to give the drugs a chance to work, Henry. If you keep on upsetting him, we're wasting our time."

"Look, I'm on your side. I've got a trial in two days, and I'd like nothing more than a coherent Raymond Boyd."

"That isn't going to happen, not in two days."

"Of course. But the point is that his reaction confirms our suspicions about the wells," Henry insisted. "The first visit wasn't a fluke."

"I'm beginning to think that the real reason you want Boyd around is for your own purposes, not his."

Henry bristled. "What does that mean? Look, I'm here at my own expense, working on a case with very limited prospects. I don't think I have to defend my motives."

"Taking him to the hospital gets him out of the way. But you're trying to break open a case in a very short amount of time. Incidents like what happened at the well speed things up. I'm not sure that's best for Raymond."

"We both know there's more than brain chemistry involved in getting Raymond better. The truth has to come out, and that could take some pushing. I think that's important for his sake, too."

"You push and things break loose. Have you stopped to think about what Raymond could get hit by?"

"Sometimes I can't think about anything else."

Harris looked troubled, but relaxed. "All right, I'll get off your back. But he has to be left alone from this moment forward. Any more incidents, and I'm taking him back with me."

"I can't fight that. You're the doctor."

Harris nodded, leaning against Henry's father's battered desk. He looked around, curiosity derailing him for the moment. "So this is your new headquarters," he said. "I call that fascinating."

"That so."

"Son takes over the father's place, assumes his mantle. Moves into his domain to complete his unfinished work. Worlds of meaning in that. I could interpret this for you, if you like."

"I'm slightly busy at the moment," Henry said.

Harris shrugged. "How do things look?"

"Ordinarily, the pressure would be on Roger. Overturning the wishes of the dearly departed is taken pretty seriously. On the other hand, most courts aren't in Cheney County."

"Worried about Crandall influence?"

Henry shook his head. "It's not Crandalls I'm worried about right now." Just then Amanda came in the door, weighed down by two large boxes. She stopped at the sight of Harris. "Is Raymond okay?" she asked.

Henry got up and took one of the boxes. "He's going to be all right," he said. "I was just about to tell the doc here about your friend Carl."

Amanda's face flushed with disgust. "I'm sleeping with Henry if he can nail him for something, even a parking ticket," she said, setting her remaining box down. "And after what we saw at the wells, I think he might do just that."

"Then something good might come out of this," Henry said, smiling.

"My God, an anthropologist could use you two to study mating rituals," Harris said. "I wish you'd just get it over with."

"I was only teasing," Amanda said.

Harris shrugged. "Fine," he said, "have it your way. So what's the story about the wells?"

Henry could feel Amanda looking at him surreptitiously from across the desk. *Having a psychiatrist around when you're falling for somebody is definitely a pain in the ass*, he thought. "Ammunition," he said. "Only we don't know what kind of gun we need to use it."

"Then why not go to the sheriff right now?" Harris asked. "Nail them before they get off the mark."

Henry shook his head. "Collier's their boy. I've got to be bulletproof. I have to figure it out first."

Harris' face clouded over. "You might not like what you find," he said. "Listen, I need to say this to both of you. You two have decided to care about Raymond, and I'm glad. It's the only reason I'm letting him stay here. But you shouldn't operate with the assumption that he's simply a victim. He's carrying an enormous load of guilt, and those feelings must come from somewhere."

"What are you trying to say?" Amanda asked.

"That he wants us both to be able to live with defending somebody who's done something sordid," Henry said.

"He could end up in jail," Harris said.

"I woke up last night with that nightmare running in my head. But I'm here to protect him from that. You need to be prepared to testify if it comes down."

"I think we can keep him out of a conventional jail, even if things turn from bad to worse. But even the psychiatric hospitals for criminals . . ."

"The way back for Raymond is through the truth," Henry said, not letting Harris complete the grim thought. "But if it turns out that he was part of something terrible, that's how it turns out."

Chapter Thirty

Frank Hesston sat behind his desk, the lights low. His office was a kind of cool tomb to him, comfortable in worn leather and dark wood, the smell of cigar smoke suffused the upholstery. Early in the evening he liked just to sit, a halo of smoke surrounding his head, secure in the fastness of his secret wealth and public power.

He had worked all day on the Crandall will, and felt he had earned this time, this tribute to his competency. Twelve million he had pried from the ground of Crandall's ranch, patiently, never rushing, not making the mistakes that led petty crooks to their inevitable downfalls. He had let the money flow slowly, not attracting attention, mounting over the years into a variety of numbered accounts from Switzerland to the Caribbean.

Flamboyant spending, the mark of an amateur, had always annoyed him. More important was the sense of security, the feeling of complete self-protection that only millions could give. He had spent some of the money, certainly, but always tactfully, and always far away from his life in the halls of state politics. The house he would disappear to, in a few years' time, was in Costa Rica, and both it and the yacht docked in Fort Lauderdale were titled in the name of a paper corporation, untraceable to him. Patience had insulated him, protected him. Patience and unshakable nerve.

But recent events had required his most intense concentration, a focus that resisted any coming apart of the discipline he had imposed on Durand and, before his death, on Tyler Crandall. Now was the time to look the greatest risk in the face and stare it down. Now was the final solution, the act that would seal all knowledge of what had really happened in a locked, buried casket. One week from now, he would be completely free.

As he sat, he became aware through the haze of cigar smoke that the door to his office was moving. He saw the brass lever go down, and watched a crease of light open on the edge of the doorframe. He leaned back, watching with a sense of calm; he knew who it would be. He had planned for it. He had created the forces that led to its inevitability.

Ellen pushed the door open and stepped into the office, her outline framed by the light behind her. "Hello, Frank," she said, and her voice betrayed a kind of defeated exhaustion.

"Hello, Ellen," Hesston said, rising. "Come in. Please, be comfortable. Sit right here."

Ellen walked in on high heels, her stiletto shoes sinking into the plush carpet. She remained standing. "I'm here," she said, not looking at him. "So talk."

"So hard," Hesston said in a hurt voice, walking from around the desk. "But I've always liked you. That will be even more clear to you when I explain why I wanted to see you." He leaned across his desk to kiss her cheek but she turned away, facing the wall. He shrugged and returned to his seat, a pale smile on his face. "I've always felt that you were the real victim in all this, you know," he said. "And I've hated that."

"Maybe you should explain that to Jimmy Waddell."

"God, I had forgotten his name." Hesston sighed. "The field hand was regrettable, but nothing compared with what you've been through. His suffering was over in an instant. A flash of sulfur, his brain choked of oxygen, the world going black. Your suffering has gone on for years. Now I want to make things right. You've been quiet for a long time, and the time has come to reward you."

"You had nothing to do with my keeping quiet," Ellen said. "I had my own reasons for that."

"But that kind of dependability deserves a reward," Hesston said. His expression softened. "Let's not fight, Ellen. You and I have always understood each other so well. We're so much alike, you know."

She turned to him at last, his wide face a place for her hatred to land. "I'm nothing like you," she said in a raspy whisper.

"We're *exactly* the same, my dear. We both want to be protected from anything this big bad world can do to hurt us. We want a wall surrounding us that nothing can penetrate. The only difference between us is how much more of what we both want I have been able to get." He picked up a cigar, caressing it between his fingers. "I know what you want, Ellen. And I'm prepared to give it to you. All you need."

"I don't want your money."

Hesston smiled indulgently. "Then call it something else. Call it the chance to start over, away from all this pain. Away from Roger, from Raymond. Away from the past. You can forget about Council Grove and everything in it and live life clean. Clean, Ellen. No ghosts to haunt you ever again." His voice was a caress. "I have the door, Ellen. Behind that door is everything you ever wanted. All you have to do is open it."

"Why do you need me? I know you're contesting the will. If you win that, you'll have everything you want."

"Not everything." Hesston set the cigar in a brass ashtray. "I want those doors closed forever. The trial is scrutiny. I don't like scrutiny."

"Then why do it?"

"To keep Mathews off my back until I can take care of things. He's a dangerous young man, and he's nosed around too much already. But Mathews or no Mathews, I don't intend for that trial to ever come to a verdict."

She looked at him, fear and curiosity mingling in her expression. "What are you talking about?"

Hesston's voice turned even sweeter. "It's enough to say that you can be a great help to me, and I am prepared to reward you for that help. I'm willing to give you a life far away from everything that's hurt you so deeply."

Ellen's voice was barely audible. "I don't want to hurt Raymond."

Hesston smiled and stood from behind his desk. He walked slowly to the bar across the office and poured himself a drink. "Can I get you something?" he asked. She shook her head. He fixed himself a highball, carefully putting two cubes of ice in a glass. He poured scotch over the cubes, watching the dark liquid begin to melt the ice. "It's not just your suffering that has broken my heart," he said quietly. "I've had to endure Raymond's suffering, too." He took a drink, holding the scotch in his mouth a moment, savoring it before swallowing. "So any solution to my problem has to help him as well."

"What does that mean?" she asked darkly.

"Right now I'm thinking of you, Ellen, of how simple everything really could be at last. All you have to do is open the door, walk through, and close it again behind you. You pass quietly into a new life. You never look back."

"You didn't answer my question."

"Think of it, darling. All the pieces of the game at rest," Hesston said, his voice sounding tired. "No more fear, no more worrying. Ever since that horror at the well you've been waiting for your life to begin again, tortured by what you know. But you can never really live, not with Raymond near you, reminding you every day of your life of what you carry with you." He crossed the room to her, and for a moment, he looked like he might take her in his arms. "You're tired. You're not young anymore. No, don't turn away. I know how cruel it is that you wasted your youth on a man who gave you nothing. But think, darling. This is your last chance. If you don't take it, you are going to die old, alone, and miserable in the same clapboard house you've lived in your whole life." He moved even closer, and his voice was all warm breath. "It's too late for games. Much too late. You have to face the mirror, my love. You have to face the lines in your skin. You have to face what your body is doing. Don't lie to yourself, sweetheart, not now. This is your life, and it's the last chance you will ever have to avoid being horrible and hateful and utterly, completely alone." His mouth was touching her ear now, lips against her skin. "I have two hundred thousand dollars for you, darling. I know what you make at the bank, Ellen. You can't save a thousand dollars a year on it. With that money no one will ever call you cheap again. No broken-down house in Council Grove, no Kmart dresses. No cheap pictures on your walls. No bad memories. All that will fade away in your new life."

Ellen closed her eyes; her breathing became deeper, slower. "What will happen to Raymond?" she asked quietly.

"I don't want you to worry about that," Hesston answered, and now he put his arm around her, supporting her weight. He kissed the side of her face very gently, just touching his lips to her skin. "I only want to protect you from anything that could ever hurt you. I want you to be safe."

Ellen's eyes fluttered. She opened her purse, taking out a tissue. Carefully, she touched the tissue to her face, wiping her tears. Her breathing steadied, and her face took on a distant expression. Hesston took her hand and held it in his own, raising it to his lips. "It's time to rest, Ellen," he whispered. "It's time to let go."

When she looked at him, he knew she was his.

Chapter Thirty-one

The trial was scheduled to begin at two o'clock, and that morning Henry stayed in his office, organizing his case and making a list of potential witnesses. If Hesston was going to break the will, there was only one way to do it: create an overwhelming case of circumstantial evidence that showed Crandall's real intention had been to leave his estate to his family. The will, in such a view, would be either fraudulent, superseded by another will either lost or missing, or made in an emotional state not representative of Crandall's true wishes. Ordinarily, such a case would be extremely difficult to prove, although Henry knew that large estates were commonly fought over. But ordinarily the plaintiffs weren't Crandalls, they weren't in Council Grove, and the beneficiary wasn't a crazy man who lived in a park.

Amanda came by with lunch at eleven-thirty. "Another Gladys special from the diner," she said. "Just a sandwich and some coffee."

"Thanks," Henry said, barely looking up. "I appreciate it."

She set the sack down on his desk. "Are you ready?"

He leaned back in his chair. "For chaos? Who knows? We have a good position. But I'll know ten minutes into the trial if that matters."

"Because?"

"Because that's how long it'll take for me to figure out if the judge is above Crandall and Hesston influence."

Amanda glanced at her watch. "Not much time left," she said. "Anything I can do?"

Henry exhaled. "There is, actually." He picked up a stack of papers. "You can run these by the clerk of the court. It'll be on the second floor, just beside Brackman's chambers."

"What do I tell him?"

"That I'm sorry they weren't there yesterday."

She laughed. "What can they expect? They dropped this on you."

"Procedure's funny, though," Henry said, barely looking up. "It doesn't care how much sleep you've had."

"All right. I'll just meet you over there, okay? And, Henry, leave a little early. There's a crowd at the courthouse."

Henry put down his pen. "Like the sheriff said, the entertainment options are limited around here. How many?"

She shrugged. "Sixty or seventy outside. I don't know how many more inside."

"Just what we need, a little circus atmosphere."

"I know. It doesn't help you to spend time talking to me. I'll see you in a couple of hours. And good luck."

Henry drank the coffee, ignoring the sandwich. He worked a while longer, and just after one made a list of his assets and liabilities. Most encouraging was the *in terrorem*; it showed that Crandall knew that his plan would cause controversy, demonstrating a clear state of mind. On the negative side, nobody had seen Boyd and Crandall speak for more than twenty-five years, at least nobody who had come forward. Moreover, the Crandalls were powerful, and they were allied with a highly competent and experienced lawyer. And there was Boyd himself; emotionally, it would be hard for a judge to let someone like Raymond walk off with what seemed so logically to belong to the family.

Henry made a third list, and headed it "unknowns." At the top was the cause of what Dr. Harris called Raymond's decompensation, the truth behind what had started him on his decline into madness; the trial was his best chance to uncover what had caused it, and it was impossible to predict if the truth would help or be a devastating blow. Ellen knew the answer, and if it was possible, Henry had decided to focus his attention on her. That was, he realized, his weak link; she was tough, and it was impossible to predict if he could pull anything of substance from her.

At one-thirty Henry packed up and walked across the square to the courthouse. The crowd had increased, and now nearly a hundred people milled about the courthouse steps, spilling out into the square. Henry circled around behind, avoiding any contact, and came in the back door with little fuss. But once he entered the building, it was impossible to avoid throngs of interested bystanders. He heard his name whispered but kept moving, pushing his way through the swinging doors of the courtroom.

The courtroom of Judge Howard Brackman was ringed by tall windows, and in the afternoon the sun beat through them, making the room uncomfortably warm. There was no air-conditioning; instead, three ceiling fans slowly spun their enormous wings, doing little but disturbing the warm air high in the room. Behind the judge's seat black-and-white photographs hung, portraits of previous occupants of the chair. They were stern, mostly, with the exception of one crazed-looking man with startling, disheveled white hair and preternaturally wide eyes. Behind the litigants was seating for about a hundred on long, wooden benches. At the end of each bench was a stack of hand fans. Henry glanced at one as he passed by; emblazoned on the front was a stark drawing of the scales of justice, with the words COURTESY OF JUDGE HOWARD BRACKMAN below it.

Henry made his way through the crowd to his seat, dropping his brief-case on the table before him. He looked to his right; Hesston was there, looking at him with an inscrutable smile. Henry walked over and stuck out his hand. "Henry Mathews."

"Frank Hesston. Welcome home."

Henry decided to peg the bullshit meter and see what happened. "Thanks," he answered. "Don't be too hard on me, okay?"

Hesston shrugged. "I'll keep that in mind."

Henry nodded and turned back to his table; in spite of Hesston's obvi-ous caution, they both knew Henry wasn't an experienced litigant. Thus far, he had done more corporate dissection than courtroom work. But he didn't have time to think about his weaknesses; at that moment Roger pushed his way into the courtroom, his mother in tow. Electricity shot through the packed room, even as it fell eerily silent. Roger had his mother on his arm, and she followed him obediently, like a dog on a leash. Sarah, conspicuous by her absence, wasn't with them. Hesston walked toward them immediately and kissed Margaret on the cheek. She stared straight ahead, as still as death. Hesston shook Roger's hand, and together they seated Margaret to the lawyer's left. Roger noisily took a seat on the other side of his attorney, and Henry studiously avoided looking at them, unwill-ing to provide a theater in which Roger could publicly show his contempt with any expressions of disgust.

Henry was opening his briefcase when the bailiff announced Judge Brackman. The roomful of people stood, a door opened, and Brackman entered. He was a short man, robed in black, with thick gray hair and eye-brows. He was smart—Henry could see that immediately—but in the cagey, down-home way that made some country lawyers particularly dan-gerous. Brackman took his seat and ran through the formalities, opening the case with a perfunctory, practiced ease. To Henry's chagrin, he addressed Hesston as though they had known each other for fifteen years, been political allies, and gone fishing together on more than one occasion. Henry was acknowledged with nothing more than a nod and the word "Counselor." Brackman leaned back in his chair. "All right," he said, "everybody knows why we're here. But before we get started I need to get somethin' clear." He nodded to Roger. "Son, you understand this *in ter-rorem* business? You straight on the fact that you're riskin' what you got to initiate this action?"

Roger nodded. "I understand."

"You understand that if I rule against you, you're excluded from this estate forever."

"I do."

Brackman looked down at his papers. "The decedent's spouse is named on this suit as well," he said. He looked over Roger's head. "Margaret, dear? You understand what you're doin' here, is that right?"

Hesston stood. "This is a family unit," he said. "Both of the plaintiffs are in agreement."

"I'd just like to hear that from her, Frank."

Hesston sat and turned to Margaret. She looked at him blankly, then nodded her head, robotlike, without speaking. Brackman watched her a moment, then said, "There's a daughter in this will too. I don't see her name on this. Don't see her in the courtroom either."

"The daughter is not seeking redress, your honor," Hesston said.

"I see." Brackman leaned back in his chair. "All right. I just want to make sure everybody understands what's goin' on here." He cleared his throat. "All right, Frank, whatever you got in mind for an opening statement, you go on ahead."

Hesston rose, his face full of deep concern. "Your honor, it's not what I have in mind, it's what Tyler Crandall had in mind." He put his hand on Roger's shoulder and nodded toward Ty's widow. "He had people in mind, your honor, real people who are going through a painful, terrible loss. He had a bereaved family in mind. *A family.* Is there anything more important in this world, your honor? Anybody who knew Tyler Crandall understands there was nothing more important to him. He worked for his family every day of his life. Your honor, I'm prepared to introduce evidence that Tyler Crandall continuously, consistently, and publicly declared that his desire was to leave his possessions exclusively to his family, and that control of the Crandall businesses was to come to his son, Roger. This sentiment never wavered over the twenty-six years of marriage between husband and wife, and it stretches any reasonable credulity that he would have written a will with the opposite instructions."

Henry settled in, taking the measure of his opponent. Over the next ten minutes, Hesston skillfully portrayed the Crandall family as the victims of a horrible fraud, the centerpiece of which was an utterly specious and inauthentic will. Although he had recently been spending his time lobbying at the state capitol, it was clear Hesston hadn't lost his touch in a courtroom. The precise management of his tone—the ebb and flow between crushed surprise and righteous indignation—transfixed the gallery. Hesston drew his comments to a close by holding up a copy of the will and saying, "Your honor, I intend to show that this will in no way represented the true wishes of Tyler Crandall. I intend to show that Tyler Crandall would have been angered and saddened by what is contained here, and would do everything in his power to see that it never saw the light of day. I personally believe that if he were here, he would light these papers and burn them before our very eyes." Hesston sat down, the impact of his superb oratorical skill settling dangerously on the crowd. The judge nodded to Henry. "All right, son," he said, "you're up. What you got on your mind?"

Henry stood, right hand in his pants pocket, his eyes on Hesston. He paused a moment with a puzzled smile. "The ability of counsel to read minds is what I'm thinking of at the moment, your honor. Mr. Hesston's power to tell us what Tyler William Crandall was thinking at the time he wrote his will is truly spectacular. But apparently his supernatural powers go even further. His claim to know what Mr. Crandall would say and do if he were to walk reconstituted and alive into this courtroom is even more impressive." He shook his head. "In my time in the third circuit court of Illinois I've been fortunate to represent some of the most powerful and accomplished people in the world, your honor. Millionaires a hundred times over, most of them. And none of these captains of industry has this extraordinary ability that Mr. Hesston possesses. Competing on the global stage in the most competitive industries on earth, they would covet such a talent, I'm sure." He paused. "But I'm doubtful that it would have occurred to even the most ambitious of them to attempt such a feat on someone sleeping peacefully in a cemetery. Mr. Hesston's ability to read the mind even of the deceased is something that has pushed all else from my brain. Although, given his extraordinary powers, he obviously is aware of that fact already."

There was some muted laughter in the courtroom, and Henry was satisfied that he had, in a single statement, reminded Brackman that his courtroom was the low-rent district, and shown Hesston that he was prepared to turn anything he said into a weapon on his own behalf.

Henry stepped from behind his table. "Your honor," he said, "a will is a sacred trust. Not far from here are burial grounds in which the Pawnee Indians laid their loved ones to rest. The government of this country, which has in many ways behaved abominably toward that ancient people, has at least regarded one thing to be inviolate and protected, no matter what the cost. That thing, your honor, is that their dead be left to rest in peace. It is, in fact, the only promise this country kept to that race, and its significance cannot be overstated. The last wish of the Pawnee to be undisturbed is something which all people everywhere understand. No person may build upon that land for any reason. Nothing must be done to disrupt the wish of those people to rest undisturbed."

Henry picked up his copy of the will. "Tyler Crandall had a last wish, your honor, as sacred as any represented by those burial grounds. He wrote down that wish with the assistance of a lawyer, so that there would be absolute clarity. He insisted that a powerful conscript called the *in terrorem* be applied, because he anticipated that there might be those who, for reasons of their own, would want to overturn that wish." He turned slightly, partially facing the gallery. "A will is a trust between those who leave and those who remain. Every person in this room will one day depend upon that trust being upheld. If we violate it, no person anywhere can depend upon the law to protect them when they can no longer speak for themselves. In spite of Mr. Hesston's claimed mind-reading ability, Tyler Crandall can't walk in this courtroom and demand that his promise to Raymond Boyd be kept. He is depending on this court to keep his promise for him." He turned back to the judge. "In the end, every person here is depending on it."

Henry glanced at Hesston as he walked back to his chair. He looked him in the eye for only an instant, but he knew Hesston received his message: *Don't fuck with me.*

Brackman cleared his throat. "All right, Frank, call your first witness."

Hesston stood. "I call Roger Crandall, your honor."

Hesston, smart enough to understand Roger's emotional nature, kept his questions simple. And he had clearly prepped Roger well; the questions were answered in short, clipped responses. *Yes, my daddy told me I would take over. The last time was four days before he died. No, he never spoke about Raymond Boyd. Yes, he spent hours going over how he wanted things handled. No, he didn't expect to die. He just wanted me prepared. Yes, those were his exact words.*

Henry wasn't surprised by the patently false image of the father-son relationship Roger described. But it felt early in the process to try to goad him into admitting his real feelings about Tyler. There was some natural sympathy for the family, especially with Margaret's presence in the courtroom. To go on the attack immediately risked alienating both Brackman and the gallery. If it came to that, he could call Sarah, whose honesty would compel her to reveal the truth. But it would cause her embarrassment and pain, and he wanted to avoid that if possible. However, if it proved necessary, he was willing to do it. For now, all that was needed was to lay some groundwork, and reserve the right to redirect. When Hesston finished Henry stood and walked to the witness box, Roger radiating loathing as he approached. Henry looked at him, letting Roger feel vulnerable for a while. After several seconds he asked, "Roger, do you remember calling me at my Chicago office the day after your father's death?"

Roger's voice was brittle. "Yeah."

"At that time you told me your father had left you a list of instructions, correct?"

"That's right."

"Those instructions directed you to call me, because I had your father's will in my possession."

"I guess."

"Is that what you told me?"

"Yes."

"So the will in my possession was the will your father believed was his real will."

Hesston was on his feet. "Your honor, the witness can't testify to the state of mind of the deceased."

Henry turned. "I can't see why not. Mr. Hesston did so in his opening statement."

Hesston turned and glared, and Brackman interrupted. "All right, all right," he said, "you made your point, son. We tend to give a little latitude in opening statements. But this is testimony. The witness is to disregard the question."

Henry smiled. "No further questions, your honor."

The rest of the afternoon went similarly; a short parade of witnesses testified that they had heard Tyler refer to Roger as son and heir, Henry doing his best to diminish their effectiveness. If, in the end, the case boiled down to a "he said, she said," Henry couldn't be sure what would happen. But when, at nearly four-thirty, Hesston called Ellen Gaudet, Henry knew the first real moment of truth in the trial had arrived. She stood and walked to the stand, hips gently swinging, in a skirt two inches too short and heels an inch too high. Hesston treated her as though she were a demure mother of three.

Henry knew what Hesston's first question would be. The first rule of trial litigation was to bring up bad news yourself, defusing its power. Hesston let Ellen get settled, and unloaded the bombshell with studied casualness.

"Ms. Gaudet, at what point did Raymond Boyd come to work at the Cottonwood Valley Bank?" A ripple moved sharply through the crowd, as Henry knew it would. Brackman gaveled it down.

"Let's keep order," he said, obviously as surprised as everyone else by Hesston's question. "Go ahead, Ms. Gaudet."

"In 1973, I believe," Ellen answered.

"And for how long was he employed there?"

"For about five months."

"I see. And under what circumstances did Mr. Boyd leave the bank?"

"He was fired. Terminated, I guess you call it."

"Why was that, Ms. Gaudet?"

There was a remote, controlled pain behind Ellen's expression. "Because he went crazy," she said. Henry started to rise, but Hesston quickly waved his hand. "Perhaps you'd better explain what you mean, Ms. Gaudet."

"He started going out to Custer's Elm during the workday. After a while, he stopped coming in altogether. That's when the bank people came down from Kansas City and let him go."

"And to your knowledge, Mr. Crandall and Mr. Boyd never had any communication from that time forward?"

"That's right."

"Were you aware of Mr. Crandall's financial dealings with the bank?"

"Yes."

"And to your knowledge was there any business or financial relationship between him and Raymond Boyd?"

"Yes."

"What was that, Ms. Gaudet?"

"Raymond was the bank manager, and he approved Tyler's loan for some land."

"Were there any other dealings between them? Any further relationship after that point?"

"No."

"You're sure about that? Nothing? No matter how insignificant?"

"Nothing," Ellen said. "Nothing at all."

"Thank you, Ms. Gaudet."

As Henry stood for his cross-examination Ellen looked at him with such a cold, dead expression that he lost his train of thought. *My God*, he thought, *I'd give anything to know why this is costing you so much.*

"Ms. Gaudet, are you a psychiatrist?"

"No," she said.

"I wonder because you were so willing to diagnose Mr. Boyd's medical condition. I believe the technical term you used to describe it was . . . 'crazy,' wasn't that it?"

"You know what I meant."

"No, Ms. Gaudet, I don't know. 'Crazy' is a very imprecise term. I'm 'crazy' about pizza, for example." There was soft laughter in the room. "So perhaps we can leave the psychiatric analysis to the professionals, would that be all right with you?"

Her answer was a low mutter. "Okay."

"I appreciate that. But just because you're not a psychiatrist doesn't mean you don't have some vital information to share with this court. In fact, there are some things you're superbly qualified to tell us." He walked across the polished wooden floor and leaned back on his table. "For example, you can tell this court what was so upsetting to Raymond just before he was dismissed by the bank management."

Hesston was on his feet, objecting. "The question is both vague and irrelevant, your honor. Ms. Gaudet is here to testify about the short business relationship between Mr. Boyd and Mr. Crandall, not Mr. Boyd's frame of mind. She's done so."

Henry smiled; Hesston wasn't, it turned out, infallible. He had taken the bait. "Your honor, you've already allowed testimony from this witness about Mr. Boyd's mental condition. I didn't bring it up. Counsel did."

Hesston very nearly barked his response, but caught himself. He gave a sideways glance at Henry, recalculating his opponent. When he spoke, his face was serene. "Your honor, the question is nevertheless vague."

"Objection sustained," Brackman said. "I'll allow the general area of inquiry, but give your question more definition, Counselor."

Henry nodded. "Ms. Gaudet, were you aware of any sudden change in the relationship between Tyler Crandall and Mr. Boyd during the time he worked at the bank?"

"Yes."

Henry leaned forward, focused on her answer. "What was that change, Ms. Gaudet?"

"Mr. Crandall told me he didn't like Raymond," she said simply. "He said that being around Raymond made him uncomfortable."

"Uncomfortable? Tyler Crandall?" Henry smiled. "That's hard to believe."

"Objection, your honor."

"Sustained."

"What made Mr. Crandall so uncomfortable, Ms. Gaudet?"

"Just that Raymond was starting to get unstable. Mr. Crandall didn't like that in a banker, I suppose."

"Very reasonable. But we're still not getting at what made Mr. Boyd's attitude change so suddenly. His decline in job performance occurred over a very short period of time, didn't it?"

"Yes. I suppose so."

"But when you think about it, we could say his job performance was never that good, couldn't we, Ms. Gaudet?"

"I don't know what you mean."

"Well, he approved a very sizable loan for Mr. Crandall when the truth was Tyler couldn't afford that loan, isn't that right, Ms. Gaudet?"

"I object, your honor," Hesston broke in. "The witness can't testify to what Tyler Crandall could or couldn't afford."

"On the contrary, your honor," Henry said, "the witness personally opened Mr. Crandall's account with the bank. She was aware of his assets to the penny."

"That true, Ms. Gaudet?" Brackman asked.

"Yes," she answered.

"All right," Brackman said, waving Hesston down. "The witness will answer the question."

"Ms. Gaudet? How much money did Mr. Crandall initially deposit with the bank?"

"It was a long time ago."

"Does the figure thirteen hundred dollars ring any bells?" Henry walked to his desk and picked up some papers. "I'll enter this into evidence, your honor." Brackman nodded. "So Raymond Boyd approved a substantial loan to a returning veteran with very little money and no collateral other than the land itself. I'd say that his job performance at that moment was extremely suspect, Ms. Gaudet. Wouldn't you agree?"

"I don't know. I wasn't paid to second-guess Mr. Boyd's decisions."

Henry walked back to his table. He was doing his best to make points, but in the end, his expertise was left with nowhere to land. Ellen was, unsurprisingly, unflappable. Her cold exterior made her a perfect witness for Hesston. He continued to try to rattle her for several minutes, but she resisted him with the perfect calmness of a stone. Unless someone somewhere let something slip, all Henry could do was circle and throw out innuendos. But a cross-examination that had been at worst ineffectual became truly damaging when Hesston got his chance to redirect; he kept Ellen on the stand, where she flatly stated that not only had Crandall not spoken to Boyd in over twenty-five years to her knowledge, but that she had personally heard Crandall refer to Roger on many occasions as "the one I want to take over when I'm gone."

Henry sat through a parade of witnesses that afternoon, hearing them all testify that they had never seen Crandall and Boyd together, and worse, that they had always understood Roger as the heir apparent in Crandall's mind. The only good news was that the sheer repetitiveness of the testimony gave it a numbing, undramatic character, and Henry was hopeful that he could unload some bombshell to shake up the court. But as though Hesston were reading his mind, he delivered another, unexpected blow; late in the afternoon, Hesston called Margaret to the stand. She stood with very real fragility, and the frightened stare in her face was so authentic that Henry had been moved himself, in spite of his position. What her presence was doing to the gallery and Brackman, he could easily guess.

Hesston walked to her and gently took her hand. "I'm deeply sorry that you have to be disturbed in such a painful, difficult time," he said. "It's a tragic situation that I would have given everything to have avoided." He paused. "Mrs. Crandall, I only have one question for you, and after that you may go, if Counsel has nothing for you. My question is very simple.

Margaret, did your husband ever talk to you about his affairs? About what he wanted for you after his death?"

Henry watched with the same fascination as everyone else in the court-room; as far as he knew, no one had heard Margaret say a word since Ty's death. When she spoke, her voice was a low, trembling vibration that barely cleared the witness box. "My husband told me that he would take care of me," she said softly. "He said that everything he had worked for was for me and for his family."

Hesston looked at her silently, his face awash in sympathy. He let her voice sink to silence, and finally said quietly, "I have no doubt he did. No doubt whatsoever. Your witness."

The thought that it would be appropriate to engage Margaret Crandall in a cross-examination never entered Henry's mind. "No questions," he answered.

Brackman roused himself from the bench. "The witness may stand down," he said gently, "with the court's deepest condolences."

Margaret nodded blankly at Brackman. Hesston, rather than the bailiff, helped her down. Roger came and took her through the gate to the gallery, but she didn't sit down. Instead, he led her slowly past the rows of people and out the door.

Brackman watched her leave. "I believe that's all we need for today," he said, when the door closed behind her. "I think we can all use a break. Court is adjourned until tomorrow morning at nine o'clock." He smacked his gavel down on a wooden block, the sharp sound jarring Henry from his thoughts.

He stood and turned to see Amanda coming through the crowd toward him, and her face showed she had heard Margaret's testimony and had been moved by it.

"It's all right," he said, releasing her. "Caring about her doesn't make you disloyal to me. I hate it, too. I'd like to crawl in a hole and vanish right now."

Amanda kissed his cheek and left right after court adjourned, unwilling to let the day end without at least checking in at her office. Henry regretted seeing her go; with the day going so badly in court, he felt that his only ally was leaving. Within minutes he discovered he missed *her*, which forced him to admit that Harris might be right: maybe they were going through some kind of ritual, the conclusion of which was becoming more and more foregone. She was breaking through his cynicism at just the right moment, when he was already thinking through his life in every way imaginable. If they had met in Chicago, with Henry secure in his position, the connection would have been more difficult. Her optimism, so valuable and attractive to him now, would have seemed naive. And he had to assume that his own calculating rise up the career ladder would have struck her as hackneyed and materialistic.

Here, in Council Grove, things were different. What he wanted in his own life was undergoing a tectonic shift, and it was reasonable that what he wanted in a woman would change with it. The merely impressive, once so magnetic and appealing, suddenly and surprisingly paled next to the real, the flawed, the human. Only in one way were Amanda and Elaine the same: they both expected the best from him. But their expectations reflected their own priorities. Elaine, looking for a counterpart, demanded brilliance and career success; Amanda pressed him toward enlarging his soul. In other words, he let himself dare to think, she actually wanted his happiness. The difference was overwhelming.

But he was relieved that nothing had happened yet that couldn't be denied. Elaine's shadow, semipermeable, was still between them, their eighteen months together making him question his timing. It wasn't that he doubted his desire; it was more an innate sense of propriety that made moving so soon toward Amanda seem rushed. He had never been able to disconnect coupling and love the way most of the young lawyers at the firm had done, even the women. The debauchery had started at law school. Casual, almost aimless fucking was the ultimate stress reliever for mostly law-abiding twenty-somethings who didn't want to sabotage a law career with a misdemeanor drug offense. But he had never played the game in earnest. It might have been, he had sometimes let himself think, that he was merely decent.

But he had to admit that he and Amanda were circling, coming closer, like skaters describing arcs that draw ever nearer. And if neither of them stopped it, they would intersect. *And what then?* To connect, to really touch; that was far different from just getting into bed. They weren't teenagers, and he couldn't imagine Amanda reducing sex to the merely recreational. She simply wasn't the type. Her heart was too big, too available for that. Sleeping with her meant life changes. There was the distance, for one thing. And neither of them, he had to admit, was very secure in their work at the moment. But his body was craving her, even if his mind was playing tricks on him to get him to go slowly.

He worked until dark, and again and again she intruded on his thoughts. He didn't regard missing her so much as entirely a good thing; to have known her such a short time and already feel the lack of her—that was the stuff of a crush, not a real relationship. But he kept thinking about her slight but unmistakable figure, and at last he indulged himself with a fantasy, letting his thoughts run unfettered.

"I'm back."

Henry looked up and saw Amanda standing in the doorway, smiling, with a bag of what looked like groceries in her arms. Considering what he had just been thinking, he was worried his face would flush with the sight of her. "What happened?"

"Let's say I wasn't needed," she said with a small, melancholy smile.

"Sorry. Kind of. I mean I'm sure that's hard."

"I felt it as soon as I walked in the place. It was twelve degrees in there."

"If that's how they feel, I can't believe they haven't fired you."

"That would take an act of God," she answered ruefully. "You know how it is with the government. So they just freeze you instead." She handed him the bag.

"What's this?"

"Dinner," she said. "I left the office, went home, and pulled a couple of things together. I hate being useless. Anyway, you can't eat at the restaurant all the time."

"Thanks. What you got in there, sprouts?"

"Hardly," she said, smiling. "Take this and I'll be back in a second."

Henry laid out the contents of the bag; there were a couple of cheeses, some good, solid bread—hard-crusted, the way he liked it—and a pasta concoction of tortellini, tomatoes, and vegetables that looked wonderful. Best of all, there was a nice merlot he recognized—not expensive, but very drinkable. He was admiring the bottle when Amanda came in the door lugging a good-sized CD player. "What's that for?" he asked.

She set the player on a table near an outlet, handed him a CD, and said, "Push the big button on the front to get it going. I'll get dinner."

"Nat King Cole," Henry said, looking at the CD cover.

"You've been too busy destroying companies the past few years to get any culture, Henry. Somebody has to do something about that."

Henry put the CD on; the sound of a small rhythm section flowed into the room, and Cole's rich tenor began singing "Route 66."

Amanda dished out portions on paper plates. She handed him a corkscrew, and he opened the wine, breathing in the scent. "I didn't realize how hungry I was," he said, pouring her a glass. He sampled the pasta and asked, "You make this?"

"The secret is letting it sit overnight, which this hasn't. It'll be better tomorrow."

"It's good now," he said, taking another bite. "You shall be rewarded. Richly."

They sat eating across his desk from each other, avoiding serious topics, feeling the novelty of being together in a quiet place. He enjoyed it; she was good company, even when they weren't working together or trying to figure out the case. After they finished, Amanda started the CD over; he looked at her inquisitively, and she smiled. "You said I get a reward."

"Name it."

She stood. "Let's dance."

"Here?"

"Yeah, here." She held out her hand, palm down, and he took it. She moved easily around the desk, coming close to him. He glanced outside; it was dark, and he was sure they would be visible from the outside.

"Hang on," he said, and he clicked off the overhead lights. The dim luminescence of the streetlamps came in through the windows, and in that dusk, the starkness of the office faded.

"Mona Lisa" started, and in the indefinite light they danced slowly, moving together. She was a good dancer; light, but not passive. He dipped her once, laughing, and in that moment he wanted her, without doubt; the way she arched her back, the soft pressing of her hip into his crotch, every sense in him alive. He moved his hand, pulling her back up to him, feeling the always surprising intimacy of real touching with someone new, tracing the spine, the shoulder blades, the small of her back. He stared at her mouth, taking in the curve of her lips. Then his mouth was on hers, a soft kiss, but very much alive, exploring.

Her hands came up his back together and with her touch he rose in earnest. Instinctively he moved to kiss her again, then stopped himself; all the reasons to go slowly pressed in on him. He allowed himself one total kiss, one great exploration of her mouth, sweet wetness and warmth. Then he turned her in his hands, feeling her backside coming against him, nestling into his hips.

"I've got to get back to work," he said. "Clock's ticking."

She leaned back, letting him support her. "I know," she whispered. But she turned back to him suddenly, putting one hand on his face and guiding it back to her, pressing her mouth on his and rocking him back momentarily with the pressure. Her tongue was in his mouth, and her fingers pressed into his back, pulling him against her. He blinked, ready to return the kiss, but she had already moved away, content to leave her mark on him, feeling her wake. She smiled at him from a few feet away—a smile suddenly demure—and then moved from the center of the room to his desk.

Lit up from her kiss, he stared at her backside, knowing the game she had played and finding himself wanting to play it, wanting to be consumed in her narrow hips, her slender but shapely arms. But she was at a distance now, and he waited for several seconds, allowing his resolve to coalesce again with the separation.

He moved toward the desk; now she was sitting in his chair, content for the moment in the power of her femininity. She ran her fingers through her hair, pushing with a habitual gesture an errant strand behind her ear. Watching her, he thought the pure loveliness of that motion would strangle him.

She left him at ten, a silent, mutual understanding that, at least for that night, her presence made work more difficult. It was nearly eleven when Henry's phone rang. It was Phillips, from the firm. "Got something, buddy," the voice said.

"Tell me."

"It's about that Ellen Gaudet."

"And?"

"Let's just say the lady's got a history."

Chapter Thirty-two

It was earlier this time when Henry dialed his old seminary professor. But one o'clock in the morning was still late enough to find Baxter in a deep sleep when he picked up the phone.

"It's Henry. I'm sorry."

Baxter came slowly to life. "This is becoming a habit," he said thickly.

"Sorry, sorry. It helped last time. I'm not choosing the timing."

"Let me wake up here a second." There was a rustling, and Henry heard Baxter get up and carry the phone into another room. "All right."

"You sure this is okay?"

"I said it was. Look, you'd get more chitchat if you called in the daylight."

"Sorry. I've got a problem. Ethical."

"That again? You're not back with your old firm, are you?"

"No, this is different. I'm still back home."

"Maybe you should have kept the job that paid all that money if you're just going to go through the same things and be poor."

"That thought's crossed my mind. At least this is my own problem."

"All right. So tell me."

"I'm trying to save my client. He needs special handling. He's . . . I want to say insane, but that doesn't quite describe it. He's just not equipped to be a part of his own defense. He's completely dependent."

"So the decision is yours to make."

"I didn't tell you I had a decision to make."

"Why else would you be calling me?"

"Okay. To help my client I have to hurt someone. No, I'm avoiding there. The truth is I have to destroy someone."

"I see."

"There's no guarantee. It's possible I could put this person—it's a woman, if that matters—through that destruction for nothing. It might not work."

"Then why do it?"

"It's my only chance. My client's only chance."

Baxter hesitated. "And you want to know if it's all right to destroy one person to save another."

"To *possibly* save another."

"I don't see how anyone can answer that kind of question for anyone else."

"I understand that. I'm ready to take responsibility for what happens. I just want some advice."

More silence. At length Baxter said, "All right, we'll talk about it. But I have to warn you that I may try to stop you, because if you destroy her and it doesn't save your client, I don't know if you could live with that."

"I don't know either."

"First tell me how hurting this woman helps you."

Henry exhaled, organizing his thoughts. "This case is about secrets, some of them twenty-five years old. So many lies have been told to keep this stuff buried there's no way to know where the truth begins. But the woman knows. She knows everything."

"And she won't tell."

"That's right. But one lie, one I never imagined before last night when I discovered it, I *do* know about. No one else knows it. Anyway, I don't think they do."

"And?"

"And if I bring it up in court it will destroy her life."

"You know that for a fact."

"Yes."

"What's the case about?"

"A will is being contested."

"So this is about money."

"No." Henry surprised himself with his instant response. "Look, of course it's about that. But it's also about the truth. It's about getting someone's life back. He—my client—got his stolen from him."

"And this woman knows how."

"Yes, but it's covered up in lies. And this part is bizarre—I think she really wants to tell the truth."

"Of course she wants to tell the truth."

"How could you know that?"

"Everyone wants to tell the truth, Henry. Lying is like an eating cancer. You think you can withstand small amounts. But your body knows how dangerous it is. Your soul knows it. That's where all the deathbed confessions come from."

"I can feel that when I talk to her. The weight of knowing and never revealing it has been slowly killing her inside. But whatever keeps her quiet is strong. She won't be easy to crack."

"Was she a part of what took away your client's life?"

"I believe she was a part. I can't prove that yet."

"That's not good."

"No. But if I can break her somehow—get her to tell what she knows—it might save my client."

Baxter paused. "Since when did you get into the saving business, Henry?"

Henry grimaced. "All right," he said, "I accept the irony. So maybe I want to redeem myself here, on some level. But I didn't think it would happen this way. I'm not comfortable playing God."

"Very wise."

"So you're saying don't go forward."

"I'm not going to say one way or another. I'm just willing to talk about it." Baxter paused. "Is there any other way to do this thing?"

"I don't know. I don't think so."

There was a long silence, nearly a full minute. Eventually, Baxter said, "You know I can't tell you what to do, Henry. If I did, I would be playing God myself, and that scares me as much as it does you. All I can do is remind you of some first principles. They're mine, and you have to decide if they're yours. One. Truth sets people free. Always, in every way. Never doubt that. Two. Deep truth almost always comes with pain. Even for Christ Himself. The truth of His mission—of who He was—hurt even Him. Remember Gethsemane, Henry. The Lord Himself sweat drops of blood to get out of facing that truth about Himself, that He was supposed to save the world. Why should we be any different? Three. Cheating the truth has real consequences, even with grace and forgiveness. Everybody wants to pretend that what's in the past doesn't exist, not just this woman. But it does exist. The past is tremendously powerful. It wants out. It's like a time bomb. We feel our sin pushing outward on our inner walls, and we think that if it comes out it will destroy us. Some of us spend our whole lives building thicker and thicker barriers between us and those explosions. But what we don't know is that it's not the coming out that destroys us. It's the keeping inside."

"You're telling me it's all right to go ahead."

"I'm not telling you that. You keep looking for me to give you an answer. I won't. Principles aren't people. You have to decide if this is right for you and right for now—for this moment in time."

"It's the last chance for everyone in this story. And everybody knows it. I can see it in their faces. If the truth stays buried through this trial, it's never coming to light."

"So you've decided. You knew what you were going to do from the beginning. You just called me for affirmation."

"Maybe. Is that wrong?"

"No. Can you live with it if you ruin this woman and get nothing?"

Henry looked up from his desk. He could see his reflection in the window and looked at himself for a moment, holding the phone. He was surprised by how tired he looked. "I believe I can."

"I pray my God to help you if you're wrong."

Henry slept for a few hours. He awoke feeling numb, and flipped on the TV to find that the circus of Judge Brackman's courtroom had grown. On the screen he saw a Kansas City station covering the case with, to his repugnance, a reporter on-site at the courthouse. She was a smartly dressed woman, very young, with short hair and a flat, slightly nasal accent. "Jeff," she was saying, "the little town of Council Grove has been rocked by one of the most bizarre cases in its history. The town's most prominent citizen has recently died and apparently left the bulk of his estate to a homeless man here, a man who by all accounts is mentally unstable. It's quite a bit of money, I understand. A couple of million dollars."

The anchor's voice came on, and the reporter pressed an earpiece closer to her ear. "Beth," the voice said, "where is this new millionaire? Can we get an interview?" Henry's heart stopped; he stared frozen at the TV.

"We're trying to locate the man now," the reporter said. "Apparently people around here call him the Birdman."

The anchorman laughed, a resonant, emotionless sound. "Why's that?" he asked.

"I'm not sure, but evidently he spends his time out in a local park here. We're heading over there and hope to have some film for you on our noon report."

"Sounds like a great story, Beth. Looking forward to seeing how it develops."

Henry flicked off the TV, threw on his clothes, grabbed his briefcase, and left the room in a trot. He floored the accelerator on his car, shooting out onto Route 12 toward the park. He drove ridiculously fast, slamming on his brakes to make turns, tires squealing. But when he saw the park he knew he had arrived in time; Boyd was there, standing under a tree, looking calmly back toward him. Henry slowed, not wanting to make Boyd nervous; he pulled up near Boyd's bench and stopped. He got out and motioned, and Boyd walked slowly toward him.

"I need you to come with me, Raymond," he said. "Right away."

Boyd tilted his head. "Junior Henry don't look too good."

Henry steadied himself with tremendous effort; they would only have a matter of minutes before the truck found its way to the park. "You're right, Raymond," he said. "I'm not too good right now. So do me this favor, will you? Come with me. Right now, Raymond."

"Junior Henry got some kinda trouble, yessiree. Somethin' goin' on. Might be the mighty hand of the Lord come down." He rocked back and forth, in no hurry to move.

Don't lie. He reads you like a book, anyway. "Raymond," he said, "there are people in town who want to talk to you. These people don't care what happens to you. They want to put you on television so they can show you to other people, like a sideshow." Boyd kept rocking, but Henry could see he was listening. "I don't want them to do that," he said. "I want you to come with me so they can't find you."

Boyd looked at him a moment, then began moving toward the car. *Good, Raymond. Good for you. You trusted me.*

Raymond got in the passenger seat of Henry's car, and Henry pulled out onto Owendale. As they turned, he could see a van in his rearview mirror drive up on the other side of the park. He eased his car out of sight, then went quickly back to the motel. He looked at his watch; he was expected in court in another thirty minutes. There wasn't time to do anything else.

They weren't followed, to his relief. But he knew the reporter would keep looking. The story was too rich for her to miss, too ripe for the kind of ridicule that reduced human tragedy to a momentary, condescending smile. They pulled up to the Flinthills Motel, Henry looking for any observers. There weren't any, and he led Raymond quickly from the car to his room. Raymond was growing more agitated and balked at entering the little space. Henry looked at him intently. "No one will bother you here," he said. "You'll be safe. You'll be alone. The important thing is to stay inside. Don't open the door to anybody, Raymond. No one but me. Do it, Raymond. Please."

Raymond walked into the room tentatively, looking around. He walked to the other side of the bed, staring at the little picture on the wall.

"All right, Raymond. I have to go to court now. Tell me you won't move from this place." Boyd continued staring, saying nothing. "Raymond?" Henry repeated. "You won't move, okay? And don't let anyone in."

Boyd turned and faced him. "Junior Henry in a hurry," he said. He sat down on the edge of the bed, his dirty pants soiling the clean bedspread. Henry looked at him helplessly a moment, then shut the door. He put the DO NOT DISTURB sign on the doorknob, and uttered his third prayer since coming back to Council Grove: *Give me time. Just a chance to do what I have to do. Then you can let all hell break loose again.*

He was a block away from the courthouse when he saw the crowd. Even more people than the day before were milling around, and he saw that the television van had returned to the courthouse. When Henry got out of his car several people called out, and the young female reporter caught sight of him. He picked up his pace, but she intercepted him at the courthouse steps. A crowd closed magnetically around them, leaning in and trapping him. The reporter nodded to her cameraman and stuck a microphone in Henry's face.

"I understand you're representing the so-called Birdman," she said with a grin that Henry found profoundly irritating. He attempted to continue up the stairs, but the crowd made moving difficult. A few people called him by name, and the reporter got between him and the next stair with a catlike move. "Mr. Mathews?" she asked. "What can you tell us about this Birdman? Is it true that he was named in the will of the richest man in this town?"

Henry stopped, gave her a withering look, and said firmly, "I'm not going to comment on the case. In the meantime, my client has a name. That name is Raymond Boyd."

The reporter, clearly surprised to discover that her subject wasn't delighted to be on television, momentarily lost her focus. Henry used the instant to escape, pushing past her and taking the stairs two at a time toward the door. She pursued, but the crowd was between them now, and he vanished into the courthouse.

The inside of the courtroom was packed, and Henry kept his eyes straight ahead as he made his way to his table. Hesston was already seated, Roger beside him saying something in his ear; they turned and faced him—Hesston with a blank stare, Roger sending him his usual malevolent look. Henry looked left, and he saw his sacrificial lamb; Ellen stared at him as he walked by, and he forced his eyes away. His briefcase had just touched his table when the bailiff entered.

"All rise," the bailiff said. "The Honorable Judge Howard Brackman presiding." The crowd stood automatically and Brackman walked in. Henry could see he hadn't been oblivious to the media attention; unlike the day before, his hair was neatly in place, and his usually rumpled robe had obviously been cleaned and pressed. *So you're the leak*, Henry thought. *You had the reporters called.* Brackman took his seat importantly, letting the crowd settle in after him.

"All right, gentlemen," he said, "let's get this show on the road. And, Counselors"—he waved his gavel vaguely in the direction of the attorneys—"let's keep things on an even keel today, if we can. I don't cotton to emotional outbursts in my courtroom."

The door opened again, and Henry turned to see the reporter squeezing into the room, a notebook and pen in hand. He turned back and saw Brackman smiling, an expression of pure, indulgent horseshit. He nodded to Henry and said, "Call your first witness, Counselor."

Henry looked at his legal pad. His throat was dry. He felt seconds ticking away, the eyes of everyone in the room on him. "I recall Ellen Gaudet, your honor."

Hesston rose, an elaborate, prolonged action. "Your honor," he said, "Ms. Gaudet has already given testimony. I can't see any reason to go through all that again."

Brackman looked at Henry with irritation. "Counsel's got a point, son. I don't want to go through any snipe hunt."

Hesston and Durand are too strong. If anyone is going to break, it's her. "The further testimony of Ms. Gaudet is absolutely essential, your honor. New information has come to light. It's imperative that she be recalled to the witness stand."

Hesston began to speak again. "Your honor . . ."

Brackman gaveled him down. "All right, Frank," he said, "gimme a chance to rule on this thing. Now, son, you're tellin' me you got somewhere to go on this thing, that right? Unlike yesterday."

"I do."

Brackman sighed and leaned back in his chair. "Tell you what. I'm gonna give you the rope to hang yourself, son. So if you got a point I recommend you get to it. We understand each other?"

Henry allowed himself a tiny smile. *You don't really mind this thing stretching out, do you, Judge Brackman? Not with reporters around, and you can boss around a lawyer who makes more in an hour than you do in a day.* "I call Ms. Ellen Gaudet to the stand," Henry repeated. "She's already been sworn in."

Ellen stood from halfway back. She looked relaxed, her expression distant, almost disinterested. She walked with her tiny steps past the rows of spectators to the gate, opened it, and stood in the witness box. She turned and faced Henry, and he almost doubted himself in that moment; her expression was so cold that she seemed impregnable. But it was too late; the die had been cast, and he reminded himself that he was fighting, in a way for her as well as for Raymond. *The truth sets people free, always, in every way*, Baxter had said. But looking at Ellen, Henry thought, *Not everybody wants to be free. Some people would rather die in chains.* Brackman's voice broke into his thoughts.

"The witness is reminded she's still under oath," Brackman said, nodding to Ellen. She sat demurely in the witness stand, crossed her legs, and smoothed her skirt. "All right, Counselor," Brackman said. "Clock's ticking."

Henry walked from behind his table. He held his first question in his mouth, tasting it, feeling its power, knowing that the simple act of speaking those words would change the life of the woman facing him forever. Once uttered, nothing in her private life would ever be secret again, and the thin veil of respectability she clung to would be ripped into pieces. That fiction, tattered and faded, was the pillow upon which she dreamed, the only thing in her world that made her able to walk down the street of that miserable little town and not feel like human excrement. It was what kept the fantasy alive, if only in an infinitesimal place in her brain, that she was a woman worth knowing. It was her air, her food, her inner life, and he was making her give it up to him on a cross. He thought of Raymond, looked up sharply at Ellen, and released his question like a depth charge. "Ms. Gaudet," he said quietly, "when did you decide to change your name?"

Brackman looked up, roused from his normal intentional expression of disinterest. There was a murmur through the crowd, and from out of the corner of his eye Henry saw Hesston set down his pen and turn to face him. Ellen stared back at Henry as though she hadn't heard the question. Then her lips parted slightly; Henry, standing near, could hear her breathing suddenly grow deeper, more labored. He let her sit, allowing the tension of her silence to work in the room. Several seconds passed, and in each Henry could detect a subtle change in her eyes; she grew more remote, as though retreating from the courtroom.

Henry repeated the question. "Your name, Ms. Gaudet. It used to be something else. I'm asking when you felt it necessary to change it."

When Ellen spoke her voice quavered slightly, a crack in her steel resolve. "I don't know what you mean," she said.

"Perhaps I'm not making myself clear," Henry interrupted, allowing a precisely measured hint of condescension to creep into his voice, as though the woman before him was wasting his time. "Your last name at one time was Cox, isn't that correct? Ellen Cox?"

Ellen looked up at the judge as though there had been a mistake, as though a pleading look at Brackman would make what was happening stop. But Brackman had picked up on the tension that had filled the room the instant Henry had asked his question, and he knew better than to do anything to deflect it. Ellen turned back to Henry, and for the first time he saw in her eyes a silent, unmistakable plea: *Don't do this. Please for God's sake don't do this.*

The sight of her simple human vulnerability nearly ground him to a halt. He wavered, and very nearly looked down. *The truth sets people free. Always, in every way.* He managed to hold his stare, and heard himself saying, "Please direct the witness to answer the question, your honor."

"The witness will answer the question."

Ellen closed her eyes for several seconds. When she opened them, she was infinitely harder, a human diamond. Then she spoke, her voice quiet, a death rattle. "That's right. It was Cox."

So it begins, Henry thought, *and together we discover your capacity for pain.* "When did you change it?"

"I don't remember."

Henry walked to his table. He picked up a sheaf of papers, turned to her, and held them up. "I believe it was in the year 1973. Wouldn't that be correct, Ms. Gaudet?"

Ellen looked at the papers. For a moment, Henry looked privately at her and softened his expression, willing her to understand: *I don't want to do this. Let me stop. Give me what I need before it goes too far.*

"I guess that's right."

"What was wrong with the name Cox, Ms. Gaudet? It's perfectly normal. Why did you feel the need to change it?" Hesston now rose from his chair, looking confident, but Henry could see it in his eyes: *He doesn't know about this. He's worried. He doesn't understand what I want.*

"Your honor," Hesston said, "I suppose this line of inquiry has some point, but as usual Mr. Mathews is keeping it a secret. I would ask the court to direct counsel to refer to matters that have to do with Tyler Crandall's will, not the personal matters of other people almost thirty years old."

Brackman looked at Hesston, then past him to the gallery; every eye was leveled at him in rapt attention. Henry could feel him calculating, comparing risks. The judge's face was unsure. "Counselor," he asked, "exactly where are we headed here?"

"Ms. Gaudet, if that's her name, is a material witness in this case, your honor. Her background is by definition germane."

Brackman sneaked a glance at Hesston; the lawyer was giving the judge a dangerous look. "I'll give you about two minutes to wrap this into something I care about, Counselor," Brackman said. "Otherwise let's get on to something relevant."

Henry nodded and repeated his question. "You haven't answered my question, Ms. Gaudet. Tell the court why you changed your name."

Henry looked into her eyes and there was another silent interchange between them; Ellen, cold and inaccessible, wanting to know how far he would push and what he knew, and Henry, his own eyes resolute, telling her that he knew everything, that he would stop at nothing. "I wanted a new life," she said carefully, quietly.

"What was wrong with the old one?"

She paused. "It was . . ."

Hesston was on his feet again, this time definitely agitated. "Your honor," he said, "I beg the court to keep Mr. Mathews' questions pertinent to the topic at hand. Yesterday the witness did a splendid job of telling us that the deceased and Mr. Boyd hadn't spoken to each other in the past twenty-five years. Now let's allow this woman to get back to her place of business and get on with her life."

Henry responded instantly, not giving Brackman the chance to rule one way or the other. "I was given the opportunity to pursue this line of questioning, your honor. Of course, if Mr. Hesston is going to be allowed to interrupt me every ten seconds he will only prolong the time it takes me to do so."

Brackman, unused to actual dissent in his courtroom, looked surly and displeased. "Your leash is getting shorter, son," he said. "I suggest you cut to the chase."

Henry picked up his notebook and strolled toward the witness box. "How did you pick the name Gaudet?" he asked.

"Out of a magazine. It was the name of a French actress."

"What kind of actress?"

Hesston leapt to his feet. "For God's sake, your honor, are you going to allow this ridiculous waste of time?"

Brackman waved his gavel at Hesston. "Hold on a second, Frank. We'll never get anywhere if you keep jumping up and down like a jackrabbit."

Henry nodded, keeping his focus on Ellen. "What kind of actress, Ms. Gaudet?"

"I don't know. She made romantic movies, I guess. Love stories."

"Of a sort," Henry said. "This particular actress ended up going to jail, isn't that correct?"

"I don't know."

"She went to jail for killing her lover, a film director who was married to someone else at the time. The murder was particularly brutal. She's still in jail, I believe. I find it very interesting you picked this particular name, Ms. Gaudet. I keep wondering what you might feel in common with someone like that."

"I didn't feel anything in common with her. I just liked the name."

You can stop this anytime you want, Henry said with his eyes, and he knew she understood him. *Right now. One more second and it will be too late.* For a moment, they locked on to each other, and he had hope; but then she looked down, staring at her hands. *So be it. God help her, God help Raymond, and God help me.*

"This particular actress took off her clothes on film, isn't that right, Ms. Gaudet?"

"I don't know anything about that."

"She was paid to act out fantasies for men, and like most women in that profession, she ended up hating them. She ended up killing the man she was closest to, in fact. Which brings me back to you. Of all the names in the world, you pick hers. You want to be named after a woman who makes sex movies and kills her lover."

Ellen's voice turned brittle. "It's just a name. I didn't think about it that way."

Henry took a breath. He had set the trap. With Brackman so ready to pounce, waiting any longer was impossible. "Then let me ask you a question you can answer. It's very simple." He paused a moment. "For what crime were you arrested in March 1973?" There was a rustle through the gallery, finally settling into a nervous stillness. "Ms. Gaudet?" Henry asked. "Should I repeat the question?"

Ellen became as stiff as wood. "It was a long time ago."

Henry held up a paper. He knew he should make her say the word; it would humiliate her, drive her closer to breaking down. There was no point now in going halfway; it was everything or nothing. "You didn't tell the court what the arrest was for, Ms. Gaudet. Please answer the question."

She looked at him, concrete hate, a thousand miles of resistance. "Solicitation," she said in a still, quiet voice. Instantly, harsh whispering broke out in earnest throughout the courtroom. Brackman, startled himself, gaveled hard, demanding silence.

Henry paused, letting the quiet settle back over the room. "Prostitution is the common word for it, isn't that right, Ms. Gaudet?" he asked.

"That's right," Ellen said at length. "Like I told you, it was a long time ago."

"Prostitution," Henry repeated quietly. "A crime where men use women for sex."

"A crime where women use men for money," Ellen interrupted.

Henry stopped. "And learn to hate them, isn't that right, Ms. Gaudet?"

"I don't know anything about that."

"I see." Henry turned and walked back to his table. "Now, I'd like to get the timing of this right," he asked. "This was March 1973, correct?"

"If you say so."

"I'm asking *you*, Ms. Gaudet."

"I guess so. Yes, March."

"And you came to Council Grove later that same year?"

"Yes."

"Where did that arrest take place?" Ellen looked at him silently. "The place, Ms. Gaudet. Where you were . . ."

"Junction City."

"Junction City, Kansas."

"That's right."

"There's an Army base near Junction City, isn't that right, Ms. Gaudet?"

For the past several seconds Henry could feel the tension increasing across the aisle from him; with the words "Army base," however, Hesston rose in thunder and lightning. "Your honor," he shouted, "this is an outrageous . . ."

Henry broke in instantly, cutting him off. "If this court has any interest in the truth about my client and this will," he demanded, "then I insist on being allowed to complete this examination without any more interruptions."

Brackman slammed his gavel down hard several times, his frustration apparent. "Right now I want you both to be quiet!" he said. He turned to Hesston. "Frank, I'm telling you for the last time to sit down for a damn minute and let me get this over with." He looked over at Henry, giving him a deeply irritated expression. "And your leash is up," he said bluntly. "You got our attention with this little soap opera, Counselor. Now make sure you do something with it. If it turns out you've embarrassed this witness with nothing to show for it, I'm going to haul you into my chambers for an experience you will truly dislike."

Henry nodded and walked directly in front of Ellen, facing her down. He stared at her, merciless, unyielding. "Ms. Gaudet," he said, "the name of that base is Fort Riley. It's the largest military installation in the world."

"I know about the base."

"I'm sure you do, Ms. Gaudet. I'm sure you did know about the sixteen thousand men stationed less than five miles from where you were living. But I'm only interested in one of those men. I'm interested in a man just back from Vietnam. Now, you testified, Ms. Gaudet, that you met Tyler Crandall here in Council Grove. You told this court that you saw him for the first time at the bank, just back from the war. But I want you to think back. I want you to think back to Junction City and Fort Riley." Henry walked to the center of the courtroom. "What I want is very simple, Ms. Gaudet. I want you to tell this court the truth about where you really met Tyler Crandall."

A wave of whispering swept through the room, and Brackman gave his bench a reverberating smack with his gavel. "I'm going to have silence in this courtroom," he said, glaring at the gallery. Hesston was on his feet again, but Brackman sat him down with an angry look. He turned to Ellen. "Answer the question, Ms. Gaudet."

Ellen seemed to diminish. "I didn't meet him there," she said quietly.

"Then perhaps you can explain how it is that less than one month after your arrest both you and Ty Crandall find yourselves in Council Grove, a place where neither of you had any family, no connections of any kind. You suddenly appear here, dropped out of the sky. Isn't it true that you met in Junction City and decided to move here together?" He held up the papers. "Ms. Gaudet, I have a copy of your arrest report in my hand. It says you were arrested at a place called Lucky's. Not very original, but then GIs didn't need much persuading, did they, Ms.

Gaudet? You were younger then, in your early twenties? So there you were at Lucky's, and . . ."

"That wasn't with Tyler," Ellen protested. "That report doesn't say anything about Tyler." She looked down, an amateur's move, the move of a guilty person, and Henry almost pitied her. Then she lied terribly, unconvincingly, utterly ineffectually. *"No,"* she said. "I never knew him then. I never went near the base."

"Tyler mustered back from Vietnam to Fort Riley," Henry said, pressing on. "I can produce that paperwork if necessary. He got back on . . ." He flipped through the papers for dramatic effect, even though he knew the date. "On February 26, 1973. You were arrested less than two weeks later."

"Not with Tyler," she said bitterly.

"I didn't say you were arrested with Tyler," Henry snapped, not allowing her to appear a victim. "I'm saying you were at Fort Riley at exactly the same time, working the base. Then, suddenly, you both show up in Council Grove—a place people don't exactly *flock to*—and your name isn't Ellen Cox anymore, it's Gaudet. How did that happen?"

"It just happened. I just moved here."

"Let me paint you a different picture. Tyler Crandall was a clever man. He was a good deal smarter than your average streetwalker, a streetwalker who suddenly gets it in her head to have her name changed. I mean, if you had been arrested for a felony, you couldn't have done that. But misdemeanor solicitation—that's a different matter. You tell the judge you want a new start, you were young, you cry a little. You snow him. It's child's play for a woman like you. You walk out of the courtroom with a new identity. Then you move away, come to Council Grove. You go *straight.* But what kind of a job do you take, Ms. Gaudet?"

"I don't know what you're talking about."

"You take a job at a bank, Ms. Gaudet. Naturally, banks ask about arrest records, even for nothing-little jobs like opening accounts. But Ellen Cox is dead, and Ellen Gaudet has no record." Ellen was starting to cry very slightly, her breaths coming in little gasps.

"Now it could be that Tyler Crandall had a reason to want somebody he knew to work at that bank. It could be that he *needed* somebody there, somebody not entirely principled. The great Tyler Crandall came here with nothing and by the time he died he owned most of this town. But what he desperately needed was someone to loan him a great deal of money to buy certain tracts of land, land that ultimately was remarkably, almost incredibly, productive." Henry paused, catching his breath, letting what had happened so far settle on the courtroom. He walked directly in front of the witness stand, staring straight at Ellen. He locked on her, holding her head up with his eyes. "So there you all are. You, Tyler Crandall, and my client. My client, who Mr. Hesston is trying to prove had no real relationship with the deceased. But you know better than that, don't you? Why don't you tell this court what really happened, Ms. Gaudet?" he asked. "Why don't you give this town its real history? Why don't you give my client back his life?"

She very nearly collapsed. For a moment, she sobbed freely, tears flowing down her face. *She's going to tell*, he let himself think for a miraculous instant. *It's all right*. But slowly, with horrifying, meticulous care, she pulled herself back together. It took some time—she regrouped in stages, first her breathing steadying, then the trembling slowly diminishing, and when she finally looked up at him she was unnaturally still, as though dead. Her appearance was shocking, with ruined mascara, reddened eyes, and sunken cheeks. When she spoke, her voice was frigid, anesthetized. "I already told you where I met Tyler Crandall. I met him when he walked into the Cottonwood Valley Bank. I never laid eyes on him before that second. And you don't know anything about whores. You've got no idea how we think."

Henry watched her, stock-still. *She owned it. She looked me in the eyes and owned every bit of it. She didn't give Crandall up*. Henry didn't get the chance to calculate his loss; Hesston, sensing the shift, leapt to his feet.

"So, now we see where this has gone," he said, pointing his finger menacingly at Henry. "This man has humiliated a woman here, and for what? She didn't know Tyler Crandall. She said that from the beginning. This is nothing but conjecture and innuendo. Your honor, I move that every word of this disgrace be stricken from the record. I don't know what this woman did in 1973, but I do know that it took courage and intelligence to start her life over, and she deserves nothing but credit for doing that. This court should commend her, your honor. She's an example of a person getting a new start in life and making something of herself. I applaud her, your honor. I think we should all applaud her."

Henry, when he saw Brackman staring at him, knew it was over. He had risked it all, and come up with . . . not with nothing, but, with Brackman so eager to keep Hesston's butter on his bread, with far less than he needed to justify what had just happened in that courtroom. "I'm going to do that," Brackman said, as always, sensing the power, feeling the flow. "I'm going to have that testimony expunged from the record. Ms. Gaudet, you may step down. The court apologizes to you for any embarrassment you have been caused."

Henry watched her stand to go, the moment surreal, slowed down. She was composed now, although she looked like she'd been through a war. But her small steps, little girl steps, were back to normal, and she was pushing her peroxide hair back in place. She didn't look at him when she passed. She opened the little gate into the gallery, and slowed a moment, feeling for the first time who she now was in Council Grove. Then she pushed on, back erect, and walked directly out the door of the courtroom.

"I'm gonna recess until two o'clock this afternoon. And, Counselor . . ." He looked at Henry, his face pure animosity. "I want you in my chambers. But I'm going to say right now that if you ever put this court through a circus like that again, I'm going to bar you from this courtroom."

The one positive thing that came from Brackman's dressing-down was an afternoon's continuance. That had come at Hesston's request; Brackman wouldn't have given Henry the time of day. But Henry didn't feel the judge's tongue-lashing; there was nothing Brackman could say that could take Henry lower than he had taken himself. *You have to be able to live with it if you come up with nothing*, Baxter had said. And what had he come up with? Not nothing—it was obvious Ellen had been lying, and that was something, however small—but not with the crack in her story that gave any real hope. And her life was over. Sacrificed on a legal altar. But he stopped himself there; no, on the altar of truth. Truth. But was truth the highest good, always best in every case? What if a lie was the only thing that makes life supportable? But it was too late now. Henry left Brackman's chambers with a thought running through his head: *Not all endings are happy. Amanda's hurricane landed somewhere else, and not every prayer gets answered.*

There was still a crowd in the courthouse when Henry appeared out of chambers, and he pushed through them without speaking to anyone. He looked for Ellen, but she was already gone. *Gone to pack, thanks to me. Her life is over here.*

He was at the steps, taking them two at a time, when the television reporter suddenly appeared in front of him. She shoved the microphone into his face and said, "Beth Harriman with Channel Five, Mr. Mathews. I'm wondering if you have a comment on what went on in that courtroom. You had some dramatic testimony about a former prostitute having a relationship with Tyler Crandall."

Henry stopped and looked at the reporter. She was so eager, so detached from any human repercussions. There was nothing he could say to her that wouldn't disappoint her, so he just told her the truth. "If you have a shred of human decency you'll leave that woman alone."

Henry found Amanda at the parking lot; she looked somber, almost gray. "I know," he said. "There wasn't any other way."

She looked at him, and silently got in the car. *At least she's loyal*, Henry thought. They sat in the car a moment, Henry glad to be entombed in its silence. "There's nothing I can say," he ventured. "It went terribly. All I can do is think that the story isn't over."

"It would take a miracle to redeem the last few minutes in that courtroom," Amanda said quietly.

He looked at her, searching for condemnation. But there wasn't judgment in her face. She was simply being honest. "I want to believe in miracles," he said, "but I don't think I do."

"Why haven't you brought up the wells? You can't just let that go."

"I don't intend to. But Roger didn't have anything to do with that, obviously. He was just a kid when those pipes were laid down. So who has something to lose? Only Raymond. And bringing it up without knowing what's behind them is dangerous as hell. Dr. Harris is convinced that there's something ugly behind it, and I agree. So give me some room. I've already sacrificed one person today. I'm not ready to sacrifice Raymond as well. Not yet."

She nodded. "All right. We need to find him. If the press gets hold of him . . ."

"He's safe," Henry said, glad to have one good thing to report. "I saw the reporters on TV before I came over. He's in my motel room."

She sighed, and he felt her relax a little. "All right. Shouldn't we go get him?"

"Yeah. But I don't know what to do with him when we do. The town's not safe for him now."

Henry drove to the motel parking lot and looked toward the street, scanning for news trucks. No one had followed them. He and Amanda got out of the car and walked quickly to the room. Henry knocked and called out softly, wanting to let Boyd know it was him. He opened the door and knew instantly that Boyd was gone.

"If the reporters find him before we do they'll eat him for lunch," Amanda breathed.

"If they haven't got to him already. Come on, we've got to find him."

They sprinted back to the car. "If he's not at the park or his house, I don't even know where to begin," Henry said.

"Let's go."

They drove the ten minutes back through town and turned onto Owendale toward the park. To their horror, they saw two white vans parked near the bench Boyd used. He could see the young reporter walking around, looking disappointed. "Not there," he said. He slammed the car into reverse and drove out the way he had come in.

It was only a few blocks to Raymond's house, but even as they rolled to a stop Henry could feel that Boyd wasn't there. He leapt onto the porch and looked inside. He called out and knocked, but the place was empty. He turned and got back in the car. "Any ideas?" he asked.

"None. But it's not that big a place. We'll just have to search it, street by street."

"All right. I'm taking you back to your car and we can split up. It won't take long to cover the town that way. Meet me here in an hour. Call me if you see anything, and stay away from the television crews."

Carl Durand was drunk. He stared at Frank Hesston's blurred face, trying to decide whether or not to go home, pack a suitcase, pick up his passport, and head for the airport. After several seconds of staring, he found himself speaking. He listened to himself as though he were a bystander in the room. "You said you had it covered," he muttered through the booze. "You said, 'Leave it to me.'"

Hesston's face shaped itself into the mask of habitual irritation he had more and more often felt about Durand. But mixed with that irritation was, for the first time, a trace of real fear. He tried to concentrate, maintain his focus. They should be celebrating; Ellen had held together, taken the shot, and left them clean. But a fog of uncertainty had descended on him, and he found that all he could think of was the sound of Sheriff Collier's voice when he had called two hours earlier. *Somebody's been diggin' over by the Crandall wells*, he had said. *"They covered up the hole but I could see the fresh dirt all right. Went down a good ways by the size of it."* And then, worse news: *"There's been a stranger in town, meetin' with that lawyer and the girl. I didn't see him, but I asked around. He's some kinda scientist."* Through the fog Hesston heard Durand's voice.

"They brought a geologist with them, Frank," Durand said, glaring drunkenly at Hesston. *"A geologist."*

"I know, Carl. I'm trying to think, if you'll shut up."

Durand took a huge swallow of whiskey from a glass. "You didn't let me take out the little freak, and we're screwed."

"Ellen stayed together. That's what's important. No matter what that weasel Mathews threw at her, she stayed together."

"People in this town aren't stupid, Frank. Even you admitted you'd have to be blind not to see she was lying."

"People in this town will do what they're told," Hesston retorted. "And on the top of that list is Brackman."

"He didn't act too goddam obedient today."

"He put on a good show for the reporters. He's a snake, and he'd bite us in the ass if he thought it was good for him. So we have to make sure he never thinks it would be good. Do that, and Brackman's no problem."

"So what's your bright idea now?" Durand wiped his mouth. "If you'd let me do what I wanted we wouldn't be in this thing."

"That's right, Carl. We'd be in Leavenworth, in prison."

"We're going to be in Leavenworth anyway, goddam it!" Durand replied. His voice was getting shrill. "For God's sake, Frank, doing Boyd now is getting more dangerous, not less. There were TV cameras at the courthouse today."

"We didn't kill Boyd because for the past twenty-five years he hasn't been a problem. Who knew Crandall was going to leave the land to Boyd? Did you?"

"No," Durand said sullenly. "If I had known what he was going to do to us I would have killed him myself."

"Of course you would, Carl. If it were up to you everybody in the county would be dead. Now listen to me. We have to keep it together for a couple of more days. Ellen's going to hang together and she's going to deliver Boyd to us tomorrow. After what happened this morning in court she has no choice. She's finished in Council Grove. She needs that money like the wounded need blood." He looked at the bottle in Durand's hand. "Give me that," he said, reaching for the booze.

Durand answered him with a scowl, but he slowly handed over the bottle. Hesston started to put it in his drawer, hesitated, then took a swig. He screwed on the lid and set it down. "This will all be over soon," he said, feeling the liquid hit his stomach. "In twenty-four hours Raymond Boyd will be out of our lives forever. Ellen's going to deliver him to Roger, and Roger is going to deliver him to hell."

"We're under a spotlight now, Frank. Waiting was a big mistake."

"On the contrary. Boyd's unbalanced, and this is the most stressful event of his life. Suicide is a completely credible end to his miserable life. And no one will be more publicly distressed about it than me."

"And what about Mathews? Him and his geologist?"

"Mathews doesn't know anything, not for sure. If he did, he would have brought it up in court."

"And what about what he suspects?"

"What about it? If the lid stays on for another day it's over. With no Boyd the case is moot and Brackman dismisses."

"You got the Boyd thing covered, right?"

"Yes, Carl. It's under control. He'll be dead within twenty-four hours."

Chapter Thirty-three

She saw him, leaning inexplicably like a drunken man against an electric power pole a block from her house. His back was to her, and she wondered if he was ill. Even from behind he looked fragile, as if a good wind would blow him off the pole and into the sky. He had a duffel bag on his shoulder. She let her car roll silently to a stop about fifty feet away from him, and he didn't turn around.

Her mouth went dry with the sight of him. She opened her door and stepped out of the car; he remained perfectly still, his arm wrapped around the pole, head resting calmly against it. She walked toward him quickly, looking around to see if anyone was nearby.

She couldn't understand why he didn't turn around. Perhaps he was lost in his own world, a thousand miles away from the street. Maybe the light pole was a ladder up to heaven, and he was resting for the climb. But for whatever reason, he didn't move, even when the sun cast her shadow over her shoulder and into his line of sight. She stood quietly less than three feet behind him, the scent of him in her nostrils, the memory of him gathering in her brain. Finally, she spoke his name.

"Raymond."

There was a pause, and then a tremble.

"I'm here, Raymond. Turn around and look at me."

Slowly, with laborious effort, Boyd pushed off from the pole and circled his body toward the voice. He stood blinking in the sun, squinting at Ellen through the glare.

For a moment, she didn't see the haggard, dried-up man before her. She closed her eyes in the silence between them, and in that instant he was twenty-six again, smiling at her in an inexpensive suit and looking embarrassed. He had stuck out his hand like a shy employee, not like the manager of the branch. Yes, she could have the job. He had only been there a few weeks himself. He needed someone right away, if she could start the next day. She took a desk within view of his office, and soon she had felt the staring on the back of her neck, an uneasy sensation prompting quick glances over her shoulder that found him rapt, adoring her silently, clumsily. She had been moved by him, in those first few weeks, to her own surprise. After a year and a half of drunk soldiers and sex that ran between the merely numbing to the truly painful, Raymond's adoration had seemed like flowers, like candy, like a high school prom. It had seemed like a life she had never had and maybe, she thought, he was normal, that his love was what love was really about and maybe she would let him do that to her and unlock whatever shred of innocence was left inside that hadn't been crushed by spit-shined Army boots. Maybe love was supposed to be sweet and it didn't matter that it was clumsy and blind.

But all she had to do was think about Tyler and Raymond disappeared. Tyler's pure, dangerous power called out to her like heroin to an addict, and she answered it in the same place that had led her to the nights at Lucky's in the first place. Tyler knew what he wanted. He was prepared to take it. If there was a man worth obeying, it was him. What she felt for him made her evil, she knew that. But there was a dark appeal in that, and given the choice between Tyler and Boyd, she had never wavered. Tyler was hard strength and badness and he touched her in her dark witch, in the warm, sickly sweet spot in her soul that demanded to be indulged. She had given in to Tyler completely, and she would play Raymond however he directed.

When at last she opened her eyes, the man Raymond Boyd had become was staring at her, the same silent adoration buried under madness but still discernible. His eyes were glimmering from underneath his hat, and he wavered there before her, listing and leaning.

"Hello, Raymond," she said quietly. "I've come to talk." Boyd shook slightly, his head bobbing. His fascination was complete and horrible to her, a vivid reminder of her own treacherous heart. He was helpless, in his way, locked in his obsession. And she had destroyed him. She was going to destroy him again.

"I've been thinking about you," she whispered, her voice failing her. Suddenly, her throat was full of bile, and she was nearly gagging. She forced out words. "I've missed you terribly. We have a lot to talk about. So much time has passed. Too much."

Boyd's breathing accelerated, the tension in his face alarming and vehement. "I have to get my blood cleaned," he said in a rasp. "It's full of gold."

"I know, sweetheart. Just come with me. I know how to help you. Everything will be fine."

Boyd smiled, and he seemed to relax. His murmuring slowed, and he held his hand out to her. She stared at his fingers a long moment, fascinated and repulsed. At last, she reached out and touched him, taking his filthy hand in hers. "Come, darling," she whispered. "Come and let me take care of you. Let me take all your pain away."

Boyd's eyes were wide, and he looked at her as though she were an angel of God. He made the sign of the cross before her. "Absolution," he said. "Fools and whores, I absolve thee."

She winced, but didn't break away from his eyes. Instead, she held him captive there, and led him to her car.

* * *

Amanda pulled her car up to Henry's exactly on time. Her report was like his: Boyd had vanished, disappeared from the earth. "At least the reporters didn't find him," Amanda said. "They've gone, too. Back to their viper's nests."

"So no Ellen, and no Raymond," Henry said. "I don't like them both going missing."

"I wonder if Collier's got them? Did you go by the sheriff's office?"

"Yeah. They weren't there, and neither was Collier. I've got to assume he's looking like we are. He's probably already covered the town, and that's why we didn't see him." Henry looked outside his car. "We can't just start looking randomly. We need some kind of plan."

"You want to split up again? Although I don't know where I'd go."

He turned and looked at her. "If Raymond's gone he's not where he is voluntarily. He doesn't *go* anywhere, for God's sake. The newspeople are gone, at least for the day. So when I think about the people who might want to take Raymond somewhere he doesn't want to be, it's a pretty short list. Collier's on it, and I want you to stay here and call me if the sheriff shows up. Right now the person I really want to find is Roger."

Roger Crandall stared at the label of the prescription in front of him in the moonlight. *Risperdol, 5 mg.* There were about forty capsules in the bottle. Enough, Hesston had told him, to take care of Boyd forever. His eyes moved up and across the gravestones at the Everlasting Rest Cemetery in Pretty Prairie. It made sense, he supposed, to have a cemetery way out in the middle of nowhere, a mile from the nearest house. But it didn't make the waiting any easier. He shifted his feet uneasily, avoiding the gravestone before him with his eyes. But he knew his father's body was several feet directly beneath him, beginning, he assumed, its long disintegration into a mass of desiccated flesh.

Hesston had insisted on the cemetery. *It's a suicide. Boyd's insane. He goes to Crandall's grave site and takes the bottle of pills. It's crazy enough to be real.* Roger shook the bottle lightly, feeling the pills rattle. There had been only one way to find out what Boyd was taking, and it meant breaking into the man's ramshackle house. That had been a risk he hadn't wanted to take. It was public, and he could have been seen. But he had managed to slip in, feeling something he hadn't expected: humiliation. His father had walked the streets of the town with his head up, fearing nobody. Now, Roger had found himself crawling on his hands and knees in the dark through the brush around Boyd's place, slithering up the porch and hoping the door would be unlocked.

The place hadn't been the mess he had expected; evidently, the lawyer and his girlfriend were keeping it up. Things were sparse, but orderly. The house had only three rooms: a living room with scratched hardwood floors and a plain table and chairs, a bedroom, with a chest and single bed, and a kitchen that contained a collection of indiscriminate junk. Roger had found Boyd's pills in the bathroom, but not touched any of the prescriptions. Instead, he wrote the names of the drugs down and slipped back out, badly needing a drink.

Roger glanced at his watch: seven-fifteen. It was starting to rain, to his irritation. Ellen should be there in a few minutes. Hesston had told him not to get impatient; it might take some time to persuade Boyd to get moving. But he would come. If Ellen asked, he would come.

Roger didn't know how Hesston got the drugs for the phony suicide, and he didn't want to know. Forty times five milligrams. He calculated in his head: two hundred milligrams. Head drugs. But in that kind of dosage it didn't work on your head. It just stopped your breathing. *Arrested it*, Hesston had said. Same difference. You were dead.

Roger stuck the bottle in his pocket and pulled a black pistol from a cloth bag. The gun wasn't for Raymond; simple chloroform would handle that problem, and he could feed him the pills afterward. The gun was for Ellen.

Roger fingered the pistol, felt the cold metal of the short barrel. As much as he hated the pills, he preferred handling them to the gun. They didn't look so hazardous, so lethal. But the gun was obviously for killing. He was sweating, and his fingers left wet little marks on the barrel. He wiped down the gun again, and put on a pair of thin leather gloves.

Hesston didn't know about the gun, and that made Roger's nerves vibrate. But Durand had called, leaning heavily. *I'll handle Frank. We need insurance in case things don't happen. The gun will be in your mailbox after eleven. Get it tonight.* Roger went over the backup plan that Durand had worked out with him: *If Ellen comes apart and tries to stop you, use the chloroform on her. Then put the gun in Boyd's hand and pull the trigger. Make sure the powder burns get on his arm. Then put the gun in Boyd's mouth and pull the trigger again.*

Ellen took the back roads toward the Everlasting Rest Cemetery. There were only two houses to pass before she could get on the road out of town, and it was nothing but deserted cornfields across the fifteen miles of country road to the graves.

Five miles out of town Raymond began to disintegrate. By the time she turned onto Highway 27 to the cemetery, his hands were clenching the armrest so tightly he was nearly puncturing the cloth. His murmuring was agitated, an eerie vocalese that crept up her spine. She looked over at him;

he was staring out the window, eyes wide. She looked quickly back at the highway, then heard Boyd give a very sad, very human moan. When she looked back, he had changed.

Boyd was suddenly, startlingly lucid as he looked back at her full in the face. In that instant he wasn't a child, and he wasn't covered over with insanity. Even through his madness he knew that something terrible was about to happen, and he was willing himself to go with her to that sacrifice. In his eyes was real terror, not a psychotic and imagined fear but a real, almost tactile awareness of danger. She saw him hold on to sanity, the madness trying to cover him again. She let the car roll to a stop, pulling off onto the gravel. "What is it, Raymond?" she asked. "Everything's going to be all right."

Boyd stared into her eyes. His lips moved slightly, and he breathed, "I love you."

She began to weep. She slumped over, her eyes welling with tears. She put her head on the steering wheel, her face turned away from him. "What did you say?" she asked in a hoarse whisper. They sat in silence for a long moment, the only sound the softly humming engine. She sat breathing unevenly, a pain thrusting through her heart until she was afraid she would die. At last she turned her head to look at him, and she saw that he had vanished again, pulled down under the waves of madness. "Get out," she said. Raymond was mumbling, not looking at her. She reached across him and opened the door. "Get out," she spat again, more forcefully. She pushed on him, and he listed over. She pushed harder, and screamed at him over and over. "Get out, get out!"

Raymond put a foot down on the gravel and swung his leg around, his bag barely hanging on his shoulder. She pushed him with all her might, and he fell out awkwardly onto the roadside. She slammed the car into gear, and was gone.

Roger set the gun on the ground and shook his arm; his hand was cramping, and he was starting to sweat in spite of the cool evening. He wiped his forehead with his shirtsleeve. Then he looked up, and saw headlights coming down the highway toward the graveyard. He crouched down behind his father's headstone, watching the car pass by and begin slowing for the entrance. It was Ellen's car.

Frank Hesston watched the rain beginning outside his window. The droplets were still small, and he watched them make tiny, crystalline explosions on his window ledge as they fell to earth. The light was fading, and he let himself feel hypnotized there, watching the raindrops die. He didn't want to hear what Carl Durand, who had just arrived, had said to him. So he just watched the raindrops, his eyes focusing and unfocusing, and time for one blessed moment stood still. Then he heard the sound of Durand downing another drink, and he was thrust back into the real world. "You've talked to Ellen, haven't you?" he said quietly.

"I didn't say a word to that whore."

"Then it was Boyd," he said. "God, Carl, if you did anything to him they'll be on us like flies on horseshit."

"I didn't do anything to him either."

"I know you've done something, Carl," Hesston said. "I know you couldn't leave well enough alone. I know you went outside the plan."

"Well enough?" Durand spat derisively. "If things had been going well enough, I would have been glad to lay low and let you handle them. But they aren't well enough, Frank. They're going very badly."

"So what did you do, Carl? Tell me what you did."

"I talked to Roger," Durand said with a shrug. "I wanted things covered."

Comprehension came into Hesston's eyes. "What did you say to him, Carl?" he asked intently. "Tell me what you said to Roger."

"I told him to go fuck himself."

Hesston got up from behind his desk, all squat muscle and finely focused hatred. Durand started to rise to face him, but the booze weighed him down. Before he could move, Hesston was on him, placing his thumb on Durand's Adam's apple. "You'll tell me right now what you told Roger, Carl. *Now.*"

Durand, paralyzed, felt the pressure on his throat and opened his mouth. For a moment, he couldn't speak. Hesston eased up very slightly, and Durand sputtered, "I told him that if Ellen didn't play ball there had to be a backup plan. I couldn't leave it to you anymore, damn it. Too much has gone down. It has to stop."

The pressure on Durand's throat increased, if anything. "What was the backup plan, Carl?"

"Do Ellen. Make it look like Boyd did it. Turn the thing into a murder-suicide."

Hesston increased the pressure, and Durand raised his arm to strike in desperation. But before he could do so Hesston had spun away in disgust. He fixed Durand in a malevolent glare. "You don't have any sense of balance," he hissed. "You shove when you only need to push. Roger! Roger couldn't shoot a man, much less a woman. Ellen's just as likely to get the gun away from him and kill him."

Durand stared. He was fed up. He had been on a straight path to the governor's mansion, and this was not a stop on that street. He was sick of Hesston's condescension, of his perfectly pressed suits and smug, self-satisfied attitude. No matter what happened in this mess, it was time to think about the future, about a time without Frank Hesston in his life. "Listen, you little bastard . . ." he began, but at that moment the door to Hesston's office blew open and Roger strode in, soaking wet.

"It didn't go down," he said, out of breath.

"What part?" Durand said.

Roger looked cautiously at Hesston, and Durand said, "He knows about it. What the hell happened?"

"None of it went down."

Hesston looked dumbfounded. "She didn't show up? I can't believe that. I had her in my office last night and she was primed."

"She showed. But Boyd didn't."

"Why not?" Hesston demanded.

"She let him go."

Durand catapulted out of his chair. "Why did she do that?"

Hesston groaned, rubbing his temples. "You don't have to tell me. The whore had an attack of conscience. God, who would have dreamed?"

Durand whirled on Hesston. "Fuck your plan," he said between clenched teeth. "I'm taking care of this once and for all."

For once, Hesston didn't try to stop him.

Chapter Thirty-four

The rain began falling in earnest around seven, just after sunset. It took an hour for Raymond to walk back to his house, and another to make his way down Route 12 to where he now stood under the darkening sky, his face upturned to the falling drops. His grizzled beard and parched lips were covered with rainwater when he lowered his head to stare down the highway. The Flinthills spread out north and east before him, a great languishing of earth that sloped away and then rose into the black at the horizon. The clouds were moving with the storm wind; gray shapes swept silently across the sky, revealing patches of stars. Boyd pulled his old cloak around his shoulders, but the threadbare fabric did little to protect him from the rain. He pulled his tattered duffel bag off his shoulder; he had checked the bag many times over the past hour, sometimes as often as every fifty yards. A disturbing idea crawled across his brain, irresistible and growing: the contents were somehow escaping the bag, dissolving through the canvas and turning to mist. Again and again he rummaged through the satchel, fingering the items for reassurance: a long emergency flare, an old wrench, large and rusty with disuse, a bundle of old rags. *Everything is still here*, he said out loud. The wind and rain swept around him, muting his voice. *Judgment is coming.*

He had been walking in the ditch by the highway, but now with the cover of darkness he moved up along the gravel side of the road. The weather was keeping traffic down, and it was good to get out of the mud. If a car did come, the approaching headlights would give him plenty of time to crouch down in the tall, wet bluestem that filled the ditch. He settled the bag on his shoulder and pushed off north up the road. He walked steadily, the rain dripping down off the edges of his hat.

Only occasionally was he forced to hide. At those moments he would sit quiet in the bluestem and let the rain fall on his upturned face until the car was past. Then he would clamber to his feet and trudge onward. Fields of barley and alfalfa stretched out to his left for thousands of yards, little furrows of green life beginning to ripen. He liked to see them, little green soldiers growing mindlessly and with perfect order. He wished he could be one of those plants, growing and turning color with thousands, millions of others. His shape would be like all the other little soldiers, safe and uniform. To his right range grass grew, unbroken and fallow. The fields were comfortingly familiar to him; much had changed during his solitary seasons at Custer's Elm, but the dark, plowed earth and ripening crops looked just as they had twenty-five years earlier.

An hour later he stopped. The rain was falling harder on him now. The moon rose pale and defiant, a crescent still below the clouds and behind him, casting a white shine on the black, wet pavement. He looked right; far in the distance he could make out the looming shape of three oil wells slowly pumping in the darkness. A sheet of rain swept past him and then the sky opened in earnest, beating on him like tiny hammers and forcing him into a slouch. He peered from underneath his hat and saw a great flash of lightning high and to the east; a second later, the ground shook with thunder. He held his arms out wide, his ragged clothes soaked. Calling out in a loud voice to the wind, he cried, *Here is rain, ye who rip and tear!* He shook his bag at the wells. *Soon is sulfur and lightning!* Without waiting he splashed through the gathering water in the ditch, climbed the fence into the Crandall ranch, and headed toward the creaking pumps.

"Come in out of the rain, Henry."

"That's all right, Sarah. I'm looking for Roger. Is he here?"

Sarah's eyes searched him. "No. What's going on? Is something wrong?"

"I don't know. I'm just looking for him. How long has he been gone?"

"Come in, Henry. Please. You'll get soaked."

"I can't. I've got to find your brother."

"Tell me what's going on, Henry," Sarah said earnestly. "All night I've felt like something bad was happening."

He moved up the steps, then reached out and gently took her arm. "It won't help to worry. Look, if Roger's not here, I can't stay. How long did you say he's been gone? Did he give you any idea where he was headed?"

She shook her head. "I don't know, a couple of hours, I suppose. But I can't be sure. I just noticed he was gone at some point. He didn't say good-bye."

"All right. I'll call the second I know something. And tell Roger to call me if he comes in." He turned and walked rapidly through the rain toward his car. He had just opened the door when he saw headlights pulling down the Crandall driveway. He shut the door and sprinted back under the porch, letting the car come into focus; it was Roger, gravel flying from underneath the Eldorado.

Roger got out of the car and stared, oblivious to the rain. "What the hell are you doing here?"

"I'm looking for Raymond," Henry said. "I want to know if you've seen him."

Roger laughed derisively as he came in under the porch's overhang. "You figure he's out here? Yeah, we invited the bastard for dinner."

"Where have you been, Roger?" Henry asked intently. "Raymond's missing. No one's seen him for hours." Roger stuck his hand in his pocket and fingered the pills. It was all right; Boyd had never showed at the cemetery. There hadn't been any real contact between them. He had nothing to fear. "I don't know where the freak is," he said. "Hopefully, somebody's putting him out of his misery."

Sarah groaned. "Don't say that, Roger. It's not right."

Henry looked at Roger's face. He was drunk, his expression that of a scared, intoxicated bully. It was utterly repellent to Henry. His own nerves were frayed, and he felt his patience leave him. He moved between Roger and his sister, his anger rising. "If you've hurt him, Roger, I'm going to take you apart, and it won't be in a court of law."

Roger sneered, listing slightly to the side. The booze was singing through him, and he was feeling brave. "Take your best shot, city boy."

Henry turned to leave in contempt, but suddenly wheeled around in anger and gave Roger a roundhouse shot to the jaw, dropping him backward several feet. Roger stumbled over the gravel's unsure footing and landed hard on his backside, his face contorted with pain. Henry looked down at him, all pity gone, feeling simple disgust. "There, Roger," he said. "Sue me."

Henry's shot and the booze turned Roger's vision black for a moment, and he leaned back, dropping his head onto the gravel. The rain fell on his face, dripping off him onto the driveway. Sarah began to cry softly, and Henry turned to her. "I'm sorry," he said. "I just couldn't take any more of him. Go take care of your mother, now. It's going to be a long night."

Raymond stood still sixty feet away from the well. Dark thunderclouds had now covered the sky, making the well a dark, vague shape of shadow. But he could hear it; a low graunching sound came from under the earth as the stomach of the field was pumped, black bile rising under forced pressure. Aboveground the metal parts squealed in protest, long overdue for lubrication. Boyd stood for a long moment, listening and staring into the shadows. Then lightning streaked across the sky, illuminating the field. The hulking shape of the well exploded in the light, Boyd's figure erect before it. He raised his fist in the air, shaking it in fury and anger. "Plague and bloodshed! he cried. My sword drinks its fill in the heavens, it descends in judgment! Ain't that right, Junior Henry? Rain and sulfur and fire from the heavens!"

Boyd dropped his bag and spilled the contents out onto the muddy ground. He picked up the big wrench and rags and walked toward the well. The mud and oil residue had combined beneath his feet into a sticky glue, and he sank into the bog as he walked. As he approached, the protest of metal on metal grew louder and more abrasive; in his brain it was the sound of robots screaming for death.

He laboriously shut the well down. When he was finished, he took the rags and rubbed them over the pipes for several minutes, eventually soaking them in oil. He then took his wrench and placed the mouth on a large pipe fitting where two lines split off from the wellhead. He pulled down on the wrench; solid from years of disuse, the fitting refused to move. He tried for several seconds, with the same result, and at last lifted his body up by the wrench handle, hanging on it over the concrete encasing at ground level. He bounced up and down and felt the wrench move slightly. Regaining his feet, he bent his knees and pulled; the fitting unscrewed a half inch, and Boyd heard a powerful hissing sound coming from under the wrench. "Now sulfur and fire," he said out loud. He bounded away from the well.

Thirty feet downwind he pushed the big truck flare deep into the ground, the spike moving easily through the sodden bog. When a foot and a half remained above ground level he pulled the cap off and wrapped the oily rags around the base. He looked back through the pelting rain at the well. *Absolution. Let there be absolution.* He pulled back the self-igniters on the flare, and the smell of burning magnesium filled the air. A flame burst up from the thin cylinder, showering sparks into the night. The heat of two thousand degrees evaporated the rain twenty feet above the flame. Boyd picked up his bag and began running to the empty highway.

As Raymond hit the highway, the flare was burning down at the well. By the time it reached the ground the rags were already smoldering, ignited by the sparks of the magnesium fire. When the heat of the flare reached the rags, the oil-soaked fabric exploded into flame, burning blue and red. The flame instantly traced outward from the flare across the ground, racing across the oily earth toward the well. In less than three seconds it had covered the sixty feet to the wellhead. Flame danced for a moment at the base of the well, sweeping in a great circle. It crept up the center shaft to the pipe fittings, and soon the entire base of the well was glowing, the blustering wind sending thick black smoke across the field and into the dark sky. When the flame licked near the opening that Boyd had cracked, the threads burned yellow for an instant; then with terrific force the entire casing of the well shaft exploded into thousands of metal pieces, disintegrating the concrete and sending iron fragments hundreds of feet into the air. The concussion splintered the limbs of scrub trees fifty yards away, their instantly superheated leaves bursting into flame in defiance of the rain. A column of screaming fire hurled itself a hundred and fifty feet high—clear and invisible at the bottom, then yellow, then orange, with startling, electric-blue tips at the top. The smell of sulfur filled the air as the flame roared upward for several seconds; then, suddenly, it began to ignite downward into the well, and the air was rent with the sound of a frantic, high-pitched, burning train.

Frank Hesston sat alone in his office, pondering how so much time and effort had been risked in such a damnably short time. He went over his approaches, relived his decisions, searching for mistakes. He had made none, he decided. Each choice was made for a reason, and each alternative would have posed a different, more substantial threat. But the fact remained that he was hanging by a thin thread that was now unquestionably spinning out of his direct control.

He alone knew the real reason why Tyler had changed his will. All that talk about guilt or growing up the boy was irrelevant nonsense, a mile wide of the mark. Hesston closed his eyes, playing over one of his last conversations with Tyler before his death. *Insurance,* he thought grimly. *Insurance to keep Carl and me honest. Anything happens to me, Crandall had said, and all hell breaks loose.* Hesston had pressed him, but Tyler had given him a dark look and refused to say another word.

Certainly Carl had brought up moving Tyler out of the loop. *We don't need him anymore,* he had said. *With Tyler out of the way we keep right on running, except the split goes two ways instead of three.* He had a point; the difference would have been in the millions. But as usual, Carl's answer to everything was the strong-arm or the shotgun. Hesston had stopped him in his tracks, before he could spook Crandall. It was too late; Tyler had already grown suspicious, sensing something shifting in Durand's demeanor. It was Crandall's gift, smelling danger before any of the others. Toward the end, he had grown guarded, cautious. That was the thing about crime: you knew you were dealing with crooks. Anyway, Tyler could add numbers as well as anybody else, and must have realized he was vulnerable. *So you change your will and turn Boyd into a threat. And I let you do it. I knew I could control Carl, and we only needed a few more years and it would have all been over anyway. And then you go and die. At fifty-six. With no warning, like the hand of God just plucked you off the earth. And you leave a mess that could take us all down with you.*

He flicked on his computer, the screen bathing his face with a cool light. Using an encrypted E-mail address, he sent a message to the private banking office of the Banque Suisse, instructing them to have two hundred and fifty thousand dollars sent to their branch on Grand Bahama Island. If and when things became untenable, a prepaid plane ticket to Miami would

put him on his boat, *Litigation III*. An overnight cruise would put him in the
Bahamas, with no traceable record of his leaving the country. He would be
just another part of the flotilla that traveled daily between Miami and the
islands. Once in the Bahamas, he could contemplate at his leisure how to
spend the millions he had amassed during a very fruitful run. But all that was
mere contingency, the kind of careful planning that had made him rich and
kept him safe so far. To walk out too early was as stupid as waiting too late;
there were millions more in the ground, millions worth a reasonable risk.

Hesston's E-mail program marked the message sent, and he closed the
laptop and put it in his briefcase. That, along with a small bag of clothing,
needed to be made ready for a quick trip. In the meantime, he would give
the trial one more day. A lot had happened, but there were pieces still in
play. Durand could well find Ellen or even Boyd, and take care of things in
his own way. If he did the winds might blow back in his direction. In the
meantime, he would show up in Brackman's court in the morning, ready to
do battle with the cocky, annoying lawyer from Chicago. But if things
deteriorated one more day, he was gone.

Raymond rummaged his way through the hedge dividing Ellen's backyard
and that of the empty field directly behind it. He quietly slipped between
the trees into Ellen's yard, the lessening rain covering the sound of his
movements.

It had taken more than two hours to retrace his steps to town, and in
that time the storm had blown itself out, moving west across Matfield
Green. Dark night descended on Council Grove, a thick blanket of clouds
obscuring moon and stars. Boyd moved like a shadow to his hideout; to his
relief, nothing had been tampered with. Once again the covering of limbs
and leaves had held up, and he lifted the canvas opening to enter. He
gazed briefly through a small slit at the back of Ellen's house thirty yards
away.

The wind and rain had blown undergrowth and wet leaves into his shelter, and he pushed the moldy piles aside to reveal a tightly wrapped parcel.
He lifted it, pulling leaves off the top. The packet was substantial, covered
in brown wrapping paper and secured with burlap string. He hefted the
package, feeling its weight. Satisfied, he sat heavily down among the leaves
and unwrapped it.

After a moment's struggle the string fell away from the package. When
he pulled the paper back, several folds of heavy, dark blue fabric were
revealed. Boyd gazed at the material a moment, his expression reverent.
His face was streaked with rain, sweat, and oil. "Bank," he whispered quietly. He rummaged through the package and pulled from it a battered pair

of black dress shoes, and another, much smaller package. He set the smaller parcel carefully down on the ground and, picking up the dark blue cloth, came unsteadily to his feet. The material unfurled itself down toward the ground, and a wrinkled suit coat appeared, followed by a matching pair of pants.

Boyd fumbled with his belt; his own pants fell down over his grimy knees, and kicking off his old shoes, he stepped clumsily out of them. The long walk through the rain and oil picked up from the well had left him a bedraggled mess. His hair hung down in long wet strands, and his legs were muddy below the knees. He bent down and put on the suit pants, pulling the clean fabric over his dirty legs. He then pulled the shoes over his soaking, thick, gray farm socks. The pants didn't fit particularly well; they were tight in the waist and seat, and he fastened them with difficulty.

Boyd brushed out the suit coat a moment, covering it with oily muck as he ran his hand over it. He put it on; it clashed harshly with his checked cotton shirt, which he had not changed. He reached for his collar and fastened it tight around his neck; then, taking from the coat pocket a light blue tie, he stood up. He tied the tie deliberately, pulling it tight and straightening it with meticulous formality. He took from the coat pocket a small mirror and a comb. He stared into the glass a long moment, his eyes unblinking. Boyd touched his scraggly beard tenderly, running his dirty fingers through his mustache and along the side of his face. He took the comb and passed it through his matted hair; it caught on a dozen tangles, refusing to move.

After a long moment he put away the mirror and comb and peered out at Ellen's house through the cardboard slit. The lights had come on in the back rooms while he had been dressing; he could see her form now, blurred through the narrow opening and the distance. She was in the kitchen, and he could make out her outline as she stood before the sink. Boyd turned toward the canvas door, his breathing shallow and rapid; without deciding, he passed from the shelter into the yard.

Ellen was taking off her high heels when she heard a muted rustling behind the house. Animals sometimes rambled up near her porch sniffing for food, but this was heavier, clumsier. She stopped, one shoe still suspended in her hand, and listened a moment. The wind creaked through the aging back window jambs, reminding her of long-needed caulking. *Never mind*, she thought. *I'll be selling soon. I'm dead in this town now.* Hearing nothing but the wind, she continued undressing, and her tight, pale green dress fell to the floor beneath her. She walked barefoot in bra and panties to her closet and stepped in, leaving the door ajar. She fingered a dressing gown, but as she pulled it off its hanger she heard movement again, more distinct and closer. An uneasy chill moved up her spine.

A word came soundlessly to her mind: *Hesston. I let Raymond go, and he's come for his pound of flesh.* She heard another sound and tried to tell herself it was a muskrat, or a possum, that any second she would hear the garbage pail crash off the porch to the ground. Nevertheless, she quietly closed the closet door behind her. She groped for the light and blinked in the sudden glare of an open bulb three feet above her head. Squinting, she looked searchingly up at the top shelf, where a shoe box lay under a substantial stack of sweaters and shirts.

Another clunk; there was no mistaking it now, something or someone was definitely near her house. Her blood ran cold; she knew that Hesston was capable of doing anything to anyone if he felt it necessary. He wasn't emotional like Durand. There was a cold, metallic quality to the man that was infinitely more frightening. She reached toward the box above her, but it was just beyond her outstretched fingers. She put her high heels back on in order to pull it down. She opened the box. A small-caliber pistol hid under white wrapping paper, beside it a new box of cartridges. Ellen sat down on the floor of the closet and slowly lifted out the gun. She poured six cartridges into her left hand, and loaded them one by one into the chambers. Her hands were beginning to tremble, and it took concentration to spin the pistol shut and click off the safety. She imagined Frank Hesston's cold, intelligent face and wondered if she could actually put a bullet into it.

Fifteen feet from Ellen's back door Raymond Boyd shook his head absently, then more violently, asking his voices for quiet. For the last thirty feet or so they had been calling more loudly, confusing him. But he knew what he wanted to do. It didn't matter now where the voices came from, if they were from inside or outside; all he had to do was push through them for a few more minutes and it would all be over.

Raymond stared up at the back door of Ellen's house from behind a cottonwood tree. He had been still for several minutes after he had strayed through some underbrush, making a racket. But he had done penance for the noise, and now he could move on. He pushed down his voices, and with a surprisingly calm movement, stepped from behind the tree and stood exposed, for the first time a direct line of sight between himself and the porch. His feet hurt in the dress shoes, and that helped clear his mind a little; he ground his little toe against the stiff leather, increasing his discomfort.

He moved forward. His head hurt brutally, and that, too, was a good

thing. Like all pain, it helped him think, and he was thinking with a crystalline sharpness now, each thought outlined in fantastically bright light in
his mind. His thoughts were tiny dots buried in his eyelids, burning laser-
bright in his own inner darkness. He glanced once again at his clothes;
bank clothes, he thought, remembering things he hadn't allowed to come to
his conscious mind for more than twenty-five years. *Bank clothes I wore,
didn't I, bird? And to church. Pews and pretty hats and the reverend people.* He
smiled, the pain in his head pulsing brightly, showering sparks against his
skull. The thought formed once again that had been boring through his
brain every day, and sometimes every moment, since the city boy had
brought the will: *The virgin awaits. She is inside.* He walked forward, pausing at the porch. He stepped quietly onto the steps, testing his weight. To
his surprise, he was sweating profusely. He didn't understand this; he felt
perfectly calm now, perfectly free. But perspiration beaded off his forehead and cheeks, beginning to drip. *The virgin awaits,* he thought, pushing
forward. He put his foot onto the second step; a loud creak came from the
dry wood. He stared, uncomprehending; he felt light, ephemeral, like a
mist. He could float. He took another step, this one silent. He looked up
into the dark sky, but no stars were visible. *The virgin awaits, and there must
be sacrifice.*

Inside the house, Ellen heard the stair creak and wrapped herself in a
robe, clutching the sides to her waist. She slowly opened the door of the
closet and looked out into the dark room; nothing was visible through the
windows. Sticking the gun hesitantly out in front of her, she stepped into
her bedroom. At that moment she heard her porch steps groan once again,
and she felt the first genuine thrill of fear. Only a person could make such
a sound; there was no longer any possibility of convincing herself of anything else. She gripped the gun tightly and crept through her room to the
hallway, trying to remember if she had locked the back door. In that
instant she got her answer: she heard the worst sound in the world—the
knob turning, the door slowly opening. Her hand was shaking, the gun
vibrating aimlessly before her. In fear, she called on her well of anger for
what could pass for courage. Years of practice made this intuitive; she had
often needed strength against predators, and her anger was always close
by, easily awakened. *I've been a victim for the last man,* she thought. *Bastards
using me, hang-dog sneakers lying to wives. Never again.*

The sound of footsteps made her legs wobble. He was inside. Here.
Now. She fanned her rage. "Damn you," she whispered, "and damn all
men. You all wanted the same thing from me." She thrust the gun out with
both hands and crouched down at the edge of the hallway. She could hear
him breathing heavily, his living, horrifying sound coming from her left,

around the corner over by the door. One step forward out of the hall and a half turn would bring them face-to-face. She wasn't going to wait any longer, not going to give him the satisfaction. Her muscles were stiff with tension as she prepared to lunge; cursing loudly, she pushed out into the living room.

Raymond felt an ecstatic happiness as he saw her suddenly materialize before him. The failing outside light did little to illuminate the room, and she coalesced out of the darkness, the virgin of the dusk, suddenly, miraculously solid. It was as it should be. His brain was singing with noises and explosions, and he felt lighter than helium. *She is here*, he thought, *here with me. There must be sacrifice.* He smiled beatifically, and in an unexpected, sublime moment, the noises stopped and he heard nothing. The whole world became utterly silent, a comfortable blanket of madness stopping all sound. The virgin, her outline backlit from the light of a distant room, shone out to him. Wrapped in that silence and pale light he thought she was more beautiful than any living creature: holy and untouched, pristine and sanctified.

The virgin was moving her mouth excitedly, but in his cocoon he could not hear her. He stood in his stillness and pulled the small package from his inner coat pocket. Papers he offered her, papers of power. He peeled several pages off the package and let them fall to the ground between them: they were covered with faded and rain-smeared writing, a hodge-podge of legal documents, bank statements, and notebook papers. They fluttered between them a moment, until at last he released his copy of the will itself, unwrapping it carefully off a long, straight razor. He watched her mouth moving rapidly as he opened the razor, and he looked in awe at the virgin, watched her trembling now, vibrating with celestial beauty and power. The virgin was shaking, convulsing, weeping sacred tears. Holding the open razor in his hand he reached strongly out to her, and in that moment he saw a flash of light come straight out from her, a star shooting from her holy body, flaring toward him like a Roman candle. A bullet passed by, narrowly missing him; glass exploded from a window behind him and to his right, showering him with bright, reflective fragments. It was more glorious, more miraculous than he could have imagined. Sparks in his brain, in his skull, in the night sky, all with the virgin before him. It was a gift from Alpha, a blessing from Omega. It was heaven. He opened his mouth to speak. "Fools and whores, let there be absolution," he spoke, and the sound of his voice shattered the air, returning his hearing. With his words the virgin's mouth stopped moving; the two stood in sudden silence in the room. The virgin was crying again, weeping tiny crystal diamonds that fell from her eyes.

"Fools and whores," Raymond said, "let peace come unto thee. Let your pain be washed into the sea of black. Sleep, now."

Raymond took the razor and quietly, serenely sliced the veins on his left wrist to the bone. Blood spurted upward in strong pulses, covering his dirty clothes. He smiled at Ellen, fell to his knees, and let the darkness overcome him.

Chapter Thirty-five

Henry, Amanda, and John Brown stood in the mud, transfixed. Behind them, a blood-red moon hung, obscured intermittently by drifting patches of gray and black. Before them, the sky above the Flinthills was being scorched red, purple, and orange. A tower of flame shot upward from the exploded wellhead, sending a shrieking, dangerous wildness out from the bowels of the earth.

Word of the explosion was spreading rapidly, and a crowd of people was gathering on the Crandall ranch. The rain had finally stopped, and Collier's black-and-white was parked fifty yards away, its headlights vanishing into the brilliance of the flame.

John Brown stared into the heat and fire. "Of course," he said quietly. "It's always so obvious once you see it." The monumental heat created a wind that blew against their faces. Brown turned to Henry and Amanda, his expression grim. "We've all been fools."

"What is it?" Henry asked over the whine of erupting flame. "What's happening?"

"Gas," Brown said. "Natural gas. A big field, from the looks of it. Millions of cubic feet. Maybe tens of millions." He stamped the ground. "Extruded limestone. Lousy for oil. But natural gas can hide there."

"But they were pumping oil," Amanda said. "There's never even been a gas strike in this area."

Henry stared at Brown for a moment, trying to work out the meaning of the geologist's words. Suddenly, his expression changed. "I have it now," he said. "The oil was just an excuse to keep the pumps moving. There has to be one more set of pipes."

Brown nodded. "That's right. A second underground set, probably much farther down." He looked at the well in unabashed admiration. "This was never about oil, not even in the beginning. They only used the oil to justify the pumps." He looked up at the erupting flame, the light of it casting yellow and orange reflections on his skin. "From the looks of that back-pressure, we could be sitting on the biggest 'undiscovered' gas field in the Midwest. For twenty-five years they bring it up, patient, not getting greedy, selling it completely off the books through Durand's distribution system. It's beautiful."

Amanda's eyes widened. "I never thought of that."

"There was a bigger payoff than you realize," Brown said. "It works two . . ." Brown hesitated. "No, *three* ways. They sold the gas off the books, obviously. That was worth a lot. But the real beauty of it was deeper down, almost visionary."

"What are you talking about?" Henry asked.

Brown shook his head. "Twenty-five years ago nobody around here was even selling natural gas," he said. "It was worthless. They would burn it off just to get rid of it. No market yet. Nobody cared about this land because there wasn't any oil on it to speak of. But whoever did this must have realized before anybody else that the gas was going to be valuable. So they bought the land on the cheap. That would have been, what, '70, '72? Just before the price of gas exploded."

"Durand," Amanda said. "He was always a big risk-taker."

"There was another reason to take the risk," Brown said. "It's the third level of the scam, the deepest one." He drew a circle with his foot and pointed to the center. "This is where we are right now, the wellhead. The circle is say, seven, maybe eight miles across. The law says when you hit a strike, all the landowners inside the circle have to get a share."

"Of course," Henry said, looking at the drawing. "The gas wouldn't stay within property lines."

"Exactly," Brown said. "You can't drill a well on one part of a field and quietly pump the whole thing dry. Not legally. The surrounding landowners have to get a piece." He shook his head. "This whole thing wasn't just to keep the gas off the tax books. That was sweet. But the point is that a field this big would have made a lot of millionaires around here."

Henry shook his head. "It would have created a lot of Crandalls, and Tyler would never have stood for that." He turned and looked into the blackness behind them toward Crandall's home. "You son of a bitch," he said. "You pulled millions out of this field, didn't pay a dime in tax, and kept out any other claims."

"How much are we talking about?" Amanda asked.

Brown shrugged. "Who knows? But more than twenty years of this . . ." He gestured toward the erupting wellhead. "With back-pressure like that, several million, with that much more ahead."

The three watched the blaze in silence for some time. The wind was coming up, and it looked like it might begin to rain again. "We're still left with this explosion," Henry said, "and what made it happen."

Brown started to speak, but suddenly Sheriff Collier materialized out of the darkness beside them. He was carrying the remains of a large flare.

"Arson," he said gruffly. "No doubt about it." He held up the burnt-out stump. "Somebody wanted to make some noise. Somebody who don't like Crandalls."

"That would do the trick," Brown said. "Even in the rain. Couple of thousand degrees, completely waterproof. If a guy knew anything about wells, he might be able to pull it off."

Collier stared at Brown, looking at him from head to toe. "I seen you around. Who the hell are you?"

"A friend," Henry said.

"I don't like your friends," Collier said, looking Brown in the eye. He turned to Henry and added, "I don't like your client neither. This stinks of Boyd. Tell me somethin', Counselor. Got any idea where the fruitcake was tonight?"

"If I did, you'd have to subpoena me to find out," Henry replied.

The sheriff was about to respond when Brown interjected, "Whoever did this, it was a desperate move. Dangerous as hell. A million ways for it to go wrong."

Collier looked up sharply. "How's that?"

Brown shrugged. "A man would have to open a live valve, just wrench it open. The gas would flow out invisibly. He'd have no way to know how much or where. With the winds the way they are out here tonight, that would be damn touchy. He could be covered in it and not even know it. Then he'd have to light the flare and physically connect it to the well. Whoever he is, he's lucky he didn't go up in a fireball."

Collier looked back at Brown insolently. "What are you, some kinda expert on starting fires?"

Brown stared silently back with a look of utter indifference. Henry said, "Mr. Brown is a geologist."

Collier stared blankly for a moment, trying to process the idea of an educated Native American. At length he said, "Well, if he had gone up in smoke, at least we'd have some bones to identify. Right now the three of you are coming with me. We're going to play questions and answers."

"What's being done about the blaze?" Henry said. "It can't be left like this."

"Containment company's been called," Collier answered. "They're going to helicopter in, be here in a couple hours." He spat at the ground, obviously disgusted. "Enough chitchat. Let's go, Mathews. You and your friends ain't gonna get much sleep tonight."

Amanda stepped toward Collier. "We've got nothing to hide, Sheriff," she said indignantly. "And for what it's worth, I don't like you either. You're a fatuous little man with a power complex and badly in need of a shower." She walked off ahead of the others, heading toward Henry's car.

Henry gave Collier a thin smile. "You've really got a knack for getting along with people, don't you, Sheriff?"

Collier grunted and followed Brown and Henry back toward the cars. As they arrived, the black-and-white's CB crackled. The sheriff sat down heavily in his cruiser and listened. After several moments he climbed out of his car with a sallow grin. "Seems your client saved me a lot of trouble," he said. "Boyd's in county hospital. Looks like he won't make it."

Henry led Amanda and John into the Cheney County hospital twenty minutes later, with Collier right behind them. Boyd was in a room in the emergency trauma area. The second Henry saw him, he was stopped cold; there was a heavy bandage on Boyd's arm, an oxygen tube in his nose, and two plastic lines dripping clear liquid into his veins. He was pale, and either asleep or unconscious. From Henry's left he heard T. R. Harris' voice.

"He wasn't taking his medication," the doctor said. "That's obvious now. Why he wasn't taking it, for God's sake, I don't know."

Henry turned and said, "He had me fooled. But I think I know why. He needed his madness to get off the park bench and do this. He would never have had the courage without the visions and the passion." His own breathing felt constricted. The awful white of the hospital room combined with the sight of Raymond lying still in the bedsheets gave him a sudden wave of nausea.

"Is he going to be all right?" Amanda asked.

"I don't know," Harris said. "The ER unit here did a hell of a job. But he practically cut his arm off there. He's lost a lot of blood." He walked over and looked intently at Raymond. "But he's alive for now, and we'll take it one miracle at a time."

Collier pushed between Amanda and Brown, full of tactless, bothersome pressure. "This man's a prisoner," he said gruffly, "and it don't make me no difference if he's here or in jail. I got his ass nailed this time."

At the sight of Collier, Harris' face became a mask of irritation. "Get out, Sheriff," he said bluntly. He gripped Collier by the arm and gave him a solid push toward the door. "Get out, all of you," he said, and the group moved together into the hallway. Harris closed the door firmly and spun on the group. "Your little circus has almost killed that man," he said angrily, "and he's off the train ride, as of right now. You . . ." He pointed at Collier. "*You* will get your officious little fingers on this man when I say he's healthy enough to talk to somebody of your idiocy. And that includes questioning. You're in my world now, and what I say goes. And for the rest of you . . ." He shook his head, clearly tired and frustrated. "Look, it was a good idea, okay? It just didn't work out. As soon as Raymond is able to be moved, I'm taking him to the psychiatric hospital in Kansas City. That's if he survives the night."

"If he survives tonight he'll stand charges for sexual assault, criminal trespassing, breaking and entering, attempted battery, and fourteen other things I'll add to the list," Collier hissed. "We got ourselves a *criminal* here, Doctor. He was found at Ellen Gaudet's. County sheriff got called over there when gunshots were heard. Turned out our boy here had a weird thing for bank tellers."

Henry was about to unleash a torrent of legal hell on Collier, but stopped suddenly. "What are you talking about?" he demanded.

"County boys found a lean-to of some kind in Ellen's backyard. Boyd's been campin' out back there, apparently. There was a change of clothes, bunch of papers and stuff."

"God," breathed Amanda.

"Tell me everything they said," Henry said. "Every word."

"Go to hell," Collier said. "It's my questions got to be answered."

Henry glared. "I have the right to know everything that those county deputies found."

"Subpoena me and I'll give you a deposition," Collier answered, staring Henry in the face. "Should be able to get to it in two or three days."

Henry barely suppressed his desire to tear the sheriff apart. "What about Ellen?" he said. "Where is she?"

"We don't know, damn it," Collier said. "She was gone by the time the county boys got there."

"Then how do you know what happened?" Henry demanded.

"It ain't rocket science," Collier spat. "He was there to rape her. She was armed, and got away. Bullet hole in the wall."

"And what about Boyd's wrist?"

"He's insane, in case you hadn't noticed. How do I know? He didn't get laid, so he wanted to kill himself."

For the second time Henry had to restrain himself from punching Collier in his self-satisfied face. "After tonight, there's going to be nothing but chaos in that courtroom," he growled. "There's a good chance this time tomorrow there's not going to be anything left to fight over."

"What the hell are you talkin' about?" Collier asked.

Henry looked at him. "You really have no idea what's going on here, do you?" He turned to Harris and said, "Everything in me wants to stay here. But I can't. Things have changed. You've got my number." Harris nodded and disappeared back into the hospital room. Henry looked at Amanda. "Let's go," he said brusquely. "We've got to find some people."

*   *   *

By the time Henry and Amanda arrived back in Council Grove it was nearly two in the morning. They sat in the car outside Henry's office. "What the hell was Raymond doing at Ellen's?" Henry asked morosely. "God, why did he have to do that?"

"Does it ruin everything for him? Was Collier right about that?"

"I don't know. I still don't know what actually happened. But it was bad enough when it was just Crandalls versus Raymond. If it's going to be Crandalls versus a rapist, God help us."

"I don't believe he wanted to hurt her."

"I don't either. I'm talking about perceptions. But the only two people who can prove what really happened aren't talking. Raymond's unconscious, and that leaves Ellen."

"Collier will be looking for her, too. She's a loose end."

"After tonight anything might happen. Did you see those flames? It was like Armageddon. *Sulfur and fire*, he said. *The judgment hand of God*."

The two sat in silence for a moment, until Henry suddenly slammed his fist down on the dashboard. "Damn it, there's something happening here, something inside of Raymond. He's only ventured out twice on his own. First, when the bird got killed. It must have taken something even bigger than that to drag him on foot to the wells. And God only knows what would make him actually break into Ellen's house."

"What do you make of the suicide attempt?"

"I hate it, but I assume it's real. That's what so tricky about all of this. I know Raymond. I know he wouldn't hurt Ellen. But I also don't know Raymond, because unfortunately he's out of his mind. So whether or not he might get it into his head to cut his own wrists is beyond my comprehension. How can you work with a client like this?"

"What are you going to do?"

"I'm trying to save him," Henry said. "Damn it, I'm trying to save him, if he would just stop being insane for a minute."

She repeated herself, her voice level and lower. It gave him a place to settle himself, and when he looked back at her he had regrouped. "Sorry," he said. "Something's torturing Raymond and I want to make it stop."

"I understand. What happens tomorrow in court?"

"This isn't about court anymore. Ten seconds after the fire containment team arrives, the whole scam is public knowledge. I have to assume some of the farmers in the area could work it out even on their own. As soon as the fire's put out, that whole area is going to get torn up. Hesston and Durand are at their most dangerous now. I have no idea what they'll do backed into this kind of a corner."

"The truth," Amanda said quietly. "God, it messes things up."

Henry nodded. "I should be out looking for Ellen right now. But if I don't have a half-dozen motions on Raymond's behalf in the morning, Collier will have him for lunch. We know he wasn't trying to hurt Ellen, but circumstantially . . . God, it looks like shit."

"The lean-to was creepy," Amanda said. "To think of him hiding back there, staring."

"I know," Henry said, waving his hand. "It's bad enough without talking about it."

"Sorry. Why don't you go work for a while, get those motions started. I'll look for Ellen, meet you back here. How long do you need?"

"At least two hours," Henry said. "What time is it?"

"A little after two," she said. "What a night."

Henry picked up his briefcase and got out of the car. "Just take my car. Call me if you see anything."

Amanda drove off, turning west onto Chautauqua. Henry entered the office and sat heavily in his chair. He looked out the front window, the dim lights of the square struggling against the dark.

Now was the time to pray, certainly. There was nowhere else to hide but in the unpredictability of God. But to what end? Was Raymond safe in Amanda's school, the nun's prayers protecting him? Or was he farther north, ready to be destroyed by a merciless wind?

"All right, damn it," Henry said to the walls. "So I pray because there's nothing else to do. I pray for some injection of hope, however irrational. I pray to the God who lets hurricanes come ashore. I pray to the God who spares some and lets others fry. I pray to the God . . ." He choked for a moment, suddenly overcome with an emotion so powerful it swept him down, submersing him. He had resisted this moment for more than five years, and when it finally pushed through, grief covered him utterly. "I pray," he said through tears, "to the God who let my parents get killed by a drunk that never knew their names and couldn't have cared less." He looked up at the ceiling. It was out now. "Do you hear me?" he cried. "To the God who let my parents be smashed into pieces. And they're dead. And what did they do that was so wrong? Are you listening to me? What was their sin? My father was a good man!" He was sobbing now, grieving openly. "All he did was work like a dog and help poor people try to hang on to a shred of dignity. But you let that truck hit them, didn't you? Would it have killed you to have just waved your hand and stopped it? Would it? Would it have disrupted your sense of order in this universe to have saved two people that I loved?"

He laid his head on the table, weeping quietly now, with no sense of time. Minutes passed, his breathing catching, letting himself go like a child. He cried for a long time, finally settling into a dull quiet. He didn't know if minutes passed or hours. But at some point, he found words form-ing in him. He didn't know where they came from, but he was certain they didn't come from within himself. They had no beginning or ending. They just were.

This is what I wanted, the words said. *The truth between Me and you. And now you know what I've known for a long time. Now you know that you hate me. Nothing can heal without beginning with the truth.*

Henry lifted his head. The words drifted away, moving through and past him. He sat still a moment, his eyes closed. He exhaled deeply, relief flooding through him. "I hate You," he said to the air. "I hate You."

At some point, he turned on his laptop and began to write. Henry didn't know how much later it was when the door opened. It was Amanda.

"Are you all right?" she asked.

Henry took a deep breath. "Yes," he said at last. "I think."

"Your eyes are red."

"I'm all right. What did you find out?" She looked at him, and to his enormous gratitude, she had the grace to release him without hovering or questioning. She merely took in his pain, and left him alone with it. It was in that second that he thought he might love her.

"I found nothing," she said. "Of course it's dark on such a horrible night. But I don't think she's in Council Grove."

"Then where?"

She looked out the window. "It's getting light. You have court in three hours."

"What a circus that's going to be. There's going to be press there. I mean real press."

"I hadn't thought of that."

"The well fire took care of that. I wouldn't be surprised to see the net-works in there tomorrow."

"How can Durand stay out of it now? It's the end for him, isn't it?"

Henry shrugged. "Lawyers," he said quietly. "The real modern miracle workers."

"You can't believe he'll get off from this."

"Who knows? He can say that it was done without his knowledge. He can say Crandall did it. It was more than twenty-five years ago. It's like dealing with ghosts." He exhaled deeply and stood up. "I have to change clothes."

"You're playing the card about the wells today, though, right?"

"Yes, which means I need to find John Brown. He's going to have to testify."

"I have his number." She rummaged through her purse, which had been left sitting on Henry's desk. "I don't know if he can be there by ten."

"It's all right. I'm going to get Hesston and Brackman in a private counsel anyway. I'm laying my cards on the table. We'll see what happens next."

"All right. What can I do?"

"I don't know. Nothing."

"Then I'll stay with you." She walked toward him. "I called the hospital. Nothing definitive on Raymond."

"Did you talk to Harris?"

"No. He had gone home hours ago. Nothing to be done, evidently. Anyway, he's a psychiatrist, not an internist. But the nurse said Raymond's condition was still critical."

"You could go to him. It would be good to have someone there Raymond knows when he wakes up."

"If he wakes up," Amanda said. But she shook her head. "I'm staying with you, at least until court. There's nothing I can do at the hospital anyway."

He put his arm around her, and she kissed him on the cheek, a motion he found impossibly tender. She continued her kisses, tasting the salt residue from his dried tears. He closed his eyes and let her bring him back to life, her lips a kind of transfusion of tenderness. She brushed his hair back and kissed his forehead. "I have clothes in my car," she said. "So I'm okay. Meanwhile, let's get you cleaned up."

Henry locked up the office; light was just glimmering to the southeast, out over the Crandall property. He could see a thin trail of smoke from that direction even though the fields were miles away. He had no doubt the fire was still raging.

Back at the motel, he felt his exhaustion as a dull, numbing ache. He looked at the bed longingly, then turned away. He heard her start the shower, and stood motionless as she came to him and began to unbutton his shirt. She undressed him, the only light spilling out from the bathroom, and he let himself be taken care of in a way he never before experienced. She led him, naked, to the shower, and he stepped in, feeling the warm water for a long time, watching it stream down his body in a kind of relaxed, numb stare. After a while she returned, wrapped him in a towel, and dried him. He stood, arms out, watching her touch his body through the cotton, feeling the pressure of her fingers as they kneaded his back, pushed down his thighs. "I'm not sick, you know," he said quietly. "I can do this myself."

"I know."

He followed her out to the bedroom, and saw a suit laid out on the bed, with socks, belt, shoes, and a tie. He dressed quietly while she sat and watched him from a chair. "You make me happy," she said as he buttoned his shirt. "I just want you to know that."

He walked to her and she stood, accepting his kiss as naturally as if they had been lovers for as long as they could remember. He picked up his coat. "Do you think Collier's been able to find Ellen?"

"I don't know. But I don't think so."

"I wish we could find out for sure. Is it just a hunch?"

"If you're right about the media, she's not going to be found if she can help it. Not after what came out."

"I hate what's happened to her." He shook his head. "No, it didn't just happen. I hate what I did to her."

"You knew there weren't any guarantees."

"I can't begin to deal with that now." He moved to the door. "I'll have to do business with it sooner or later, of course. When I do I don't plan on being in a courtroom. Right now it won't help Raymond if I fall apart."

Henry drove toward the courthouse, feeling once again like he had a loaded gun in his briefcase. Yesterday, it had been the secrets in Ellen's past. Today, it was the scam that had probably netted Crandall and the others millions off the wells. Frank Hesston was about to get his nerve tested in a way he had never experienced. But the killer instinct of a litigator wasn't rising up in Henry. Nailing them or watching them slip away wasn't going to be his job; that was criminal work, and the district attorney would handle that. Which suited him, because in his heart, he didn't really care about Hesston or Durand. Finding out the real secrets of the wells didn't mean a thing unless they connected the dots to Raymond.

Henry pulled into the square and caught his breath. There were at least ten news vans parked or circling, drawn magnetically by the well explosion and Raymond's suicide attempt. Directly in front of the courthouse was a CBS truck, looming over the local affiliates like a mother ship over her satellites. There were at least two hundred people milling around, and to Henry's particular disgust, several locals were being interviewed by the media. He could only imagine the picture of Raymond they were painting.

There wasn't anywhere to park in the square itself, so Henry turned around and headed off behind the courthouse, hoping to come in the back door. But suddenly, he wheeled south out Pawnee, driving fast. He went west on Highway 27, and looked at his watch: it was ten after nine, fifty minutes before court started.

He covered the seventeen miles to Pretty Prairie in just under twelve minutes. But he slowed when he saw the Everlasting Rest Cemetery approaching on the left. It was a hunch, and nothing more.

He saw her sitting on the grass, her back to Ty's gravestone. She didn't move when she saw him. She looked at him, expressionless, watching him walk slowly through the graves in her direction as though she were already a corpse. "It came to me on my way to court," he said. "I wasn't sure. But I hoped."

"I'm here because I'm dead. You knew where to look because you killed me."

Henry stopped, took the blow, and quietly said, "I'm sorry that you were caught in this. I never wanted that."

"Is Raymond alive?"

"He is. He's getting everything possible."

"I want to be with Tyler. We can be dead together."

"I was just looking for the truth."

"No matter what happens to the people."

He knelt opposite her, feeling the moist grass on his fingers. "I have a client who still doesn't have a history, and a very uncertain future. I'm going to keep pushing until he has both."

She looked at him with derision. "And do to him what you've done to me."

Henry paused; if revealing the truth did to Raymond what it had done to Ellen, then Raymond's truth was dark, indeed. "It's too late to stop. It's the only way for Raymond to find himself. It's the only way for him to live a real life."

"You do all the choosing, don't you?" she said bitterly. "You choose for me. You choose for Raymond. What does this cost you?" She shook her head. "Nothing. It costs you nothing."

Henry looked down. This was his own place of pain. "I know I'm choosing. It's not fair, but we're all getting used to that now. It has cost me something, but I'm not going to compare wounds."

Her eyes flickered briefly with interest. "What did it cost you? I'd like to know that you suffered something in this. That would give me some happiness."

"I don't think you'd understand."

"Try me."

He closed his eyes a moment, gathering his thoughts. "All right. Before I came back here I had my own lies to tell myself. Lies about why I got up in the morning and worked sixty-hour weeks to become a person I don't even like. Lies about a woman I thought I loved. More than anything else, lies about the death of my parents and the God who let it happen." He looked at her. "That whole world is gone now. Blown up, with Raymond's wells. So I'm like you. I'm suspended in air, with no place to go." He looked out across the grass. "Just toward the truth. That's all I know to do."

They sat quietly together; for a moment, there was a kinship between them, and he felt some of her animosity drain away. Henry breathed deeply, collecting in his lungs the invisible scents of the growing things that surrounded them. He looked up; the sun was startlingly clear, as though the air was of prehistoric purity. He felt inexplicably relaxed, as though he had cast a die and could do nothing now but wait and see how God acted.

"What can I do now?" Ellen asked in a cracked whisper. "What can I do with my life?"

"You're almost home, I think," Henry said. "We're all almost home. Just a little farther."

She laughed morosely. "It's worked out so well up until now."

"There's a way you can redeem all this pain. You can come back with me and tell the court what you know about Raymond Boyd."

"And that would redeem my miserable life?"

"No. It would be the first step in a new life. A brave life."

"I'm old, Henry." She looked it; she obviously hadn't slept, and her makeup had worn off long ago. Her clothes were wrinkled. She looked as though every day she had lived had been a hard one.

Henry saw the truth and let it cut into her, revealing her inner bone and flesh. "Then this is your last chance."

She looked at him and he could see her practiced composure cracking, falling to pieces. "That's what Frank told me," she said. "I don't want to cry anymore. Can't you all leave me alone, for God's sake?"

"No. You lost that right more than twenty-five years ago."

She sat with her head up, looking straight ahead, tears streaming down her face. "Do I have to do this out of the goodness of my heart? Because there isn't any."

"What did Frank Hesston tell you, Ellen? What did he say was your last chance?"

"He wanted me to hurt Raymond. I wouldn't do that."

"Hurt him how?"

"I don't know. God, let me rest, can't you?"

Henry watched her for a long time, comprehension creeping into his face. "He was using you, wasn't he? Using you to bring Raymond to him."

"He offered me money. I need it. I need it thanks to you." Her sobbing wracked through her again briefly, and she said between gasps, "I can't start over again, can't you see that? Where am I supposed to go? What am I supposed to do?"

He put his hand out and touched her hair; she reached out and grabbed it with startling force, squeezing the fingers so hard he grimaced. "You did this to me," she spat. "You killed me."

"You can put a stop to it," Henry said. "You can finally see that justice gets done."

"Justice!" she said. "That's a stupid word." She relaxed her grip in exhaustion, letting his fingers fall.

"I need you, Ellen. Raymond needs you. This town needs you. There isn't much time."

"I've been protecting people so long, it's like a bad habit. I just keep my mouth shut."

"Then it's time you found your power."

She smiled bitterly. "Having power isn't something I know about." She shook her head. "Carl would never let me live to tell what you want me to say. I was stupid to think he would. I'm a loose end."

"Then strike first."

She hesitated. "And what about Raymond? You don't want to know his truth."

"I can't protect him from the truth anymore. I don't want to do that."

"Because it's the only way he can get better."

"I believe that. Dr. Harris believes that."

She stood slowly, rising from the grass of the graveyard. "Your so-called truth has taken everything I have from me."

"I'm sorry."

"I'm dead. I don't care." She stood, looking out across the gravestones. "I'll say what you want if it hurts Durand and Hesston. I'll do it for hate." She looked down, taking in her disheveled, dirty dress, the grass stains on her arms. "I don't want to go looking like this."

He was moved almost to weeping at her glimmer of self-respect, still intact after so much assault. "Then we have to leave right away," he said. "Amanda will help you."

"That girl you're with?"

"Yes, that girl. Can you make it?"

She nodded, wiping tears from her cheeks. She followed him across the grass, unsteady but determined. He gave her his arm, and she leaned on him as they walked.

Henry dialed his cell phone when he got to the car. He heard Amanda pick up. "It's me," he said.

"Where are you? You have court in twenty minutes. I was just leaving."

"Then I barely caught you. Good."

"Yes." There was a pause. "What do you need?"

"Just for you to be kind to someone. Do you have any makeup?"

"A little. I don't wear much."

"Whatever you have will be fine. I've got Ellen with me."

"You found her," Amanda breathed. "Is she okay?"

"She's had a hard night. But she's going to testify. She wants to clean up, and I don't want to take her back to her house after what happened."

"I understand."

When they arrived at the motel Amanda was there waiting, and she took Ellen by the hand and led her into the room. Henry waited outside, pacing, continuously glancing at his watch. At last the door opened, and when Ellen emerged, she looked better, but still exhausted. There was some color on her face, and her eyes were no longer red. "Thank you," he whispered to Amanda as they walked toward his car.

Amanda got Ellen into the back seat and leaned across the car. "She's very brave," she said. "It's like Mary Magdalene, going back and facing those people after everything's come out."

Henry nodded. *Yes,* he thought, *the town whore back from the dead, trying to be born again.*

They arrived at court ten minutes late. Henry led them in through the back, and the few people on that side fell away, staring openly. Henry was able to get Ellen inside the building before any reporters stopped them, and he pushed open the courtroom door and vanished inside with Ellen on his arm. Amanda followed in Henry's wake, squeezing into the crowd at the back of the room.

Brackman was scowling, ranting, Henry had no doubt, at his tardiness. Henry caught his eye, and Brackman stopped in mid-sentence. He took in the two of them in a sweeping glance, processing and weighing what he was seeing. "Approach the bench," he said after a moment. "You, too, Frank."

Henry gave Ellen a seat just behind his barrister's table. He caught his first real look at Hesston as they walked toward the front of the room. Hesston's face was pure, malevolent hate. But Hesston wasn't interested in Henry; he was looking straight through him, boring his eyes into Ellen.

Brackman leaned forward and quietly said, "I thought you had learned your lesson, son. I'm this close to having the bailiff cuff you right here and now for contempt."

"On what grounds?" Henry asked.

"On *her* grounds, damn it," he hissed. "Are you out of your mind? If you so much as say her name I'm going to cite you."

Hesston interrupted. "I'm going to initiate proceedings against you at the bar association," he ground out to Henry. "You are a disgrace to the legal profession."

Henry looked back at Ellen, taking her temperature; she looked nervous, but was sitting quietly, her eyes down at the table. "The witness insists on being heard," he said. "It's her decision. She wishes to amend her previous testimony."

"Amend!" Hesston said, a little too loudly. Henry looked sharply at him; the first pebbles of his stone face were beginning to crack away, the beginnings of what might become an avalanche. "Why don't you just say she perjured herself, then," Hesston said, controlling his voice. "Because if she changes one word of what she said I'm going to see that she goes to jail for it."

Brackman looked at Hesston closely, weighing the implications of the attorney's outburst. "Don't get wound up, Frank," he said, his eyes searching. "You've been wanting sonny here to hang himself. I don't see how you can complain if I let him do it."

He turned to Henry. "I'm gonna ask your witness if she really wants to do this. If she doesn't, I'm going to put you in jail for contempt without another word. If she does, then I'm going to give you five minutes. If she doesn't deliver something in that amount of time, I'm still going to have the bailiff haul you into my jail. Then I'm going to see you don't ever practice law in this state again. That's the deal."

"I accept the terms. May I call the witness?"

Hesston raised his hand. "Listen, Howard . . ."

"Let it go, Frank. Let's get this over with."

Brackman looked toward Ellen. "Ms. Gaudet, you mind standing for a minute?" Ellen slowly rose, her face blank and withdrawn. "Mr. Mathews here says you got somethin' to say to the court. Is that right?"

Ellen looked at Hesston, then at Henry. At last, she nodded. "Yes," she said in a small voice.

"Now this is somethin' about Tyler's will, that right?"

"Yes."

Brackman looked a last time at Hesston, the lawyer communicating a silent threat, the judge receiving it. But the situation had changed; after the well explosion and the media attention, it wouldn't pay to be on the wrong side when the remaining secrets came to the surface. Brackman wasn't a fool, and he wasn't going down to protect somebody bleeding to death before his eyes. "The witness will take the stand," he said. "She's reminded she's been sworn in."

Hesston stood motionless as Ellen walked past him, as though moving a single muscle would destroy his carefully balanced self-control. He was hanging by a thread, moving with the utmost care, unwilling to jostle even his thoughts. When he spoke, his voice was so still and brittle you could bounce a quarter off it. "I want it on the record that I object to this further humiliation of the witness," he said. "On the record."

"So noted."

Ellen sat with infinite stillness, her hands folded in her lap. Henry, unwilling to force her to say anything, extended to her the one scrap of self-respect that was his to give. He would empower her to end her own life. She had extended her arms; he would hand her the knife. He walked from behind his table and stood before the witness stand. He looked into her face and asked, "Ms. Gaudet, what was your relationship with Tyler Crandall?"

Ellen looked past Henry to a quiet, dead place. "Tyler and I were lovers from 1973 until shortly before he died." The courtroom rumbled, but no one existed for Henry in the room but Ellen. He was a lawyer allowing an already dying woman to spill her remaining lifeblood in one lethal stream.

"Tell the court about your relationship," he said quietly.

"We met at Lucky's, near the Army base, like you said. Tyler liked to be there, around the Army guys. He liked to watch them dancing with the working girls. We used to sit there with a buddy of his and he'd think about his Army days."

"Who was this buddy, Ms. Gaudet?"

"Carl Durand. They had been in the service together."

Of course, Henry thought. *Durand was the expertise, but he couldn't buy the land himself without tipping the whole county off. He needed Crandall to front the operation. One piece of the puzzle at last.* "Senator Carl Durand? Of Durand Oil?"

"That's right."

A collective gasp rushed through the courtroom, but Brackman did nothing to suppress it. His eyes had been gleaming for the past several minutes, as the implications of what Ellen was saying began to sink in. With the mention of Durand's name, however, he began to positively glow. Those words moved his courtroom from an insignificant back-water to the center of the media universe, producing a Pavlovian response. Henry looked over at Hesston; the lawyer was watching them both with vacant, frightened eyes. He was simply along for the ride now, and both he and Henry knew it. Either Ellen would give him up with Durand or she wouldn't. But to protest now was impossible. Even to move an arm would be to betray himself, and he became an implacable statue of marble.

"We'll get back to Mr. Durand," Henry said. "Did you continue this relationship with Tyler, even after Mr. Crandall married?"

"We didn't stop the affair because of him getting married."

"In your relationship with Mr. Crandall, did you ever discuss Raymond Boyd?"

"Yes."

"What was the nature of those conversations?"

"Tyler told me that Raymond was in love with me." Another ripple rushed through the crowd.

"And was he?"

"Yes. I knew that already."

"Did you love him?"

"No."

Henry walked back over to his desk and stared at a legal pad. "Why did Mr. Crandall care that Raymond Boyd was in love with you?" Henry asked. "Was he jealous?"

"No."

"Why not?"

"He knew that I didn't feel that way about Raymond."

"So why did he bring it up?"

"He wanted me to do something."

"What kind of thing?"

The tiniest break in Ellen's expression told Henry that he had arrived at the center of her pain, the axle around which everything revolved. "He wanted me to go to bed with him," she said. Ellen's confession landed on the gallery like a spell. The real history of Council Grove was being spun out before them for the first time.

"Why would Tyler Crandall, who was already your lover, want you to do that?"

"Because he thought I could make Raymond do something Tyler wanted him to do."

"What was that thing?"

"First, to loan him money."

"To help set up his oil operation?"

"Yes. To buy the land."

"Why would your sleeping with Raymond make him do that?"

"Tyler told Raymond that he was going to give me to him," she said.

"Did he have the power to do that, Ms. Gaudet? To give you to another man?"

Another pause, this time longer. "Yes."

Henry stopped a moment, letting both himself and Ellen regroup. Then he returned to the wells. "Was it only to buy the land that Tyler needed Raymond Boyd's help, Ms. Gaudet?"

"No. But once Raymond made the loan, it was easier to get him to keep helping. Raymond knew he had done wrong. It was a kind of trap, I guess."

"What else did Tyler want Raymond to do?"

"They needed help to put some extra pipes down in the ground. It had to be done in one night, Tyler said, and it would take at least four people to do it. And he wanted to get Raymond involved so he would have to keep quiet about the loan."

"Four people?" Henry asked. "So far we have Tyler and Raymond. Who were the others?"

"There was a field hand, Jimmy Waddell. They needed him to make the connection. Tyler said it was dangerous, and he didn't want to do it."

"The roustabout who died during the drilling of the Crandall wells."

"That's right."

"So there was Raymond, Tyler, and the roustabout. That's three. Who was the fourth?"

Ellen closed her eyes. "Carl Durand."

Henry had never felt so in control. Brackman was on his side. Hesston could do nothing. "Why was Carl Durand there?" he asked.

"He knew all about wells. Durand had to be there to supervise the whole thing. Tyler said it was complicated, dangerous. He said they were taking a big risk."

"Then why use Raymond? Didn't they just need a pair of arms? Why involve someone from the bank?"

"Tyler said they needed Raymond to be in on it. They had a lot of other ideas, and Tyler said having the bank in his pocket was a good thing."

Henry walked over toward Hesston's desk, casually, as though the proximity was incidental. But he looked into Hesston's eyes for the pure pleasure of witnessing a bully tasting fear. He didn't know how far Ellen would go. She had already gone further than he had dared hope. But for now, he was in no hurry to close the noose. It was like a drug just to know that Ellen Gaudet, for more than twenty-five years powerless and used, held Durand and Hesston in her lined, overly tanned hands. "Ms. Gaudet, what else did Tyler tell you about that night?"

"They got all the pipe laid in like they planned. But Durand didn't like loose ends. They couldn't do anything about Raymond. They needed him anyway. But the roustabout had to be taken care of."

"Taken care of?"

"He didn't have any family. That's why they picked him."

"So you're saying that the story about the roustabout dying in an accident isn't true."

"There was no accident. I know who killed him."

Henry walked slowly to the witness box, trying to hold her focus, hoping and even, for one second, praying that she would stay strong. He reached the box and gripped the edge of the gate. The destiny of everyone involved in Ty Crandall's will was about to change forever. "Ms. Gaudet, who killed that roustabout?"

Ellen began to cry slightly now, little tears escaping her resolve to feel nothing. But when she spoke, her voice was clear. "Raymond Boyd," she said. "Raymond Boyd killed him."

Henry leaned against the witness gate, feeling her words like a blow against his chest. *Guilt*, the doctor had said, *enough guilt to fracture him and drive him to the park. Enough to slowly unravel his mind.* "How do you know that Raymond Boyd killed him?"

"It was all planned. Durand told Raymond to turn a wheel on the well-head while the roustabout was down in the hole. He turned it, and some kind of gas came out."

"Sulfur gas?"

"I think that's right. It killed the roustabout in just a few seconds. Durand told everyone it happened the next day while the man was alone working on the well. He said oil rigs were dangerous, and it was just one of those things."

"You're saying that Raymond Boyd murdered the roustabout."

"He didn't know what the wheel was going to do. That was a part of the plan."

"How can you be sure Raymond didn't know what the wheel would do?"

"Durand and Tyler didn't want to be the ones. They set it up for Raymond to do it."

"So that was another reason to have someone else there? To take care of Waddell?"

"Yes. Tyler said they would get Raymond to kill the roustabout and make it so he could never say anything. Then they could use the bank whenever they wanted."

"Use the bank for what, Ms. Gaudet?"

"To clean the money."

"That part didn't work out, did it?"

She looked down. "No," she said. "Tyler didn't really understand Raymond. He was right about Raymond not being able to tell anybody what had happened that night. But he was wrong to think Raymond could stay and pretend. He wasn't a killer. He wasn't strong like Tyler. So he made himself quiet inside. He covered up everything he knew in his craziness."

"He moved to Custer's Elm."

"He did that to stay near me," she said quickly. "He couldn't bear to be apart. He couldn't bear to see me either. He knew that I had betrayed him."

"Why didn't you come forward? Why didn't you tell what you knew?"

A wave of anguish swept across Ellen's face. "Tyler told me he would take care of me."

"What did he mean by that?"

"That we would be together if I kept quiet."

"You mean that he would divorce his wife?"

She smiled, a hard, thin curve of her mouth. "I suppose."

"You've known that wasn't going to happen for a long while, haven't you, Ms. Gaudet?"

"Of course."

"So once you realized you had been used, why did you keep silent? Were you afraid?"

"No. I don't know."

"Then what kept you from telling the truth, Ms. Gaudet?"

"Raymond."

"I asked you once before if you were in love with Raymond Boyd. You told the court no. Are you sure that your answer was correct?"

"Yes."

"Then tell this court why it was so important for you to protect him."

Now, at last, she broke her long, unfeeling stare into space. "Because somewhere along the way I realized that he was the only man in the world who had ever actually loved me." With those words she released herself and began sobbing gently, her body heaving in small convulsions.

Henry let her cry a moment, hoping she could hold herself together just a little longer. "Ms. Gaudet, I have one final question. Was there anyone else who knew about what had happened that night at the wells?"

Ellen's crying subsided as she willed herself back under control to answer. It took some time, and Henry waited, hoping that, having lost her pride, she might find her courage. When she spoke, her voice was very still. "Yes," she said.

"Who was that person, Ms. Gaudet?"

Ellen lifted her arm, pointing a long, slender finger toward the table across from Henry's. "He knew," she said. "Frank Hesston was behind every bit of it."

Henry exhaled and closed his eyes. "Thank you, Ms. Gaudet. I have no further questions."

Chapter Thirty-six

Frank Hesston was cuffed where he sat in the courtroom, Brackman giving the order. As the bailiff led him from the courtroom, he had stared, dumbfounded, not at Brackman or Henry, but only at Ellen, eyes locked on her until he passed out of the room.

Carl Durand was stopped by U.S. marshals as he entered the Kansas City International Airport. He was wearing cowboy boots, a Kansas City Chiefs sweatshirt, sunglasses, and a dark jacket. He was carrying seventy thousand dollars in cash.

What happened to either of them afterward didn't matter to Henry. What mattered was Raymond, and when Dr. Harris called to say that he was out of immediate danger, Henry let himself think that God had heard Amanda's prayer.

Closing up his father's office took less time than reopening it. He and Amanda loaded the fax and copy machine into Henry's car, and all the papers from the case fit neatly into a couple of boxes. Before they closed the door, Henry surprised himself by rearranging the furniture a last time. He pulled the desk over to the side where his father had placed it, and pushed the filing cabinets behind. He flicked off the lights and pulled the door shut. "So that's it, then," he said.

"And what's going to happen about Raymond and the money?"

"The will is validated, obviously. But there will be practically nothing left. With the cost of the fire containment, the back taxes and penalties, it won't be much."

"But something, right?"

"A little, I hope. It depends on how things go. It's Margaret I'm worried about."

"That wasn't your fault, Henry. You never wanted her name on that court document."

"I know. It's just another reason to detest Roger, as if I needed it. At least she has Sarah, and some family of her own, I assume. Between that and Social Security she won't starve."

"And the criminal charges on Raymond?"

"The DA says they're not pressing charges about the roustabout. He says he's suffered enough."

"Anyway, he didn't know what was going to happen. But he did know about the wells, Henry. Breaking the law for love isn't a defense."

"The statute of limitations is long past for that," Henry said. "Of course, for murder, it's indefinite. But for everything else—the bank loan, the wells—he's clean."

She sighed. "So that's all right. You really are finished."

"Yeah."

"So now what?"

Neither of them had spoken about the future, and he was grateful for it. But that talk couldn't be put off forever. "Well, my immediate plans are to show you how grateful I am for your help on this," he said. "That could take some considerable time."

She laughed and kissed him, a kiss warm, sexual, and full of promise. "I'm a patient woman," she said. "And after that?"

"Not sure," he said. "Any ideas?"

She looked down, obviously uncomfortable. "I played with this stupid idea for a while. That you'd open up this office again and practice here."

"Dr. Harris would just love that, wouldn't he? Him and his oedipal theories." He looked across the square. "But no, I can't do that. This place is behind me. I can't live here again."

"Even if they need you here? Think of what you could do, Henry. You could defend these people in a way your father never could."

"Maybe," he said. "But it's a mistake to think of yourself as a savior. I don't want the job." He looked at her, feeling her sense of exposure and wanting to relieve it. "Anyway, you weren't the only one with crazy ideas," he said. "I kept wondering all morning how you feel about Chicago. The day we met you told me you loved it."

She took his hand. "I do. But we got Durand, Henry. And the man who's taking his place on the oil and gas committee—Sam Coulton—he's wonderful. He's promised to push for full funding for the agency. I can finally do what I've been fighting for the past two years."

He looked at her, feeling her dedication, knowing that no plans between them would be right if they pulled her away from her cause. "Then we'll just have to keep thinking," he said, putting his arm around her. "I hate to think of the phone bills."

She smiled, and then said with a start, "Henry, your cell phone bill through all this—it'll be a thousand dollars."

Henry got a faraway look. "What day of the month is it?"

"I don't know. The twenty-third, I think."

He smiled. "Paid to the end of the month by the firm of Wilson, Lougherby and Mathers. God, I love irony."

She laughed out loud. "Are you sure they won't sue?"

"They can't turn on the lights for a thousand bucks. I'm home free."

She kissed him again, more lightly, and said, "Then come show me how grateful you are."

Henry's room was quiet. They had passed the day together, and now it was evening, the light fading through a sliver of curtain onto the bed. His fingers touched her back, tracing downward in lazy circles. He watched her skin yield to his touch, a soft indentation that traveled under his fingers, supple, soft, and warm. When at last his fingers reached her buttocks, her breathing deepened, and he began to kiss her back, lips open, tongue gently flicking. He breathed her in, closing his eyes and letting his own inner protections begin to collapse. He wanted inside her, not just a penetration but an abandonment of soul. He wanted to enter her place where time and light stopped, and only the warm, dark caress of tongue and nipple and entwined fingers remained.

She turned over and looked at him, taking in his body deliberately, her eyes staring unabashedly at his crotch, his legs, his shoulders. "I want to feel your weight on me," she said in a whisper, and he moved, happy and obedient, to cover her with himself. Their hips met and she was touching him, teasing and guiding him. There was a low exhalation of his breath and they began moving together, tentative at first, then a rhythm emerging. They gained speed slowly, a cycle of tempos growing like a storm. He opened his eyes and saw her looking at him, her hair errant and wicked, her smile childlike and determined. He grabbed her buttocks and drove into her, breathing hard as tiny droplets of sweat formed on his face.

He closed his eyes again and he was floating above himself, he didn't know for how long, his vision tunneled and focused utterly on the one thing. Then, as he released an explosion of breath, he heard her muffled gasp and felt her open mouth on his shoulder.

No secrets were shared afterward, and none were necessary. Neither moved, and Henry had no recollection of coming apart from her. Only sleep as dark as starless midnight, and the bliss of utter, abandoned nothingness.

When the sun came up the next morning Henry turned to feel Amanda in his bed. She wasn't there, and he opened his eyes to see her sitting across the room in a chair, looking at him with a smile. "Good morning," she said.

Henry breathed deeply, taking in her scent from the pillow and sheets around him. "Yes, it is. Very good."

"You're up early."

"So are you. But I'm glad. I have somewhere to go, and I want to be there early."

"Of course. We'll go to the hospital together."

Henry sat up, pushing a pillow behind his back. He licked his lips and ran his hand through his hair. "Not the hospital. And I need to go alone, if that's all right."

"Alone?" She looked surprised and disappointed. "If you need to."

"Look, I know it's bad timing." She nodded, and he said, "It's just something I have to do before I leave. It won't take me long."

"Can I ask where you're going?"

"Yes, and I'll tell you. But I'd rather you didn't. It's just personal."

"All right," she said, turning to the sink for a hairbrush. "Then you'd better get started."

Henry pulled the sheets back, stretched, and stood naked behind her. He reached down and kissed her on the back of the neck softly, then again on the cheek. She turned and put her arms around him, pulling him close. "I'm just getting used to you," she said.

"I know. I can tell you that where I'm going doesn't have anything to do with us."

She looked at him a moment, then kissed his cheek, releasing him. He walked to the closet and pulled on some underwear, blue jeans, and a tan pullover. At the door he said, "I'll meet you here. Give me a couple of hours." She nodded silently, and he pulled the door shut behind him.

Henry got in his car and drove west on Highway 59, the morning silently opening up outside his windows. He settled into a cruise, passing through tiny towns of only a few hundred people. After a half hour he pulled into Caldwell, the town where his father had been born. He turned left onto a gravel road at the outskirts of the place, and rolled to a stop in front of a small clapboard church. Off to the right he saw the small, neatly kept cemetery that adjoined the church lawn. He got out and walked underneath a cast-iron arch that marked the entryway.

Henry walked through the little graveyard slowly until he stood before two side-by-side plots sharing a single wide gravestone. He looked down and read the inscription: HENRY AND KATHRYN MATHEWS, HUSBAND AND WIFE. FROM EARTH TO HEAVEN'S SAFE ARMS. He kneeled in front of the stone, running his fingers over the granite letters. He didn't cry. He was simply still for a long time, feeling the breeze on his skin and the warming sun on his neck. He saw his mother, holding the house and family together on a shoestring. He saw his father, struggling against the injustices he found in the world, losing more than he won, forever dedicated, forever optimistic. *For every deep truth, there is pain. Even for the Christ.* He finally stood up and reached in his pocket. He pulled out the key to his father's office and laid it on the headstone. "I got the bastards," he whispered. He walked to his car without turning back.

Amanda was ready to go when he got back to the motel, and had packed his belongings as well. She didn't ask where he had gone, and he kissed her gratefully. They reconnected easily, and the drive to the hospital in Kansas City was sweet. The Flinthills unwound beneath them, the sun arcing between cloud cover across the plains in enormous sheets of light. The outskirts of Kansas City finally appeared, and they made their way through town to Raymond's hospital.

They found Harris inside, talking with a nurse at the entrance station of the psychiatric ward. The doctor looked up, saw them, and answered their question before they had even asked it. "He's doing remarkably better."

Henry relaxed. "That's good news."

"He wasn't responding to what we had him on, so I put him on Clozapine. It's helping."

"Is he lucid?" Henry asked.

"He's not out of the woods yet. But he's doing well. I had what amounted to a fragment of a real conversation with him last night."

"You're kidding."

Harris smiled. "Know what we talked about?"

"What?"

"General George Custer. And you."

"Me? What did he say?"

"Not a lot. But I made sure he understood what you had done for him." Harris turned, leading them down the hospital corridor. He stopped in front of a door. "He's not alone," he said, smiling. "He's got a guest."

Harris pulled open the door, and Henry saw Ellen sitting in a chair across the room from Raymond, reading a book. "He's resting," she said, looking up. "We were talking, and he just nodded off."

Raymond was sleeping sitting up, his back propped up with pillows. Harris walked around the bed and picked up Raymond's arm. At his touch, Raymond's eyes fluttered open. "Junior Henry," he said. "The mighty arm of the Lord."

Henry smiled. "Hello, Raymond. How are you?"

He spoke lethargically. "Brain pumped full," he said. "We'll see what we see."

Amanda walked up and touched Boyd's arm. "Hello, Raymond," she said. "It's good to see you."

Raymond nodded. "Raymond Boyd," he said quietly. "That's who I am."

"You can't imagine how good it is to hear you say that," Henry said.

A nurse entered the room and nodded to Dr. Harris. "I'm just checking his drip," she said, crossing to Raymond.

"All right, Raymond," Harris said, intervening. "We can talk later. If you're resting, we'll leave you to it."

Harris gently prodded Henry and Amanda toward the door, but Raymond's voice stopped them. "Junior Henry?"

Henry turned around and Boyd looked into him the way he had when Henry had been just a boy, watching the rituals and sermons to the air.

"Knew your father," Boyd said. "He was a good man."

"Thank you, Raymond."

"You're his son."

Amanda took Henry's hand, and they left the room, Ellen sitting quietly, watching Raymond settle back into sleep.

They walked down the hallway and Henry asked Harris, "Can those two possibly have a future?"

"Together?" Harris shrugged. "Who knows? Her concern is real. She's hardly left the hospital."

"Where else would she go?" Amanda said. "She's a stranger in her own town now."

Harris nodded. "It's healing her to be with him. I don't know if they need to be together like you meant it. But for now, she's finding herself again."

Henry stuck out his hand. "Thanks. For everything."

"You're welcome. Best case I've had this year. I'll be in touch soon."

Henry and Amanda walked out of the hospital together, winding their way through the parking lot toward his car. The sunlight was bright, and the sound of traffic filled the air around them. An ambulance sat in the emergency entrance, its rear door left open. They were back in urban life. "So where to?" Amanda asked. "Tomorrow life will start happening again. We have tonight."

Henry stood by his car, staring at her face, every cell in his body leaning toward her. But he resisted the temptation to press her to him, enjoying the delicious anticipation of feeling her body again, the sensation still too new to take for granted. He thought for a moment, wondering what beginning would lead inexorably to the conclusion they both wanted so much. "I have a suggestion," he said at last. "Dinner for two, at Skunk Pepper's. We'll call ahead, and have him put the Cristal Roederer on ice."

She smiled and kissed him full on the mouth, her lips covering his with sweet, feminine warmth. "Perfect," she said.

From the Author

The town of Council Grove does exist, although not precisely as I have described it. Significant liberties were taken, both in geography and in citizenry. No disrespect is intended to the fine people who live there.

Custer's Elm still stands, although it's only a smaller, misshapen caricature of its glory days during the Indian wars. A lightning strike forced it to be cut back. I like to think the lightning was sent by Crazy Horse, just to make sure nobody else gets comfort from the tree that shaded Custer's men. If you look carefully, it's still possible to see the huddled ghosts of the doomed mercenaries on their way to their deaths.

My grateful thanks are extended to the coincidentally named Boyd Brown, a retired oil wildcatter, from whom much information was gained about drilling and geology generally. Any technical errors are entirely my own. Also thanks are due to all at Jane Dystel Literary Management, especially to Jane and Miriam. "No, Jane, it's not too early to call." A special thanks to Jake Morrissey at Scribner for his conscientious editing and friendship.

God, inscrutable and mysterious, brought us all together.

For more information or to contact Reed, please visit:

www.reedarvin.com

About the Author

Reed Arvin is a respected Nashville-based music producer and award-winning composer who has worked with Amy Grant, Michael W. Smith, Rich Mullins, among many others. He is the author of a previous novel, *The Wind in the Wheat*, an inside look at the music business. Born in Kansas to parents who are lawyers, Arvin now lives and works in Nashville.